RHYMER: HEL

BAEN BOOKS by GREGORY FROST

RHYMER
Rhymer
Rhymer: Hoode
Rhymer: Hel

To purchase these titles in e-book form, please go to
www.baen.com.

RHYMER: HEL

GREGORY FROST

BAEN

A Baen Books Original

Baen Publishing Enterprises
P.O. Box 1403
Riverdale, NY 10471
www.baen.com

ISBN: 978-1-6680-7260-8

Cover art by Eric Williams

First printing, May 2025

Distributed by Simon & Schuster
1230 Avenue of the Americas
New York, NY 10020

Library of Congress Cataloging-in-Publication Data

Names: Frost, Gregory, author.
Title: Rhymer. Hel / Gregory Frost.
Other titles: Hel
Description: Riverdale, NY : Baen Publishing Enterprises, 2025. | Series: Rhymer ; 3
Identifiers: LCCN 2024059680 (print) | LCCN 2024059681 (ebook) | ISBN 9781668072608 (hardcover) | ISBN 9781964856223 (ebook)
Subjects: LCSH: Thomas, the Rhymer, 1220?-1297?—Fiction. | LCGFT: Fantasy
fiction. | Novels.
Classification: LCC PS3556.R59815 R593 2025 (print) | LCC PS3556.R59815 (ebook) | DDC 813/.54—dc23/eng/20241223
LC record available at https://lccn.loc.gov/2024059680
LC ebook record available at https://lccn.loc.gov/2024059681

Printed in the United States of America

10 9 8 7 6 5 4 3 2 1

DEDICATION

In Memoriam, to Timothy R. Sullivan and Tom Purdom,
two lights of science fiction who lit up Philadelphia
for quite some time.

ACKNOWLEDGMENTS

The three Rhymer novels—and this one in particular—would not have made deadlines had it not been for the edits, feedback, and meta insights of my writing colleague Oz Drummond as she combed through the text. Thank you once more for the many, many hours of conversations, Zoom discussions, and heaps of notes at so many critical points during their creation.

Anyone who wants to write a novel set in Elizabethan London can do no better than to utilize Liza Picard's *Elizabeth's London*. Picard knows everything about everything. Likewise, Park Honan's *Christopher Marlowe: Poet & Spy* covers everything you could want to know about the more shadowy aspects of Marlowe's short life.

Finally, once more my thanks to my ever-tenacious agent, Marie Lamba, and to my editors on this volume, David Butler and Toni Weisskopf, for further fine-tuning of Thomas's adventure.

PART ONE:
THE PLAGUE DOCTOR

I. Lost in Þagalwood

Thomas Rimor has glamoured himself to blend into a pocket of deep crimson shadow on the pathway through Þagalwood. Armed with bow and arrows, he plans to ambush the Yvag knights who'll be escorting the latest *teind* to Ailfion for sacrifice. It's something he has done repeatedly over the years with mixed success.

In all that time he has become more and more attuned to the ördstone he carries—that black, scalloped, alien "skipping" stone decorated with peculiar blue jewels—to where he can sense when the time for a new *teind* is drawing near. The stone almost speaks to him. His scalp crawls with the sensation of its pulsing when it heralds that the Yvags and their captive are on the march—as it's doing even now.

However, this time as he waits, invisible in deep shadows and surrounded by the grotesque trees that populate this wood, instead of the escorted *teind,* he is surprised when, far up the pathway in the opposite direction, a single Yvag emerges from among the wood. Like a pale ghost, the Yvag simply walks out and onto the wide pathway, turns and departs.

Thomas hastily draws an arrow, but then hesitates to shoot. The Yvag hasn't seen him and it isn't leading some unfortunate ensorcelled man or woman toward a slow descending death in the fathomless pit called Hel. Nor is it dressed in the usual black-and-silver Yvag knight's armor as he is, although it's too far away for him to make out the details of its costume.

Nevertheless, the pale distant Yvag has impossibly just come out of the depths of the wood.

He is aware that these bone-white trees watch him. The whorls and knots of their trunks are like weird inhuman faces; their branches join overhead to form an archway above the path—the branches directly above him rub together, producing odd, whispery, clacking words, in this instance, *"Let be, let be, Thomas Rimor. Let her be."*

He lowers the bow.

The numberless trees used to call him names such as *"lonely"* or *"friendless one"* while they invited him to join them, which is to say, to die by straying from the path and attempting to enter the wood. He knew better than to listen to that invitation. He once watched a man named Gallorini deviate from the pathway to be immediately overtaken by living roots and tendrils like tentacles and consumed, stripped of skin and muscle until nothing but a bleached bone skeleton remained. It is still here, far back along the pathway, but has itself grown gnarled and distorted over the centuries and now is simply one among the hundreds or thousands of such trees that fill this place called Þagalwood.

At some point over time the wood began to acknowledge him by name. When he steps through a gate now, the rasping branches whisper to each other excitedly that *"Thomas is among us, look, look."* It's as if he is here to entertain them. For all that they've taken an interest in him, at no time have the trees ever betrayed his presence to the Yvag, which makes him wonder if they want to see him triumph over the elves of Yvagddu. Centuries have passed, and he still can only speculate as to why they are here and what they really are. It's not as if there's anyone he can ask about them.

Ahead in the distance, the pale Yvag has been swallowed up in the ruddy darkness. Thomas remains in his pocket of shadow awhile longer, watching in both directions for the anticipated company of knights and victim. Still, no one else appears.

He wonders if the knights have avoided him, have cut a gate straight into Ailfion itself. He's suspected them of this for awhile, has thought about lying in wait for them above Hel's plaza—risky, yes, but they would be as unprepared as he is now.

The ördstone continues to skritch against his skull. The *teind* is happening . . . somewhere.

Finally, he tires of waiting for a procession that's not coming. He walks up the pathway himself to where the pale creature emerged.

Given that to step off the pathway into the wood is a sure way to die, how has the one he just saw not been consumed? Maybe it truly was a ghost?

Then it occurs to him that the trees called it *her*. Mostly the elven seem to have no immutable sexual characteristics, or any such at all that he can perceive. Their queen, Nicnevin, adopts whatever gender suits her; but that certainly wasn't Nicnevin, not as he's known her. For one thing, she travels only with a retinue as befits a Queen.

The place where the Yvag ghost exited is just black soil, typical forest floor, and undergrowth, nothing exceptional.

He tugs at the leather thong round his neck to retrieve the stone from its pouch. It lies, blinking in some complex sequence, upon his palm. His entire hand glows blue as the small jewels in it ignite. The stone, he's learned, is full of surprises. It does far more than simply cutting portals, gates into and out of Yvagddu.

He holds it before him, and the ördstone casts a thin beam of light at the ground, illuminating a line of footprints; he traces their circuitous route backward into the depths of Þagalwood as far as he can see.

Thomas has a mad idea. He puts away his arrow, straps the bow across his body, draws a black barbed Yvag dagger he carries, and then with great caution takes a first step off the pathway, ready to slash and leap back if wriggling wormlike roots sprout to seize him.

To either side of his foot the soil does rise and shift. Tendrils poke out but immediately withdraw again. None threads up where the Yvag walked, or where he now stands. It could be a trick, certes. Þagalwood might be leading him into its inescapable depths to make a meal of him, but why would it have waited all this time? The trees observe him, a curiosity in their midst, a unicorn.

He takes another step along the trail the Yvag made. Still nothing reaches for him.

Centipedes and creepy-crawlies churn the soil ahead alongside and between the blue footprints. The blue insect trail looks to wind deep into the wood.

Overhead branches shift and scrape in a nonexistent wind. The scraping sets his teeth on edge: *Vital one, yes, come, come deeper.*

He peers up. Did it just call him "vital" or "fatal"? Either way, he's not turning back.

He continues along the ghost's trail, whoever she was. It does seem that insects thrive in the soil where she walked and do not stray far off it, or else the insects were here first and showed the ghost the way.

Deeper in, Thomas soon finds himself surrounded by peculiar lavender flowers, with petals that look meaty and thick. He bends down to pluck one, and the scraping voice of the wood warns, *"Kanerva, poison! Poison to the Yvag! Poison to you!"*

The large flower doesn't look poisonous. Still, he's glad to be wearing Yvag armor, which covers his hands as well as the rest of him.

He lifts and cautiously inhales the flower, and is nearly dropped to his knees.

Coughing, he pushes the blossom away from himself. Pulls his head back, blinking tears. The scent still burns in his nostrils.

His dizziness lasts only a few moments. Even the perfume of *kanerva* is hazardous, it seems, but it's also familiar.

This taste was in his mouth as "Sir Richard" carted him to Kirklees Priory with the intent of having the Yvag Zhanedd finish him off. The creature Bragrender masquerading as Sir Richard had used no more than a tiny needle's worth of the poison hidden in a signet ring, and Thomas lay paralyzed for hours, close to death. It's deadly to the Yvag as well, is it? Good. He can think of a use or two for such a poison.

With great care, he holds the flower away from himself as he continues forward. The trail winds deeper still, well beyond any place he has seen before. Behind him, the main pathway is lost in the dimness, too. He wonders how vast can Þagalwood be.

The trail winds around and around until he is absolutely lost, and consumed by a growing terror that the wood is intentionally toying with him.

Then, at the moment when panic nearly overwhelms him and he's ready to run back the way he's come, the footprint trail dumps him out onto the main path again. He is exactly where he entered. His own footprints show where he entered.

This is impossible. If anything he has been plunging deeper and deeper in among the broad white trunks, away from the single safe pathway. How can he have been this disoriented? Þagalwood has taken him for a journey, and led him where it likes; but in the end it hasn't taken his life.

Still, no *teind* has passed this way. In the dirt there are no three-toed prints of Yvag beasts or prints of Yvag feet. Nothing has passed by. He can't have been in the wood but a quarter hour surely. Back in London, no doubt whole hours will have elapsed, but he's used to that.

In Alpin Waldroup's company that first time, this place terrified him and for so many years after, even though it's somewhat akin to the King's Way through Sherwood Forest: a main route between critical points, along which regal cortèges drag captured *teinds* to their death—or did until he started interfering. That's the difference between the two woods, he supposes: wherever you cut into it, that's where Þagalwood somehow begins. He thinks of all the red tunnels he's seen, and how all of them, when you walk them, deliver you onto this path. That only changes when you concentrate on a destination other than Þagalwood.

He kneels, the flower set beside him. Thomas looks down at the stone. It's cold and dark; none of the blue gems twinkles. The collecting of a *teind* has already taken place. Somehow, he has missed it. The stone offers no clue.

"Wake up," he tells it. "We need to go."

He stands and concentrates on his destination. It should still be night in London, but he is cautious as he slices open enough of a portal to look upon his destination—indeed the interior of the Lazar-house in Southwark is dark. They've no patients, and no sisters from St. Thomas the Apostle Hospital are on hand.

He finishes the cut and steps through the gate into the house where once upon a time lepers were kept isolated from the populace. Nowadays, plague victims have taken the place of the lepers in the houses.

Thomas turned and sealed up the gate. As he'd anticipated, it was still night, but also surprisingly chilly.

There were a few places he could have chosen—mostly open fields—but he didn't want to walk about in London with the *kanerva* blossom. Who knew how long it might remain potent once plucked or what effect the air here might have on it compared to that of Yvagddu.

He set to work. Stored in the back of the Lazar-house was a crate he'd brought from his own apartments. In it, packed in straw, was his alembic, acquired during the time he'd studied with the alchemist Hieronymus Brunschwig in Strasbourg nearly a century ago.

He had used it perhaps four or five times since to distill elixirs for his patients.

Now he took out the flat-bottomed cucurbit and dusted the straw off it.

Carefully, with both hands in gloves, he tore apart the *kanerva* flower. He stuffed the thick chunks of petals into the cucurbit, and mashed them down with a stick. The smell of them was still powerful. Twice he had to set the cucurbit aside and go out and breathe fresh air. To his amazement, the night air was cold enough that he could see his breath. Not a typical August night at all.

In some confusion, he went back inside the Lazar-house.

When he'd packed as many petals as he could into the cucurbit, he filled it with Coventry mineral water out of a bucket.

Under the ashes in the central hearth, there were embers. Apparently, a fire had been going earlier. Everything about that was wrong, but he would take the time to look into it later. For now, the embers made it easy for him to stoke a new fire and set up a trivet for the cucurbit.

He set the cucurbit over the low flame and placed a glass cap on top of it with a tube extending off the side. Beneath the end of the tube he placed an empty flacon. In short order the distillate began accumulating, dripping into the flacon. The *kanerva* scent surrounded him, and he grew dizzy just standing close by. Quickly, he propped open the doors to draw the noisome fumes out, then went outside awhile himself.

Altogether, the process took a few hours. The flacon by then was over half full of poison. The remains of the *kanerva* blossoms were nearly charred. And Thomas was satisfied he had gotten as much as he could of the distillate. He replaced the glass stopper in the flacon and set it aside.

When the cucurbit cooled, he would rinse it out, pour the mass of leaves out in the yard, and then repack the whole alembic in its straw and return it to storage. In the meantime, he used the ördstone to cut a gate to his apartments on London Bridge. He would only be there a few minutes.

By the greenish light cast by the fire circling the open portal, he retrieved all of his arrows, then returned to the Lazar-house and sealed up the portal again.

One by one, he dipped the arrowheads into the flacon and then stood the arrows against the wall to dry.

These arrows were distinctive, of his own design. Yvag armor had always been resistant to penetration by traditional arrows, especially at any significant distance, and he had fashioned these—narrow iron triangles that could punch through the exotic armor—and he made it a habit now to retrieve them after any skirmish with Yvags rather than leave them as evidence, or some sort of calling card. The less they knew about their attacker the better. Even when the arrows did kill one of the elven, the creature might nevertheless resurrect unless Thomas made certain of its death, usually by parting head from body, and it was extremely rare when he had that opportunity, especially in the middle of rescuing a *teind* from their midst. The addition of this poison, if it was as lethal to them as to him, might change all that. No doubt he would eventually have the opportunity to find out.

And he would have gone to sleep then, blissfully focused upon that eventuality, except that the ördstone chose that moment to thrum again, alerting him to the taking of a *teind*. The cold weather, the fire, and now this alarum—Thomas arrived at an ineluctable conclusion regarding just how much time had passed while he'd been lost in Þagalwood.

Exhausted as he was, he filled his quiver with the new arrows, took up his bow, and prepared to hurdle across worlds again. This time he would risk the location.

II. The Untimely *Teind*

The portal the Yvag knight opens hovers at the top of a rise that overlooks the glittering city of Ailfion. Thomas is already seated in the tall blue grass behind the portal, himself glamoured as more grass, barely distinguishable from it. But no one is looking his way in any case.

A second knight emerges. Crossing over, each of them unglamours, casting off the appearance of Elizabethan guards in steel cuirasses and baggy leggings, becoming spike-faced and golden-eyed, and wearing shiny black armor that's edged in silver sections—like flexible carapaces that only highlight the oddness of their jointed limbs.

Following behind the two, a blond young man of perhaps sixteen years stumbles nakedly through the opening as if tied to them. Thomas can't see much of his face, but knows it will be slack, his eyes unfocused. It's impossible for him not to think of his long-dead brother, Onchu. Behind him comes a third and final Yvag. The knight transforms as the two others have, bends double at the waist, and seals up the gate with its own glittering ördstone. Rising, it tucks the stone away in the breastbone pocket of the armor.

Thomas, his bow laid across his lap and three arrows at the ready between his fingers, does not move so much as to breathe.

Within moments a horde of tiny, flying creatures reaches the knights and their captured *teind*. He thinks of them as hobs or fae. Some green, others a dull earth-red, they have strange heads like mushroom caps, teeth as fine as fish spines, tiny wings, and claws as sharp as miniature sword blades. The first one he ever encountered, with Waldroup, proved to be some kind of little flying machine that dissolved when cut apart. They acted as though alive, however.

The hobs circle the knights and their captive, then fly straight back toward the fantastical city to announce the *teind*'s arrival. The squealing bastards love open portals; he has no idea why.

The knights close up around their *teind* to head down the grassy hillside.

Now is the moment.

Exhausted as he is, Thomas rises up. His shape is like a deformity in the nocturnal landscape. He draws and fires all three arrows in quick succession. The slender points puncture the slick armor, and all three knights drop where they stand. One quivers violently an instant, then stops.

The naked *teind* remains, precariously upright, robbed now of both will and guidance.

There is no time for more. Quickly, Thomas circles him, bending again and again to snatch back the arrows. Only one of these catches on something, and he rips it free. He wraps a rag around the tips and shoves the arrows back into the quiver, then digs a hand into the chest pocket of his own Yvag armor, drawing his ördstone, and slashes the night.

Nothing happens.

He slides a finger across the stone, cups his palm. The stone is dark, none of the tiny jewels glittering—but, no, one does spark and then immediately fades. Dead. The stone is dead.

Something has happened to it, or this is a trap. Either way, he's stuck on this hillside above Ailfion, with a glaikit *teind*. He risks a glance in the direction of the plazas, sees the domed top of the Queen's massive summer house.

The fae horde wheels about over the plaza of Hel and streaks right back for him. Oh, they're easy enough to kill individually. En masse, though, they'll shred him to pieces in a few seconds' frenzy.

Thomas quick drops to one knee beside the last Yvag knight that emerged, pulls the body closer, and reaches into its sheathlike armor, grabs its ördstone. This had better work.

The stone flickers, its jewels run through a sequence he has viewed a hundred times.

He stands, focuses, and slices up across the night. A thin green fire follows his hand, flexes and pops open. Beyond it lies a wide path enclosed between rows of monstrous white trees. Taking hold of the naked *teind*, Thomas launches him through the open gate, and hangs on, using the *teind's* momentum to yank himself in after.

The youth sprawls in the middle of the Þagalwood pathway. Thomas cuts down, sealing the portal behind them, his last view that of the hideous little hobs swarming ever nearer.

He scoots over to the youth, shakes him. The *teind* remains stupefied. They don't have the luxury of time here. He presses the stolen ördstone up to the boy's face. "Wake up, you!" he insists.

The *teind's* eyes flutter. Open. They slowly and with some confusion regain their focus. When they do, the naked *teind* yelps and scrambles back. He reaches the edge of the path before Thomas can grab him and shout, "Stop!" He quickly concentrates and unglamours, becoming visible in his own Yvag armor. He pushes at the helm and it pools at his throat.

"What's . . . ? Where?"

"Yes, yes, I'll explain it all. Just allow me a moment." He stands, holding the stolen stone, and concentrates hard on the destination that had been chosen for—well, for whenever that had been. He still doesn't know what happened with his walk through Þagalwood. He will find out, but after this little adventure is over.

He cuts then a sliver, just enough to ascertain that it's night. He can only hope for the rest. He cuts down. Immediately the smell of brine assails them. "Go on," he urges. "Go through, quick now before they find us here. They will come after us."

"Who?" He's covering himself, or trying to, his hands pressed over his genitals.

"Yes, you want all the answers, naturally. Come on." He leads the way, and the *teind* can only follow him out into the oceanside night.

Thomas seals up the second portal. They might find it, he knows, but it should take them a good long time given the thousands of cuts that have been made by the Yvags themselves into and out of Þagalwood.

He has done this before, but dear God, has he ever been this tired? What has happened to his stone?

Thomas sloshed out of the marsh not far from Hythe. No one seemed to have been keeping watch. He had concentrated on the hut he owned here, but between the borrowed ördstone and his exhaustion, he'd arrived near rather than in it. At least they'd arrived unseen, which was all he could ask for.

"It's *cold*," complained the naked youth.

"I know, and I do apologize. What's your name?"

"I'm called Piers. But—"

"A plowman's son, no doubt."

The boy blinked, clueless.

"Never mind. Come on. There's a hut up ahead we're going to. It's not far. I have clothes for you there."

"You have clothes for me? I understand you not at all. I mean, how did I come to be naked and here? And where is here and where were we just now—those trees? They were trees?"

"Best you never mention them to anyone at all," Thomas replied. He took that opportunity to glamour himself in a respectable outfit with a ruff. Piers seemed too busy being naked and confounded to react to the change that had taken place.

The first hint of dawn was just coloring the edge of the sky, and he could make out the shape of the hut he owned, which stood perhaps a mile from St. Mary's Church and the village of Hythe.

"Here we are." He found and opened the door to the hut. It smelled like vermin had been living in it, which they probably had, though there should have been nothing to sustain them in here. No one had informed the mice.

Thomas took out the borrowed ördstone and navigated by its blue light. He found the shelf, high up, where he'd stored the bag of clothes, and handed that to Piers. "You'll find something in there. They may not fit well as I could hardly foretell your proportions, but 'twill do until you are safely arrived in Calais or elsewhere on the coast and can make your way deeper into the Low Countries perhaps, or France."

Blond Piers pulled a pair of braes out of the bag, then a shirt and padded doublet. "France? How so France?"

Thomas had placed his bow up on the high shelf. "Just now you can't go back to—where did they find you?"

"Chel-Chelmsford." The question seemed to have unsettled him. "What happened to me?" Holding the doublet, Piers stopped. "Tell me how I came to be naked and here. And where indeed *is* here? And who are you that has rescued me?"

"Yes, of course." Thomas drew a breath. "Tell me first, was there a priest or an alderman perhaps in Chelmsford who took a special interest in you?"

"There's Alderman Fleetwood."

"Fleetwood. Mmm." He must remember that name. "Well, through your friendly alderman, you were chosen by the elven to be sacrificed. He selected you, and as likely, he it was ensorcelled you, stole you from your home, and had you removed to Ailfion."

"Fleetwood. But he's—"

"A good man? That is how it always seems. In truth, though, he's neither of those things. You are the fruit he picked, and the proof of this pudding is that you are here, which, as you ask, is Hythe, if you know it, the central of the Cinque Ports on the coast, not too far from Romney. I had made plans, but I suspect they are not in place any longer. We'll have to seek a ketch that will carry you across the narrow neck of ocean."

Piers seemed still to be thinking about all that Thomas had told him. He said, "Fleetwood's not a man?"

"Well, his skin and bones are those of a man. It's his soul the elves own."

The doublet was too large for Piers, but it would serve. Thomas reached out to him with a leather purse. "Tuck this in under your doublet and keep it hidden. It's sovereigns and ryals, enough for you to tour all of Europe for a year, should you prefer. And also to buy clothes that fit."

He took the purse, stared at it. "Where did this come from?"

"Under those boards there." He pointed into one corner.

"I—who are you?"

Thomas replied, "Best if you can't answer that. Enemy of the elven, that's enough to know, for you, for them. But, then, they're unlikely to have the opportunity to hunt for you when their tithe is now overdue. At least, that is my hope. Time and *teind* wait for no elf."

Piers tried on stockings and then looked at the shoes. There were three pairs in the bag. He found one that fit.

Thomas nodded. "That will do, certainly for the time being. Let us see what we can find for you. We may have to pay a wherry to take you as far as Hastings to get you across. I'm sure once the Brede Inn is fully awake, we'll get something to eat and then locate you some kind of transport." He put his quiver of arrows up on the shelf, then replaced the bag to cover the weapons.

In fact, to their good fortune, at the inn was a boatman who knew of a ketch anchored at Romney this day that was bound for Dieppe. They walked with him to his skiff, and Thomas paid him two shillings to see that the youth got on board.

"Will I see you again?" Piers called.

"With luck you'll never need to. Travel safely, young Piers."

As the boatman steadied the skiff, Piers climbed in, and off they went.

Thomas watched for a few minutes, then turned and walked back to the inn. He desired a room. One with a bed in it.

What month and year this was could wait until he had slept for a day.

III. Jeu de Mail

"Who?" asks Nicnevin just before she whacks the hard wooden ball. "What mortal hand and eye is so well set against us? Against *me*?"

The Queen's buzzing thoughts blare across the tableland of shorn blue grass encircling her domed summer house—a peculiar distinction in a location where it is always summer, the outer world manipulated and controlled by subterranean forces greater than even she comprehends. The Unseelie grant the Yvags pleasant environs. It's one more reason that owed tithes must be paid on time.

Nicnevin's elaborate, paneled gown is sheer where it isn't transparent, and beaded with pearls that seem to wave and flutter on wisps around her. She dresses to parody the ostentation of the latest mortal Queen.

Her taloned feet are bare as she strides the stone walkway through the grass. Trailing her are some of her advisors, counselors, and assets. Everyone carries a long-handled mallet. The counselors are glamoured as if in costumes representing other species they have known. One is even shaped as a troll. The assets on hand are the disturbing Bragrender, and transforming Zhanedd, who struts about without armor, naked from the waist up to display the long and vicious scar that runs from throat to belly, a pure white badge of honor so far as she seems concerned, a reminder of what's been endured for Ailfion. Most any changeling would have succumbed to such a wound, but Zhanedd refused to die—in fact, throughout her long recovery spoke only of pursuing and killing, as she put it, "the changeling going by Robyn Hoode." He who had opened her up.

It was a near thing: The wound was too severe for Yvag regenerative powers alone to overcome. The changeling—if indeed he was a changeling—had inflicted what should have been a mortal wound. Bragrender brought her back from the priory. Someone needed to be blamed for the failure to take Robyn Hoode, and it wasn't going to be him.

Instead, Nicnevin had him hand the dying Zhanedd to the subterranean Þagalwood beings as a last resort. Those entities then performed their abstruse surgeries on Zhanedd, opened her up further and filled the damaged part of her with a harvested segment of the same material that comprised them. They are creatures or machines whose parts seem to know instinctively what they are to do, and join together accordingly.

The white segment in her flowed into place. Its bourn immediately sprouted thousands of connections finer than hairs, plugging intricately into her, each tiny connection an agonizing jolt, until the electric pain of being joined to the Þagalene symbiont engulfed her.

And then, as suddenly as it began, the agony stopped.

Zhanedd is become part-Þagalwood. Between the two vertical rows of breathing holes down her torso, the whiteness flows like some amorphous parasite, binding the changeling together. Symbiotic, transformed, but in any case alive.

By the time the subterranean organisms completed their repairs of her and she recovered, many years had passed in the World-to-Be, and the one called Robyn Hoode was either long dead or had moved on without a trace. However, others embracing variants upon that name turned up repeatedly as if to replace him. While Queen Nicnevin sealed off Sherwood Forest as a source of further *teinds*, a whole gaggle of "Robyn Hoods" arose there. The name became synonymous with outlaws.

Initially, recovered and remade Zhanedd took some small satisfaction in eliminating the imitators at every opportunity. She ran across none of the original Sherwood outlaws who had stood against them. None remained alive outside the ballads and tales.

And yet *someone* continues to interfere arbitrarily with the selection of their *teinds*. Either more than one enemy is involved, or else this nemesis is unaccountably long-lived, which would again seem to support Zhanedd's original notion of a rogue changeling. Evidence suggests that the current one is yet another archer—it seems to be a requirement for the rôle—and like his predecessors, he tends to take his arrows with him. However, the latest incarnation of the archer has somehow laid hands upon *kanerva* poison. Now victims of the unknown assailant cannot be reanimated. Nicnevin has three Yvag knights too dead to recover; the sacrifice they were escorting has vanished; and it's too late for the Queen to contact her various Yvagvojas—her skinwalkers—to select another candidate: this enemy would force her to pick one of their own as sacrifice, reducing their number further. The addition of the poison makes it seem as if the enemy lives *in* Þagalwood.

Bragrender strikes his ball too hard. It flies over the Queen's ball and clouts one of the court counselors squarely on the side of the head. Two of the others drop their mallets and catch him as he falls, his glamour extinguished. Bragrender laughs at them. Outraged as they are, they can hardly make themselves look his way, so disturbing is he with his flickering, warping form.

Nicnevin tsks. "I did not request you to take off their heads, Bragrender."

Her offspring frowns.

Zhanedd speaks up then. She proposes they change their pattern and start collecting *teinds* ahead of schedule. "We could keep them in the septenary prison, so there is always someone held at the ready, impossible to rescue. Any attempt to do so would trap our nemesis in the prison, too."

Nicnevin considers that as she lines up her next shot. "An expedient solution," she buzzes, "going forward." Then she knocks her bright blue ball through the grass. A hole opens up in the ground ahead and the ball drops in. She has won, of course.

Bragrender throws his mallet, just managing to hit no one. Still, all eyes turn to him, if only peripherally. With a disdainful air, he takes out his large ördstone and casually cuts a slice in the air as if it were nothing. The other side of the fire-edged ring is dark, lit by torches, an interior of stone and wood, bars and shackles. A foul, choking reek pours out of the portal.

The grotesque Bragrender ducks through the ring. Shrill screams of horror echo from the far side. A moment later he tosses a small human back out, who tumbles and sprawls; Bragrender steps out after, turns and seals up the portal. The man he's ejected through the gate is filthy. He has raw wounds on his ankles from wearing shackles. His clothing is in tatters, his hair and beard greasy, teeth almost green. He looks up at them all in terror. "Use this one," Bragrender advises, his voice harsh and unpleasant.

"Where is he from?"

"Newgate Prison in their city of London." Bragrender bends down to wipe his hand clean in the grass. "Matters not if they saw me in there. They're all adjudged mad or worthless. No one listens and no one will think on him as anything but an escaped lunatic, if they think on him at all. This one was due to be hanged tomorrow so none will hunt for him very hard."

"And how is it you can cut a gate into this prison?"

Bragrender, or one aspect of him, smiles deviously. "Oh, I visit it now and then to terrify them. It's fun." He sneers at Zhanedd as if to say *See how vastly superior is my idea?*

Approaching the small captured man, the Queen covers her nose. She nudges him with her mallet. "Why must they all stink thus?" She tries glamouring their captive. For the most part he transforms into an Yvag knight, though there are gaps in the image due to his extreme filth. "I would reshape him, but it would certainly turn him inside out. Still, I suppose he'll do." She gestures at two of her guards. "Take him, strip and bathe him. Then we'll see how well he glamours and give him to Hel immediately. Go." The Yvag knights stride forward and drag the terrified man away.

Nicnevin thrums. "Your solution is a good one, even more expedient than Zhanedd's, Bragrender."

"Hers is stupid. We would have to feed her *teinds*." What mote of camaraderie might have existed between them in the brief aftermath of their battles with Robyn Hoode, it burnt out long before she even recovered.

Zhanedd for her part ignores his taunts. She seems to have learned patience since she gave up hunting Robyn Hoodes, just as she is becoming ever more noticeably pale. Some transformation is occurring within her, about which she says nothing.

"We still have an enemy who glides in and out of Þagalwood, kills our knights, and knows our world well enough to know its poisons, and so may have even consorted with trolls. Is there an unhinged changeling in the wood who fled Ailfion and now, misguided, attacks us when we pass through? This I would know."

Zhanedd steps forward to steal the attention from Bragrender. "I have set traps for such a one. I would meet him."

Bragrender chortles. "And yet have caught nothing."

"Then for the moment that is settled," says Nicnevin. "Zhanedd will hunt our marauder, and Bragrender will try not to infuriate me further. These are less significant matters than that which continues to irritate: the elimination of this violent queen they have placed upon their throne. She promised tolerance following the abbreviated reign of the Mary creature, but obviously dissembled as any worthy monarch might. In the wake of her strict anti-Catholic laws, we've already lost half a dozen deeply invested skinwalkers to the axe and the scaffold cage. She is as merciless as her father proved to be when he didn't get his way. Too many of our voja have gone to ground and are unable to put any agenda in play. Some hide in sympathetic houses near and in the city of London. Most, however, have sailed to safe havens such as Brugge and Leyden, hiding among and instructing others who would gladly eliminate this Elizabeth."

"And what about her witchcraft ruling?" asks one of the advisors. The question, notes Nicnevin, is aimed at pale Zhanedd, but she seems preoccupied, her thoughts elsewhere.

Bragrender harrumphs. "Goes against us to be sure, but we have already infiltrated the witchfinders' ranks. They're as intolerable and ignorant as the inquisitors of Spain and France, therefore easily worked. Maneuver them just a little, and we can keep investigations pointed where and at whom we like. They will do our bidding and never suspect."

"So-o-o," begins another counselor, glamoured as a sea creature and sporting a tentacled headpiece, who glances around, seeking at least some looks of support. "Eliminating a powerful monarch—we have discussed before the ways this could inadvertently reveal us to the mortals if we are incautious."

"Oh, yes, yes, Panguramin, but you worry far too much of invasion," says Nicnevin.

"It happened before. The Unseelie—"

"Tush, humans pose no threat anywhere comparable to the

Unseelie. We'll make no bargains with *them* before any universes collide or collapse."

"Very well, Majesty. How do we eliminate this interfering queen?"

Nicnevin smiles broadly. "Assassination is the natural course. Enable the humans to do everything for us. We stir the pot and our voja report on the conspiracies that take shape on the isle and in the so-called Low Countries across the water and elsewhere. So many of them want her eliminated, we have to do hardly anything other than encourage the right ones, guide them to connect. Plots will manifest, and out of half a dozen or so, we need but one success. This is what I mean, Panguramin. Humans see whatever we wish them to, and are led to perform as we instruct. Never will *they* gain dominance over us."

"Majesty." A tall counselor glamoured as a pink, long-necked bird bows before her and gives a silencing glance at rotund Panguramin, whose tentacles appear to warp and writhe in frustration.

"Yes?"

"I am far more concerned regarding the protracted wait for each new *dight* in our armaments. We need to scour some of these Protestant leaders in order to control both sides in this back-and-forth, as it seems to be the dynamic we must anticipate going forward. That which was steady—"

"Until the queen dies," Bragrender interrupts. It's difficult to be sure, given his ever-shifting visage, but he seems to be wide-eyed with delight at the idea. To which queen he refers is as opaque as he is unsettling.

"Well, and to that desired end," replies Nicnevin, "our voja who inhabits the *lich* called Mortimer is at work on a simple scheme that should soon enough bear fruit."

She hands away her mallet now that she has won the game.

To Bragrender as she passes him, she whispers, "Find me Ritarenda. Do it now."

IV. The Plague Doctor

The plague doctor stood by himself at the front of the ferry, a shallow-bottomed hoy, and leaned motionlessly on a rough kebbie staff. Sheep surrounded him, bleating, nervous—due in large part to the pigs sequestered (barely) at the opposite end.

What he was thinking, no one else on the ferry could tell. The long-beaked mask he wore beneath his wide-brimmed hat disguised his features entirely and made the other passengers keep their distance from him. The blue-glass lenses hid even where his attention lay.

The sight of him, shaped by his black oiled cassock, was like a glimpse of Death out for a casual boatride up the Thames. He had not been among them on the rough channel crossing—at least, not in that grotesquely avian costume. And he had not stood among the farmers waiting to load their animals on board for the trip to the slaughter. Where had he come from? Had he been waiting for the ferry in the shadows at Gravesend? Surely he hadn't emerged from King Henry's device fort there ... unless there was plague in the fort? And there could be, and who would tell them?

No one was certain as to who had gotten on and who had disembarked at Gravesend.

He shouldn't have had such an effect. Plague in London in the summer months was as common as fleas. So-called community plague doctors abounded. Most of them had little if any medical training; a few were young physicians just starting their careers. He had observed and interacted with them for so long now, he felt he could spot the good ones even while cloaked and masked. Most were only useful at recording deaths.

One thing was certain to those looking on as he passed by: Whatever herbs and fruits and spices he was breathing, they smelled immeasurably better than the stink of the miniature stockyard the animals were making of the long ferry.

Greenwich approached on the left, with the red-and-white royal palace of Placentia perched above. A long straight stairway led from the palace down to the river, beside its immense watergate, behind which could be discerned the royal barge: The Queen herself was not on the river today.

After that came the steeple of the church at Rotherhithe, and then a scattering of small landing stages below various alehouses. The plague doctor observed the few ships anchored there, crews gone up the steps for libations while they awaited word of a berth secured farther upriver at the Custom House docks.

Almost immediately, on the starboard side of the river, the gibbets at Wapping-on-the-Woze came into view. As it was near high tide, all that could be seen of any hanged and drowned pirates there was the tops of their cages, one of which appeared to contain a pair of hands, tied at the crossed wrists and clinging to the top of the cage.

On the left-hand side, the home of the Earl of Sussex, Bermondsey House, passed by, followed by three corn-grinding windmills. The plague doctor could recall when Bermondsey had been a quiet Benedictine monastery as he could also recollect when King Henry VIII changed all that.

The breadth of the river shortly became speckled with wherries and canopied tilt boats scooting around larger ships. Most of them had gathered near Billingsgate—the legal quays and Custom House on the north side of the river—unloading or awaiting their turn to unload. The Tower, an island unto itself, slid silently past as the steersman navigated between anchored ships and headed for a space where he could put in at the quays away from the cranes at wharfside.

They tied up against one nearly empty quay and laid out a plank onto which the animals were to be herded. Most of the passengers hurried ahead of the livestock to disembark.

The plague doctor didn't move, but stood watching as if fascinated by the cranes—a trio of little cabins on stilts that maneuvered cargo off the nearest ship and onto the Custom House quay. Inside each cabin, a man walked inside one of two side-by-side wheels either to raise or lower the rope attached to a pulley overhead. The ropes, ending in hooks, lifted tuns, crates, and other cargo from a ship and held onto it until the cabin was rotated about and the man within stepped from the raising to the lowering wheel beside it. The cabins reminded him tremendously of the treadwheel cranes he had once helped operate to lift and set blocks of stone in the construction of abbeys and cathedrals. Not much had changed in all that time save that the cranes had become a little more sophisticated. *Alpin Waldroup*—it had been awhile since he'd thought of that name. Far longer since he'd spoken to Waldroup's ghost—a spirit he could no longer resurrect if he tried.

Avoiding the livestock, the plague doctor walked along the quay then around the harbor of Billingsgate and a carrack unloading there. He lingered as if to watch the activities, but really to confirm that none of the others off the ferry were watching or following him. They weren't. He strode to the quayside and quickly hired a wherry to row him up to Fresh Wharf on the north side of the river just below London Bridge.

After paying his penny, he climbed the steps and entered the bustling bottleneck of people attempting to push their way onto the bridge. The twelve-foot-wide roadway across the middle of it generally left little room to avoid sliding through the crowd coming from the south. Pickpockets flourished here and did very well for themselves, but even they gave the disturbing plague doctor ample room.

In the middle he passed what had once been the chapel of Thomas à Becket and was now a grocer's shop, just one of the two hundred shops and abodes edging the length of the bridge, which included the ruff shop above which the doctor lived; for now, however, he passed it by as well.

At the south end, he walked beneath the Traitor's Gate, where impaled heads and body parts were displayed overhead. Woe betide you, should a fresh mount drip its gore upon your person. Originally, the traitors' parts had adorned the bridge's drawbridge, but it had been torn down some years before, and the Southwark Gate became Traitor's Gate.

He emerged to set off down Long Southwark. A main thoroughfare, if he'd kept going the road would have taken him all the way into Kent; as with London Bridge itself, walking down Long Southwark would have had him navigating against flocks of pigs and sheep, and gaggles of geese, all being driven to market. He would also have been rubbing elbows with disguised Catholic priests and spies on their way into the City of London from the continent and making use of the teeming main road to blend in. Knowing as he did how they had infiltrated the Church over the centuries, he suspected there were Yvags among the priests who walked Long Southwark. But this afternoon he'd become The Doctor, a man concerned neither with glamoured elves nor with Catholic infiltrators, only with disease and death.

Like the travelers on the ferry and the bridge, the people walking toward the river all parted before him as he strode down Long Southwark. As with those who'd eyed him on the ferry, he represented the very embodiment of the plague in an unsettling if not monstrous form. No one knew what lurked beneath the long-beaked mask. Medicine for them was a variation of witchcraft, simply a state-sanctioned variety. He might easily have been a demon in its employ.

Finally, without St. George's Bar, he turned left onto Kent Street and headed for the Lazarus-house where he served. The house had been here since the 1300s, originally an isolation hospital for lepers. Now it was become one of various plague hospitals, in this case associated with nearby St. Thomas Hospital. In the guise of Dr. Gerard he divided his time between the two. As had been the case with the lepers before them, there was little anyone could do for the victims of the plague except isolate them. The afflicted who showed up at St. Thomas were directed here. The assorted available "cures" were at best harmless, at worst quite capable of killing a patient who would otherwise have recovered. The only real cure the plague doctor knew of was to leave the city until the weather turned bleak and the plague died out. Those who could afford to summer in the countryside were generally still alive come the autumn.

Outside the Lazarus—or more popularly named Lazar—house, a horse-drawn cart stood. A white stick poked up beside the driver's bench—the warning sign that the cart contained plague, but this wasn't a dead cart for hauling corpses. This one belonged to the Viewers—two old women who went from house to house to tally the dead and record the causes for the parish clerk. He could have done without a visit from them, but he nevertheless hurried up the steps and went inside.

All the people who beheld the plague doctor might have considered him the embodiment of the plague, but in truth the two seemingly harmless Viewers were the disease personified: To record the manner of death for their parish, they set foot in every single house where someone had died and thus by direct contact marinated in every ague and fever, shrouded in every miasma filling every plague-infested room. Rarely did the women last long in the rôle of Viewer, but at tuppence for every body recorded, they made enough money to stay off parish relief in the months or weeks before they eventually succumbed. Thus, a collective of sickness hung about them wherever they went. The parish officials, aware of it, insisted they leave their reports in an isolated box to be retrieved at a later time.

These two particular women had been at the job for going on two months. What data they'd collected thus far hinted this would be a mild plague year. The worst he'd seen since moving to London was 1563, when it had consumed 20,000 hereabouts. And that hardly compared to 1348, when nearly everyone around him had died.

In that year he'd speculated at first that the plague might be a disease conjured by the Yvag to wipe out the human infestation occupying the world they wanted. Soon enough, however, he realized he was encountering one felled skinwalker after another, and came to understand that this so-called Black Death played no favorites. The Yvagvojas themselves might be immune, but their lacunal human conveyances were no less susceptible than anyone else. It was chaos for them as it was for unoccupied humans. Nevertheless, the Black Death had drawn him into the world of medicine, the study of humors and herbal remedies for a variety of afflictions—all of which had hardly changed in three centuries.

Inside the Lazar-house he removed his hat and mask, and with a handkerchief wiped the sweat from his face, pushed back his hair. The world went from smelling of cloves, lemons, and lavender to a vague sourness. Fresh rushes for the floor were needed to clear that sick smell away; he must send someone to purchase some at first opportunity.

Thomas unbuttoned and removed the oiled cassock. Beneath it he wore a long mutton-sleeved shirt, baggy breeches to his knees, and silk stockings.

As he lay the cassock down, his nurse, Mme Bennet, wearing a yellow dress and white apron, came up to him. She reached over and tied the strings on the ends of his sleeves. "The parish Viewers are here," she told him, as though he wouldn't have realized that already.

He thanked her, then walked around the corner into the hall, leaving Mme Bennet in the entryway. The two elderly women awaited him there.

The nearest Viewer said, "God protect ye, Warden."

"And you. Who have you brought?"

"Family," she said.

She made room for him to pass. He became immediately concerned with the second Viewer, who appeared to have developed a swelling on one side of her neck. She saw his stare, and touched a hand to the swollen gland as if to hide it from him. He said nothing as he passed by and entered the open chamber.

It was a small room, containing a single bed and chair. Another woman, sunken-eyed and hollow-cheeked, either starving or afflicted, lay abed. Beside her sat either her husband or son—given both their states he could not say for certain. The young man was drawn and pasty of countenance as though he might collapse beside her at any moment. Behind him, a dark-haired girl of perhaps twelve stared down at her mother, then up at Thomas. If she had plague, it was not obvious yet.

Behind him, the Viewer said, "These folk been shut up the full twenty days. Parish fed 'em. Dead cart took away the 'usband and parents of 'im and another boy. This elder boy, Mathias, 'e's strong, outlastin' it so far, though his mum might be gone in the night. And the girl, called Syndony, she been with the rest but ain't showin' no signs at all. Thought us mebbe she's a *special* one." He glanced around and she smiled in gap-toothed amusement. He knew what she meant— that the girl might be a witch. She knew better than to say so directly. "We could take her with us."

The girl was staring at him with her large cobalt-blue eyes, her expression shocked, as if surprised to see him. They held each other's gaze for so long that he thought perhaps she was mute. Then, too softly for him to hear, she mouthed what looked like the word "red" before turning back to her mother. He went on watching her a moment longer before turning back to the healthier Viewer.

"Thank you for your attentiveness, we'll look after her as well." He drew his purse from out of his loose breeches, counted out twelve pennies, and leaned forward to hand six to each of the women. The second Viewer held out her palm, which gave him a closer look at the swelling on her neck, which only reinforced his opinion.

How long did he suppose she would last? Longer than the mother lying here? She must already be experiencing symptoms. She took the money and said nothing. Her eyes dared him to suggest that she might be ill. As a Viewer, she knew what her chances were once she was walled up. The other woman would know, too.

"They are in God's hands now as are we all," he said, and gestured for them to go.

The Viewers took their money and left. Mme Bennet came in to stand beside him.

"We need some fresh rushes," he told her. "Can you see to it?"

"Oui," she said, and went back out.

Thomas walked back to the room with the family. The son looked up at him with tired eyes.

"Young man," he said. "Young man, do you have any family in the countryside, away from the city?"

The brother nodded, finally with some effort making eye contact with him. "Horsham," he said. "Roffey, that is. Near Horsham. Got a cousin."

"Name?"

"Wyntour, same's us."

"Well and good. I want you to come lie down. I shall arrange with the hospital for a wagon that will take you to your cousin. It's not that far, Horsham. Might e'en have you to 'em by day's end, and the healthier for it. Come." He reached out a hand and the brother all but fell against him. He caught the boy and walked him to the next room, placed him on the pallet there, unconscious. Then, with hands pressed to him, Thomas closed his eyes.

The first time he'd done this, forever ago with Janet, his wife, he had felt an abnormality in her and by some means he still didn't understand had pummeled it into nothingness. Whatever had afflicted Janet, however, it hadn't been plague. With victims of plague, there was far less that he could do. If they weren't too weak, he could make them sleep, and sometimes that sleep proved restorative. This boy had resilience, as the Viewer had said, and seemed to be fighting against the disease.

After a while, he got up from the brother, who was sleeping peacefully now. In the doorway he found that the girl, Syndony, had followed them and stood watching. He told her, "Your brother is sleeping. I need to see to your mother. You should go sit with him."

The girl walked boldly past him, unafraid, and stood over her brother. She lifted his hand and held it. Watching Thomas, her head tilted in curiosity, she waved her free hand about just above her brother and repeated the word "Red," then turned her head to stare at him again.

A special one, the Viewer had said. Perhaps, thought Thomas, in this instance she was absolutely right, although he'd no idea what the girl saw.

Mme Bennet had gone to St. Thomas the Apostle Hospital and arranged for a wagon to come collect the family.

The driver, named Hughe Lothey, had provided his services on numerous occasions before this for the hospital, and as much as he could trust anyone under the circumstances, Thomas trusted that Lothey would deliver these three to the hamlet of Roffey near Horsham. Short of going there himself, it was all he could do.

Lothey told him, "We'll make Dorking today anyways."

Within Lothey's hearing, Thomas told Syndony and Mathias, "When this summer is past and plague's in retreat, I shall come look in on you and see how you've fared." He clasped the boy's hand, taking him aside, and gave him three shillings. "To help with your keep and welfare meantime," he said. "Don't say anything to Lothey, he'll be paid well upon return." Mathias seemed to understand. He tucked the coins away, then climbed up and lay back beside his mother. His sister sat cross-legged, and studied him as if trying to figure out what he was.

From the doorway, Thomas watched them roll off in Hughe Lothey's wagon. In spite of his assurances that he would pay them a visit, it turned out that events would conspire to send him off in another direction entirely, and he would not reach Roffey at all.

V. Christianne

Christianne Maddock drew back the curtain and tumbled in beside Thomas Gerard in his four-poster bed. She'd just visited the third-floor privy, and had to say it was quite the luxury. There was something to be said for living in a London Bridge house, and one was that the toilet emptied straight down into the river, dispensing with the need for chamber pots and close stools. One had only to descend to the third floor.

Christianne was nineteen. She had been on the game for five years before she had encountered the physician whose bed she now shared.

She had worked at the Cardinal's Hat brothel in Bankside not far from the Bear Garden. Somehow in that time she had managed to avoid contracting syphilis—one of the numerous perils of her profession. Gerard treated the women for various ailments, including two she knew who had contracted syphilis and two others for pregnancies. One had kept her child; the other made use of an abortifacient the doctor had procured, made with rue. For the syphilis there was only mercury, and it only seemed to help when the affliction was caught early; yet miraculously Dr. Gerard's ministrations seemed to banish even the pox. Others he treated for wounds and injuries suffered mainly at the hands of their customers. She'd had her share of those sorts, but usually could get them drunk enough to make them pliable and easy to evict. If it hadn't been for Threston, her relationship with the good doctor might never have evolved into anything.

The owner of the Cardinal's Hat was named Urquhart. She thought him by and large a fair man, not one to sample or even handle his own merchandise. His passion, if it could be called that, was gambling, at which he was not particularly lucky.

One night, playing cards in an upstairs room, he had lost heavily; the final pot had included co-ownership of the Cardinal's Hat. The morning after, it was all any of the women could talk about.

The man he'd lost to, his new partner, believed that every girl and woman working for him was also required to service him if and as he chose. Unfortunately, what he, Threston, seemed to enjoy most was causing pain. Within a few weeks, other girls had been variously whipped or caned, kicked down the stairs, and in one instance burnt with a poker across the backs of her thighs.

Whereas Urquhart might protect the women in his employ from a violent customer, nobody was going to protect them from the new co-owner himself. When Threston finally got around to her, Christianne scorned his invitation and in return received a beating that broke her nose and cut her lip and nearly dislocated her jaw. She was fortunate not to lose any teeth.

Thus did Threston see to it that Christianne met the physician Thomas Gerard outside of the Cardinal's Hat.

She sought the Lazar-house where Gerard often worked. Another of the doxies, named Ellen, accompanied her to make sure she met up with Gerard.

Christianne doubted Threston would notice her absence, but to be safe, she hid in the early morning shadows until she spotted Gerard returning from St. Thomas Hospital a few streets away. She had not announced her presence to the French woman who arrived there first. The woman might have taken her in, but Christianne did not know her. Instead, wearing an old, stiffened hood, she approached him. He saw her swollen face, crooked nose, gashed mouth, and heavily bruised jaw. Asking no questions, he led her inside.

It would be days before she was even recognizable as herself again. Gerard treated her cuts and bruises and carefully set her nose, which adjustment caused her to pass out. While he treated her, he asked her repeatedly who had done this to her, but she preferred not to say. This was her situation to deal with, not his.

When she woke, the doctor explained to her that as the Lazar-house currently contained no plague victims, she was welcome to remain there while she healed—at least until that situation changed.

She could assist Mme Bennet in cleaning and purifying the rooms if she felt a need to pay for her keep. The floors always needed new rushes. Under no circumstances was she to return to the Cardinal's Hat. Christianne objected. She complained how much money she was failing to make because of what Threston had done. Gerard asked how much that might be. He really seemed to have no idea. She replied that she could be making ten or even fifteen shillings the week, but "looking like this, I'll be lucky to win a penny to buy a loaf." She flexed her jaw and winced. "Like maybe though I couldn't eat it if I did."

She had no family, at least none she was going to admit to. That life had hardly been better than what Threston offered. Gerard, on the other hand, proposed to try to find her some suitable employment while she healed. "Even with no particular skills, I'm sure you could make three pounds a year as a maidservant."

She gave him a tolerant smile but shook her head carefully. "Take from me my thanks, but I'll go back to what I know soon enough. Other than Threston I been doing just fine at the Cardinal. Look out for each other, we sisters do." He nodded but seemed to want to say something more, probably how, since Threston's arrival, more of the women seemed to *require* looking out for.

Instead, he replied, "At least allow *me* to do you some kindness. Be our guest here until you heal. Mme Bennet will look after you. You are far less trouble than any plague victim."

Yet, a mere three days later, it seemed that the far-off plague had arrived, and the beds began to fill up again. Gerard explained, "A light plague year unfortunately doesn't mean a year without plague." He described the disease as imitating the ocean, arriving in waves. Why, he did not know. No one knew. There were any number of theories, he said, but many more questions than answers: Why did far more men contract plague than women? Why was it that foreign ships arrived off the high seas with a crew already plague-ridden? How had it found them at sea? Had they carried it aboard, a secret cargo, from their port of origin?

Christianne knew of a brothel on the far side of the river that had been shut because of Italian sailors who had brought plague into the house. Upon arrival, they had shown no signs of it.

"The Lord Mayor," said Gerard, "unhelpfully blames the irregular outbreaks on Londoners' fondness for theater-going—especially those awfully corrupted souls who attend plays in the new playhouses erected over in Shoreditch. You know the sort. They absent themselves from church services on Sundays. And yet the Queen herself loves and patronizes theater, even has her own company of players. But that is another matter. My concern is that we must move you elsewhere for your safety."

She dismissed the problem: She would simply return to the Cardinal's Hat despite that Threston remained there. She'd had a visitor from the brothel the day before who warned her that Threston was threatening to garnish her earnings for a year for having run off. At least he wasn't hunting her down yet.

The swelling was much reduced in her face, and her bruises, while tinged with yellow and still a source of pain, were beginning to fade. Her friend Ellen came looking for her, and she prepared to leave, to return to the Cardinal's Hat. That was when Gerard abruptly intervened.

He stepped into the doorway of the room where she stood with Ellen. "Fool that I am," he said, "I should have thought of this before. My own apartment lacks the services of a good maidservant. What would you say to my proposal that you remain awhile in my employ and take care of my house? Just until you're completely healed or you tire of the position, the work. Threston need know nothing of it. And I can afford to pay you well, let's say a sovereign a week for this? More money than you can expect to make at the Cardinal's Hat. Truly, after a year, you might even *buy* the Cardinal's Hat and evict Threston."

Christianne looked first at Ellen, who shrugged, then at Gerard as if she'd never seen him before. Finally, Ellen placed a hand on Christianne's wrist and gave her a slight approving nod. "I will wait outside. Don't rush nothin'."

When Ellen had gone, she asked, "A sovereign? Each week?"

"That's right." A gold sovereign—she wasn't certain she had ever held one in her hand. He might as well have promised her a myth. She knew him for a kind man, but she could not trust that there was no catch to such a contract.

"What shall I be, then?" she asked him. "Nursemaid? You have children, need caring for? A wife who needs someone to help with the cooking and the cleaning? That what this is about?"

"If that were the case, would that be so bad?"

"For a sovereign, it hardly matters. I just want to know what it is you think you're acquiring."

His expression told her that he could understand her mistrust. "Very well," he said, "there is no one else. I've no family for you to look after. No one at all." He bowed his head. "I'm sure if anything it will be quite boring. If you want to leave at any time, you can. It will always be up to you, although I find the Cardinal's Hat the poorer option. You'll have your own chamber in my house, your own bed. Granted it will be a trundle bed until I can get an oak frame made to suit. But I swear to you I won't interfere with you."

She smiled, winced at the twinge in her jaw, and then answered, "Why not?"

That was how she ended up in his apartments on London Bridge.

It took them a half hour to walk amongst the tight, milling crowd, passing through one underpass after another and the various shops on both sides of the central throughway, then beneath the prefabricated jewel of the bridge, Nonsuch House, before arriving at his own house. "Nonsuch," he told her, "was assembled here where the drawbridge tower used to be. It's not quite the same size, and there are some planks of drawbridge remaining. You see?" He led her over to the wall to look downriver. "The drawbridge hadn't worked in eighty years. Watch this step here. This board is dangerously rotten. They should really put up a barrier around it before some sheep or person finishes the job of splitting it in two. Of a clear morning, from here one can see all the way to Rotherhithe. Of course, I have a better view up on my roof. Come." He took her hand and led her back to the twelve-foot-wide bridge road. According to Gerard, nineteen arches spanned the river below, all supported upon starlings of elm, some larger than others. With no drawbridges remaining, this had become the farthest point up the river that tall ships could sail.

Thomas Gerard occupied the top two floors of the next four-story house on the east side after Nonsuch. Another, similar structure occupied the side opposite. Both structures leaned toward each other. He pointed high up to where two large posts wedged between them. "If those weren't there, I think my house and that one should have met for a kiss in the middle."

The hanging sign above the ground-floor door read THE RUFF SHOP. As the name implied, the shop made and sold ruffs of every size and color. It did a brisk business as well in pins. The second floor housed the shop-owner, his family, and his apprentice.

Bertelmeeus Van der Paas sat behind his counting table. He had reddish-brown hair receding at the sides of his forehead. Thomas led Christianne around the shop, introducing the ruff-maker's sturdy wife Jutte, and his two daughters, Susan and Lettice. The latter girl was shy around the young, blond apprentice, who was named Fulke. The three of them worked at two long benches clustered near a small hearth where a fire was burning despite the warm day.

While Gerard explained to the proprietor that he had hired a maidservant, Christianne wandered over to the two benches to watch the trio at work.

Fulke and Lettice folded a long strip of material that had been sized, cut, and stitched by Van der Paas; they each used a warm iron poking stick with which they made pleat after pleat in the material around a central "neck," turn by turn creating the cartridge pleated form of a ruff, so skillful in their efforts that each fold of figure eights was nearly identical to all the others. Susan concentrated on brushing a slightly bluish paste of starch over and into each gather of a completed ruff before setting the whole thing aside to dry and stiffen.

Finished ruffs stood on display throughout the shop, some consisting of hundreds of pleats, a few the size of serving platters. The most impressive one on display stood an elaborate three tiers high, and each pale tier was of a different color and decorated with jewels and pearls. "The b-bottom layer," Fulke explained to Christianne, "contains six hun-hundred pleats."

Christianne stood transfixed by the process going on around her. From where he sat, Van der Paas looked her up and down with some concern. She had pushed back the hood of her cloak, revealing the damage done to her. The ruff-maker looked critically at his landlord. Gerard shook his head, then walked over to her.

"Perhaps," he said to her, "later you will want to pick out a new ruff or two for yourself. A sovereign goes a very long way."

"She will want some pins, too, I think," Van der Paas called out. "Yes?"

Christianne gave him a crooked smile and nodded. They continued on to the back of the shop and the stairs.

The third floor comprised a broad hall, with a high ceiling. The hall contained an old but sturdy trestle table, four solid chairs, a smaller side table, and a counter table with till drawers as if Thomas performed accounting here (he explained that it was a secondhand table, a castoff from downstairs after Van der Paas bought the larger one he was using now). This one supported a pitcher and a bowl for washing the hands. A tray on the trestle table offered cheeses and fruits. A house servant, whose main employment was in Nonsuch House, had been and gone already. So, Gerard already had a servant, thought Christianne.

The walls here were covered in carved linenfold panels, which gave it the look of a library filled with books all of the same brown color. Two of the walls were mostly covered with tapestries. A stone floor circled out from the recessed fireplace, situated directly over the hearth in the first-floor shop, no doubt sharing the same chimney. Beside it was a doorway to a modest kitchen and pantry. Most of the hall's plank floor was covered in matting, and sprinkled with fresh rushes and herbs, making the rooms smell inviting—especially important given the small privy chamber clinging like a distended wasp's nest to the outside wall beside the kitchen, its lid-covered wooden seat revealing a straight shot down into the Thames. One of her jobs as maidservant would be to replace the fragrant rushes as they dried out. "There is a shop near the north end of the Bridge sells them," he told her. He led her up to the fourth floor.

That floor was divided into three more rooms, the smallest hardly more than an open closet. The medium room, being used for storage, contained very little—a small travel chest, satchels, cloaks, pairs of boots. The walls here were covered in a repeating paper pattern that had been in place when he purchased the property, according to Gerard.

The room had a sloping dormer ceiling on one side. At the end of the dormer a small door opened onto the flat rooftop of the third floor. A low parapet curved around the rooftop. Wind off the river below buffeted them. She stood at the edge and looked down. The bulge of the privy was discernible past the parapet.

As he had promised, the view of the river was spectacular.

The largest room on the top floor contained his bed and two chairs. The opposite side of the dormer slanted away here. Another door opened onto the third floor roof. From underneath the oak frame of his bed, Gerard pulled out a trundle bed. The trundle was more of a cot—a smaller, narrower frame that fit snugly under the bed. It was made up with a smaller mattress, a pillow, and a wool blanket. He reiterated that Christianne was to have a bed of her own in the other chamber before many days had passed. "The carpenter who provided this one for me is quite reliable. I've no doubt he'll have something with posts already carved or else we shall have him situate and carve them here."

As neither of them had eaten much throughout the day, Gerard insisted on taking her to the Sun Tavern on New Fish Street.

It proved to be a raucous evening, as the Lord Admiral's Men were there celebrating a performance by one of theirs, an actor named Edward Alleyn, at the newest London theater, the Curtain. From what she could overhear, Alleyn had acted an astonishing female lead in whatever play they were celebrating. Given how much they were laughing, she guessed it must be a comedy.

Gerard ordered assorted meat pies, savories, and a sealed quart of wine. The two of them ate ravenously, and mostly ignored the cheering and shouting of the actors, who themselves ignored everyone who wasn't in their company, save for one, who glanced her way a few times. She was fairly sure she'd had him and not all that long ago.

True to his word, Gerard left her on her own in the house while he tended to an increasing number of plague victims at both the hospital and Lazar-house. Simply as something to do, she cleaned the house and replaced the old rushes. Each day upon his return, he seemed to expect her to have gone, just as each day he seemed delighted that she wasn't.

Twice in those first nights she attempted to climb into his bed with him. The first time, he politely declined: "As I swore, you do not owe me any sexual favors in trade either for the work or the money." The second night, he insisted more adamantly still.

"If it's boys you prefer, Doctor, I can recommend two who are very good."

He started to reply but then seemed to give up. He thanked her for her offer, but declined.

Two nights later, she waited until he was asleep. Then she carefully climbed in so as not to wake him. In the morning, she stirred lazily and opened her eyes, as though his looking at her had roused her. Then she rolled over and climbed atop him with purpose. He said, "How can you be so petite and yet weigh on me like a boulder?"

She, stroking his passion until it equaled her own, leaned down and whispered to him, "I'm not doing 'is out'a some debt. You need ta understand that perhaps *I* want something, too. And wanting it, I mean to take it." She promptly proved her statement.

The night after that when she came to his bed, he put up no fight. She said, "I ain't ashamed of my skills. This is my choice, so not your place to reject it. You did offer me the freedom to choose, yes?"

"I did," he agreed.

By the fourth day, a carpenter and his assistants arrived with the sections of a bed frame for her. As Gerard had predicted, they brought posts that were already elaborately and beautifully carved. The doctor purchased a large coil of rope, which the carpenter used to thread and tie off in lengths supporting the mattress. Then he lay the feather-stuffed mattress upon them. Now, he said, she had a bed of her own in place in a separate, if slightly cluttered, room and she need not come to him again. She did anyway, night after night. "People aren't meant to sleep alone," she said. "At the Cardinal's Hat, the other girls and I slept together often, shared our beds. Especially once Threston arrived."

At the end of the first week, she received her promised sovereign. She was by then keeping house for him and even sometimes cooking. London Bridge was practically its own market. Cattle and fruits and vegetables from Kent crossed the Bridge on their way to Leadenhall or Cheapside or one of the other markets. The clogged thoroughfare ensured that there was always time to barter and almost always something of interest to barter for.

The second time she received her sovereign, she asked for two weeks more in advance, and he gave it obligingly. It was obvious from his expression that he expected more than ever she would be gone when he returned.

Instead, she spent the next day in Van der Paas's ruff emporium, handling one of the heated rods and intricately but somewhat clumsily pleating a ruff under the guidance of no less than Van der Paas himself. It was warm working with the rod so near the hearth, and Christianne had removed her sleeves, her pleated skirt, and bum roll, leaving her in shift and apron. Her dark hair, loose, hung halfway down her back. She looked up at Gerard when he entered, and grinned.

The ruff-maker pursed his lips and vigorously nodded. "She might become very good at the pleats, I think," he said. "She has—what you say—the knack of it? She wants to learn starching, you know, as well and, while I can teach her, she should go to Antwerpen and the employ of Diones Welfes, who is the queen of the starching. That will make of her an expert. In great demand."

That afternoon they returned to the Sun Tavern. She revealed that she had spent his sovereigns to pay for her apprenticeship in ruff-making. She intended, she said, to learn everything about the trade and then open her own shop. "That would be—that is, I would be pleased to see that."

A week later, while Gerard was at the Lazar-house, Threston turned up at the Ruff Shop.

He came through the shop door dressed in adequate finery—doublet, baggy leggings, and an absurdly large codpiece. He had the furious bleary-eyed look of an insulted bear in his cups. He wore no cloak, and his ruff was dirty and half-unpinned.

Her back to him, Christianne stood in her shift and apron in the shadows of the shop, bent over a length of silk she was attempting to work into the appropriate shape. The form had gotten away from her. Lettice, beside her, clucked her tongue at the uneven folds and told her to start it again, and she would have, only she heard and then saw Threston where he stood berating Van der Paas himself. He hadn't yet seen her. She laid the poking stick down on the bricks of the hearth. To Lettice, she whispered, "Tell me when he leaves."

Van der Paas said, "You seem to be in need of some pins, sir."

Threston's lowery gaze fastened on Van der Paas as the man in charge. He pressed one hand into his collarbone. "You," he said, "I'm told a doctor name of Gerard lives above here. That so?"

The proprietor replied honestly, "The physician is not at home. You to St. Thomas Hospital should go."

"I know *that*. It ain't 'im I'm lookin' for. It's the girl 'e brought 'ere for 'is own."

Van der Paas could not overcome the natural instinct to glance her way.

Threston followed that glance. Christianne didn't even have to see him to feel his attention. She glanced at Lettice, who shook her head, but Threston had already started across the shop.

"*There* she is," he said loudly, as if she were an old friend.

She turned around to face him.

"Well now, girl, we been holdin' your space but you hain't turned up to earn your keep. A small fortune you owe The Cardinal already. You think you're gonna go off an' make ruffs nah, do ya? This your new livelihood? Not what you're for, is it?" As he passed one of the displays, he shoved the elaborate ruff on its stand onto the floor. Van der Paas cursed him and ran forward. Threston ignored him and circled the table at which she'd been working. "You're an investment, like, you know. You don't get to leave before you've paid the balance."

Christianne backed up to the hearth, Lettice beside her. Van der Paas shouted, "You get out of my shop, vandal!" Threston turned to deal with him.

That was when Christianne grabbed and whipped one of the hot iron poking sticks against his face. Threston sprawled across the table, knocking strips of material, pins, and neck forms every which way. He rolled over and stood up. A red welt cut across his cheek and the bridge of his nose. The stick had somehow spared his eye.

Christianne fled past Van der Paas and out into the crowded thoroughfare. The only thing she could think to do was spare the family from this bastard. She glanced back, to see Threston lurch out of the shop after her. He immediately encountered a large flock of sheep being driven across the bridge to market. The sheep trapped him.

She thought of running all the way to the Lazar-house, but decided she was tired of running from him. She turned and made sure he saw her as she fled toward Nonsuch House. He shoved and kicked the sheep aside. Their herder cursed him. He ignored the empty threat. From one voluminous sleeve he drew out a short baton that he gripped beside his leg. She knew that when he caught her this time he would beat her to death.

Christianne ran to the edge of where the old drawbridge had been, the spot where Gerard and she had stood. It might work. It was all she could think of to do.

Threston charged after her. She still had the poking stick and she still held it as if promising him a fight. Given the chance, she would stab him. He leered. There was going to be no chance. He was going to toss her into the Thames, and she knew it. He would watch her fall all the way down. He was that sort. But not until he'd punished her for gashing his face. He touched his cheek, looked at his bloody fingers, then licked them, and grinned at her again.

He marched straight for her, crossing the same boards as she had done, but the same boards proved less inclined to support a fifteen-stone lout than an eight-stone woman. One moment Threston was there, and in the next the plank Gerard had pointed out to her had snapped with a loud crack and Threston was gone. Someone in the crowd may have screamed, but it might only have been a sheep bleating in triumph.

Uncertain she could believe her own eyes, Christianne walked carefully to the jagged hole in the drawbridge plank and peered down. Threston hadn't reached the river. He'd landed on one of the large piers and rolled down to the stone and brushwood starling. His head was canted oddly.

She edged around the broken board and made her way back along the side of the bridge road to the shop, ignoring the catcalls her half-undressed state provoked. Once inside, she marched to the table where she'd been working. Van der Paas, his daughters, and Fulke just stared at her in awe. She set the poking rod down on the hearth to warm it again, and then, as if they'd not even been interrupted, said to Lettice, "Now, please show me what I did wrong."

Gerard returned to his apartments late in the afternoon. Christianne told him immediately what had happened. Confession finally cracked the stoic façade she'd managed to hold onto. She began to tremble as she described what had happened by Nonsuch House. She knew Threston would murder her, but had nowhere else to run. She clutched at Thomas Gerard and cried, releasing all that she'd been holding in, maybe since Threston had beat her. She expected now that she would be arrested for luring the villain to his death. When she cried herself out, Gerard took her back downstairs and left her with Susan while he went to see for himself.

Returning to the shop, he informed her that the tide had come in and had swept Threston away. "I can't imagine anyone at the Cardinal's Hat will miss him, and you can stop worrying that someone might be coming after you. From here you make whatever life you want."

VI. The Dying Priest

By August, the Lazar-house overflowed with bodies half a step away from being corpses. This was still shaping up to be a mild plague year, but "mild" hardly meant plague-free. Thomas, in his doctor's mask and cassock, remained anonymous in public, one of a number of such garbed physicians about London. Through St. Thomas Hospital, rumors spread that more victims of plague recovered in this particular Lazar-house than any other. People of means who had survived twenty days of isolation paid to be taken there, whereas others with more money and the knowledge to bribe the right authorities, could avoid isolation altogether and be delivered directly to the Lazar-house. Inevitably, the house's reputation and that of the practitioner Thomas Gerard became intertwined. That was how he came to encounter the priest named Mortimer.

The priest arrived in a small plague cart as if he were already dead. The cart driver must have been paid well to remain after delivering the afflicted priest. A spindly man, he watched Thomas arrive in his cassock, hat, and mask, then climbed down. The driver said, "You're the doctor, Gerard? 'Is Grace heard about you from a parishioner what credits you with saving his life. Wants you to see to 'im, and nobody else. 'Is name's Mortimer. And he's paid me to wait 'ere and take him back home, and you ta see 'im."

He proffered a small purse. Thomas said nothing, although he thought the priest mad to think he was going to be fully cured of the plague in short order and would ride out of here sitting upright in the

43

cart. Nevertheless, he took the purse and, upon entering the house, handed it to Mme Bennet. She looked tense, strained.

Thomas hadn't even removed his mask and cloak before an intense chirring filled his head, as if two or more nearby Yvags were shouting at each other. He winced, and paused in his tracks. Had the driver been paid to deceive him, send him into a trap? How could the creatures have found him here? He'd been careful, wearing this costume in public, seeming sometimes tall and thin and sometimes shorter and rotund beneath it. He remained anonymous in mask and cassock to keep people away. He looked over his shoulder, but no one was behind him, no one followed after; but he understood why Mme Bennet looked strained. No doubt she sensed something of the rage pouring forth. "Please," he told her, "wait here."

The Yvag chatter ahead was vituperative—not the whispering communications of elven knights lying in wait, but a stream of invective fueled by rage against many perceived insults. More surprising was that the name *Nicnevin* wove through the cursing. This was not an ambush nor anything like it, but an argument that did not even include him.

Thomas continued along the hall. Another hapless plague victim occupied the first chamber, and was attempting to cover his ears and curl up tight to escape the screeching dispute.

Thomas walked on to the last room, amazed that Mme Bennet had been able to endure the inner turmoil that long. He stepped into the doorway.

The afflicted priest lay barefoot on a pallet. He wore an embroidered smock, and somehow still had a sleeping cap on his head, which rocked side to side in his delirium. The priest was a skinwalker host, and in such dire straits that the two personas of priest and Yvagvoja had fractured, severed by the plague. The voja clutched onto small lucid moments here and there but could not keep his detaching conveyance from deteriorating. From that alone, Thomas knew the priest's time was short. Probably, he had ignored the buboes and other signs of the plague, thinking himself so far above mortality that he needn't concern himself.

Thomas couldn't have helped him if he'd wanted to. And he didn't want to.

He was, however, interested in the seeming backflow of rage the plague had triggered. The human host was in a state of delirium, of course, but the voja, wherever it lay, wasn't clamping down on their communication, either. The Yvags, like Thomas, would normally be immune to the disease. Mortimer's voja had made the mistake of assuming his occupancy of the human host would protect it. Now all the Yvag could do was ride out the storm or for the sake of its own sanity try to withdraw prematurely by killing the *lich*, the occupied body. It might have waited too long. The fever had spread.

Thomas backed away from the fiery squabble. He walked out to where the cart driver waited. "I am sorry," he said. "Someone has exaggerated the curative powers of our house. We will make your priest as comfortable as we can while he's here, but at this juncture, there is little anyone can do other than pray for his soul."

"Is 'e—" the cartman started. "Is 'e yellin' at God, sir?"

"I can't say. His soul has torn in half."

The driver crossed himself, then looked nervous that he had done so. "God 'ave mercy on the poor man," he muttered.

Thomas assured the driver that he would do all he could to aid the priest. "Which church is it he represents?"

"St. Botolph, sir," the man replied.

"Any one in particular? There are four such in London."

"In Billingsgate, sir."

Thomas nodded. "God's blessing that your parish recovers." He handed the man a shilling. "No need for you to wait."

"Thankee, sir." The cart driver tucked the coin away, then brushed his hands down the front of his dirty jerkin and hurried to his cart now that he had permission to drive off.

Thomas assured Mme Bennet that he would be fine, but that she mustn't come in, because the dying man was far too infectious. Then he returned to the priest.

Mortimer had sweated through and vomited upon his smock. Even through the barrier of flowers and herbs in the mask, the stink was mephitic.

Coming up beside him, Thomas lifted the priest's left arm, studied the wetness beneath it. The blackened armpit was freely leaking pus and blood into the smock. Delicately, he turned the head to view the swollen, bulbous neck clearly, and finally lifted the smock to peer within. If there had been any doubt before, the prominent buboes in both armpits and groin confirmed the lethal state of the plague. It was a wonder the priest wasn't already dead . . . except, of course, he was.

He lowered the smock. At last the priest focused upon him with eyes sunk deep in two pits, then erupted in laughter as if amused by the long-snouted mask. "Only thing worse than spies is the death," wheezed Mortimer. "Both so treacherous, hey?" He grinned.

"Fatal," Thomas agreed.

The priest grabbed him by the wrist and began to speak in French. "You will not save me then, physician?"

"You're a prelate. Surely, you know more about salvation than I." He carefully pulled himself free of the priest's hand, pushed it back onto the pallet. "Your corporal self cannot now be saved withal."

"No. But you could hurry it along." The priest grunted dismissively, then drifted off, eyes closed. The chirring quieted. The voja seemed to lose its connection to the body, and Thomas anticipated he was about to die. Then suddenly, the priest glanced up at Thomas again and momentarily came to his senses. With sudden intensity he asked, "What is the day?"

"'Tis a Thursday."

At that, the priest visibly relaxed. "Then it is tomorrow and I've missed it not."

"*What* is tomorrow?"

In singsong, he answered, "The Queen's barge, it travels the river, the glorious Thames, all glitter and gold." He tittered. "Oh, the Lambeth bells do ring out . . ." He seemed to lose the thread of it. Then he asked, "From here we can hear them, can we not, the bells?"

"Whenever Her Majesty sails the river, we hear the bells, yes. You hope to live that long, do you, to hear the bells ring out again?" It seemed an odd thing for a skinwalker to fixate upon.

But the priest wasn't listening to him any longer. "At Deptford *praematurus* ends the reign, rejoice, rejoice! Hosanna!"

In his head the chirring intensified, *lich* and passenger lost in some form of giddy, incoherent raving. Thomas leaned over Mortimer and prompted, "Deptford? What happens in Deptford?"

Sunken eyes focused on the blue lenses of his mask. "Bird doctor, in the marsh near the creek, you can stand on one leg and watch our assassin, ay. Oh, he'll be quick and not miss such a doe when it presents. One shot wherefore all the banishéd come home, carrying silver spoons to sup on her corpse." The wheezing priest seized up then. A shudder traveled through his body.

Here it came.

Mortimer's heels kicked at the pallet and then stopped. Thomas pulled back before a watery red mist erupted out of the smock only to rain back down upon it. As he looked on, the body decayed, its festering liquids leaking into the pallet, its skin turning gray and coriaceous.

No point in rushing to St. Botolph's now. The voja would be active immediately. Even if it was suffering any aftereffects from contact with the plague, it would open a portal and vanish long before he could make his way across the river.

The only remaining question was whether he understood correctly that the Yvags intended to assassinate the Queen. Mortimer, while not a part of the arrangement, had been privy to it, and a beneficiary of its successful enactment. Some unnamed assassin would await her barge, tomorrow near a creek in Deptford.

VII. The Deptford Deception

The day was blustery, the wind kicking up a fine spray off the Thames as Thomas hailed a four-foot-wide wherry from the south shore below the Bridge. The boatman rowed over. Thomas climbed aboard and asked to be taken to Deptford. He placed two pennies in the boatman's hand.

Thomas held his unstrung bow wrapped in muslin. The quiver at his belt angled out from the fullness of his hose. Fortunately, in London there was nothing odd in someone well-dressed going about armed for archery. The Queen herself had made it mandatory for all respectable men to practice archery regularly, though the main spaces for that practice lay on the north side of the river, in Finsbury Field and across the Spital. Still, for all the oarsman knew, his passenger was off to practice at Bermondsey or some other such location where rich men dallied.

Thomas glanced back up the river. Right now the Queen's barge was somewhere above London Bridge, so he still had time to seek for the assassin that Mortimer had babbled about. Deptford wasn't too great an area to search. There were fields, meadows, but much of it along the water was shipyards now. And the priest had referenced a creek.

As they got closer, the oarsman said, "Y'know, there's a fine beer house in Horsleydown, got some targets set up even, last I knew."

"Yes, I know of it, but deliver me below the shipyards and I'll give you a groat to spend at the Beer House yourself."

This must have appealed to the oarsman. They shot along the river, the wind blowing gusts of spray over them, in and out among the hundreds of wherries and awning-covered tilt boats, and then around the ships at anchor at the Custom House wharf, and still others resting below the southside taverns. The oarsman navigated them out past all those. Glancing back, Thomas spotted the Queen's barge and an entourage of smaller boats all swarming just below London Bridge.

The wherry gave wide berth to the King's Ship Yard, where one ship like the ribbed skeleton of a whale sat up on blocks. Men, tiny by comparison, swarmed over it. One after the other, the boat passed the upper, middle, and lower watergates.

The oarsman pointed to a bluff ahead. "Tha's the Deptford common green," he said.

"All right. Put in there."

They pulled up alongside the first dock below it. Thomas handed the boatman his bonus, and climbed out, tugging his cloak around him. Off the dock, he headed up toward higher ground. Before climbing up, he paused to cast aside the muslin and string his bow, then headed east in the direction of Deptford Creek.

On his left along the river lay more docks and wharfs and, on the elevated ground behind them, another two taverns. Sailors from anchored ships occupied tables on the lawn and watched him pass by. Ahead, the wharfs came to an end. Then there was just river mud and reeds, much of which would be immersed at high tide. The marshy land beyond sloped up to a meadow.

He glanced back the way he'd come. The Queen's barge had reached the middle of the river now and looked to be abreast of the Tower. Wouldn't be long before the efforts of her dozen oarsmen brought it even with the meadow. And he still hadn't come upon any creek. He hastened up the rise behind the second tavern—and there was met with a strange sight.

At the edge of the bank overlooking the Thames, a well-dressed young man stood aiming a caliver musket out across the river. The caliver's barrel perched on a fork rest stuck in the ground. That struck him as odd, because the caliver didn't require such support—except that this young man stood and held his musket as still as a statue.

Thomas crouched low, bow drawn, as he approached. He found there, lying unconscious in the meadow grass, three other figures. Each of them had a mug beside him as if they were resting between servings of ale. Other than the grass, the only thing moving was the slowly burning match cord of the caliver. Even if the musket were to go off momentarily, it was aimed at nothing. This made little sense.

Thomas rose to his feet beside the young man, whose glassy brown eyes continued to look out across the water, unfocused as though he slept, his body as motionless as if he'd been carved in this position. He stood exactly like someone who'd been ensorcelled as a *teind*.

Gun poised to fire but aimed at no target—here was the perfect scapegoat, no doubt, but where were the Yvags? There was no open portal, no signs of a gateway at all. Given that this spelled young man wasn't going to shoot anyone, where was the true assassin? The creek—where was the creek?

Thomas hurried on through the meadow grass toward a line of white poplar trees. Past those, he made out a glitter of water snaking away from the river.

The lower sections of the poplars were dark and gray, the upper bark white and smooth. Between the darker, crooked boles of the first tree, a figure hid, dark gray clothes and cap blending into the shadows there. Thomas just made out a bearded face. That man was aiming his own musket at the river, its barrel braced against the tree.

With a quick glance at the river, Thomas spotted the approaching barge. Below, the barrel of the second caliver moved in a slow pivot as the shadowy figure tracked the barge's approach.

The lone assassin remained utterly focused upon the barge, sparing no glance anywhere else. After all, who was there to interrupt his perfectly executed act? He had put all the others to sleep.

Thomas broke into a run toward the trees. He fired his first arrow. It nicked the poplar's trunk and struck the rifleman, who must have pulled the trigger and set off the charge in the same instant. The gun blasted, and a bluish cloud of smoke filled the air. Thomas couldn't look to see what if any damage the shot had done. The assassin turned and stared at him now, wide-eyed and angry. Behind Thomas and up the rise, the young spellbound man's gun also discharged. Perched as he was at the top of the bank in full view from the river, he would be the one pursued and arrested. There was no helping him just now.

In the trees, the assassin turned to run.

Thomas's second arrow caught him high up in the shoulder. His gun went flying and he tumbled down toward the creek.

He scrambled up again and ran, but, reaching the trees, Thomas had a clear shot at him now, and his third arrow found its mark dead center. The man's cap spun away as the body seemed to leap down into the creek.

Thomas glanced back. On the promontory above, the young man was stumbling about in place. Probably the sound of his gun discharging had awakened him from whatever spell had been cast. He dropped to one knee, then got unsteadily to his feet again. The tall grass swayed and thrashed, so presumably the other three prostrate figures were stirring as well. They wouldn't know what had happened, either, wouldn't know to flee.

Thomas headed down to the creek as two of the tilt boats that had accompanied the barge beached. Men in black jerkins and wide-brimmed hats bounded over the side and charged up the bank. Some carried guns, others polearms. One group came running straight at him. He stopped.

The men neared, and he called out and pointed. "The real assassin's there. *That's* his gun!" At which point one of the queen's guards reversed his musket and struck the butt of it against Thomas's chin; the world exploded with elaborate fireworks.

VIII. In the Tower

They left him in a room within the White Tower—a wood plank floor, two padded stools, one of which might have been there for him to kneel and pray upon, and a small table. Otherwise the room was bare. There was a single mullioned window, the lancet panels far too small for him to fit through, but they were also barred as if he might try. If he'd any remaining doubts about the nature of his detention, the bolt-studded door with a single small observing screen conformed to the idea of a cell, not an apartment.

He'd tried to explain the situation as they sailed him across the river and through the so-called Traitor's Gate and onto the moat, but the guard who'd struck him the first time turned as if about to hit him again, so Thomas fell silent and let them take him wherever they intended. That turned out to be a landing on the west side of the keep. He stepped out, needing no prodding by anybody's halberd. They had his bow and his arrows. He hoped someone had retrieved the dropped caliver and investigated the creek. All he knew for certain was that the ensorcelled young man and his three companions had similarly been carried off in a different boat, a miniature version of the Queen's barge rowed by four oarsmen, and been taken out on the Tower Wharf. He could remember when it was called the King's Quay, but mentioning that seemed likely to get his jaw broken.

He speculated on what would come next. If they interviewed the ensorcelled young man, who knew what story he would tell? It wouldn't include Thomas, but he couldn't say if that was going to improve his chances with the Queen's soldiers or not. He could see from their perspective where the simplest solution here would be to execute everybody, especially given that nobody's story was going to make much sense. Dead enemies eliminated all need for clarity.

When at last a key jangled and turned in the lock, Thomas had dozed off seated on one of the stools, with his back against the wall. He got to his feet as the door opened. Two guards with polearms entered and took their places, one on each side of the door. Then a tall, lean man ducked through the opening.

The man wore a long black robe. He had ruffs at his wrists as well as his throat. His face was thin, his short beard neatly trimmed, the ends of his mustache turned up, which might have suggested a smile except there was no hint of one on his dark-complected face. His brown eyes were doleful, the eyes of someone who had handed down many difficult and harsh sentences and acknowledged the weight of each. He wore a black skullcap that left a trim widow's peak showing on his forehead. He might easily have been the devil, here to claim a few souls.

His pitiless eyes studied Thomas thoughtfully.

"You dress like a gentleman. May I take it that you are?" Thomas wasn't sure what to say to that. The man continued, "You were not quaffing warm ale with Thomas Applegate and his louche companions, else you vanished your cup."

"Is that the young man's name?"

"It is. He and they claim not even to have beheld you. Nor—and upon this they swear—did they fire upon Her Majesty's barge." The robed man watched him intently.

Thomas replied, "Yes, I believe that's true. His weapon discharged over the river but he was not the one who fired upon the Queen. Is Her Majesty—that is, no harm befell her, did it?"

"The shot, for there was but one needs accounting for, broke a glass pane of the barge. It passed through the forearms of the Queen's helmsman. Quite terrible wounds that our physician anticipates will heal. The helmsman will of course have to retire from his position but he will never want for anything hereafter—this by her decree, although he was simply standing near her. He did not intercept the musket ball on her behalf." The dark eyes fixed upon him again. "Did you fire it?"

Thomas shook his head.

His inquisitor nodded. "No, you arrived with bow and arrows, although there was nowhere a target set up in Deptford today for the practice of archery. That would be in Finnes Burie or Moor Field. How do you account for being on the wrong side of the river? Are you a foreign traveler, do you not know your way about London?"

"I know London exceeding well."

"And what do you know of Salisbury Court, monsieur?"

The question startled him. He had to think about it for a moment. "The French Embassy—you think me a French agent provocateur? That I urged—what was his name, Applegate?—to fire upon the Queen?"

"Stranger things have been known."

Thomas silently agreed with him on that point.

Despite his odd interrogation the man relaxed then. "I myself know of something more than passing strange. Would you care to see it?"

"Assuredly."

"Accompany me, then." He turned and ducked back through the doorway. One of the guards followed. The other waited for Thomas to exit.

The robed man awaited him in a stone corridor, then fell in just ahead of him to lead the way. The guards brought up the rear. "Know you to whom you are speaking?" asked the man.

"I am not certain of your identity, sir, suspicious only."

"Let us cure you of suspicions. I am Sir Francis Walsingham, the Queen's Secretary of State. Now, to whom have I delivered this information?"

"Thomas Gerard," said Thomas, "of London Bridge."

"Ah. You are a merchant?"

"A plague doctor. I work out of a Lazar-house in Southwark."

"And you choose to practice archery midday on Fridays, hmm?" Walsingham glanced back with a slight smile before entering a spiral stairwell and descending. His voice floated up as Thomas followed. "You gave no lies in your interview—your eyes looked nowhere but at me. There was no reaching for an explanation, a dodge, a prepared answer. I would have noticed. And so, despite the peculiarities, what prevails is a drunken Applegate who discharged a musket harmlessly without being conscious of the act, while hardly being drunk enough to be so fuddled, his beer so warm in fact, it would seem to have sat heating in the sunlight long enough to sour, and all members of whose party never saw you as you fired two arrows into a second musketeer whom they also deny seeing, although they do share a vague recollection of *some*one leading them up the hill from the tavern."

"Three arrows. The first only knocked him off balance. But you found him, then, in the creek."

"Lucky for Applegate and you that we did. A cloak caught on a fallen branch kept him from being washed into the Thames. Otherwise, the gun lying in the mud would accuse you, and the two calivers taken together, well, they would seem to cement your relationship to Thomas Applegate, and you would all very likely be headed for nooses at Tyburn come Tuesday." Walsingham exited the stairwell. His footsteps echoed around him. The space smelled fishy and vaguely putrid. They had emerged onto a stone platform supporting two massive columns, and beyond them a solid wall that must have been part of the foundation of the white tower. A stripe of murky water off to the side that splashed and sloshed, lit yellow by two wall torches, would be a part of the Tower Moat.

Walsingham signaled for the guards to remain in the spiral stairwell; then he walked around the columns. On the far side of them lay a corpse. It was the man he'd shot: two arrows still protruded from the body, one from the shoulder, the other from the spine...except that, as he neared, Thomas could see it wasn't a man at all, but an Yvag dressed in water-logged fashionable style, with a full-circle cloak over his upper body, its tasseled cords looped around the elf's throat as though the cloak had strangled him; the patterned leggings were twisted, one shoe gone missing. The silvery hair halfway covered the scabrous face. Of course the glamoured assassin was Yvag. What was amazing was that he had carried out all of this alone.

"Might you be able to explain to me how it is you killed a demon with your unique arrows? They *are* specific, are they not?"

He hadn't lied so far and he was sure Walsingham would know it if he were to start now.

"The tips are of iron and also dipped in an extract lethal to them. It keeps them from...reanimating."

Walsingham's eyebrows raised, but otherwise he betrayed no surprise. "They are capable of such a thing?"

"They are. In this instance, it's a happy coincidence that I used those arrows, for I didn't know with certainty that the marksman was Yvag, only that they were behind it."

"Yvag?"

"Of an elven race," Thomas explained.

Walsingham gave Thomas a skeptical glance and stroked his goatee. "Were I not looking at the proof of what you say, I should have you dragged off this minute to Bedlam. It's not far from here. Perhaps I should do so in spite of what my eyes behold."

"I am acquainted with the hospital, Sir Francis, although not yet as a patient. Methinks you would have to share my cell there now in any case."

Walsingham tilted his head back as if he might laugh, but did not. "I should summon Dr. Dee to behold this corpse and give his opinion. He claims all manner of association with the unnatural, yet I believe this will set him on his heels. The conjuring of demons through sigils and goetic seals falls shy of the notion of demons that exist when and where they see fit, necessitating no human agency to bring them forth. Without doubt, he'll be inclined to bring in a witchfinder."

He tapped the tips of his index fingers together while he thought.

"I would hear everything you have to say on the subject of these . . . Yvag, beginning with how you learned of this attempt on the life of the Queen."

Walsingham indicated the way back to the spiral stairs and up. The waiting guards once again followed.

"Do not worry," he said. "I am keeping the body on hand for now. There are secrets yet to be learned from it. You and I shall exit by the West Gate and walk to Seething Lane, Mr. Gerard, where you will give up all of those secrets you have, providing me everything there is to know about these creatures that would kill Her Majesty."

He extended a hand, indicating the way Thomas should go.

"Please," he invited.

IX. Seething Lane

They exited through the West Gate and walked across the open green of Tower Hill. It was coming on night now; Thomas had been held in the Tower most of the day.

As they passed the hill, he could not help observing the permanent scaffold and gallows there, unoccupied for the moment, but there had been plenty of days during the Civil Wars and as recently as the reign of the Queen's father, where he had stood among the crowd and watched beheadings. The day they had executed Thomas More, for instance. A great man to be sure, the lord chancellor. However, Thomas hadn't been there to watch More end his life; he had been on hand, as he always was, to try to identify the elven among gathered priests and figures of state. Skinwalkers especially collected at public executions. They seemed drawn to them, perhaps a result of their being immortal themselves. They watched and buzzed, expressing a frisson akin to sexual frenzy at the moment when the axe fell.

Up on the street now, he and Walsingham rounded the graveyard and then the church of All Hallows Barking, then turned to walk up Seething Lane. It proved to be a short street of large and stately houses. From the street the only thing that distinguished Walsingham's house was the amount of candlelight glowing in its windows. It was as if each room of the several stories was occupied, which as it turned out proved to be the case. Walsingham must have had his own candlemaker on retainer, just for this house.

Throughout Walsingham's house, agents were everywhere scattered. Multiple rooms contained decipherers, seated at tables, some with large code charts pinned up on the walls. Walsingham explained how each decipherer worked to break coded communications from one source or another, adding to their collective knowledge of dispatches they had intercepted. Other rooms held code writers, who were busy fabricating letters to enemy agents utilizing those same codes. Here were female as well as male agents, imitating the handwriting of particular individuals. Walsingham led him through one room engaged entirely in breaking a code in use by Mary Stuart and her supporters in Scotland. It was slow going: The codes shifted regularly.

"I have double and even triple agents in my networks," he told Thomas.

"How does a triple agent work?"

"Oh, they report to Germany or Spain or France as well as to me *about* Spain or France, but then I learn who else is collecting the same data, which can be useful of itself. It potentially guides me to install someone else further along the chain. Oftentimes I find it is best to let information arrive at its destination unscathed, intact but read, and watch what happens."

On the second floor one large room contained a map of the Low Countries, and France and Spain. Green flags stuck into the map represented known and suspected enemy agents, while other flags, red and blue, represented Walsingham's assets in the field, many of them in and around Rheims and Paris and Amsterdam. Small painted portraits hung beside the map. Thomas inquired as to their identities. Walsingham identified a few for him, including one of Fernando Álvarez de Toledo, who was leading the Spanish army in the Low Countries.

Another room displayed a map of all Europe and Turkey, with more flags.

In a smaller room, men seated at benches were at work on mechanical devices: at one bench three men worked side by side devising signet rings with hinged stones concealing tiny hollow compartments for messages, or poisons, perhaps—he could not help thinking of the ring that had nearly been his undoing in Barnsdale Wood. Elsewhere, Thomas caught sight of a walking stick being fitted with a spring-loaded blade in its tip, while across the room a man wearing a peascod-bellied doublet struck a strutting pose and his voluminous belly loudly fired off a pistol shot that seemed to hit nothing. The belly itself caught fire and had to be doused. Farther on, another man detached his ruff with remarkable ease and flung it side-hand at a wax manikin. The wobbly ruff bounced off its target, missed the tapestry that had likely been hung to blunt its effect, and instead embedded in a wall, splitting the paneling. Walsingham winced but made no comment as they walked by.

Almost unacknowledged, they wandered through more rooms of active spycraft, arriving at a set of double doors—the last room on the hall, Sir Francis's own private chamber.

He closed the doors after them. Here he had a desk, a few chairs with arms and cushions, and a draw table, its leaves unextended. He offered Thomas a seat beside the table. From an oak livery cupboard, he brought a decanter and poured two glasses of port. Handing one to Thomas, Walsingham finally and with a deep, weary sigh, sat down with his own glass. He took a sip and closed his eyes in pleasure. When he opened them again, he stared intensely at Thomas.

"If I did not trust you by now, you would have seen none of that." He set down the port. "How much do you know of the plots against the Queen?"

Thomas perhaps knew more than many people did and suspected others; no doubt some of it was inaccurate, as talk in alehouses and even Inns of Court was often speculative if not outright fabrication. But the question posed was simply Walsingham warming up to his subject. Thomas made a small shrug and replied, "I know there have been plots, at least since Pope Pius had Her Majesty excommunicated in his *Regnans in Excelsis*."

Sir Francis nodded solemnly. "Before that, actually. What I call the Northern Rebellion, and Burghley styles 'the Revolt of the Northern Earls,' preceded the Pope's declaration of war by some years. Mary of Scotland had been deposed following her husband's death and she fled from France to England. The Queen ultimately 'rescued' her by putting her in the custody of the Earl of Shrewsbury. She knew already that Mary was a schemer, not to be trusted. There are letters—so-called casket letters—that, if truly written by Mary of Scotland, would prove that she helped murder Lord Darnley, her own husband. And there is no question she receives intelligence from abroad.

"But to the rebellion. Several Roman Catholic earls in the north saw Mary's presence in England as a means to recover the throne and make England a Catholic land once more. They were dangerous men, conspiring against their Queen, and she was right to show them no mercy. We captured and executed Percy. Charles Neville, the Earl of Westmorland, fled across the water, but forfeited titles, lands, his marriage. He lives now by the grace of others, who are still at work to undermine the Queen. Pius's papal bull didn't arrive until after we had smashed the rebellion, but it has subsequently given Westmorland and the rest carte blanche to scheme away. We know they communicate in code with Mary of Scotland and she with them. They would prefer to find her a suitable new Catholic husband, one who might also lay claim to England's throne." He lifted his glass again. "What they perhaps do not appreciate still is how Pius's excommunication only stoked the fires of suspicion: Her Majesty perceives *all* Catholics as enemies now. The tolerance she showed them initially has been poisoned, while the plotting against her has never for a moment stopped, witness the intelligence we continue to gather here and abroad."

Thomas said, "Your task seems daunting, plots and conspiracies emerging everywhere. 'Twould be impossible to chase down every one of them."

"Yes, and that is why I need more operatives all the time. But for the moment, I have gone on long enough about these Hydra-headed schemes. Your creatures are certainly a new head, a serpent that has been playing a part undetected before this . . . You must tell me all of it."

"All of it" was exactly what he could not tell Walsingham: centuries of thwarted Yvag intrigues and machinations, and a far greater number of occasions where he'd been defeated, including the many *teinds* he'd failed to rescue. Then there were his dialogues with the woman the Burgundians had handed over to the English forces, who called herself Jehanne la Pucelle, and these days was called "the Maid of Orleans." Glamouring had afforded him opportunities to converse with the condemned young woman about demons and Yvags and angels. She had described her visions and prophecies to him; they were not dissimilar to his own prophetic riddles and fits, and many did come to pass.

She was martyred by Bishop Cauchon, not an Yvag himself but

certainly in league with some in ecclesiastical garb to discredit her—in particular Father D'Estivet, an Yvagvoja whom Thomas had dispensed with himself, leaving the bastard voja's corpse in a sewer.

Nor could he discuss with Walsingham his participation as a soldier in the English civil wars. He'd been on hand to see Lincoln killed at Stoke Field, after which he had hunted down a complicit skinwalker named Symonds. All of the kings he'd watched rise and go down—the fall of the Plantagenets, followed by the rise of the Tudors—he could not mention. Three hundred years observing and participating in various affairs of state, he could not disclose, else reveal that he was no more human than the Yvags.

What he did tell the spymaster was of the plague-infected bishop, Mortimer, whose desiccated corpse still lay in the Southwark Lazar-house. Mme Bennet refused to enter the same room with the body. "Had he not been delusional, dying from the plague, we would not even know of the plot these creatures concocted, and the Queen, I fear, would have been slain this day. It was a simple and cunning plan undone by indiscriminate illness."

"This bishop. We can assume he is a Catholic sympathizer?"

"What, because he might have had property taken away by the Crown?"

"You understand me, then," said Walsingham.

"I know that the Queen's father stripped the Church of most of its wealth and possessions, especially its property."

Walsingham made a gesture of dismissal. "The city continues to rebuild itself upon those very properties."

"Would St. Botolph's be one such? That's from where the cart driver delivered him." He remembered something else. "It is also possible," said Thomas, "that he had recently arrived here from France—in his pyretic babbling, he slipped in and out of French as well as Latin."

That appeared to catch Walsingham's attention. "And you are certain Applegate knew nothing of any of this?"

"I am certain his innocence is real. I suspect he was deceived by a friendly face, likely someone he thought he knew—he and his cohorts. These creatures upon a whim might look like anyone at all and nothing like their true selves. Or perhaps the group's drinks were dosed with some elixir by one they mistook as their server. Or they were all simply ensorcelled. These things I do not know. The specifics whereby the elven selected Applegate, I cannot even guess. Mayhap it was that he owned a new caliver and readily could be persuaded to demonstrate it, which was a necessary feature if the plot was going to work."

Walsingham frowned. "This innocence of his will pose a difficult problem, as the Privy Council has already determined his guilt and intends to execute him and his associates come Tuesday. You are fortunate in that I shielded you completely from their inquiries."

"For which I do thank you."

Walsingham waved away the gratitude. "Oh, I assure you my reasons were entirely selfish—I wanted to know who and what you were, and what our enemy is, before Burghley's or Leicester's networks got their hands on you. We may all be comrades in arms, but I will have information before anyone else clutches onto it. Also, this way thou art beholden to me for this courtesy. I can hand you over to the other two services or the Privy Council at any point in the future." He said it casually, as if he was stating a simple fact, and Thomas supposed that, effectively, he was. "These Yvag—if they're going to interfere with my work, I will know everything about them that you know."

"Then you're going to want at least another bottle of port."

The spymaster smiled, but his gaze focused inward. "Applegate, though, I have to do something with him. He cannot be allowed to go free when the story of his attempt on the Queen's life has already escaped, and word of her helmsman's bravery—Her Majesty's depiction of the event, you understand—is already being celebrated at court. We must be seen to act decisively in the matter. There must be consequences of some sort." He sipped from his glass.

"But he's innocent."

"Innocents have perished before this. Fifteen thousand at the hands of fanatic Catholics in the St. Bartholomew Massacre alone."

Thomas hadn't expected mention of that. It was one of the many things he had chosen not to reference nor reflect upon. Twenty years earlier, the time Walsingham alluded to, he had been in Paris. The spymaster's words dredged up awful memories.

"Small children disemboweled Admiral Coligny where he lay," Thomas said distractedly. "The mob burnt Huguenot bibles and then choked their victims with the charred remains."

Walsingham looked at him with astonishment. "You were on hand for it, too? Surely you couldn't have been but twelve years old."

"I'm a bit more aged than I appear, Sir Francis." Thomas emptied his glass. Yes, it was quite dangerous mentioning "everything" he knew.

"Nevertheless, Dr. Gerard, the fate of Applegate is a conundrum that you will help me resolve. Once that is accomplished we can investigate the parameters of our mutual arrangement." Walsingham refilled their glasses.

"What arrangement?"

"Why, is it not obvious? Our separate concerns overlap significantly, so much so that I see no reason for you not to be in my employ. I do pay my assets well."

"I have wealth enough."

"Yes, you dress and comport yourself as if you are used to it—a gentlemanly façade that is exactly what I need in an agent. That, and the ability to think on your feet, which again you have already demonstrated in saving the Queen's life today."

"I have a life of my own."

"Family, then?"

He thought of Christianne, who was certainly someone he cared for, but not as family, nor even a devoted lover. If anything, the past few weeks she and Fulke, Van der Paas's apprentice, seemed to have become involved, a development he was honestly glad of. He replied finally, "Well, as it happens, no. No family."

Walsingham opened his arms as if to say *Where is the impediment?* He said, "So. You can continue to oversee the expiration of those afflicted by plague and do your rounds at St. Thomas Hospital. Nothing will change there. In fact, your very occupation may well prove useful to us again before we're done."

Thomas started to speak, but Walsingham held up his hand. "No need to answer me now. Think on all of this and consider what you might do to aid Applegate. Let us solve that conundrum first, and let everything else follow as it will." He raised his glass. "To the Queen," he said.

"To the Queen," Thomas replied. As he drank his port he considered that his first impression had been right and that he had just made a bargain with the devil himself.

X. The Blackwall Rescue

On Tuesday morning, with blustery winds tearing hats off heads, the group of Thomas Applegate and his friends were grimly marched from the Tower along the waterfront of Portsoken Ward, and through Ratcliffe and Limehouse. Their jerkins were for the most part unbuttoned, and their ruffs had been removed—a clear indication of their looming fate. As they went, a crowd collected behind them, following along, knowing or guessing the destination of four men being led by soldiers along streets nearest the river.

In Limehouse, they turned south, heading across the Isle of Dogs, past shops of rope-makers and sailmakers and other rigging specialists and the houses and hovels of fishermen, past a string of windmills, and toward the causeway and the curve of the Thames called Blackwall Reach.

From across the fields of the East Marsh of Poplar they spotted the gibbets that had become permanent fixtures above the river. Two of Applegate's friends tried to turn back then. They wailed and pleaded, tearfully beseeching the guards marching them to their deaths to let them go, swearing that they had done nothing to warrant their being arrested in the first place. They had drunk some ale with a stranger who had paid for the drinks, and then fallen insensible. They hadn't even heard their friend Applegate fire his weapon. The guards remained unwavering and ushered the shackled young men along. By now their families had caught up with the procession, and set about begging the same guards to let their sons go, with as much success.

Thomas, walking along beside the black-gowned Walsingham,

thought it all a cruel act, but knew, as Sir Francis had outlined, that all must be carried out exactly as planned if they were to deceive the enemy. As Thomas himself had surmised, there was one sure way to handle this situation that would not appear suspicious to the Yvags and other enemies, who would be watching, and were probably mixed into the crowd even now. He glanced around at the crowd, half of whom seemed drunk and excited, and half of whom wailed and wept in earnest. Listened for the thrumming of Yvag communication in the wind, but could make nothing out in such a gathering.

Arriving at the gibbets, the guards held back Applegate's friends along with the crowd, and marched him alone out of the mud and up onto the low platform of the first gibbet. A short ladder leaned against the post. Young Applegate turned about to face the crowd as the hangman stepped forward.

Trembling mightily, Applegate spoke to the crowd. "God is my judge, I never in my life intended to hurt the Queen's most excellent Majesty. How it came to pass, I know not. I swear my innocence, and I am penitent and sorry for my good master, Mr. Henry Carey, who hath been so grieved for my fault, suffering unjust rebuke for the same. This was no plot, no—" And here he broke off, his emotions overcoming his ability to continue.

Members of the crowd, likely his family, pushed forward, calling, "Stay! Stay!"

The hangman guided him step-by-step up the ladder as he sobbed, then finally fit the noose around his neck. In a moment he would be pushed out from the ladder to swing free.

There came a tumult at the back of the crowd, someone pushing their way through. Thomas and Walsingham turned as one to watch a well-dressed and handsome figure come forward. Sir Christopher Hatton, the Queen's Vice-Chamberlain, whom Sir Francis had earlier referred to as "the Dancing Chamberlain," climbed onto the platform beside the hangman and turned to address the crowd. "By order of Her Benevolent Majesty, Thomas Applegate is hereby to be set free, and all charges against him and his companions dismissed. The Queen has determined that, while foolish and wicked in his actions, Thomas Applegate meant her royal self no harm and thus she pardons him for his actions. His life is hereby spared." Hatton folded up the paper and gave Walsingham a slightly arch look before descending from the platform. Behind him, Applegate cried out, "Praise God and praise Sir Christopher Hatton!"

"And thus is justice served," said Walsingham to Thomas. "The Queen exercises her magnanimity, a foolish but harmless young man is set free, the Privy Council maintains its retributive judgment, including the councilor—and Applegate's employer—Henry Carey. To the outside world, it appears only that the queen has been generous. Your Yvags will assume precisely that, foolish or not, she has allowed the boy to go free. No one is the wiser as regards our knowledge of any plot to murder her or of their part in it. It is really quite ingenious."

"Letting information arrive unscathed?"

Walsingham laughed, and bobbed his head.

"As I've said, you have a mind for the sort of subterfuge on which my service depends, Gerard—a skill set that cannot be taught, sir. Let everything hereafter follow as it will."

Thomas replied, "I promise to consider your offer, Sir Francis, and to give you an answer anon."

"Do not take long. Events will not wait."

The crowd dispersed, some running across the muddy ground to surround and embrace their saved sons, others no doubt uninterested now that no one was to be hanged.

"I am curious about one thing, Sir Francis," Thomas said.

"Only one thing?" Walsingham asked.

Thomas smiled slightly. "For now," he said. "Why do you call him 'the Dancing Chamberlain'?"

Walsingham chuckled. "Sir Christopher *became* Sir Christopher by dancing the galliard at a masque put on for the Queen. She found him, let us say, appealing to her appetites, and in short order he was knighted, made a member of the Privy Council, and made Vice-Chamberlain of the royal household. Furthermore, the Queen bestowed upon him the house of the Bishop of Ely. Of course that meant she turned out the bishop, who is still complaining two years on. He *should* rejoice that he got to keep his cathedral. And his head."

"I see."

Hatton was walking ahead of them, and patted Applegate on the back.

"He'll be the Dancing Lord Chancellor before he's fully unfurled.

He's done very well using what attributes God has given him. Mary of Scotland accuses him of being the Queen's lover."

"Is he?"

"Not for us to say. But, like him, you have attributes that must not go to waste."

Thomas replied, "I am persuaded that you will only accept my assent."

"Then you understand me well." They walked on behind Hatton and Applegate. "Right now, however," he said, "Her Majesty wishes to meet you."

"What? Me? Why?"

"Oh, you cannot be so obtuse, Gerard. Single-handedly you saved her life, a fact which you know perfectly well."

He wanted to object but could find no substantive argument. Assuming the assassin did have some skill with the caliver, Thomas *had* stopped the Yvag from shooting her. But the last thing he desired was to have his profile elevated for it.

"Right now I am to take you to Placentia Palace where the Queen awaits. A tilt boat for us is at Limekiln Dock."

"Sir Francis, I seek no renown for what I did."

"Of course not. That is the last thing you want. If they are as clever as you've said, then some of these demons might have infiltrated the Queen's household and will be watching."

"You know that and yet you—"

"I do not say no to Her Majesty where her mind is made up. That being the situation, I am curious if anyone should give their true nature away, to me if not to you."

"So I'm bait as well," said Thomas.

Walsingham gave a sort of shrug. "The Queen's summons is a *fait accompli*; I merely choose to make the best use of it in the circumstances. You should do the same."

The tilt boat let them off at the landing that jutted into the river below the red-and-white palace complex of Placentia. Crenelations capped the walls and towers of the entire structure. Ahead of them were its tallest, octagonal, towers.

Thomas followed Sir Francis Walsingham up the steps. On the river, the spymaster had explained that, save for her so-called progresses across the countryside, Elizabeth preferred to spend the whole of her summer at Placentia. She had been born there. The palace and she were as one.

As they crossed the paved yard, everyone bowed before Walsingham. They passed beneath an archway that ran from front to back of the palace and entered there.

Already Thomas was listening, watching every face for any hint of odd expression. But how was he to be sure of anything? From centuries of interaction with them, he knew how well the elven could disguise themselves. They could glamour for perhaps days, or reshape themselves for hours of perfect mimicry; whereas Yvag skinwalkers might navigate a human host for decades and never give away their true selves. Under his breath he muttered an old, old riddle of his: "They who own all, brows never ringed—counselors to kingdoms, never a king." They were the highborn, the influential, the sorts of people whose attention he made a point not to draw, but Walsingham was effectively putting him on display here. Servants and staff might be harmless enough, but among the courtiers it required but one to identify him, while he could hardly go from courtier to courtier, laying hands upon each in order to force connection and hear their infernal buzzing thoughts. And that only covered the Yvags.

As Sir Francis had explained, most certainly there were spies embedded among her staff—some reporting to Mary of Scots, others to the French or the Spanish ambassadors. When Thomas asked why Walsingham didn't sort them all, he replied, "First, Gerard, you must understand, on any given day the people in attendance might number a thousand. Spread throughout the palace is an entire town. Second, and of far more importance, it can be useful to observe a spy who believes they have not been found out. All manner of information can be gleaned from them, whereas an arrested spy is no more than that, their usefulness at an end."

Led inside, they were met by four Gentleman Ushers, dressed in black frock robes, each carrying a white rod. The ushers fell in beside Walsingham and Thomas, and led the way through two corridors and then into a Great Hall, where surely a hundred people stood milling about. Thomas's apprehension expanded into almost tangible dread as various individuals and groups turned to watch him escorted through their midst. Walsingham was known to them, but he was not, and all eyes tracked him across the hall. Walsingham all the while quietly identified various individuals among them. He nodded at a man with a wispy mustache, who was eyeing them intently, "There 'tis the Duke of Norfolk, and there Dudley, Earl of Leicester." Robert Dudley, in an ivory doublet, scowled as if they had affronted him. Another, identified by Walsingham as "the Earl of Lincoln," had a weathered face and white beard, and wore a tall black cap.

Then they entered another short corridor and, finally, a smaller hall, the Queen's Presence Chamber. Woven rush matting covered the floor. The walls were painted with floral swirls and curlicues, and enormous stuffed cushions lay off to one side. Three women sat upon these as if taking their leisure. They, too, focused upon Thomas.

Across the chamber, the Queen stood before her throne. Both it and the cushion upon it were bright red.

The Queen herself wore a white gown with lines of scarlet trim that curved like stems off which were embroidered small red leaves. Her sleeves puffed up at her shoulders. The gown was fitted with a filmy gray gorget and ruff, which matched the gray material that emerged from the slits in the sides of the gown. She stood tall and still, her severe face pale as ivory. Her red-gold hair had been worked into rows of small curls around her face, above her ears. A cluster of gems and pearls nestled atop her hair, while a necklace of pearls was strung as if by casual accident around her. There must have been another dozen people near her, but in her presence he hardly noticed them. His fears fell away, not as if they left him but more as if he could no longer hear them. What he thought of in the presence of Elizabeth was Nicnevin. Here was the same poise, and the same effusion of power. And in any case, he acknowledged, by now everyone had gotten a look at him. There was little point in panic.

Thomas took his lead from Walsingham in approaching her. Sir Francis had been adamant that, whatever he did, Thomas should not turn his back on her, even if it meant walking backward when they departed the chamber.

Sir Francis made a leg and took her hand as he bowed.

"My Moor," she said affectionately to Walsingham. Then she focused past him, straight at Thomas. "Is this he?"

"It is, Majesty," Walsingham answered, gesturing to him. "Thomas Gerard."

"You are quite lovely to behold, Thomas Gerard. I know not your name, but I see your breeding clearly." She smiled and, as Walsingham stood aside, extended her hand to Thomas.

He likewise made a leg, took her hand, and lightly pressed his lips to it. As he did, he noted spots and shallow divots upon her hand. She'd suffered smallpox at some point in her life. He said nothing about it, but fixed her with his blue gaze. She was lucky, he thought, that it had not scarred her face.

Elizabeth said, "Sir Francis has described how you brought down the assassin who very nearly murdered me." Her dark gaze slid from him and took in everyone in the room. "What tribute can I pay to you, Thomas Gerard, for all you have done?"

"Nothing, Majesty. I did not act for a reward."

Her smile broadened. "Well, there's a rare sentiment. Still, what would you have if you could ask for anything?"

Thomas glanced at Walsingham. Finally, he faced her again and said, "I should hope one day to dance a galliard with you."

Her gaze sharpened for an instant. Then she laughed quietly. "So, you would have a knighthood of me," she said, and laughed again. This time Walsingham and then others joined in. "Sir Francis, I shall expect you to arrange this."

"Majesty," Walsingham said in affirmation.

Back in the tilt boat, Walsingham told him what a good job he'd done. "The Queen likes clever men who can entertain her with their wit. You played a dangerous card referencing Hatton, but you did it slyly and successfully."

"Thank you."

"The whole court will be buzzing even now with mention of you. Which means those in league with Mary will know your name. Your elvish demons, perhaps, as well. We have succeeded in kicking the hornet's nest."

"Yes, I'm aware," he replied joylessly. He reviewed the many faces that had watched him pass. "What do we do now?"

"Now? Right now I wish to see the remains of this bishop who launched you in my path. I've sent already instructions to Mortlake that Dr. Dee should join us at your Lazar-house. It is time for me to hear what the great demonologist has to say about these creatures of yours."

XI. Dr. Dee & the Skinwalker

It took Thomas and Walsingham nearly an hour just to navigate the crush of London Bridge. Walsingham used that time to ask what Thomas knew of Dr. John Dee.

With care he replied, "I know that he was imprisoned for casting horoscopes during the reign of Queen Mary of both the queen and of the princess, Elizabeth. Treason, wasn't it?"

"It was elevated to treason, yes, followed by a Westminster Star Chamber examination. They handed him over to a Catholic bishop, Edmund Bonner, for religious examination because of his occult leanings. Instead of damning him as was anticipated, Bonner and he became friends."

Thomas asked, "This would be the same Bonner who refused the oath of royal supremacy?"

Walsingham raised his eyebrows. "You do know your affairs of state remarkably well for someone so uninvolved with government business, Gerard."

Thomas made no reply. He knew of Bonner because, a decade earlier, he'd suspected that Bonner had at some point during his multiple imprisonments been turned, occupied by an Yvagvoja, though ultimately Thomas had been unable to establish it, as Bonner had remained locked away in Marshalsea until his death. If he was a voja, he'd become ineffective, trapped by the obstinacy of his human conveyance. "Did the bishop's friendship cause Dee trouble?"

75

"It did not. Dee converted to Protestantism and now he is Her Majesty's principal astrologist and advisor in natural philosophy. He is a much greater thorn in the side of Baron Burghley, whom he has petitioned for patronage, with repeated attempts to convince him that Dee has secret knowledge of a treasure hoard hidden in the Welsh Marches. That Burghley himself has proudly linked his lineage to the Cecils or Seisyllts of the Marches was my contribution to Dee's knowledge, which allowed him to play upon Burghley's vanity."

"Truly?" Walsingham's confession of manipulation amazed him.

Sir Francis replied simply, "It keeps him occupied."

Mme Bennet met them at the door of the Lazar-house. She nervously babbled in French about the strange tall gentleman who was moving from room to room, studying and speaking to the four remaining plague victims as if he was an attending physician. Clearly, Thomas was supposed to be incensed by this news. Bennet liked her routine and didn't care to have it interrupted, much less interrupted by arrogance. Plus, she'd found the transformation of Mortimer unholy, and had insisted Thomas have the ghastly remains carted away. He'd promised, but after Deptford things had progressed in such a way that he had committed to housing the body until Walsingham could see it for himself. Already she'd spent an uncomfortable day here aware of the unnatural remains lying in the tiny rear room near her, and imagining all sorts of things she didn't even want to say aloud for fear she might cause them to come to pass. Plague was awful enough; matters of magic and the devil were not to be tolerated at all.

Thomas reassured her: Once these gentlemen had scrutinized the body, he would see that it was removed immediately to the churchyard in Billingsgate.

"The bedding as well!" she insisted, and he promised they would take that, too. Of course, of course. He squeezed her hands reassuringly.

Dee was studying one of the plague-infested, a man Thomas had already tried to give some relief. At their approach, Dee turned and stood upright. He was tall, more so even than Walsingham. Beneath his plump ruff he wore a long flowing black gown with layered shoulders and slits along the sides for his doublet sleeves. Like Walsingham he wore a skullcap but in contrast his face was pale and unblemished, his beard pure white and trimmed to a point below his collarbone. His brown eyes were wide and expressive of his keen interest in the sick patient.

"I thought to probe his swellings but then speculated upon the liquids contained within, that they might themselves be a sea of contagion, yes."

"An astute observation," was all Thomas could think to reply; all other imagined comments ended with *You must be mad, sir.*

"It is not for speculation of plague I called upon you, Dee," replied Walsingham. "Ours is a different affair altogether, one more aligned with your expertise in matters occult." He glanced at Thomas for affirmation. Thomas nodded and did not voice his own doubts regarding John Dee's exchanges with demons.

"This way, sirs," he said, and led them into the central hall. Mme Bennet looked on from the front of it, keeping her distance until "ça corps" was gone.

Thomas led them to the back. "I bundled him with his bedding. I believe you'll understand why." He opened the door on the small narrow room.

It was barely wider than the pallet on the floor. The body was mostly covered by a sheet that Thomas now drew aside.

Even prepared for it, Walsingham gave a small gasp at the leathery figure lying on its back, its flesh and fluids having liquified and dried into a brownish oval stain on the pallet around it.

"A trick, sirrah. You've dragged this from a crypt, have you not," said Dee sharply.

"Sir, I have not. Three days ago, this was a bishop named Mortimer of the Church of St. Botolph's in Billingsgate. He was in a state similar to that man you were just viewing, though much closer to death."

"Surely, no. This body has been dead for years," Dee insisted.

Thomas nodded. "Yes, that also is true."

Dee expressed confusion.

"Why doesn't it look like the other one, from Deptford?" asked Walsingham. "Whatever its age, this is a human corpse, not a gray and scabrous monster."

Dee said, "What—"

"That is because they're two different things," Thomas replied. "The assassin in your custody was . . . *is* an Yvag, glamoured by magic to appear human while alive. This bishop was a skinwalker, by which I mean his corpse had been inhabited and directed *by* an Yvag, one hidden someplace else."

"Yvag?" asked Dee. "Does that specify the demon? For this is witchcraft, surely."

"Not demons. A race of elves," Walsingham explained as though it was obvious. Dr. Dee looked back and forth between the two men as if he could not be certain of either of them. His expression suggested that surely they mocked him.

Thomas said, "The glamoured ones maintain their false shape for a short time only—that one in Deptford just long enough to ensorcel poor Applegate and his friends. Skinwalkers, however, can inhabit their human conveyance for a very long time, for years. I suspect the dead bishop had been displaced a decade ago or longer, possibly prior to the Act of Supremacy. The Church has been a reliable haven for the Yvags over the centuries. They wish to accrue power and wealth, and use it to change, corrupt, and remake this land to their specifications. The stability of the Catholic Church allowed them to forge many alliances and accrue great wealth—in particular, in the form of property. When King Henry broke with the Church and began confiscating their wealth, he was also destroying a fabric of manipulation and control that had been woven with care across those centuries."

"But to what end their manipulation?" asked Dee. He seemed to Thomas to have grasped the key points.

"To the elimination of all of us and the reshaping of this whole world to their liking."

"Another race, working to displace *us*?" Dr. Dee was shaking his head, eyes on Walsingham, who looked as dour as ever. "This is sorcery."

Thomas replied, "You don't have to believe in every aspect of it, Doctor. If you prefer, then think of them as what your own philosophy allows: demons will do. They share a commonality. *Your* demons want to claim our souls." He gestured at the desiccated corpse of Mortimer. "These demons can strip us of them altogether."

"And Dee," Walsingham interjected, "their every goal just now is to eliminate the Queen."

"Were it not for the intrusion of plague," added Thomas, "Bishop

Mortimer's cohorts would have succeeded in shooting Her Majesty on her barge at Deptford."

"There are more, then?"

"At least one who we possess."

"You must show me."

"I shall," Walsingham agreed, "but you're to make no mention of this to Burghley. For now, he is not to know. Gerard, you will..."

"Forgive me, I'll leave the viewing of the other body to you. I've promised Mme Bennet to remove this one posthaste."

"Very well, but I expect you at Seething Lane. We must further engage with what we know. And mayhap Dr. Dee can use his skill to scry some shade of a future event, once he's beheld the true nature of the enemy."

"More like, I shall call upon a magistrate to act as witchfinder in this matter and hunt down the guilty conjurer."

Thomas refrained from telling him how thoroughly he was wasting his time.

They left Thomas to bury the dusty bones of the late bishop. He sent to the hospital for a death cart to transport the body across the river, and meanwhile in back of the Lazar-house built up a pyre and burnt all the bedding, as the law required in the case of plague victims. The house had a fire pit behind it for just such items. Fresh bedding would need acquiring.

The cart arrived, its driver grim and gaunt. The white stick protruding off the front of it could clear the congestion on London Bridge like Moses parting the waves. Thomas stopped only at the Ruff Shop long enough to tell Christianne that he would likely be late returning.

At St. Botolph's a messenger from Walsingham awaited him with a note: The body they had left below the Tower had vanished. Tower guards insisted no one had even attempted to come down the stairs, and the gates letting onto the moat had been locked, yet someone had stolen into the space and carried off the corpse without being seen by anyone.

Thomas had an idea how it had happened but could not verify his suspicions until he and the cart driver had hauled the bones of Mortimer, wrapped in a sheet, down into the church crypt. There they found the nearest vault opened as if expecting the bones. Thomas knew why, and apparently the cart driver reached a similar conclusion. He set down his end of the sheet and sprang up the steps as fast as he could go. Thomas followed. He paid the unnerved cart driver a handsome bonus, then watched him drive quickly away before returning to the crypt. From experience he knew that both the Yvag that had been sleeping in it and the little hob that would have guarded it were long gone. It would be someone else's problem to see the new remains interred. Probably, they would conclude that vandals had displaced these bones from the vault, and so place Mortimer's remains in it identified as whoever they thought was buried here.

He exited the church and strode off down Thames Street for the Tower.

At the West Gate he could not find a guard who remembered him, and finally used his letter from Walsingham as a form of introduction. He didn't want to go to Seething Lane to drag Sir Francis back to the Tower Moat; what he had in mind to do needed to be carried out in private, otherwise it would generate any number of questions that he was disinclined to answer—and that assumed he could explain any of it at all.

One of the guards led him down the spiral stairs and beneath the Tower. At that point he had to insist that the guard follow him no farther. When the guard asked why, he answered, "I am looking for clues as to how the body was stolen." While this failed to explain anything at all, it sounded like a why and wherefore. He had long since learned that something which seemed like an answer usually worked to satisfy such a query, as with Jehanne la Pucelle where he gained access to her by insisting to her warder that she wanted to confess to him. That he was glamoured as a priest helped, but the explanation was still nonsense.

Once away from the guard and past the two massive columns, Thomas drew out the small pouch that hung round his neck, opened it, and took out his new ördstone. Its blue gems flickered, then stopped. He knew what the old stone could do—not merely open gates between or through worlds, but also preview portals and even retain some essence of people who had meant something to him, generating simulacra that spoke with him as if present and that only gradually faded away. It had taken him a long time to understand it: They were portions of people he'd known, united fragments. The memory of his wife, Janet, had lasted two centuries before finally falling silent. This new stone contained none of those fragments.

The question was, was it attuned enough to him yet to reveal a closed portal? He positioned himself near where the body had lain and floated the stone on his palm, aiming it first where the body had been. Then he turned in a slow circle.

There.

Almost hidden by the nearest column, the faintest distortion appeared in the air a mere ten steps away. It was vague, but he couldn't imagine what else it could be but the ghost of a portal. So, they had come and retrieved the body, probably here and gone in under a minute. He didn't need a clearer picture, and attempting to get one might draw more attention than he desired. The last thing he needed was an army of alerted Yvag knights pouring into the world beneath the Tower.

He replaced the stone in its pouch. Quite likely the assassin had possessed an ördstone, too, that had led them to it. In all the business of being arrested, educating Walsingham about the Yvags, and seeing Applegate freed, Thomas had been unable to take care of a few critical details that normally he would have dispensed with immediately. That stone was one. The body stuck with two poison-tipped arrows was the other. The Yvag had them now.

Between his appearance at court and the secrets the recaptured body was about to give up, it would not be long before someone came hunting him.

XII. Bragrender Underground

Bragrender accompanies the body of Ritarenda across the Queen's Court Plaza and toward the nearest glass-and-steel spire. The body floats on a clear panel beside him, his ördstone channeling his directions to the panel so that it turns and glides at his pace. As he reaches the spire, its wall flutters, parts, lets him and the body through. Only on the far side does it become obvious that the spire is itself a projection, a reminder of what their homeworld once was and will be again after they've scraped the humans off the World-to-Be.

Inside the projection of a hundred towers, a field of inverted U's stretches across the landscape. The projected towers above are in essence a memorial. Beyond are the true towers and pyramidal fortresses and ziggurats that house the People. One citadel, abandoned, sits on a promontory, its outer wall fallen in places, the inner towers in partial or complete decay, a home now only for the blue-winged passerines that have learned better than to drift near Ailfion itself. The crumbling citadel has been left as a cenotaph to remind the People of the foregone war with the Unseelie, though the truth is, that war occurred long before they escaped to here. The ruin is just a ruin.

Below is where the machinery of the city lives and never sleeps. He steps onto a platform, which grows sides to surround him and the floating panel; then silently the sealed platform sinks. He watches the surface rise up above and close over him. He and the body are bathed in red light. Then the doors open before him and he steps out into a vast pathway. It appears to run straight to infinity. He and the body continue their journey along it.

The side tunnels are full of life—if Þagalwood creations can qualify as living. All manner of the bone-white creatures glide and roll and trundle along around him. They appear to be a melange of common parts, stacked and fitted in a myriad of forms according to task, all moving with purpose, all self-replicating and self-guided. After his birth, it was not long before he grew weary of being both ogled and spurned by those above. Once he discovered the way in, the entire subterranean world of Ailfion opened to him. With these creatures he had far more affinity than with the Yvag to whose society he ostensibly belongs. The assemblages took little notice of him and when they did, they were neither repulsed nor amazed. He was just another self-actuating entity in their midst. Whatever the consciousness of Þagalwood is, he feels attuned to it now, at peace among these strange automata that keep the world of Ailfion running. So he is hardly surprised when one of the creatures glides up beside him and extends one of its arms. It holds out something to him, an offering. He does not hesitate to accept it. The creature spins about and glides away.

Bragrender studies the gift: Shiny black like the armored carapaces the knights wear, this is a hand larger than his own, ending at the wrist in a thick ring bespeckled with tiny gems, like an ördstone is, but stones of dark red rather than blue.

The ring is empty, the hand hollow. It's a glove. He slides his hand into it. The ring seems to lock into place. He can sense it probing, attempting to connect with him in some manner, placing images and instructions in his head. Is this a prototype, experimental? The instructions hint at that, as they also hint that he should deliver it to Nicnevin. Although she hasn't specifically asked for the glove, it is to her that any new device ought to go, that she might decide to whom it's given. He is supposed to act as courier. Well, there's a part of the instruction he'll overlook.

He glances around for something to test the glove on, finally settles on the railing ahead, concentrates and extends his hand, palm down, in accordance with the instructions. The tiny lights flicker in sequence. Then his hand judders; his fingertips glow and a narrow beam of light reaches out from them. It seems to etch the rail for a moment, until he thinks, *Enough.* The glove goes silent, cold. The railing where it has been etched seems to lose its coherency. What was solid crumbles before his eyes and sprinkles to the floor as dust. How delightful.

Two of the white creatures race up to the point where the rail has vanished. The one with snakelike appendages reaches over to where the rail still exists and connects with it. After a moment, it begins to extrude a new rail across the open space, as if it and the other creature knew what Bragrender was going to do—and maybe so, maybe the glove communicated his intent.

Bragrender draws off the glove, and like full suits of elven armor, it goes soft, almost shapeless. Oh, he might share this, but not with the Queen, not yet. He has a body to deliver.

He sets off again along the pathway.

It's not long before he takes a side tunnel. Doors part to let him into a dark and quiet chamber.

Once upon a time, or so he has been told, this entire wing of the undercity lay all but dormant. So rarely did any of the People perish that the services of the mortuary were nearly forgotten. It's only in the time since just before his birth that Yvags have been forced to confront the prospect of their mortality. In the past fifteen cycles more than four dozen of them have been rendered lifeless, more than in the past thousand cycles, since the War with the Unseelie. Most of the four dozen perished in what is now called "The Battle of the Forests," when for a time a whole army of humans seemed amassed against them, until the Queen finally conceded defeat and sealed off all of the ördways into that region. It is a dead zone now. Raging Zhanedd alone defied the Queen's dictum and returned to the forests of Sherwood and Barnsdale time and again until she had eliminated every self-appointed "Robyn Hoode" that sprang up—and for a time there were quite a few of them. The name seemed to carry some deeper meaning for the humans. Zhanedd was allowed to hunt them seemingly because of her unique status of hybrid: not only a changeling but now part-Þagal as well. She was becoming a bridge creature, linking worlds. He's wondered if the Þagalwood part of her would bring them closer together, but no, she still loathes him as she seems to loathe everything. He has little regard for his mother's counselors, too, and they for him, but about Zhanedd there is something wrathful, something wrong that cannot be fixed. After all, he rescued her from that original Robyn Hoode, who tried to kill her; yet never once has she so much as acknowledged it.

Bragrender admires her stubbornness, but he hates her for thinking herself superior to him as well as the rest. Absurd. Which of them terrifies the other Yvags without so much as a word?

From the ceiling the mortuary automaton descends, a bone-white cylinder formed of tightly woven coils. These unspool as the mortuarian lowers itself to stop just above the body. The unfurled coils have become twenty strands of cables, some ending in small fingerlike digits, sharply tipped but delicate; others resolve as devices, blades, containers. Some of them slice through the costume Ritarenda wore in disguise. Four pierce the body and slither deep into it. Beginning where they've entered, a blackness rises up and up until all the cables turn black, and hardly a few moments before the last of that blackness is drawn up, leaving behind pristine white cables once more.

The remainder of the cables have harvested the core of the assassin as still others have hardened and sealed his form that he might serve as the next *teind*. He will descend into Hel with honors. The Queen will say, "He served the People well." It is what she always says.

Bragrender would challenge this ritual, but no one seems able to supply him with facts about the Unseelie and how the People came to be subservient to them. The truth, it appears, is lost in time. Even Nicnevin—even his mother—insists that she does not know; the relationship between their races began long before she was made queen, and that was an eon ago, before the People had migrated to this world, centuries before they set their sights on this other, this Earth that they would remake for themselves. He has questions as to how that happened: For instance, for an ördstone to open a gate, one must provide it the intended destination, as with his hops into Newgate Prison, or Ritarenda's own ördstone, providing the signal on which they converged. That being the case, how was the first leap to the World-to-Be accomplished? As with so much, either no one knows or else no one who knows will tell. All anyone does seem to know is that the very first gate was called *Malros*.

It has all evolved into a kind of game now, the remaking of that world, a game of slow and steady transformation. They acquire pieces and move them across the board, into alliances that will ultimately cause as much chaos as possible, forging more alliances, tilting everything off-balance while the sheeplike denizens wander about, ignorant of it all. Whatever he thinks of his mother, she is a conniving manipulator.

Right now she wages a campaign to acquire more changelings in order to repopulate all of Yvagddu. It's out of fear though, he thinks—fear that, somehow, the Changeling Pool will become contaminated again or, worse, dry up altogether. Fortunately, as Yvag influence has spread outward from where they first breached the World-to-Be, so has their opportunity to snatch changelings from many more locations.

His drifting thoughts are interrupted by the mortuarian. Two of its cables have plucked something from the corpse. Bragrender is familiar enough with the processes here to know that the core intelligence is handing him foreign objects found in the body: in this case, arrows. Two of them. The coils release and drop them into his upturned hand, then withdraw.

The arrows are interesting. He has not seen their like before; in particular he studies the slender triangular points of solid iron. He has seen wounds such as these would make, notably on knights escorting a *teind*.

The mortuarian interrupts again. It communicates its data to him silently. The body of Ritarenda expired permanently as too much of its lifeblood is irretrievable, but also because that blood is thoroughly contaminated with the poison *kanerva*. The mortuarian proceeds to discharge all of the collected fluids.

Kanerva! He knows where that grows: deep in the heart of Þagalwood. It's so poisonous that he sets down the arrows, even though they've been sterilized after analysis by the mortuarian.

So far as he knows, Bragrender himself is the last Yvag to have used *kanerva*—a ring containing barely a drop of it with which he stung that crafty Hoode. He knows exactly how lethal the stuff is. So who has harvested the the toxic flowers, and when?

Somehow this unknown assassin has stolen into the wood and out again without dying.

He would ask the voja who inhabited the human priest Mortimer about this, but the Yvagvoja is still delusional from its exposure to the disease that practically devoured Mortimer. The voja barely managed to open a portal and fall through it. This plague of the humans has played havoc with them before. It's not as if they're unacquainted with its effects upon a host and its operator. It means, though, that Bragrender has to bide his time before he can ask about their enemy.

All he has is maybe the name of a hospital, nothing as to who treated Mortimer, who might have communicated with him.

The presence of *kanerva* means there is a great deal more to find out.

Finished, the mortuarian wraps itself up and ascends into the darkness. Bragrender turns and walks back through the doors and out the lane, threading his way to the surface again.

Someone killed Ritarenda with unique arrows coated in a poison that can only be got in Þagalwood. Plague-mad, Mortimer volunteered details of Ritarenda's scheme to someone attending to him, who in turn must have informed the assassin, who, based upon these two arrows, most probably is the very same archer who has been interfering these past cycles with their normal harvesting of *teinds*.

The presence of the poison would seem to support Zhanedd's theory of a renegade Yvag changeling living within the wood. If so, it's a very clever changeling. The arrows prove one thing for certain: there is an enemy out there, perhaps a network of them—able to dance between Ailfion and the World-to-Be. Interesting, too, that this has all occurred at the same time as Zhanedd has withdrawn from the court, hardly appearing at all any longer.

Even as he contemplates this, one of Nicnevin's council is crossing the plaza of Hel and gesturing to get Bragrender's attention. It's the counselor Valtuustmaj, dressed in flamboyant robes and looking right at him, which is the oddest aspect of the approach, because Valtuustmaj can almost never manage to look squarely upon Bragrender's ever-shifting form.

"Hail, Bragrender," says the counselor. "Fortunate am I to encounter you."

"How so?" He enjoys how the counselor winces at his voice.

"Word comes from one of our voja embedded in the court of the Elizabeth. They claim to have beheld someone credited with the slaying of Ritarenda. It seems he was fêted and much celebrated by the court."

"Human or one of us?"

"Unknown. They could not get close enough to the archer to tell. The humans celebrate him as one of their own, but then they would. Their queen confessed to being smitten with him."

"Has this archer a name?"

"It was given as 'Gerard.'"

One aspect of Bragrender smiles seraphically. "I shall start with that."

Valtuustmaj bows but seems reluctant to withdraw.

"There is more?" Bragrender asks.

"I—it is a question I have. The humans' court, it is so very like our own. Do we think the humans created such in imitation of us? We, after all, infiltrated their political stratum and so surely shaped and influenced the very nature of governance. Or is it that we are influenced by our association with them? Our apparel, our appearance, seems modeled upon theirs. Is the Queen's a reflection of theirs or are their specifics some backscattering of Nicnevin?" Sheepishly, Valtuustmaj adds, "It all seems to blend together, so many voja returning from World-to-Be having worn the skins and thus the costumes of mortals, the shapes of which they might then convey to the automata."

Bragrender nods as if pondering the matter. But instead of addressing it, he finally says, "You've done well today, Valtuustmaj. And you'll do better still to tell no one else the news of this Gerard. Yes? Not just yet." He pats the counselor on the arm, then walks off across the plaza.

Whose fashion influences the other—that is the matter of great concern to the council. He takes only a few strides before he begins to laugh.

XIII. Thomas Hunted

Among the governors of St. Thomas the Apostle Hospital in Southwark, Lord Covington rarely put in an appearance. A mistress of his had given birth there a few years before, and he had solicitously arranged everything for her, including providing her a room away from the venereal wing. After she was discharged, his lordship seemed to forget the hospital altogether. So it was of some surprise to the fifteen sisters on duty—the nursing staff, their collective title being a leftover from earlier times—when he showed up one sunny, warm August morning, demanding to speak with the matron.

Covington was a short, stocky man, and this may have made him more imposing to the nurses, in that they had to face him at eye level. Lizard-like, he rarely blinked. That morning he was dressed in a fine doublet, and in his case the jutting peascod belly probably matched his own. He stood bow-legged in ivory tights. A feathered cap collected most of his curly hair, and the ruff at his throat was so wide that, had he tried, he could not have viewed his own shoulders.

The sisters fetched Matron Ives, governess of the hospital. Taller than Covington, she strode down the stairs from the second floor in her layers of yellow and white. Covington seemed not even to notice her approach. Nurses hung about in the shadows to listen, whilst trying to be invisible at the same time.

Matron Ives said, "Your Lordship?"

Covington turned about and replied, "Matron, I delight in your presence. I have a matter of some urgency to discuss with you." He glanced at the women lurking about. "Perhaps not in a hallway, however."

The matron clucked her tongue at them and nodded to him. "Please," she said, "follow me."

She led him down the hall to an unoccupied room. "Now, please, tell me why you are here, lordship."

"I am curious about a prelate brought here some weeks ago, afflicted, I am told, with the plague. He was seen by your physicians, the resident surgeon here perhaps?"

"No, Your Lordship. I know the man to whom you refer, and it was evident immediately that the bishop—for, bishop he was—suffered from plague. Quite advanced plague at that. We did as we do with all such cases and sent him to the nearby Lazar-house, where that affliction can be managed appropriately and he poses no threat to everyone else. Were we to keep plague victims here, the entire hospital would empty in a week. Surely, you understand. Forgive me if he was your friend, but the bishop could not be saved."

"Friend? Oh, hardly." He manufactured a look of concern. "Then, if none of your physicians here, who did attend to him?" asked Covington.

"That would be Mr. Gerard, in charge of our Lazarus-house. He is skilled at palliative care, which is what most plague victims need by the time we see them here."

"Mr. Gerard is the doctor, I see." Covington seemed delighted. "Skilled, I have no doubt. Well, I wish to meet him, your Mr. Gerard."

"Then," said the matron, "you must go to the Lazar-house. It is nearby."

"Direct me, please."

The matron led him outside and pointed the way back to Long Southwark. "On the far side," she said, "down Kent Street."

He bowed. Then with a spiderlike gait, Lord Covington walked down the steps and off toward the main thoroughfare.

Two of his patients had perished overnight, a sailor off a ship from Lisbon and a woman who'd tended to an afflicted neighbor—her kindness had been her undoing.

Thomas called for the plague cart and paid two young messengers to carry the tragic news to a ship's captain and a family respectively. The death cart would carry the corpses and their bedding to the Pardon plague pits for burial.

He refused to allow Mme Bennet to enter the chambers where the two had died. The Lazar-house matron was hardly immune to the miasma of plague, whatever it was, however it traveled, and he did all he could not to imperil her. He sent her off to purchase more rushes for the two rooms. When the hired cart came, he and the driver loaded the bodies into it, and it rolled off.

In her absence, Thomas gathered new bedding for one of the vacated chambers. It was as he came out into the hallway that he heard a gentleman's voice inquiring if the doctor was about. That meant Mme Bennet had come back, but he wasn't listening for her reply: Beneath that question, like a breath of wind, came the softest chirr of an Yvag, one whose anticipation was more intense than it could control. Even after centuries, the shape and intensity of that contact was too familiar.

Bragrender, the grotesque Yvag that had nearly done for him.

Mme Bennet told the Yvag to follow her. Thomas was trapped here around the corner.

He stepped back into the empty room, and threw himself upon the new bedding. He dragged the linen sheet over himself. Then, concentrating hard, he glamoured himself as the woman whose body he had just sent off to the plague pits. He might not resemble her exactly, but it wouldn't matter. Plague had distorted her features in any case.

He lay perfectly still.

They turned the corner of the hall, and Mme Bennet said, "Oh," from the doorway of the room. "Why, it appears the dead cart came for only one of them."

The "man" must have attempted to push past her.

She said, "No, no, you mustn't, Lord Covington. Do you not see that this woman died of plague? You do not want to become close to her."

"Forgive me. I..." Footsteps crackled on the rushes as the Yvag stepped back. "Of course, madame. But I do not see this Mr. Gerard of yours."

"Oui, that is because he is not here," she told Covington as if he was an idiot. "He will have traveled with the cart, of course. He does that sometimes. The dead man was from a Portuguese ship, and he worried that more plague will follow from it. I'm quite certain he will have gone with the body to look for more infection."

"That's extraordinarily brave. Not afraid of the contagion himself?" She made to answer but he must have waved her to silence. "This Mr. Gerard—is he a bowman?"

Mme Bennet to her credit snorted a laugh. "A what, m'sieur?"

"An archer. You know, does he practice the art of archery?"

"But it is the Queen's opinion that *all* gentlemen in London should practice the art of archery."

"Yes, of course, but does *Gerard*?"

"I have never seen him do so, m'sieur."

The more she was goaded and annoyed, the more the French side of Mme Bennet emerged and the more stubborn she became. Thomas had to suppress the urge to smile.

Exasperation dripping from his voice, Lord Covington asked, "This plague cart, it would be crossing to the far side of the Thames?"

"That would depend, m'sieur, where this ship from Lisbon has weighed its anchor, oui? Plague has come into the city this way. It has happened before."

"And you have no notion of where in the river this ship is anchored."

"Aucun, oui."

The chirring grew more intense. "Mr. Gerard, he lives where?"

"His home? I do not know this, though I believe he walks some distance to arrive here each day."

"You know not where his home is?"

"I have had no cause to ask him." Indeed, he had never told her.

The chirring roared but then stopped, as if Bragrender had managed to master his temper. "Very well. Thank you, madame," Covington said. "I shall return another time." His footsteps marched down the hall and out. Mme Bennet followed after, probably to ensure that the fellow left.

Thomas remained on the pallet awhile in the guise of the dead woman just to be sure Bragrender had gone.

So, it was as he had feared: Walsingham had used him as bait, and the enemy had taken it. The Yvags had pieced things together. The assassin's body beneath the Tower gave them the poisoned arrows, which no doubt linked the nobbling of their *teinds* to the foiled assassination attempt. Then, presenting himself to the Queen and her hundreds of attendants had erased any remaining anonymity. Add to that whatever information the bishop's voja might have been able to provide; it was enough for the Yvags to forge a link to the hospital.

And Bragrender now would not let up. Of that he could be certain.

It had tracked him here. He must assume that it would learn all it didn't know soon enough.

Thomas threw off the sheet, got up, and cautiously glanced down the central hall before turning to exit through the rear door and past the burning pit. He watched a dozen people pass by before selecting one and glamouring himself as that individual. Then he walked in the opposite direction, from which he gave a backward look at the Lazar-house. He was going to miss the daily outrage of the contumelious Mme Bennet, but every other option would place her in mortal danger. If "Lord Covington" returned, she needed to be ignorant of everything. Bragrender would surely know if she lied. The same would be true for Van der Paas and Christianne.

It was past time to go.

XIV. Ruff Treatment

A herd of pigs being driven to market took up most of Long Southwark road. There was no getting around the squealing creatures, and so it took Thomas a frustrating hour to make the short journey back onto London Bridge.

Well into the dark passageway through Bridge House, Thomas unglamoured, one instant a scruffy traveler in old and unkempt clothes, the next himself in his actual doublet, ruff, and cloak. The plague doctor's costume he'd abandoned in the Lazar-house. Its presence there might keep the Yvags as well as Mme Bennet believing he would shortly return; and though like everyone around him he seemed to be out enjoying the day, he was listening warily for any hint of the masquerader who had asked after him—the thing called Bragrender that had once contorted itself into the form of Sir Richard atte Lee and almost killed him. He'd no idea what it looked like now.

How long did he have before the creature finally tracked him down? Already Thomas was cataloguing the few things he owned and would need to take with him. Convincing Christianne to accompany him might take a little longer. She might be safe with Van der Paas, but her occupancy of the third and fourth floors of the house would entangle her sooner than later with these creatures, in which case she likely would end up in the well between worlds in Ailfion. No, he would see her comfortably set up in Antwerp before that could happen.

As he hurried through the archway of the recently fabricated Nonsuch House, he formulated what he would say to her; after all, he had been planning for this day or one very like it ever since Van der Paas had suggested she would benefit from further training. The timetable had simply been stepped up.

The Ruff Shop was doing a brisk business as he came in. The old proprietor was conferring with someone who looked wealthy enough to purchase all of the stock on display. Thomas made a point of brushing clumsily against the man as he squeezed past, but sensed no inner alien voice.

Van der Paas's daughters and Christianne assisted a young couple who appeared to be buying ruffs as mutual gifts, while other people milled about unattended. None seemed to take any notice of him.

Thomas didn't see blond-haired Fulke anywhere. He'd reached the bottom of the stairs when Fulke appeared from the back, carrying a pair of sprung shears he had just sharpened. He smiled and nodded as Thomas passed. Courteously, Thomas turned sideways to let Fulke pass in the narrow space. That was when he thought he glimpsed, just for an instant, a flicker of attention from a slim man with long dark curls whose back had been to him in the far corner of the shop, almost against the hearth. The look was there and gone so quickly that Thomas very nearly dismissed it. He started climbing, taking the stairs two at a time, but slowly, as he reviewed what he had seen.

The fellow had been there when he entered, hovering over one of the ruffs on display, despite which, he had looked up in that moment as Thomas passed Fulke.

Had he actually witnessed that? He'd heard no bombilation as he might from a skinwalker. From here, among this throng, he wouldn't necessarily hear a glamoured Yvag. But how could the Yvags have found his dwelling so quickly, when a mere two hours before, Bragrender had *wanted* to know where he, Gerard, lived?

Thomas rounded the landing on the second floor, where he heard but did not see Madame Van der Paas in her kitchen. From the shop below, there was no disturbance, and no footsteps came thundering after him. Maybe he had seen nothing at all. As he continued his climb, he countered his own rationalization: *When ever had such covert attention meant nothing?*

Reaching the third floor, he paused to listen to the space. The kitchen lay behind him, and the main hall to the left and ahead. His traveling chest, removed from Christianne's room upstairs, sat shoved aside in a corner of the hall, half-obscured by one of the two wall tapestries. Nothing appeared to have been disturbed. Maybe one of the customers in the shop was an Yvag, but the creatures hadn't invaded his rooms.

Bragrender had been seeking the doctor who had treated Bishop Mortimer. Things would have been different had they come face-to-face, he and the Yvag monstrosity. Three hundred years would have compressed in an instant. If the one downstairs was Bragrender, Thomas doubted he would have made it across the shop alive. But there was nothing familiar there. Whatever else, that was not Bragrender downstairs.

All the same, when two Yvags came looking for you within hours of each other, it was definitely time to be elsewhere. That was how he'd survived this long, and damn Walsingham for putting him on display for the Queen. It was bad luck to invite the attention of gods, devils, and elves. Not doing that was how he'd lasted this long. But Walsingham didn't care—he was shaking all the trees no matter what fell out.

Well, it wasn't going to matter in the end. He would gather his essentials and be gone before any alarm was sounded.

Thomas picked up the chest from beneath the tapestry and carried it across the chamber. He set it down and went to the kitchen.

Knives, colander, pipkins, large cooking forks, and a bowl of three oranges and six dates—he should give the fruit to Madame Van der Paas on the way out. It would only rot up here now. The carving knife would do him fine. He grabbed it and returned to the dining hall.

One aspect of the ornate linenfold paneling that comprised the walls of the dining hall was how the panels were never quite alike, but all gave the appearance of glazed standing page ends of books, covers alternating with spines. The frames were carved to include faux hinges at the top and bottom of each "book" panel. It was a simple matter to incorporate a few panels that opened on actual hinges.

Along the side of one he inserted the knife, then pushed carefully. The panel swung open.

Thomas repeated this maneuver on the next two panels below it. Behind the three panels lay a single vertical recess tall enough to accommodate his unstrung bow, which he carefully removed, sliding it over one horizontal frame and out. Next he lifted out his belt and quiver of arrows, which he stood on the floor beside the bow. Then, crouched, he reached into the bottom panel to collect the Yvag items he kept there: the black puddle of a wadded-up suit of their armor, two other ördstones belonging to deceased Yvag knights, two of their barbed black daggers, and finally a cloth bag containing a single *dight*. He looked inside the bag at the small green pyramid. *Were a spinner*, he heard Little John say as if it had only been this morning. He'd kept possession of it since his time in Sherwood Forest, a seemingly foolish thing to do, but he'd had a premonition that he would put it to use one day. He had never been closer to having the Yvags recover it than now. The *dight* he also placed in the chest.

Next, Thomas carefully closed the three panels again, making sure they remained indistinguishable from those around them. Then he picked up the chest, bow, and quiver, and hurried up to the fourth floor.

From under his bed he retrieved another dagger, a bag of coins including more gold sovereigns, and an oilskin wrapper containing various letters of credit, his accumulated wealth, effectively spread across half of Europe. The letters fit into a hidden compartment in the bottom of the chest. Everything in there was going with him. Clothing, plates, utensils, furniture he could always buy more of anywhere.

He had just started to descend from the fourth floor again when a tiny spot of green fire appeared in the air below him. The spot expanded to a line, but before it had time to flex into a circle, Thomas retreated back into his bedchamber, shoved the chest beneath the bed, belted the quiver, took the bow, and as stealthily as possible unlatched the door to the rooftop. Then, instead of going out onto the roof, he climbed up into the bed and drew the curtains all around. In the darkness he bent and strung the bow, laid an arrow across it, then balanced upon the mattress, waiting.

The Yvags not only knew where he lived, but they'd cut a portal there? How? He'd never ever jumped from here to anywhere... But, no, he *had* jumped to here. The night he'd acquired the *kanerva*. It hadn't been direct, but if Bragrender or another had scanned the Lazar-house, they would have located a single gate.

Something slapped against the curtain, startling him out of his reverie. It batted the curtain again. He heard a tiny raging voice and knew exactly what was outside the bed. Drew his black dagger. He hoped the hob's Yvag companion was still investigating downstairs.

Tiny claws found and parted the curtain. Goggle eyes stared in, blinked. As the hob stuck its head through the opening, Thomas swept his dagger quick across and cut the head off. He caught the body by one wing and flung it past him. It smacked against the wall. He paid it no mind but kept his attention focused ahead. Now the side curtain was slightly parted and he could see the doorway into the chamber. On his right, the door to the rooftop he'd left ajar was caught by a gust of wind off the river. It swung loose, then swung closed with a loud report.

Two Yvag knights in black armor with silver trim came charging up the stairs. He could hear their internal chittering clearly as they neared. They burst into the room. *"The roof!"* one exclaimed. It charged across the room and threw open the door. The other hung back, staring at the bed, its head tilted. It held one of their coruscating "leaping" swords. He hadn't seen one of those in a very long time, but he hadn't forgotten how they worked. The creature's armor looked different, too—adorned with more spikes, while the silver trim seemed applied with a purpose he could not yet discern, but something beyond mere decoration.

Thomas tilted his drawn bow and with one tip poked at the side curtain. In response to the movement the Yvag thrust its sword, which sliced through the curtain and into the wall, pulling half the curtain back as it recoiled. Thomas shot the Yvag through the head.

He slapped the front curtain aside and jumped out, turning for the second knight. The other Yvag had gone out onto the rooftop.

Keeping the interior door in view, Thomas circled around the open access to the roof. He had to crouch as he walked beneath the angled dormer. The knight on the rooftop had backed all the way to the parapet overlooking the river. It was straining to see if its quarry had somehow climbed up onto the fourth floor's setback roof. It only caught sight of Thomas in the open door at the last moment, and started to draw its sword.

He fired and the arrow struck the knight solidly in the chest. It stumbled back and over the parapet wall without a sound. Thomas closed the door, then stood still, listening. Would they have sent just the two? He couldn't imagine Bragrender allowing *any* others to do the job of capturing or killing the assassin of their assassin, yet here they were and no sign of Bragrender. Was this group acting independently? When these two failed to return, whoever had sent them was sure to know why and where Thomas was. They would come seeking to finish him.

He tiptoed across the bedchamber and peered around the doorjamb. The flicker of green fire was gone.

Thomas nocked one arrow and fitted two more to hang between his fingers. Nothing moved below, but the sense of a presence emanated from there.

If he attempted to descend those stairs, any hidden Yvag would simply need to wait to pick him off. He would be an easy target, exposing his lower body first. One dancing sword blade would cut a leg off before he ever had anything like a shot.

Instead, he knelt, then lay upon the rushes and slid over until he could see a portion of the third floor. No one in sight. Nothing moving.

Likely the Yvag would be in the kitchen or beside the privy, two places Thomas could not see from here. Sooner or later, someone would come up from the first floor, and it might well be Christianne. Whoever appeared, the Yvag would surely kill them. How was he to get below it?

Then he remembered the rope he'd purchased that the carpenter had used for the corded bedstead to support Christianne's mattress. A great coil of unused rope lay piled in the smaller room.

Crawling back, he got up and crept away.

To gather up the rope, he had to put away his arrows, knowing that should the Yvag choose this moment to ascend the stairs, he would be a helpless target. But the stairs stayed empty. The creature was no doubt doing what he was doing—listening for every movement. Thomas stealthily returned to the roof.

Around the side of the roof there was a much narrower lip, where the fourth floor was smaller than the width of the third floor. There was just enough room for him to place one foot after the other all the way round to the middle of the bridge side. Two thick beams ran between his building and the one directly opposite across the bridge. The beams were anchored in place and braced with struts in order to keep the two facing walls from leaning into each other as some on the bridge already did. There were fifth stories where someone on the top floor could climb through the window of the opposite building, the two canted so steeply toward the middle.

Precariously, Thomas leaned out and draped the rope around one of the beams. Then, with the bow slung against his back, he swung a leg over and lowered himself down carefully onto the beam. There he sat, a leg to each side, while he gathered up the rope and tied one end of it tightly around the beam. He couldn't be certain how long the rope was, but thought it might reach to the second floor. It looked like it from here. He steeled himself.

Curling one leg around the rope, he started his descent. Hand under hand, with one leg out for balance, the other looped in the rope, he slowly, incrementally slid down. His palms felt like they were being flayed, but he held on. He had to hope the third Yvag was watching the stairs and not looking out a front lattice window as he descended.

And then he ran out of rope.

He swung somewhere near ten feet up. By now people on the street below had caught sight of him and a crowd had gathered below. If he let go and dropped now, he was certain to land on somebody. They might break his fall, but more likely he and they would break each other's necks.

A wagon laden with sacks of grain was crawling along the twelve-foot-wide roadway. The driver yelled for everyone to get out of the way, but nobody much moved, which slowed the wagon's progress to a snail's pace.

Thomas hung on. The wagon rolled directly below him.

He let go.

He thudded against the grain sacks, knocking the wind out of him. The bow jabbed at his side, and he thought a rib cracked. Miraculously, he lost no arrows nor landed on the quiver.

People cheered and pressed in on the wagon, much to the ire of the driver, who was trying to reach the north end of the Bridge and get his grain to market. Thomas rolled off the sacks and stood up. For a moment he swayed a little dizzily, and a few people propped him up. One of them, beside him, said, "Her 'usband's gunna catch up wi' ya an ya tary long here."

He laughed, winced at the pain this brought, gripped the man by the shoulder, then pushed off through the crowd. Straightening his ruff presentably, he charged back into the ruff shop.

Clients still swarmed the floor, including the man with dark curls, who seemed to be waiting for word from upstairs. At the sight of

Thomas in the doorway, the man bolted through the shop and into the back. He slapped Christianne aside. Fulke, beside her, yelled and gave chase. He was still holding the sharpened shears, and managed to stab the fleeing Yvag once, mostly slicing its costume, but for an instant its glamour flickered, and its goblin-like face and golden eyes glared at them.

The Yvag bounded up the stairs, Fulke in pursuit. Thomas drew Christianne to her feet. "Stay here," he said. "Don't let anyone come up."

He took off after the Yvag and Fulke. The thunder of their steps beat like drums. He yelled for Fulke to wait. He could hear Yvag chatter now. The one on the stairs was screeching its warning to the remaining one higher up. Thomas rounded the second floor, bow nocked, arrows ready.

Above, the Yvag bounded up the stairs for the fourth floor, Fulke in blind pursuit. Thomas shouted again, "Fulke, stop!"

Maybe he didn't hear. Maybe his fury at Christianne's mistreatment was too hell-bent.

Fulke was above him on the stairs to the fourth floor when the beam of light as from an ördstone but bright red struck him and the wall behind him. Fulke shrieked, but only for a moment, and then he was simply gone, crumbled to dust. Behind him a great stripe of wall dissolved at the same time as if a horde of insects devoured it.

Thomas spotted the fourth Yvag, in its black shiny armor. Its nearest hand was disproportionately large. Its wrist glittered as if with rubies. In the same instant, it saw him and pointed that hand at him. Furiously, Thomas fired two arrows into the creature. It tilted back, arms flung out. The glove went dark and nothing happened.

The disguised one that Fulke and he had been pursuing scrambled for its dying comrade, arms outstretched, hands grabbing for the weird glove. Thomas unhesitatingly shot it in the back, and it sailed on past the other, skidded on its face, and tumbled to a stop.

Behind Thomas the disintegration of the wall over the stairs slowed, then ceased somewhere near halfway up. Structural boards jutted out of the hole. Through it he could see Nonsuch House. A cloud of particles that had been the wall and perhaps Fulke floated through the opening to scatter off on the wind.

Thomas dropped down on the steps and hung his head.

✠✠✠

In the aftermath, Christianne crept up the stairs, both hands on a pair of shears in front of her, ready to stab. Thomas remained slumped there. The wall behind and above him looked as if a cannonball had torn through it.

Thomas looked up and said, "Stop, Christianne. Just stop. You don't want to—"

She stepped around him, saw the two bodies on the floor. "Fulke?" she asked, somewhere between calling to him and asking if one of these bodies could be his.

He answered, "No," but she was already crossing the room, not awaiting his reply. The knight's helm had receded, revealing its metallic silver hair and gray goblin's face. The formerly resplendent lord nearby similarly was no longer human, but instead some grayish gargoyle dressed in rich man's finery. Black blood pooled beneath them both.

She turned back to Thomas. "Where is *Fulke*?" she asked him.

From where he sat, he replied, "Gone. Dead."

She almost doubled over from the punch of the word. He shared her anguish, knew that he could say nothing to soften the blow. "They killed him—that one"—he pointed at the knight in black and silver—"killed him. Did this." Loosely, he waved behind himself at where the wall was missing. "The other one—"

"Lord Covington?" Her eyes brimmed with tears, but she was fighting them.

Thomas blinked, taken by surprise by the name. How many with that name were wandering London, looking for him today? He shook his head. "He's not Covington, but he was watching for my arrival downstairs. It's me supposed to be dead, not Fulke." He focused on her again, let out a long sigh. "After this they'll be very cautious, but eventually they're going to come back."

"But what be they? Devils?"

"As good as any word for 'em, given what they do."

They remained in silence like that for a moment. Then she asked with surprising calm, "Who are you, that devils and demons hunt you? *What* are you?"

"A threat," he replied bitterly. "A danger to all who know me." He stood up. "I have to go. You and I, *we* have to go. I'd hoped to elude them, or at least lead them away from here, from you, Fulke, everyone.

A single day and I would have been safe and gone." *And all because of Walsingham.* He must have said the name out loud.

"Walsingham?" she asked. "The Queen...he's... You've met the Queen?"

"I should never have agreed to it."

She stared at him as if she'd never seen him before. "Why must *I* go, too?" she asked.

He pointed at the gaping hole in the wall. "That's why. After this you can never visit these floors again any more than I can. They'll return. And if they find you...they'll twist you up, take you apart, to learn my whereabouts. 'I don't know' will only get you dismembered more slowly."

"But how, from whence?" She was nearly in tears "How did they get in at all? They never come upstairs. I woulda seen."

He sat another moment before he dug a finger into his ruff, hooked it round the thong looped around his neck. She'd seen it and the small pouch he wore on it any number of nights in bed with him. He pulled open the pouch and took out a scalloped black stone no bigger than a cupping of his palm. "I don't know what it'll show. It's not yet reliable as my old one was."

At the bottom of the stairs he held out his hand palm up and turned to face her. Small jewels in the black stone lit up blue, and a beam of blue light no thicker than a thread shot from it straight into the kitchen. Christianne went around behind him, and he continued to turn. The light played its narrow beam over the surfaces of the walls. When he faced the stairs, however, the thread of light spread to reveal the ghost of a circle. It looked something like a round window. Whatever it showed was almost invisible. He couldn't see what was on the far side, but he knew already.

"There," he said. "That's how they got in." He did not add that it was a circle he had created or that it would take them into the Lazarhouse.

He lowered his hand. The apparitional "glass" vanished.

As he tucked the strange stone back into its pouch, he told her, "Through that gateway, they can return anytime at all. If you're up here, they'll take you. Tomorrow, the next day. They can tear you to pieces one particle at a time, make your torture last years, centuries. Once I've gone, nothing would stop them from coming for you."

"Once you've gone." She repeated. "But Van der Paas—"

He shook his head. "Cannot know what we know. And anyway, he resides below, not up here. If I've vanished, they'll let him be in the hopes that I'll return. Once it's obvious I'm not coming back to this house, they'll cast their attention elsewhere."

"You can't know that."

"No, I suppose I can't, finally, though I have walked this pattern many times now, and they have reacted in the same way each time. They have limited resources and methods."

Christianne said, "I thought you so kind, gentle-like."

"Not where they're concerned. Not ever." He shook off the gloom. "Now, you must go back downstairs. Keep Van der Paas and everyone there. Tell him this man we chased killed poor Fulke, threw him off the roof. We don't know why."

"What will you do?"

"Set right what I can, which is very little. Then I need to go out for a while." She started to turn away. He gripped her arm. "You keep to the lower floors. Don't come back up here without me for any reason."

She looked hard at him again. He could read her very thoughts from the look. He was someone she'd thought she knew but now appreciated had only presented one thin layer of himself, and that was a defensive wall around his true and bitterly cold self.

Wiping at her eyes with the palm of one hand, she turned and descended the stairs. He had no idea how she was going to tell Van der Paas about the loss of Fulke. He should be the one, but first there was work he must do.

Alone, Thomas knelt beside the knight and inspected its armor. The silver-edged sections did seem as if they would come free. He tugged at one and as it pried loose, it reflowed into a disc. He looked at it, touched it. It was razor sharp, and small enough that he could easily throw it. He touched it to the suit and the disc returned to its former shape. It seemed the armor itself contained perhaps half a dozen weapons, a significant improvement on the one he'd kept all these years.

When he pulled at the oversize hand, it slid free, a separate glove. The glove had killed Fulke. He was briefly tempted to put it on, but had no idea how that might work. He might accidentally destroy the rest of the apartment before he had mastered it. For the moment he set the glove aside.

He shoved and worked his arrows out of the two corpses. Then he stripped the new armor from the knight. The armor, pliant now, was already knitting together around the holes the arrows had made in it. The poison had no effect upon the material.

He dragged each body up the stairs, through his bedchamber and across the short roof. He threw them one at a time over the edge into the Thames below.

The tide was going out, creating a spillway through the arches. The bodies vanished in the churning water. He repeated this with the first one he'd killed. Four Yvags consigned to a watery grave—yes, they would be wary of invading this space again for a time.

Now to the large glove. Its powers reminded him greatly of how their sacrificed *teinds* broke apart in Hel—disintegration, but faster, almost instantaneous. A wind roared through the hole above the stairs, causing tapestries and bed curtains to flap.

An idea formed, a way he might protect Van der Paas.

On the third floor again, he stood where the new ördstone had revealed the ghost gateway for Christianne. He drew on the glove.

The ring around his wrist flickered. He could feel it in the same way he'd felt his ördstone, the soughing in his mind. He thought of what he wanted to do, what he needed the glove to do. He pointed the glove at the gateway, palm up. His fingertips began to glow, the gems in the wrist circlet ran in a sequence, and then a beam of red light, thin as a reed, jumped from his fingers to define the gate. Then, slowly, it shrank in toward the center, devouring all evidence of the Lazar-house gate in the process.

At that point the glove became lifeless on his hand. Removing it, he wondered if this or something like it was what Nicnevin had used to seal all the gates of Sherwood.

Thomas added the glove and the new suit of armor to his travel chest of possessions, then shoved it back under the bed. Time he spoke to Van der Paas about Fulke and Christianne, and to make him understand that he was about to inherit ownership of this building. Thomas would be leaving the old proprietor short two apprentices, though he really had no choice if the remaining one was going to stay alive.

❖ ❖ ❖

At Seething Lane, a servant had him wait outside the door. After a minute, Sir Francis came out to meet him.

"Well, Gerard, what carries you to my door?"

"France, I believe," he answered. "Or Flanders. You said events could not wait. Where exactly was it you wished me to go?"

Walsingham made a sly smile. He replied apologetically. "The situation has changed."

"Oh." Thomas thought he heard dismissal in that. "I see. For me as well," he said. "I must leave London." His thoughts turned to how he might cross the narrow sea and at least deliver Christianne safely into the bosom of Antwerp before he took up residence somewhere well away from here.

"I take it our gamble with the court has paid off, then," Walsingham remarked. "They've come after you?"

Our gamble. He liked that. Walsingham was a scheming bastard. All the same, he calmly said, "Yes, they've come after me and in such a way that it necessitates I depart these shores immediately. I came only to tell you this as a courtesy."

"Well, yes, and I appreciate that you would do so. I think before you set sail for parts unknown, however, you should first come in and allow me to tell you *how* matters have changed and what I would ask of you now. From the sound of it, what I want and what you need might prove to be mutually satisfactory." When Thomas just stared, he extended a hand. "Come in, physician. Hear me out at least, before you decide what your future's to be."

Thomas went in.

PART TWO:
THE RIDOLFO
PLOT

XV. The Florentine Banker

"Tell me," said Walsingham, "what if anything do you know of a man named Roberto di Ridolfo?"

They were seated in the spymaster's private chambers at Seething Lane, where Walsingham had apparently been studying maps of the Low Countries.

The name caught Thomas off guard, and he knew his expression gave away his familiarity with it. Walsingham had surely seen that. No point then in attempting to dissemble ignorance.

He replied, "Roberto di Ridolfo, merchant banker from Florence, where his family is well-regarded. He has properties in Brussels, a relationship with the House of Fugger at least where the production of mercury is concerned, and since 1555 he has maintained a residence here in London."

"Heigh and bravo," said Walsingham. He leaned back in his chair. "I am impressed."

Thomas wondered if he would be as impressed if he knew that Thomas had letters of credit with Ridolfo in all three cities, enabling him to replenish his fortunes between here and Italy. He owned many other letters of credit as well, but that wasn't relevant; why, he wondered, was Walsingham interested in Ridolfo of all people? He could not see how the banker was tied to the attempt on the Queen's life. What else did the spymaster know of him? Then Thomas remembered something else. "I believe Signor Ridolfo is also a friend of William Cecil's, your Baron Burghley. Is that to do with this?"

Now Walsingham's eyes almost glowed. "It is everything to do with this. Burghley has borrowed money from him, and thus been gulled by the fellow's amity and so pays him no mind at all. It has escaped his notice that this banker's habitual travels back and forth between Brussels and London make of him the perfect courier."

"You think he carries notes to and from Mary of Scotland?"

"To and from her supporters at the very least, yes."

"You know this to be fact?"

"It is my supposition, based on various inferences and convenient coincidences, that he is a papal agent. Your job would be to prove me right or wrong. The facts are for you to uncover."

"I was unaware that I am allowed to prove you wrong, sir."

Walsingham gave him a Machiavellian smile. "Oh, I insist upon it. It is all too easy, Gerard, to be led off into the brambles, wasting critical time in pursuit of a false narrative. By the time the mistake is self-evident, it's often too late to retrace one's steps. Here, given the Queen's life hangs in the balance, I need to see the proof no matter what it might be, so if there is nothing to Ridolfo, then it is essential to know that and know it sooner rather than later after valuable resources have been redirected uselessly."

Thomas took all that in, nodding. He leaned forward upon the cluttered desk. "You're sending me to Brussels then?"

"Lovely city, Brussels. I take it from what you've just told me, that a trip to Brussels might be just the remedy for your situation. Am I mistaken?"

Thomas breathed a sigh of relief. "Quite the opposite, sir."

Walsingham tapped his forefingers together. "So you will go to Brussels. Meanwhile, we know that the Queen's court is infiltrated by at least one of these elven creatures, who has identified you to . . . Who have they identified you to?"

"Others of their kind."

"In this matter, I rely entirely upon your instincts. We must get you away, and I need you elsewhere. On good authority I have it that Roberto di Ridolfo sets sail tomorrow for Brussels. If you hurry, you might even manage to make the crossing on the same ship as he."

Thomas thought he could accomplish that. "And what do I do once I arrive there?"

Walsingham rose up like black smoke out of a chimney. He crossed the room and opened a small door in his ornately carved livery cupboard. Turning, quite suddenly he tossed a purse of coins to Thomas, which he caught. "Find me evidence that Ridolfo is engaged in something traitorous. You seem to know much about him. See what he does, mark with whom he associates. If you can bring me proof of an unfolding plot, so much the better. Once he's back on English soil, with such proof in hand we can arrest him outright, or, as I always prefer, turn and run him."

Thomas found it all extraordinarily commodious, as if Walsingham had fomented his troubles in order to force him into this situation. "Might I ask, Sir Francis—had I not arrived here conveniently today, who would you be sending in my place?"

Walsingham had a tell when he was lying, Thomas was beginning to appreciate: He waved a dismissive hand through the conversation as if erasing it out of the air. "Oh, well," said he, "I've a man stationed already in Dover, one who watches every crossing—in fact, he will be watching you. And an asset in Brussels, one who listens for any disturbances, but otherwise has no ties to the banker. Surely he knows less than you just recited, and would likely do a very good job, but again, hasn't the range of knowledge you've already displayed. They are, I suppose, alternatives."

Well, he thought, he'd put his oar in the water of this spy game; he could hardly afford to withdraw, when it was getting him out of the city. Besides, Antwerp was a stop on the way to Brussels, a perfect solution for what to do about Christianne, too, providing Van der Paas had the connection he claimed.

"I might need to leave a few items behind. I would prefer to leave them under your care."

Walsingham seemed to have fallen into other thoughts. He blinked a few times, and said, "Of course. Bring your items. I will see them safely stored here."

Thomas stood. "Sir Francis," he said, then bowed himself out of the chamber.

The purse proved to be full of gold sovereigns.

"I don't understand," Christianne said in frustration. They stood beside the table in his large third-floor hall, having established that nobody else had come up here since Thomas disposed of the bodies.

Thomas and Van der Paas had already surveyed the damage on the floor above. His carpenter would return next day to start the extensive repairs on the wall. Meanwhile, they had shored it up. They were fortunate that most of the destruction had been to a cross-section of wattle and daub wall, and not the actual frame of the house.

Thomas had contemplated seeking lodging elsewhere for the night, but decided finally that here was likely the only place he knew for certain there were no remaining portals, whereas anywhere else might contain hidden gates or be public enough for him to be tracked. Better for this one night that he stay here. None of the Yvags who had seen him here had opportunity to pass that knowledge on. Bragrender would remember his appearance, but Bragrender wasn't here, an admittedly puzzling development that he would have to figure out later.

Thomas replied, "It's simple, Christianne. Van der Paas has written a letter of introduction for you to Mme Diones Welfes in Antwerp. He did this some weeks ago, after he'd voiced the opinion that he considered you had a natural talent with the ruffs, and thought you would benefit from studying with the greatest starcher in the world."

"I know. He's dropped plenty hints to me how I ought to study with her," she said. "Says she can teach me things even he doesn't know how to do."

"Antwerp was always going to be your next step given what you want to accomplish and what he wants for you. Van der Paas insists once you finish your apprenticeship with Mme Welfes, you can go anywhere you like and name your price."

Tears were welling in her eyes. If anything, she looked angry.

"Is this not what you wanted?"

Christianne nodded, and stifled a sob. "But not like this—forced out because of Fulke, because of those creatures."

"No, of course not. It is unfair, but now we're all forced to act, to change whatever plans we had. I have to leave, too—to protect you and Van der Paas and his family. 'Tis hardly what I wanted. At least traveling to Antwerp gets you what you desire."

"You know so very little of what I desire, Mr. Gerard. Fulke and I—" she started to say, then stopped. She seemed to resign herself to the situation. "You are coming with me then?"

"As far as Antwerp, in order to present the letter of introduction to Mme Welfes and speak on his behalf, and yours."

"But you are not staying. And you daren't tell me where you're going."

"As a result of what's happened here, it's better if . . ." He gestured at the hole in the wall above, but no words came. Sharp ice shot through his brain. He grabbed at his cloak, tried to warn her. Formed "I—" but could not find the next word. He lunged for the counter table and managed to collapse upon it before the seizure splintered him. His last thought was *It's happening again.* Then he passed out.

He woke, still on the bench, on his back, Christianne kneeling at his side, her eyes fearful. He touched her cheek. "It's all right," he said, and wiped at his lips. "Happens to me now and again, ne'er so often as once it did, but I receive no warning. Fits and riddles, they come when they come."

"You spoke, but strangely."

"No doubt. Could you tell what I said? Could you repeat it? I would know if I heard it right."

She continued to eye him worriedly, but recited:

> "*The sleeping palmer travels far through time,*
> *yet knows not the day the witcher*
> *slays the scoured soul,*
> *so close he cannot see it.*'"

He nodded. It was what he'd heard, as abstract and unhelpful as any riddle he'd ever uttered. He asked her to help him stand. After a few moments, the lightness in his head passed. He straightened and gathered his cloak again.

"What did it mean?" she asked.

"I have no more idea than you. Who or what is the sleeping palmer? A pilgrim? Is it supposed to be me? I see with no clarity. There's no code to interpret by. In all likelihood it will reveal itself eventually. That is, most of them do in some fashion."

She continued to look concerned.

He explained, "I used to suffer these fits all the time. Now I can go years without one and then suddenly I'm taken by surprise and there's a mad prophecy or riddle or whatever it should be called. A curse, really, I suppose, for it advantages me not at all." He started for the stairs.

"All your answers seem riddles to me."

He stopped. "Yes, I imagine they do." There was so much he dared not share with her, and harsh as it was to acknowledge, he knew it was because nobody could be trusted, not even she. "If I were to say that is to protect you and Van der Paas?" *And myself?*

"Mr. Gerard, when have you needed to protect me?"

"Point taken, but Threston was merely a bully. The Yvags would peel you like skinning a rabbit. We must be gone before the demons send some other glamoured Lord Covington to lead an army of their kind through Van der Paas's and up these stairs. So, we are off in the morning, and when we reach Antwerp, I will pay Mme Welfes for your training."

"You told me that's not how apprenticeship's s'posed to work."

"Yes, well, this one's a little different."

Like him she had little to pack, and little that couldn't be left behind, especially without Fulke. Apparently, they had dreamed of going to Antwerp together. Thomas, tangled in his own intrigues, had hardly noticed.

Across the Mer du Nord they traveled as a couple, which made the matter of watching Ridolfo simple. Then arriving at the port of Antwerpen, while they gathered their belongings, Thomas watched the banker meet a contact, a man with soulful eyes and a long beak of a nose. A narrow patch of white hair dangled from his chin to a point just above his pale yellow ruff. He might have been a cleric; his gown was simple and black, much like the ones Walsingham wore.

The two men spoke animatedly, old acquaintances. Thomas probed for anything unnatural thrown off by them, but both, it seemed, were human. Then again, he'd had contact with Ridolfo exactly twice himself in some twenty-odd years—glamoured the second time enough to suggest that he'd aged. The banker was mortal and most likely so was his companion.

Carefully, and keeping his back to the two men, Thomas maneuvered himself and Christianne nearer to where they stood until he could make out some of what they were saying. The other man told Ridolfo, "Alba will provide us ten thousand." And Ridolfo replied, "That will sweeten Norfolk's bitterness. He will be faithful to our—" He stopped mid-speech, and Thomas turned his head just enough to see that the men had noticed his and Christianne's nearness. The two walked off out of earshot. He did not try to get close again. If Christianne took any notice of what he was doing, she didn't acknowledge it.

Mme Welfes's shop lay near the Cathedral of Our Lady, its tower visible from the wharf. She greeted Thomas imperiously, wary in accepting his letter, but as she read it, her expression softened. Her eyes sparkled, and she turned to regard Christianne anew. "Van der Paas speaks grandly of you," Madame told her. "You are gifted, he says. And Van der Paas rarely thinks anyone is even conscious." She glanced at Thomas again. "He says you have payment?"

Thomas reached into his cloak, drew five sovereigns from Walsingham's purse, and placed them in her oustretched hand.

"Most generous. I have at this very moment room here for two apprentices, so it is fortuitous timing for us all." She folded up the letter. To Christianne she said, "Say your goodbyes, then, and after, let us see what my old friend has taught you before now." She took her money and retreated to her counter table.

Thomas removed a few more sovereigns from the purse before offering it to Christianne. "What?" she said. "You already paid her."

"Yes, but you will want to see the city, and treat yourself to something, a fine dress, mayhap. Or set it all aside for when you strike out on your own."

"But what will you do? It is your money." It was Walsingham's money, but he saw no reason to involve her in that subject.

"In Brussels I will collect more before I go. So worry not, I'm hardly insolvent."

Her eyes were wet again. A single tear rolled down her cheek. "Why do you do this for me? Everything you have done?"

He opened his arms and embraced her. "Because you are worth it," he whispered to her. "You need to remind yourself of that every day." Stepping back, he studied her face. After this he doubted they would ever meet again. He was going to miss the pleasure of her company, and, he had to admit, his own eyes burned. "God be with you, Christianne," he told her, and kissed her forehead. Then he picked up his small traveling chest and walked out into the street, leaving her in the shadows of Mme Welfes's shop.

✠ ✠ ✠

Ridolfo stood on the wharf along with three others awaiting river transport. Thomas strolled behind half a dozen stacked puncheons and glamoured himself. Assuming Ridolfo would never have met Fulke (and certainly was never going to meet him now), he emerged from the stacked barrels with a mop of blond hair and freckles, and casually joined the group hiring the small boat to take them down the Senne to Brussels.

Like London and Antwerp, Brussels was a walled city that had outgrown its containment, although while London simply spilled new parishes across the landscape, here they had tried to keep up with the city's growth by adding a second, more expansive, set of walls. Also like London, the walls contained gates, which could be prodigious. Halle Gate, for instance, was at least four stories high and inhabited, with a working, though disused, porticullis and drawbridge. It made Thomas think of the dismantled drawbridge of London Bridge, and of Newgate, Ludgate, and even the Tower itself—massive structures incorporating or turned into prisons.

Soldiers seemed to be everywhere about, far more prominent than in London, but then all of Flanders was in effect at war, a situation exacerbated by conflicting treaties signed just this year, which essentially pitted the northern provinces against the southern, and William of Orange against Spanish rule over the Netherlands. England wasn't the only place where Catholicism found itself under assault. The war showed no signs of ending anytime soon, either.

Yet, business in Brussels carried on as if none of this were ongoing around it.

The boat let its passengers out below Halle Gate. Thomas hung back, maintaining his seeming obliviousness of Ridolfo as they disembarked. Another man met the banker here. This new man was short and round-faced, his dark hair pasted to his head. His clothing looked less than fresh, and he seemed slightly unsteady on his feet as they conversed, as if he'd spent the hours awaiting Ridolfo's arrival in a tavern with a pitcher of wine. The banker reacted as if this was to be expected, and the two of them headed off toward the hill on which perched the magnificent royal Palace of Coudenberg. Thomas let them walk away. Ridolfo's residence, he knew, was on the western side of the palace, and not far from there lay an inn, The Black Swan, where he'd stayed the last time he'd done business in Brussels with the banker. He hoped it was still a going concern. Their pancakes had been delicious.

The proprietor of The Black Swan, Andries Engelbrecht, didn't recognize him or the name he gave, Rafe Lindsay—the same name he'd used on his previous stay—but that was hardly surprising given that nearly two decades had passed since then. Engelbrecht's wife, Margriet, was a plump woman. She had only just married Andries when last Thomas had stayed at The Black Swan. Now she had gray in her hair, and two grown children—a son, Aelbert, and a daughter and namesake, Griet, both of whom assisted their parents with the inn.

The tavern part of the inn was a room containing three tables with benches and a few triangle-backed rough-hewn chairs with cushions to make them at least minimally comfortable. Kegs of ale were stored under the stairs that led to the two individual rooms on the upper floor. Wine in square glass coolers stood in the corner of the short entryway to the kitchen. The proprietor and his family lived in a smaller, adjacent building accessed by a rear door leading to a yard where someone had set up pins to play the game of quilles.

The second-floor room they rented to Thomas was small, with a thick pallet on the floor, a washbasin and pitcher on a small stand, and a close stool. The angled thatched roof accounted for half of the ceiling.

Upon being led to his room by the young, sturdy Aelbert, Thomas happened to catch a glimpse of the other traveler staying at the inn, who was just emerging from the second room. It was the round-faced man who'd met Ridolfo. Over the chest he carried, Thomas nodded as he might at any stranger. The man, closing his door on his way out, nodded back somewhat warily before descending the stairs and leaving the inn.

To Aelbert, he asked who the man was. "I think I may know him from somewhere," he explained.

While his parents might have refrained from gossiping, young Aelbert was only too happy to talk. "A Scotsman who insists he's Fleming. He speaks our language fairly well, too. His name is, ah, Charles Bailly. He is a strange little man, I think, given to intrigues of some sort. Very fond of our wine. He comes and goes at all hours."

"Bailly, hmm." He set down the chest beside the pallet, and stretched.

"We have housed him a few times. He has…visitors. Important-seeming men."

Thomas placed a sovereign in his hand. "You must alert me if any such visitors arrive while I'm here."

Aelbert grinned, wide-eyed, at the gold coin. "*Yes*, m'sieur." He formally bowed and went out, closing the door after him.

Thomas would have liked to follow Bailly right then, but hurrying out now would call attention to him, not to mention that he would need to glamour as someone else if he wanted to keep Rafe Lindsay disconnected from any prying he might need to do. Rafe would be visiting Ridolfo, and probably within a few days.

In fact, it proved to be eight days before he had cause to make an appointment with Ridolfo, but by then he'd learned that he wasn't the only person interested in Charles Bailly.

Each morning, Bailly went out for a constitutional stroll through the park below the palace. In following him, Thomas would exit through the rear door of the tavern and enter the street through the narrow alley separating tavern and family home. In the alley, Thomas glamoured and then emerged onto the street. Bailly's route took him through a bustling street market. Thomas remained a complete stranger as he tracked Bailly through the park. In any case, Bailly did not seem to be paying him any attention.

By the second morning, however, Thomas recognized that a second man trailed after Bailly. Of medium height and with auburn hair, the man walked slowly along and wherever Bailly paused, the fellow turned away and walked in a large circle through the crowd, once, twice, as many times as necessary before Bailly set forth again. Each time, the man passed close enough for Thomas to see his unkempt countenance and frustrated expression. Like Thomas, he seemed expectant that Bailly was about to meet with someone, or perhaps receive something.

Steps led from the park up to the Royal Palace, but Bailly never climbed them. He remained at the bottom, against a low wall overlooking a rectangular pond. It seemed an obvious location for a clandestine meeting, but Bailly met no one. He remained by the wall, as if utterly carefree, until he finally turned and headed back across the park, taking one circuitous route or another, but always returning to The Black Swan in time for the afternoon repast. The second man never entered, but strolled off up the street to a nearby alehouse.

On the fifth day, Bailly took his usual stroll, and after perhaps half an hour beside the pond, he set off again. This time, however, his course back to the inn took him along a narrow, curving street that ended in a circle. The other man had maintained some distance from Bailly, and now found his quarry emerging from the loop at the end and headed straight back at him.

Thomas drew up and in the shadows of a narrow alley quickly glamoured himself as one of Walsingham's code breakers, a face Bailly would never have seen before.

Caught out, the other man had no choice but to walk straight past Bailly and along the road as though ignoring him, but it was clear to Thomas that Bailly had already taken notice of his pursuer. Approaching Thomas, Bailly repeatedly looked back at the receding figure, his gaze fearful. So unsettled by the encounter was he, that he nearly ran into Thomas, who sidestepped him. Bailly muttered, "Oh, beg pardon," but hardly gave him—a stranger—a glance. After that, Thomas let Bailly wander away, and strolled off elsewhere for an hour.

Back at The Black Swan, Thomas entered unglamoured to find Charles Bailly seated alone at a table with a wineglass and cooler before him. Bailly looked up, and Thomas, returned to the guise of Rafe Lindsay, pretended to respond to the motion, looked his way and gave a courteous nod, but continued straight up the stairs to his room.

There, he tried to make sense of it all. Walsingham had said he had a second man in play. If that's who the other man was, he was sloppy at shadowing. If he wasn't Walsingham's man, then who the devil was he? Who else might be interested in Bailly?

Perhaps he, Thomas, was supposed to focus strictly upon Ridolfo while this other agent tracked Bailly? There was no obvious way to learn the answers to his questions, no instructions to acquire, but the clumsy stranger was proving to be unhelpful. If nothing else, he had made Bailly aware of being watched by *somebody*.

Thomas's instinct was still to follow the Scotsman: Given Bailly's daily routine, he wondered if that first day the nervous little man hadn't conveyed a verbal message to Ridolfo and his companion and was awaiting a response that had yet to arrive.

When Thomas went down for a meal and a mug of ale, Bailly was gone. He hadn't come up to his room—Thomas would have heard him pass by.

He sat down at one of the small tables, and Andries Engelbrecht served him a platter of four fried pastries. "Sparrow," he said. "Very good with our ale, m'sieur." That turned out to be true, and Thomas enjoyed a second ale. A curious scent wafted his way, and he glanced around. A stranger at another of the small tables sat puffing on a long-necked clay pipe. He eventually turned the pipe over and knocked it against a small bowl. When he spied Thomas watching, he reached over, holding out the pipe and a leather envelope. "*Tabaco.*" Thomas shrugged. "Herb de la reine?" he tried.

Having no idea to what that referred, Thomas raised his hands and replied, "Thank you, but no. I'm quite sated." The stranger shrugged and proceeded to refill his pipe bowl with more of the stringy herb while Thomas looked on.

An hour later, Bailly returned. He crossed the floor unsteadily, bumped into the pipe smoker without seeming to notice, and clutched the rail as he climbed the stairs up to his room. Wherever he'd gone, it seemed he had continued to partake of the comfort of wine.

One afternoon, Aelbert knocked on his door to replace the pitcher of water for washing. Once inside the room, the boy said quietly, "Bailly has two visitors. Englishmen both."

Thomas thanked him. He'd heard the footsteps pass his door. He pulled his jerkin over his shirt before exiting the room and descending into the tavern. He called for a pint pot of ale, and settled down at one of the tables, but then moved to a chair at another table where two men were playing the game of Irish, positioning himself so that he was also facing the stairs. They shook their cups, rolled out their dice, and moved their men along the points of the board. Thomas set down a wager of a penny on one of them.

Within the half hour, the two English strangers came down the steps. Bailly was not with them, but his presence wasn't needed to confirm the men's identities. The first man, with a dark, receding hairline, had a widely spaced and somewhat wispy mustache and a prominent lower lip that gave him a supercilious affect. There was no mistaking Thomas Howard, the Duke of Norfolk. Walsingham had pointed him out specifically in Placentia Palace.

The second man wore a black cap with a jeweled band; his face was more severe, with a short beard, dark brown eyes, and a sour expression, as though the whole experience here was making him dyspeptic. Thomas was fairly certain he was looking at the Baron Lumley. Two English noblemen in The Black Swan seemed uncommonly unlikely, even more so that they were there to see Charles Bailly. As they passed nearby, Thomas tilted back his pot of ale and pretended not even to notice them. They went out the door.

After a moment, Thomas stood up, handed his empty pot to Margriet Engelbrecht, then crossed the room and went out, too. He took one look around, establishing where the two men had gone and that no one else was walking nearby, turned so that he faced the door, and glamoured himself as one of the men he'd just left playing Irish within—the one whose back would have been to the noblemen as they departed. Then he pushed away from the door and headed along the cobbled street, strolling as if leisurely in the same direction they'd gone. When, a few minutes later, they turned from the wider road to Leuven, he slowed up, knowing exactly where they were going.

Just to be sure, however, he walked to the intersection from where he could watch the two men enter the house of Roberto di Ridolfo.

XVI. The Letter of Credit

Thomas hurried back to the inn, unglamoured along the way, and went directly up to his room. He opened the chest he'd brought with him, removed the majority of the contents, mostly clothing. He pressed a secret catch along the bottom of it, which released a portion of the bottom, revealing a wide, shallow compartment containing an oiled leather sleeve. He unfurled that, and then carefully went through the various papers it contained until he found the one he wanted.

The handwriting was crisp and clear.

He replaced everything in the chest, closed and locked it, then got up. The intrusion he planned would only work once, but he could think of nothing else that would provide him with as much information for Walsingham; at least at this very moment he knew where three of the participants in the evolving plot were located. For the rest he would improvise.

He put on the doublet he'd worn upon his crossing. It still had a ruff attached to the wire *supportasse* at the neckline. He buttoned it. adjusted the ruff so that it looked fresh, then carefully slid the legal document up into his left trunk sleeve before draping himself in the sleeveless, braided, knee-length black gown he'd brought. Now he was dressed respectably.

Returning to the street, he headed for Ridolfo's house again. Norfolk and Lumley might have gotten a look at him as they left the inn, but with luck he had just been part of the scenery, dressed like the men playing Irish, not like a proper gentleman and thus beneath their notice. Nevertheless, as he walked up the narrow street, he concentrated, adding lines to his face, gray to his hair, and more to his beard, much as he had done centuries ago to "age" alongside his wife.

A servant answered Ridolfo's door. Out of sight, a conversational debate was going on. Someone said loudly, "Even if he has not been exposed, we must treat him as compromised."

Thomas told the servant he was here to see the banker Roberto di Ridolfo. The servant ushered him inside and must have assumed he was part of whatever was taking place, because he led Thomas straight to the door of the room and held the door open.

As Thomas entered, the conversation within came to a halt, and the ördstone around his neck seemed to shiver.

The room proved to be a dining room, with pale yellow walls and dark beams, a long table off to one side that could seat eight, two cupboards, sixteen mullioned windows, a dark plank floor, and a Persian carpet running between the table and the large hearth.

Norfolk and Lumley were there, both on their feet. Ridolfo sat at one end of the table, with a quill and inkpot before him, and papers, two of which were already folded into packets and sealed with red wax. Two chairs farther along the table sat a fourth man, with a high forehead, a bent nose, and a small mouth, mostly hidden in his mustaches. His trim beard ended in two points. Beneath his ruff and high collar, and over his fur-edged gown, he wore the chain of the Order of the Golden Fleece. Thomas realized he was looking at Fernando Álvarez de Toledo, the Duke of Alba, whose portrait was among those identified by Francis Walsingham at Seething Lane.

"Alba will supply us with ten thousand"—suddenly the overheard words had context. The four men stared at him critically. He stared back. The ördstone seemed to be warning him that one of them was an Yvag. It might even be Ridolfo, but he didn't think so, and in any case he hadn't the time to puzzle that out just now.

Thomas smiled in feigned embarrassment. "Sirs, I am regretfully sorry. Your servant mistook me for someone else, I think. My name is Rafe Lindsay, and I have an open letter of credit to Signor Ricardo di Ridolfo." He slid the document from his sleeve and held it out as if not knowing to which of them it should be handed.

Norfolk exclaimed, "This is hardly the time—" but Ridolfo raised a hand to silence his objection.

"You are quite right, Signor Lindsay, Jaan has confused you with someone else," Ridolfo said, rising to his feet. He took the proffered document and looked it over. "Ah, I see. 'Tis I who must apologize to you." He handed the letter back to Thomas. "Might I ask you to return in one hour, at which time I will be available to honor your letter?"

"Of course," Thomas replied. To the remaining trio, he said, "Gentlemen," and then withdrew, back through the entryway, where a seated Jaan the servant lurched to his feet to open the door to the outside.

Thomas left.

What had he just seen? Two Englishmen presently colluding with the Italian banker and a representative of Spain? How else was he to characterize it? Was Alba delivering money, or had they been referring to an invading force of ten thousand men? He couldn't be certain how to interpret that line out of context, but it would surely be enough to prompt Walsingham to act. Their conversation, what little he'd heard of it, seemed to refer to Charles Bailly. He was the likely subject who'd been "compromised." The word suggested that, after encountering his other shadow yesterday, Bailly had panicked in fleeing to Ridolfo's house.

As to whether any of them was Yvag, Thomas couldn't be sure. He and the ördstone were still learning to communicate.

An hour later, having passed the time in a tavern and stew, Thomas returned to Ridolfo's house. Jaan ushered him in again, this time to a room containing no conspirators. Only Roberto di Ridolfo remained. The packets of letters that had been on the table were gone as well. There was no reaction from the ördstone. Ridolfo was not the Yvag.

Ridolfo stood and said, "Signor Lindsay, please." He gestured to a chair and they both sat. Thomas handed him the letter of credit again. Ridolfo read it over, nodding. "Yes," he said, "Signed in London a decade ago. I do remember this. A relative?"

"My late uncle."

"He is almost fixed in my memory." He peered at Thomas. "You resemble him, I think."

"Yours is an astonishing memory, then. It's true, I do resemble him."

Ridolfo got up. He asked, "Might I offer you something? A fellow in Amsterdam, Lucas Bols, has begun distilling an interesting drink called gin. It's perhaps an acquired taste, but, eh . . ."

"Thank you, yes."

Ridolfo went off. A few minutes later, Jaan entered with two small glasses and a tall, corked stoneware bottle. He filled the two glasses, left the bottle, and then departed.

The drink was cloudy and slightly pink. Thomas waited for his host to return.

Ridolfo entered and sat back down. He placed a large purse of coins before Thomas, then lifted his glass. They drank. The warm gin burned. It had a curious and spicy herbal flavor. His eyes watered. His host seemed not the least bit troubled, and smiled as Thomas recovered. "An acquired taste, as I said."

Thomas replied breathily, "It may take me some time to acquire it."

Ridolfo set his own glass down. "So," he said, "where does your uncle's money take you?" He gestured to the purse. "One assumes you are traveling."

"You assume correctly. Yes, Paris is next. Eventually I hope to reach Florence."

"Lovely city, Florence, my true home."

"Really? Do you return to it?"

"Now and again, yes. Not often enough. It is a long journey."

"Mayhap I will encounter you there." He studied the glass. "First, though, I may have to pay a visit to Amsterdam. Bols, you said." They traded smiles of appreciation before he downed the rest of his gin.

Thomas anticipated that Bailly would be away as soon as possible, and packed his belongings, ready to hire a cart.

Instead, the following morning, Bailly was back to his previous routine. He walked to the park below the palace. Thomas looked for the shadow who'd followed Bailly before, but the fellow did not put in an appearance or else had learned to conceal himself more successfully.

Bailly's morning routine was repeated for another three days. It was obvious he was nervous, and that whatever he waited for, it should have occurred by now. Most likely the conspirators had warned him not to contact Ridolfo directly again.

Thomas ran through a repertoire of glamoured faces and costumes, different each morning, and remained intent upon scanning the strolling crowd for the shadow or anyone else showing an interest in

Bailly—so intent in fact that he almost missed the moment when a small parcel passed into Bailly's hands.

The stranger who delivered it wore a hat with a gathered crown and a brim, and just might have been Jaan, Ridolfo's servant, but he couldn't be sure—the face remained obscure in the shadow of the hat, and the exchange itself was almost invisible. The stranger walked on past Bailly without acknowledging him at all and climbed the steps up to the palace.

Bailly then wasted not a moment before striding off in the opposite direction, back across the park.

It would have been far too obvious for Thomas to return immediately, even though Bailly should have no reason to suspect him of anything. He allowed a quarter of an hour to pass, then returned to The Black Swan.

Bailly had gone. Thomas was glad he'd packed up his own belongings earlier. He paid his bill, folded his cloak over one arm, then carried his travel chest down the street in search of a cart he could hire to take him to the Scheldt, where he hoped to hire a boat to take him to Antwerpen. He didn't know how far behind he might be. If Bailly arrived in England ahead of him with whatever package he'd been given, he might easily elude them all. Walsingham's network had significant gaps in it.

The cart he hired took him to a village, Rupelmonde, where he could hire a boat to take him up the river, but not before morning. The driver told him that various houses took in travelers heading to or from Brussels—travel in and out of Brussels was a going concern in Rupelmonde. He was left on the banks of the Scheldt next to a large castle. As the cart rolled off, Thomas stood admiring the castle. He counted seventeen towers on its walls. While he stared up at it, an old man passing by told him, "Imprisoned Gerardus Mercator in there seven months for heresy, they did."

From a family named Duerincx, he rented a garret room for the night. After a light supper of soup and bread, in the twilight he took a stroll about the village, watchful for Bailly, but did not see him anywhere. Finally, he turned in.

Early the following morning along with two other travelers, Thomas hired a boat to Antwerpen. Unloaded on the wharf there, he learned that transport to a crossing ship was not yet present, and so he milled about among a dozen others. Bailly was not among them, either. He feared that his quarry had either changed his mind or somehow arranged passage the night before. He decided it was more important to alert Walsingham than to pursue Bailly.

From the wharf in Antwerpen, he and the others were rowed out to one of two dozen ships anchored in the port, a carrack. From farther up the wharf another boat also set off for the ship.

At the carrack, Thomas climbed the rope ladder onto the deck; sticking his head up, to his surprise he found himself face-to-face with Charles Bailly. He kept his own reaction in check. Bailly glanced at him but gave no sign of recognition; he stood fingering his ruff as if interminably bored, and finally turned away.

Thomas's small chest was hauled up, and he collected it. Bailly carried with him only a leather bag, something like a saddlebag, thrown over one shoulder.

Thomas walked across the deck, set down the travel chest, and then settled himself upon it. Others were still climbing up. He watched as an arm reached over the gunwale and another familiar face rose into view: auburn hair, and the same leather shoulder cape over a maroon doublet. Bailly's shadow didn't recognize Thomas, but his sights locked onto Bailly, who at that moment was across the deck and looking out as if he could see his destination in the distance. By the time he turned back, his shadow had worked his way in among the other travelers where Bailly wouldn't spot him.

Well, well, thought Thomas. *We're all going to Dover after all.*

XVII. Marshalsea

On their crossing the Strait of Dover, Bailly's shadow seemed to vanish. Thomas did not see the man anywhere and suspected he was now lurking belowdecks. Bailly spent the crossing opening and closing his leather satchel, as if he felt the need to confirm over and over whatever it contained.

The chalk cliffs, which began as a white line painted along the horizon, grew ever thicker. Soon the castle above that line was visible and then finally shapes comprising the town itself below it.

At last the crew prepared for the passengers' departure, furling the sails, dropping anchor.

A few wherries from the town met them to convey the handful of travelers to the shingle banks beneath the town. *Conveyances*—the once-innocent word was now joined for him forever to the notion of skinwalkers, the Yvagvoja who inhabited humans.

As he awaited a wherry to convey him to Dover, Thomas reflected upon this first assignment for Walsignham. He had no experience carrying out others' assignments. Even back in the days of Sherwood, the schemes had mostly been of his devising. He had acted in coordination with others, but not upon their direction. He recognized now that he didn't much like being directed by someone else, and even less being constrained by them. He worked alone—really, he always had, ever since the day he saw Alpin Waldroup buried. So it should not have surprised him that he felt unsatisfied now.

If Alba did prove to be a skinwalker, he would, Thomas supposed, go on a list—one naming Yvags he must revisit another time.

Meanwhile he tried to imagine what plot collected the likes of Ridolfo, Norfolk, Alba, and Bailly—men drawn from such very different strata who would normally have little or no contact. He hoped Walsingham would make sense of it all, because he could not.

In the end, he paid his ten shillings for the crossing and climbed aboard a small boat that contained neither Bailly nor Bailly's shadow. They had boarded some other wherry. For the brief journey to shore he paid another two shillings. Two young men ran into the surf, caught the prow of the boat, and dragged it up onto the shingle for him and two others to climb out.

Yet even as Thomas was stepping onto the pebbles, he watched Charles Bailly, farther up the beach, being arrested, put in cuffs, and his closely guarded leather satchel confiscated. It was all being done at the direction of the man in the maroon doublet—Walsingham's other agent and a shadow no longer.

Furious, Thomas wanted to intervene: In one go, the fools were undermining an operation he'd spent many days observing and analyzing; he'd identified the players, and he still knew only a part of it. Idiots! Now he might never know where Bailly would have led him.

"Charles Bailly is a member of the household of Mary of Scotland as well as being an agent of Pius V," explained Walsingham as a simple matter of fact. He sat at the draw table in his private room, where he had received Thomas. "For quite some time, I have known of his other occupation. He is an obvious go-between for the likes of Ridolfo, able to carry messages directly to his employer. This is hardly the first time he has eluded us and then returned. It is, however, the first time that no less a personage than Cosimo I de' Medici, Grand Duke of Tuscany, has warned Her Majesty of the plot against her. That number you overheard, the one relating to the Duke of Alba, referred to ten thousand *soldiers*, the armed force Alba has promised to supply for an invasion."

Thomas had given his full report on the events in Brussels, naming Norfolk, Lumley, and the Duke of Alba as part of the broader scheme that seemed to be implied. Even so, he hadn't imagined an actual invasion might be in the works.

Astonished by what Walsingham was telling him, he could not contain his ire: "And yet you *arrested* him?"

Walsingham's eyes flashed. "Oh, not I, master Gerard. Like you, I would have given him his lead and followed him all the way home before I confiscated his secrets—if I confiscated them at all—at Chatsworth House, in the presence of Mary of Scotland to drive home the point whilst establishing once and for all her part in these machinations. To my everlasting frustration, Her Majesty rejects our every attempt to establish Mary's knowledge of and participation in such schemes.

"No, 'twas Burghley had him arrested. He was found to be in possession of a book printed in Liège and written by the bishop of Ross advocating for Mary of Scotland to be made queen, that on top of a group of letters that I expect are written in a code Mary would have deciphered for us if only they'd been allowed to reach her. While I share your frustration and displeasure over this fiasco, mostly I would like to know what is in those letters. They will be transcribed for me shortly and the originals continue their journey to Chatsworth. I can only hope that part might still bear fruit."

Walsingham continued. "But you, in the same period of time, have penetrated Ridolfo's network. From your description of him, the other man you saw in Antwerp was probably Lesley, the bishop of Ross himself. I imagine he was handing off the copy of his book they took off Bailly."

"And Bailly?" Thomas asked.

"Oh, he is currently being held in Marshalsea prison."

"Then who's the damnable fellow who had him arrested? That followed him?"

"His name is Herle, William Herle. He's been Burghley's agent in this for some time. Usually as a prison informant, but in this instance allowed to roam. Cecil must have him on a leash."

"Well, he's not much good, is he?"

"I understand, you're incensed that he interfered with your own surveillance and undermined us. I assure you that, between my network, Burghley's, and Leicester's, this is likely to happen again. There may be more spies abroad right now than there are agents of the church. 'Tis often hard to separate them as, incognito, they play the parts of sworn enemies of Her Majesty."

"Yes, I do understand that, Sir Francis. What I meant, however, was that Herle's not much good because Bailly spotted him days ago.

Tricked him into revealing himself. And I myself had observed him even before that."

"What? Both of you?" Walsingham goggled at him.

"Almost certainly Charles Bailly informed Ridolfo of his presence, too. I think that must have delayed his crossing back to England. He stalled for days, you see. Now I think it explains why Ridolfo didn't accompany him, or Baron Burghley might have laid hands upon the banker as well."

Walsingham touched one hand to his mouth. "Mon dieu." He stared at Thomas. "When was your audience with Ridolfo?"

"Four days before Bailly finally received his anticipated parcel, which was four days longer than I expected."

"And you are certain you saw the sealed letters at that time?"

Thomas nodded. "Quite certain. As I said, his servant mistook me for one of the conspirators and showed me in. Ridolfo had the letters in his possession."

"Four days," mused Walsingham. "More than ample time to revise and code new letters. Far less incendiary letters, too, I'll warrant."

Thomas saw what he meant. "Bailly's become a decoy," he said.

"I imagine the originals have already arrived at Chatsworth House by some other means."

"Norfolk?"

"Or the bishop of Ross. He kept himself available but entirely removed from the nexus of intrigue. Or possibly it's someone we do not yet suspect." He rose to his feet. "That is for other assets of mine to investigate. As we have him in our possession, we must now focus upon Bailly."

Thomas stood, too. "How so?"

"In four days they will not have changed the code, but merely penned new missives with it for us to decipher. If we can persuade him, Charles Bailly may yet be of service to us."

XVIII. The Rack

The rack was referred to as "the Duke of Exeter's Daughter"—a sly reference to a former constable of the Tower. It stood in a room on the Tower's lowest level. The small chamber otherwise contained only a small table and chair. There were two mullioned windows letting in a subdued light, with thick sloping wells beneath them.

The metal-and-wood frame of the rack contained three cylinders. The main one, with a long handle attached, lay in the middle and was separated from the other two by horizontal slats. Heavy ropes were secured around the main cylinder with two leading up and around the top cylinder and two connected around the bottom one. The ropes ended in loops for the wrists and ankles of the prisoner.

The guards who led Charles Bailly into the room made him stand beside it while they conversed quietly with the operator of the device, allowing time for Bailly's situation to sink in, for his imagination to do half their work for them.

When they decided he'd had enough time, they ordered him to lie on his back with his arms above his head while they placed his hands and feet in the rope loops and tied them securely. He was not a particularly tall man, and the distance between wrist and leg cords was close to his full range already.

The guards left and another man arrived, a hunched-over scribe well known to the Tower guards and carrying papers and an inkpot and quill. He took his place at the small table, sorted his papers, and almost immediately began asking questions in his nasal voice.

"Charles Bailly, who conveyed your letters to Mary of Scotland?"

Bailly replied, "I know nothing of what you speak. I'm an innocent man caught up in something beyond his ken."

The scribe cocked his head. "You would suggest what? That you did not know you carried treasonous correspondence?"

"I did not, sir, not until I was arrested."

The interrogating scribe held up a torn piece of paper. "Yet you wrote a letter to the bishop of Ross, whose conspiratorial book was found in your possession upon your arrival in Dover. You warned the bishop that, and I quote, 'we are all betrayed.'" He turned the paper toward Bailly as if he could read it from there. "You see? It's a remarkable thing for an innocent courier to say in the absence of some plot or other. How else can you be betrayed?"

Bailly made no answer. The interrogator seemed disappointed. He gave a nod, and the operator of the rack pushed on the handle, advancing the cylinders a full circuit. The ropes went tight and began to pull Bailly's arms up, his legs down. He winced and let out a small noise. His shoulders burned with the tiniest ache, his hips and knees as well. The cylinder stopped turning.

The interrogator stood up and came around the table. He carried a different sheet of paper, one that had been folded and sealed with wax. With both hands he held it above Bailly's face. "I show you this letter now which was found in your possession, a page full of gibberish to anyone unacquainted with the necessary code key to decipher it. Now, if you assist me in its translation, matters do not have to go this way." He gestured at the rack. "Be wise. Survive."

Sweat trickled along Bailly's forehead. Nevertheless, he stared up at his interrogator and said, "Wise men ought to see what they do and examine before they speak."

"Oh, but we wise men know what *you* do, papist. It's you whom we examine." He gestured for the operator to push on the lever again. The cylinders rolled.

Bailly's shoulders and knees flared with pain so sudden that he cried out. His shirt became immediately soaked with sweat. Sweat pooled in and stung his eyes.

"Decipher this. You know its content. Help us, and your misery ends. Otherwise . . ."

Bailly shook his head.

"Otherwise, you will soon lose the use of your limbs forever," the interrogator warned. "And for what?" He sounded genuinely regretful.

"I. Am. Innocent."

"No one is innocent."

The cylinders rotated another clanking spin. The ropes snapped tighter. Bailly, lifted slightly above the supporting slats, screamed and blacked out.

His passing out stopped the torture before his shoulders dislocated. Returned to his cell and lying on a layer of rushes, Bailly tested his arms cautiously. His elbows and shoulders ached so much, he feared moving them. When he drew his legs in, his knees burned. Respite from his agony was all he could think of.

Bound up in his pain he did not notice the moment his visitor arrived, but eventually became aware of a dull light coming from behind him as if a candle had been carried into the cell.

With some effort he turned onto his back.

Inside the door of Bailly's cell stood a tall, robed figure, with hands bound before him. Above the robe was a gaunt, bearded face, with wisps of hair on its crown, thicker around the ears. The face was solemn, woebegone, and known to Bailly.

It was John Story, or, rather, Story's ghost, for the figure was glowing softly as it looked down upon him. Bailly knew Story well enough—their paths had crossed a few times. They were part of the network engaged with the Duke of Alba to dispense with Elizabeth and place Mary upon the English throne. And like Bailly, Story had foolishly gotten on a boat in Antwerp and ended up in the Tower, condemned as a traitor and, if this specter reflected truth, was already dead.

"Story?" He barely produced a whisper, cleared his throat and repeated the name.

The ghost of John Story came and knelt beside him. The bluish light thrown off by the ghost fell upon Bailly; he could make out the shadows cast by his own arms. "Why did you attempt to warn Lesley?" asked the icy voice.

"Story, the bishop wasn't with us at Ridolfo's house. If they were pursuing me, surely they sought him, too. I knew him to be in Antwerpen. Their man, the one's in Marshalsea now, he would know him."

The specter frowned. "Ridolfo knew already you were found out, non? You told him, did you not? He it was should have revised the plan, sent you away and entrusted the letters to someone who had not been compromised."

"But he did, man. Lord Cobham took them to the bishop. They wrote new ones that reveal almost nothing, and swapped 'em in Antwerpen before we sailed."

"Of course," the specter said. "Do you not see how Ridolfo has thrown you to the wolves while the other letters reach their destination?"

"He had no choice, Story, my—"

"Do not martyr yourself, Bailly. The letters are no longer threatened. They have made their way to their destination. Why let these men snap your arms and crack your legs? Confess to Burghley and assist him. Admit everything. You have suffered so, they will all believe your change of heart." The sorrowful eyes bored into him. "Think upon it."

Then the figure of John Story rose up and silently, slowly walked back across the cell and into the darkness.

Alone in his misery, Bailly told himself that Story's ghost was right. Let them translate the new letters with his aid. They would learn next to nothing from them. Ridolfo had rewritten them to be harmless. He was tired and in pain, and Ridolfo had used him the same as all of them used him, had left him to be followed and taken so that someone else might escape scrutiny. His life was forfeit for Cobham, or soon would be.

One monarch was no better than another.

In the corridor outside the cells, Thomas unglamoured as the luminous ghost of John Story. If Bailly should ask of his guard, he would learn that Story had been hanged and quartered in the time Bailly had been in Brussels. His head currently occupied one of the spikes on Traitor's Gate on London Bridge, which had at least given Thomas some grotesque sense of the man's appearance.

He'd asked Walsingham who Bailly's associates were—who might have been part of his network. John Story was the perfect candidate, the more so because he was dead.

Everything Walsingham and Burghley wanted to know, the ghost of Story had found out. The letters—the real ones—had made their way to Chatsworth House by other means while Bailly provided a diversion, one that Burghley's foolish man Herle had bought into. With luck, persuaded by the ghost, Bailly would now assist with deciphering the replacement letters, which, if Walsingham was right, would provide the elements needed to decipher the other batch of letters once his network had obtained them. Thomas did not doubt that they would be obtained. Walsingham, he recognized more and more, was merciless.

Beyond that, and although he would never have expressed it to the spymaster, Thomas did not want to see anyone else broken upon the rack.

In 1546 he'd witnessed the burning of a woman named Anne Askew as a heretic after she had been tortured on the very same device they'd just used to stretch Bailly. In Askew's case the torture had not been interrupted. They'd dislocated her shoulders, hips, elbows, and knees. She'd had to be carried in a chair to Smithfield for her burning, and the executioners had chained her to a post to keep her upright. Her agony had been so obvious well before the kindling was lit that he doubted the flames did anything but grant her quick and blessed release.

At least one of her torturers, Lord Chancellor Thomas Wriothesley, had been a skinwalker, turned sometime late in the reign of Henry VIII. He was a schemer who thereafter seemed to delight in all manner of torture and cruelty. Thomas regretted he'd never gotten the opportunity to dispatch him. Fortunately, it seemed that nature had been equally repulsed, and had brought Wriothesley down through illness, though not swiftly enough to save the poor woman Askew.

XIX. New Digs

Thomas sat in the yard of the Long Southwark tavern and pretended not to be watching the Lazarus-house down the road. Sir Francis had cut him loose now that the focus had turned to Bailly and deciphering the coded letters. Thomas had been advised only to "keep out of sight" until called upon again, which he found almost amusing. He was glamoured now as he had been since leaving Walsingham's house as flaxen-haired John Chandos for whom he'd fought as a longbowman at the battle of Crécy, a face he still vividly recalled two hundred years later.

Watching the house, he couldn't be entirely sure about the man strolling down the narrow road but turning at New Rents street and plodding casually back, idly and repetitively as if the streets circumscribed his world. He might have been anything from a madman to a relative of someone with plague being provided hospice by Mme Bennet. From here it was impossible to say with any certainty whether the man was Yvag or not, but the danger Thomas would likely put Mme Bennet in if he so much as approached her wasn't worth the risk. Of that he was certain.

He had tried to be careful for so long now not to make friends, or at least to do so in such a way that allowed him to disengage with ease, securely separating everyone from any association with the entity known to the Yvags as Thomas the Rhymer. Time and again he'd erased the evidence his enemy might acquire by which to track him back to anyone nor they to him.

Even with such precautions, close acquaintanceship sooner or later threatened the other person: Waldroup, Janet, Little John, Isabella Birkin—even as casual an ally as Sir Richard atte Lee fell prey inevitably to the elves and their schemes, ultimately paying the highest price possible just for knowing him. Despite all he tried to do, time and again the presence of Thomas spelled doom for those nearest him.

So he had made of himself a ghost, a spirit, one that struck swiftly and became smoke, connected to no one. He'd hoped to keep that ghost linked closely with Þagalwood, where Yvag soldiers themselves feared to stray from the path. He played upon their belief that he was part of the Wood or one of their own, a changeling gone wrong, and in a sense he supposed that was reasonably accurate.

Now, thanks to the plague and a dying skinwalker's chance encounter with his current alter ego, he had jeopardized those who knew him in London—all because he had not been able to retrieve two arrows from an Yvag corpse, while allowing himself to be displayed to the Queen. He might as well have been presented to Nicnevin on a plate.

Two weeks gone from London, and it looked like they were still watching for him. The Yvags didn't know where he was. This fellow going back and forth along the road would be glamoured, not a skinwalker. They wouldn't waste a skinwalker on so menial a task. But they were watching.

He drank his ale and moved on.

At Van der Paas's shop, glamoured, he claimed to be in search of new ruffs and pins. He allowed Lettice Van der Paas, the ruff-maker's youngest daughter, to show him a few samples before he casually dropped that he had been acquainted with Thomas Gerard, who lived above the shop, and he wondered if his old mate happened to be home.

Lettice nervously glanced to her father, but he was otherwise occupied with a customer himself. Finally, she said, "You are the fourth 'friend' of the doctor who has asked after him in a fortnight, where no one ever asked after 'im afore. You going to ask when 'e's expected to return?"

"So," he said, "he is not at home." She glared at him. "When is he expected to return?"

"*Never*," she answered furiously. "Gave the building to my father, know you that? Never is he coming back, having killed our . . . our friend." Her eyes were full of hurt.

"That—" he began but stopped. It was what she believed, and better in numerous ways that she did so. "I am sorry to hear this. Sorry for the loss of your friend."

"Least you haven't trespassed when we was closed, as if we made up our story."

"Someone did that? Broke in? How do you know it was the same person?"

"*I* know," was all Lettice said. "'E wanted to go see upstairs even as he were asking. Told him no, what with the carpenters workin' to fix the wall."

"Wall?" In the end, Thomas purchased two new ruffs, one golden yellow and another with a pattern that made it look embroidered, adding a hundred pins before leaving Van der Paas's—items he would in fact need if Walsingham sent him somewhere on the continent. He had established to his satisfaction that the Yvags were looking for him here, too, even to the point of invading the house to satisfy themselves that he wasn't about.

There was no denying it: the Yvags were hunting for Thomas Gerard. To confront them would gain him nothing, would in fact increase the likelihood they would pursue and find him. And if they were invading here already, he could only endanger everybody he cared about. Tortured or with a daughter or two threatened, Van der Paas would give up Christianne in Antwerp. The creatures might get one step closer to him, but with her or any of them, they would reach a dead end. Of course, they would probably kill her, too. If he wished to protect them, Thomas had one option: The plague doctor, Gerard, must completely vanish and stay invisible.

The means to this end was a foregone conclusion. Brussels was only going to be the beginning. Meanwhile, he could either rent a new apartment or fall upon the mercy of Walsingham. And given that it was Walsingham who had effectively destroyed his anonymity, it was only fair that Walsingham provide him sanctuary.

"Now verily I do see," said Sir Francis Walsingham. "Your willingness to spy for me had nought to do with Queen and country. Rather, the demons mingling in Her Majesty's court identified you as the assassin of their assassin."

"Indeed not," Thomas replied. "You put me on display in the Queen's court and they came hunting. The body they stole back contained the evidence they sought, which is to say, the arrows."

"And you dare not go home because they watch now for Gerard's return."

Thomas nodded. "Everywhere. And you need to send me elsewhere."

"One sympathizes, of course, having lost sight of any number of enemies whilst in pursuit of them for their machinations." He shook his head at the situation. "I cannot say I regret in the slightest how circumstance spins you like a weather vane back to my draft."

They just stared at each other then, Thomas all but willing Walsingham to die. "Bailly, half-frightened out of his wits, has already provided Phelippes the complete code key to decipher the letters we took off him and thus the ones delivered to Mary. He's proving so very helpful I fear we might even have to let him go in the end. Much would I like to know how you imitated John Story to terrify him thus. One of *my* guards claims to have caught sight of you leaving Bailly's cell and was so affrighted at your appearance that he fled his post. He says you *glowed*."

Thomas almost cringed. He'd insisted the guards all withdraw. Trust Walsingham to post an observer even so. All he could say in reply was, "I have some small familiarity with theater, props, and effects."

To his surprise, at mention of this, the usually dour Walsingham smiled warmly. "Indeed," he said. "I thought that might be so, else you prove to be supernatural yourself. I myself love plays and theater, as does the Queen, do you know. We champion a few of the finest companies. They play at court." He seemed genuinely delighted by this addition to Thomas's repertoire. "No wonder you've adapted to our game so well. Deception and disguise thrive in your blood, don't they, Gerard?"

He didn't know what to say, so remained stone-faced.

"Certainly, when you come back, we must take in a play or two at Burbage's Theatre."

"When I come back, you say." He was suddenly, keenly interested. "Then you *do* have an assignment for me."

"Currently, I require someone with your skills to infiltrate the English College, the one which began life in Douay, but has since been relocated to Rheims. Do you know of it?"

Thomas shook his head.

"Then allow me. It is a college run by Doctors Robert Parsons and William Allen. Allen in particular believes that men of all faiths can and should be brought together to discuss and debate humanities, philosophy, and jurisprudence, which sounds the very standard of educational perfection. And I believe, for Allen, it is. Unsurprising then that it is something of an extension of Oxford linked to the university in Douay—or was until university and college fell out. That's due to Parsons. His determined goal, unlike Allen's, is to establish the light of Catholicism over all other faiths. Nothing short of conversion. The college, it would seem, is breeding Jesuit heretics with the intention of unleashing waves of martyrs upon us."

Infiltrate the college—that suited Thomas fine. Jesuits, Catholics, Yvag skinwalkers. They were all of a piece.

"Evidence suggests that graduates of Parsons' program have been sequestered already in various houses by families in the north. I tell you, another plot is brewing, Gerard, as sure as we sit here. I should prefer to stop it by nurturing, shaping, and guiding it where we want it to go; however, I can only do that if I have a clear sense of what goes on within. The first order of business, then, is to have eyes on the inside, and that is where you enter.

"I would have you embed yourself among the *juris studiosi*, collect the names of those with whom you associate—lecturers and students alike—and pass those names on to me. They are comparable to your disguised demons: they look just like us but they are not us. Parsons is training a secret army." He tapped his index fingers together. "Your French is impeccable, as is your Latin. You are a little older than the usual Cambridge recruits persuaded by their agents to attend. Perhaps you can use your theatrical skills to look a bit younger. Then again, the younger men are plastic, easily molded. You could be someone who has thought through your choices, an older, wiser, dedicated convert who reminds the younger men of Ignatius of Loyola himself. Yes," he said thoughtfully, "with your theatrical bent, I am persuaded you will work a few small miracles along the way."

Thomas made no reply to that.

"Once embedded, you must use every advantage, remain in play. This will be for months at the very least, I'm sure. It should align nicely with your express desire to disappear from London until they stop looking for you.

"I've already one agent installed at the college, a young wit and poet by the name of Thomas Watson. He will vouch for you to them. Other operatives of mine believe him to be a double agent, so his endorsement of you should lead them to conclude you are also a Catholic schemer. While I wish you to remain independent of each other there, you can rely on him if needed, but upon no one else, even beyond the school. Regrettably, the English embassy in Paris is itself a molehill. Our poorly paid civil servants trade or sell as much information as they collect for me and for Burghley. Commodities of fact can be sold fresh to multiple buyers, all of whom are of course assured they alone are receiving the bounty. Even my most trusted, a fellow named Seys, might for all I know be selling secrets to anyone and everyone. Be assured, the paths of such buyers and sellers of information will certainly cross your own at the college."

"Then you have many agents placed there?"

Walsingham smiled indulgently. "You and Watson are the first in what I hope will expand to a greater network."

Thomas wondered if that was in fact the case. Walsingham was always guarded and said what he wanted you to know. Safer for others, if others there were, that they were not named, not even known to exist. Would they in turn know nothing of his existence there? Thomas doubted that Sir Francis trusted anyone entirely. Then again, in his position how could he?

The spymaster added, "*Pro tempore*, until you depart, there is a safe house you may use in Aldersgate Ward by St. Martin's le Grande. Unlikely anyone would ever tie you to it. I shall see a key is provided you. And we must find you a new name, both for your residency and for your travel." He leaned forward, picked up his quill, and began to write.

"Thomas Creighton," he suggested.

Without looking up, he replied, "Spell it for me."

Thomas did.

"Yes, that's a perfectly sound name, and distinctive. Good."

When Thomas remained standing there, Walsingham leaned back. "Was there something more, Creighton?"

For a moment he'd been tempted to reveal his own ability to glamour, an impulse he recognized now to be ridiculous. "No," he said, "I—thank you, Sir Francis."

"Needn't give thanks. You will give service enough before you're through," promised Walsingham.

That was certainly true. Walsingham cared about nothing else.

XX. Bragrender Underwater

An incensed Bragrender storms through the high blue grass above the plaza of Hel, the energy thrown off by his rage withering the stems below and beside him, carving a dead path of his route. He, glamoured as Lord Covington, had identified the assassin he's sought forever and was a mere step away from confronting and killing the creature—at which precise moment, one of Mother's little emissaries turned up to say that she required his immediate presence. Oh, how he wanted to snap the neck of the intrusive herald. Instead, he passed the glamouring of Lord Covington to one of his knights, Taistellejan, and as quickly as possible made the jump.

Across the open plaza he marches toward its center, where the Queen even now sits holding court. Two armed escorts march up beside him as if they could do anything about it were his intentions to kill her.

Her massive throne projects out of the plaza pavement as a huge winged structure that dwarfs the other eight seats of her counselors. They are dressed in the current fashion, which emulates and to an extent enlarges upon that of the current Londoners: Ruffs have become the rage here, and Nicnevin's counselors all look like heads on plates perched atop sloping falls of crushed velvet.

Nicnevin has always been one for excess, so it is impossible to know where or even if her purple, flowing gown reflects anything but her own taste. The layers flutter, glinting with pearls and gems that seem to glow from within. She has chosen, too, to style her abundance of red hair in a parody of the human queen against whom they all sit and plot. Assisting mortals in conspiring to kill the Elizabeth has become her council's exclusive pastime.

For what matter of state, discussion, or concern has she brought him here when he was about to pounce upon the slayer of Ritarenda, who as well killed their *teind* guards? It had better be astonishingly critical.

Even now in the pestilential city of London that lesser knight (they're all lesser than Bragrender, after all), in a glamouring of his own design, will be claiming *his* victory—the head of their nemesis. He would like to take the two guards and throw them into Hel. He may be obedient, but he knows down in his marrow that he's sacrificed that opportunity for something that's going to prove insignificant to everyone but Nicnevin. This is what she does. It is how she fractured pitiful Zhanedd's devotion to her. Whatever Mother requires is the most important thing, even when it is the least important. She will assure you that you are in charge, and in the next breath assign someone else to hobble you. Adversity builds character.

His escorts stop smartly.

The Queen turns to face him as if she hasn't bothered to notice his aggrieved approach. "Ah, Bragrender," she says.

"Ah, Jumalatar Nicnevin Ní Morrigu," he replies, his voice deep and painful to hear, the sound of a rusted hinge. He gives a small bow, mostly watching her twitch at his utterance of her full name. Just then if he were to choose he could exercise control over her through the binding of names, but he allows the moment to pass. The power of the spoken name dissipates like fog. It is enough to have her appreciate his indignant state of mind and how he could make her do something foolish if he chose to. Bragrender has become a master at manipulating his mother the Queen.

Nicnevin fingers the gold torc at her throat, gathers her composure, and says, "We have been discussing how our good cousin Zhanedd has been acting peculiar for some time and we seek your opinion, as you have spent more time in the Below than any among us." Her gesture at the circle is met with nods.

This is why he's been sabotaged: Because no one knows where Mother's pet changeling has gone? He seethes. Damn Zhanedd. If he had any sympathy for her before, this has torn it.

He says, "Other than delivering her to the Below when she was wounded I have not so much as beheld her once upon the tiers there." And that is true: Zhanedd has retreated to the same realm as he? It's news to him. Although now he wonders why. What has become of his experiment? He seems to have lost track.

Nicnevin dismisses his counterstatement. "Even so, you know more of the sentient machines' domain than any of the council here."

What he knows is that he *prefers* the company of those machines to that of these trucklers. Surely, Nicnevin is cognizant of that already. It's not as if he has dissembled otherwise.

"I'm unclear what you desire, my queen. You want me to confront her? Ask her to elaborate upon the Þagalene part of her?" He cocks his terrifying face. "Fear you it—she—is not homogeneous? I am truly at a loss."

"I would know, Bragrender, if she is governed now by impulses she cannot understand."

"That, I'm certain, is apparent just in that you refer to her as *she*, which itself sets her apart from all other changelings in Ailfion, whose former human selves you never mention. And here I speak plainly what others think and never say." He glances accusingly at the counselors. "There is something of your shaping"—he would like to say "interfering" but restrains himself—"about Zhanedd, *dear* Mother, just as there is of me. We are of the People and yet we are not of them in the slightest. We are outsiders. Others."

He starts walking around the circle of stone seats as he continues. The counselors' fearful oblique gazes track him as he does—nobody wishes to look upon Bragrender directly for fear they will behold some intimate or terrible aspect of themselves, one they would deny; but they also fear when they can't see him at all.

He asks, "When you say 'for some time,' you are referring to the many cycles since I carried her out of battle? Or is there some still more recent change that I wouldn't know, given that I've spent little time in her company since saving her life, nor kept watch upon her after handing her off to the machines, nor in the aftermath of the Þagalene graft that saved her? She did not invite my attention, nor expressed any gratitude. I have my own important—"

"Yes, we are aware of your quest. But this is of concern. She has withdrawn from us."

He thinks, *That would be because you betrayed her authority time and again, undermining her at every turn.* How different the quest for the one called "Robyn Hoode" would have gone if Nicnevin had allowed Zhanedd to have the reins she was promised. He says, "You would know 'Does the graft rule her?' Have none of these useless appendages of yours the capacity to undertake such observation on their own? Aware of my quest? Is it as abstract as that? I believe I have managed to discover and track the murderous abductor of many of our *teinds*, and am—*was*—very close to catching him so as to learn whether he be errant changeling himself or something we've never seen, a life-form not previously taken into account."

"Such as . . . ?" asks Nicnevin.

Can she really have no notion? "For instance, what if there lurks a multitude of secret enemies scattered across the World-to-Be? We've half-identified *an* enemy, but what if he is part of a network? I would like to know that. I was about to uncover whether that was the case. Yet, at so critical a juncture, it's Taistellejan in my place who even now encounters him—all *my* efforts are handed off to another to puzzle out, simply because your poor Zhanedd *might* be in some altered state, a parasitic symbiosis with the Þagalene or—" Bragrender pauses. The truth of the Queen's request is suddenly clear to him and he laughs. "Ah. You fear she's succumbing to the Unseelie, because of how Þagal is sourced."

Nicnevin grows visibly angry with his churlishness.

Bragrender sweeps a deformed claw at the circle of counselors. "Surely," he says, "among these eight there is somebody capable of following Zhanedd down into the Below." He closes that grotesque hand as it points to her again. "Or perhaps the prospect is too terrifying."

The Queen's golden stare is ice-cold. "There were nine counselors previously," she says.

"Oh, so you investigated already and it's cost you. Were you going to tell me of that?"

"Zhanedd dispatched my envoy."

"One can hardly blame her. I would be inclined to do the same."

"Enough!"

"I'm sure whichever of them it was will regenerate."

"That is not the point."

"No, of course not." He shakes his head, makes a "tch" of disappointment leveled at all of them. "Very well. I will speak with her if I must. *If* I can find her. As I said, I have seen nought of her in the Below and I do not seek her out." With that, he glances sidelong at her over his shoulder. "Am I done here? Yes, I believe I am."

He stalks away from the plaza as if it is poisonous, which for him it is. Political machinations rarely achieve anything but a thinning of sound judgment.

Where is Zhanedd, then? He cannot believe she is hiding in the Below, in *his* world. She has retreated to his universe and remained unseen by him? Well, there are nearly an infinite number of levels, so many pockets of creation and cessation, and guided by an intelligence as opaque to him as to anyone—even so, he feels he would know of or sense her. He'd thought her consumed with revenge upon all the "Robyn Hoodes" and utterly immersed in Sherwood Forest with the gates all sealed.

But it has been a long time since Robyn Hoode slit Zhanedd wide open and Bragrender saved her by dragging her back to Ailfion. The machines with which he left her had not been employed in centuries. Can anyone recall even one Yvag with any implanted, symbiotic Þagalene material? Zhanedd became his grand experiment, in effect a new life-form created by him, and no doubt Mother is right to be concerned, even fearful given that Zhanedd was already . . . unusual. His competition, even his nemesis. What might the Þagalwood part of her direct Zhanedd to do?

Perhaps he should be worried, but he's much more interested in the answer to that—how has it altered her—just as he wants to know right now what Taistellejan learned, wants to hear how his substitute killed the creature that called itself Gerard and have the body presented to him, like a gift.

He wanders through the levels, returns to the surgical and reabsorption sectors, where nothing is in operation, but she is not to be found in any of the places he looks (although he does find the rejuvenating counselor she slew in the care of the mortuarian). Zhanedd is not wandering the levels like some ghost. She has come and gone. He doubts Nicnevin has it right at all. She is not dwelling here and he is not going to waste more time on her.

He has looked and established where she is not. He will look again perhaps, later. Right now is time find out how Taistellejan dealt with the human killer.

Bragrender draws his large ördstone and concentrates it upon the location of Taistellejan's own stone. After a moment, a portal appears before him.

He tunes the lens to see past the gate. Oddly, nothing clear shows. It might simply be night, save for the dark swirling beyond the lens as if he's looking into the center of a very murky cyclone. He's looking at . . . water. Muddy, murky water. A few almost colorless fish swim across the face of the portal. Near the bottom of it a wan blue light pulses. With care, Bragrender makes a small low horizontal swipe. Filthy, stinking muck pours through the slit, a spewing waterfall around his feet. It spits out the dim blue lucency. The stink and silt tell him everything.

The far side of the gate comprises the foul and muddy bottom of the Thames. He hastily seals the slit back up, then reaches into the odious muck and picks up the ördstone of Taistellejan. Brown goop drips between his articulated finger joints. If his soldier's lifestone is at the bottom of the Thames, it's fairly easy to guess where Taistellejan himself is, as well as the knights he commanded. They are not riding back to Ailfion in triumph. And the gifted glove he entrusted to Taistellejan, it's not here, either; washed away in the river or even possibly in the possession of their enemy. But gone.

Bragrender erases the gate. No need to revisit that one ever.

He turns, and there is the rejuvenating counselor. Bragrender crosses to the body and tears out the black tubes, flings them against the wall. The mortuarian spins to life and rises out of his reach, so Bragrender grabs the body of the counselor and hauls it out onto the walkway, flings it over the edge. They want to put him back together? It's going to take them a little longer than planned. One dead counselor for one failed knight. Seems fair. The knight won't be returning even if the counselor does, eventually. Just now, though, it feels as if he has balanced an equation.

He would not have failed as Taistellejan did, nor lost the glove. Nicnevin pulled him away at the most critical juncture, undermining him as she always does, as if her little pathetic problems outweigh his efforts. Now they *still* do not know their enemy beyond a name, and in all likelihood that name has already been discarded. It is the closest he's come to having an answer to and possession of this adversary since . . . well, since rescuing Zhanedd at the priory. Had he just let her die, he would have had his adversary then and all this would be over and done. So whatever he's done to Zhanedd—however the Þagalene material has altered or corrupted her—is fine by him. Let the Queen go chasing after her. He will answer no more of these imbecilic calls. And when he takes power, as one day he surely will, he will squash all the idiots like bugs.

Keenly aware of the disadvantage he's been put at, he strides through the squishing muck and away from Reabsorption.

The assassin will have changed his name and location. No more Gerard the plague doctor. What will he become next? What would he, Bragrender, have become? *King.* True, but not a helpful answer.

INTERMEZZO
XXI. The Haunted Wood
(150 years earlier)

The image she returns to time and again is of her killer watching her be carried through the gate, his jaw set, the Yvag dagger he holds dripping with her black blood. Those icy-blue eyes hold her as if they know her. They were not the eyes of an Yvag, nor the changeling they had imagined at all. He was something else, something unique.

And then Bragrender was sealing up the gate. She shortly lost consciousness. Half her gills had been severed. Nobody recovered from such a wound. And too much of her blood remained on the gate's far side. While she drifted in and out of awareness, Bragrender sliced another and then another gate. At one point she saw above her the stricken face of Nicnevin and she thought jubilantly how the Queen did worry over her, did truly care, although the question of why remains unanswered.

That view of Nicnevin lasted a single moment; in the next the Queen was gone and instead white-bone skeletal machines probed and pried at her naked form. They reached deep within her. Was there pain? She thinks she screamed and lost consciousness again possibly more than once. The limbs of the machines flexed and flowed, clearing out a cavity within her. The things leaned over her as if focused upon her body, though eyes they had none.

Finally, a coldness poured into the terrible wound, or maybe it flowed into the new space they'd made within that wound, and immediately she was enveloped in a soft singsong voice that has not left her since: *Yes, yes, little one, sleep now. Give us your past to hold; we will return it a hundredfold.*

No one stood near to account for this voice; no one was there at all—just the swirl and bustle of those faceless white constructs attending to her. Even Bragrender, once he'd deposited her in their care, did not reappear, did not give her a second's thought. But the disembodied voice wrapped her as if in a fresh and soothing cocoon.

After that, Zhanedd began to dream. In the dreams she seemed to hover in the air like one of the fae except that no one in the dream noticed her presence, peering over their shoulders, hovering above them. She beheld a human woman who looked something like her, a girl really, being joined in marriage to the *lich* of an Yvagvoja. Unlike the girl, she perceived the voja's sharp features overlaid upon the face of the possessed husband, who was in reality a wretched, waterlogged corpse already dead before being scooped out and repurposed; no one save Zhanedd's floating ghost recognized his true nature, and she was not even there, was she?

By what miraculous process she didn't know, the *lich* got a child by the bride. The girl went home to her family, parents, and servants, including the ghostly presences of two brothers, one of them a seeming idiot with sharp blue eyes. Soon her pregnancy was making her ill, and she retreated to her bed, afterward almost never left it until the end when the *lich* brought her home with . . . well, not with her child, not with Zhanedd. They had made the exchange by then, the alderman and the rotting husband, and Zhanedd had been deposited in a broad meadow, a landscape dotted with tents and, oddly, with a set of doors like two enormous shells erected in the middle of the field standing against the curious sky. When finally they opened, they revealed that the meadow was somehow boundless sunny outdoors and a contained room within Ailfion at the same time.

Some part of herself wondered why she recalled this particular dream—what had the family of dead humans to do with her? She'd known no memories of life before Yvagddu. She had never dreamed before this. So was this series of collapsing realities death, then? She could not say, but the dreams themselves crumbled and blew away, to be replaced by silence.

Zhanedd awoke alone, naked, her armor long since peeled off and repaired. It hung beside the shelf on which she lay. Armor was easy to stitch back together. It bore only the memory of its wearer.

Looking down at herself, she found her entire repaired side become bone white. When she touched it, gently exploring with her long fingers, the whiteness shifted, flowed in the cavity like an eel, alive and unmistakably threaded into her via thousands of insubstantial strands: She didn't feel it moving even as she saw it do so—as if she beheld someone else's terrible injury. Here, however, was proof she hadn't perished. The instrumentality of Þagalwood had saved her. Bragrender, who routinely despised and dismissed her, had executed this. It would be some time before she had opportunity to ask him why, only to have him answer dismissively, "I wanted to see what you became. I didn't expect you would survive."

The constructs kept her in the underground for a long time before they released her back into the population of Ailfion. There something had changed. People fell silent at her approach. Golden eyes lowered or looked at her askance, as if no one was sure how or whether to acknowledge her. She had never been one of them, always queer and suspect. Did they all know what had happened to her? Even Queen Nicnevin, who had subverted her authority on so many occasions, seemed unsure of how to approach her now, as if in her recovery Zhanedd had gained an unnatural aspect they all sensed. Was it all due to the Þagalene symbiont? In a moment of insight, she thought *This is how they react to Bragrender, the same furtive glances, the discomfort, the . . . fear.* They had always viewed her as dubious; the addition of fear gratified her. They *should* be afraid. Much more than they feared Bragrender.

The People do not know what she is anymore; they only know she is different. She is starting to appreciate her difference, too, although not what it is they're sensing just yet. The Þagalene voice whispers but its message remains subliminal.

By the time she is capable of seeking revenge for what was done in the priory, the individuals have all melted away.

Most of them have died. Nevertheless, doggedly, she pursues every mention of "Robyn Hoode"—at this stage it becomes her life's purpose, but that name has become a badge that anyone can wear. It's passed around Sherwood like a goblet from which anyone can drink. Anyone accused of poaching from the King's Preserve or thieving on the King's

Way gives that name rather than their own. Those living in the forests are all Robyn Hoodes now, but none is the one she seeks.

Zhanedd cares not. If they take the name, they accept the consequences. She tracks and slays each without pity. In all the time she hunts them down, however, she never manages to cross paths with that blue-eyed one who almost ended her. He is gone. Dead, most likely, a mortal like everyone in the World-to-Be. And yet . . .

During Zhanedd's recovery in the Below, Nicnevin's soldiers continued to battle in those forests, hunting Hoode, but more specifically the rumor that he and his fighters still had one or more *dights*. Finally, though, no *dight* was ever recovered, and Nicnevin had lost too many soldiers to a seemingly well-organized resistance in the forests. It simply wasn't worth pursuing.

The Queen sealed off all the gates across Sherwood and Barnsdale. There were plenty of other places to hunt *teinds* in an ever-expanding world, not to mention the continued need to take possession of figures of power if they wished to promote their agenda.

Zhanedd alone pursued the hunt there. Nicnevin couldn't have stopped her and had the sense not to bother trying. Bragrender taunted and dismissed her, the tedious bore. He wanted her appreciation despite admitting he hadn't cared whether or how she lived. He'd simply used her.

Rumors of the fate of Zhanedd's Robyn Hoode swirled like smoke: He'd gone away, joined a crusade; he was asleep like the mythical Arthur and would one day return when the humans needed him again; he was still about but had taken another's name or gone off with someone named Marion. Stories begat stories begat stories.

She even hears her own story thrown back at her in distorted forms—the tale of a prioress who poisoned or bled poor trusting Robyn to death.

In some versions, she is a witch, in others his cousin or sister, and in others simply a cruel nun. The ballads, the stories, all clutter up the landscape until even the idea of seeking revenge grows tedious. It becomes akin to trying to slay a ghost. What ultimately causes her to let go of the question of Hoode is that after many travels in and out of Þagalwood, she has discovered something far more intriguing.

She knows, as does every Yvag, that to stray from the path in Þagalwood is to invite death: The sentient roots from those trees would wriggle up out of the soil to coil around and through the feet and legs of anyone who divagated, binding them to the spot to strip them clean of flesh and tissue, rendering them into a new distorted white-bone addition to the unnatural woods. Only during harvests are these rules held in abeyance.

According to Nicnevin, enough mad, failed changelings have attempted to escape into Þagalwood that their horribly transformed skeletal remains serve as markers, warnings to any others who might be inclined to stray. Zhanedd, seeing them directly, cannot distinguish their supposed remains from the rest of the grotesque bleached boscage. How can anyone tell them apart? She has stared and stared at the "remains," and there is no distinction. In the same sense, her own experience of the voice of the Wood runs counter to what she is supposed to believe.

Nicnevin and the elders of the court maintain that Þagalwood began as a dominion under the control of the Unseelie. According to them, most of the things growing there are in fact the dormant remains of ancient warriors killed in long-ago, forgotten battles with the Unseelie and planted as a reminder, and no one can say for sure whether they constitute Yvag or Unseelie losses. To Zhanedd this fumbling explanation explains nothing at all. If one begins asking questions in response to these upheld truths, one gets no answers that make any sense, and very soon no answers at all.

If they are Unseelie, how can it be that knights of glorious Ailfion come to harvest parts of them to populate or assemble the subterranean Below with a myriad of freakish constructs that design everything, run everything in Ailfion? For that matter, when did this begin? If those machines have always directed everything, has there ever been a time when they didn't exist? And the timeline makes no sense. The war with the Unseelie began well before the Yvags retreated to this world. How then and why is a graveyard of Unseelie warriors here?

And how is it that when new machines are needed, Yvag knights are allowed to leave the path in order to break up, chop down, or in some other way disassemble one of the tree creatures? Does the Wood identify its offered constituent in some manner? To whom is this knowledge given? To the Queen? The entire process is opaque, a closely guarded secret. But why?

It has become clear to her that none of those who might ostensibly know are willing or able to share the truth of the trees. Zhanedd suspects that they are all lying to her. And it's a great, vast lie. The Queen and these counselors have no more knowledge of the processes underlying Þagalwood than she does.

In the end, it is the whispering voice that leads her astray. *Follow,* it says. *This way, Zhanedd.* It knows her name.

So comes the day when she gives herself freely to the Wood. Nicnevin has undermined her too many times. Sherwood Forest is all but off-limits now. And Bragrender pursues his own quest to chase down some shadow figure—and it's not as if he is inclined to share what he knows with her anyway. She is beneath his interest. The voice has inveigled her enough times. It shows her the contempt with which they all dismiss her; *changeling* becomes a belittling term, a way to keep her down.

The Wood leads her to a spot and invites her in. She stands on the main path from which all others open and peers into the gloom out of which the skritchy voice seems at its loudest.

Behold, it says.

What is she supposed to behold? she asks. The voice does not say.

She stares into the depths until her eyes ache. Nothing emerges. Nothing appears. Frustrated as much as ever, she gives up.

Looks down.

There in the soil before her, the insects, annelids, myriapods, and other scavengers of the Wood crawl and slide, burrow and skitter along—but only within a narrow reach. The insect life acts as if innately sensing the boundaries of safety; instinctively, they turn aside at the edges, creating (though it is only just now obvious to her) pathways leading into the depths of Þagalwood. The primordial creatures have worked and traveled the paths of the Wood since . . . probably since there was a Wood, only, no one has ever thought to observe them. If she's right, it's so absurdly elemental, hiding in plain sight. *Behold.*

Emboldened, Zhanedd dares to take a step onto the insect path before her.

Beside where she has placed her feet, wriggling tendrils rise out of the ground as if to ensnare and incorporate her; they try to reach but almost as quickly retreat into the soil again. Nothing touches her save for the millipedes and woodlice that cross her feet.

The path remains invisible, yet easily followed.

She takes a second step on the new trail and then another and another. The insects continue to scatter, burrow, and flee ahead of her—a miniscule procession showing her the way. Tendrils rise up and withdraw. The way ahead defines itself as a path. She follows it.

The spectral voice of the Wood lures her deeper still. It might be luring her to her death, but it could have done that with her first step. Why tease her to take the fiftieth or five hundredth?

In the depths of the Wood all about her, the rare and poisonous blossoms of *kanerva* grow in abundance. The trail weaves itself past them, too. She thinks: Bragrender might know something of this to have acquired the *kanerva* he used on Robyn Hoode. There are questions he should answer, which in all likelihood he won't. Then again, maybe the blossoms are harvested the way the trees are. It occurs to her to wonder whether the Below reaches beneath Þagalwood. Why wouldn't it? What if the entire Wood is itself a construct?

She threads her way among the patches of lavender and continues to follow the self-generating track deeper.

The first time she enters, the trail leads her back out again onto a different part of the main path. As she steps out, the symbiont within shifts. She clutches her side, almost doubles over from a sharpness more exquisite than pain. It lasts for only a moment—something within her disconnecting from the Wood. She glances back, and knows that she will return.

She cuts a portal home to Ailfion.

She has spent no more than a few hours in the depths of Þagalwood. Yet, upon arriving in the plaza, she learns that she has disappeared for more than a week. Despite the best efforts of the Queen's soldiers, no one has been able to locate her.

She experiences the same displacement as humans who've been kept awhile in Yvagddu and then returned to the World-to-Be. Where has she been? they ask her. She says simply, "In Þagalwood." Those asking fall silent. Some glance uncertainly at the elongated *S* of Þagalene matter that fills the side of her torso. She knows by then the source of the voice she has heard, but not why she heard it.

She abandons the quest for Robyn Hoode.

Repeatedly she returns to Þagalwood. Every time she enters, a new trail leads her somewhere she has not been before. She discovers that the Wood is much deeper, and stranger, than anyone recognizes; each time she returns, it is to discover she has been absent much longer than she knew. Yet the notion of retreating is untenable. She cannot back out now: The Wood is leading her someplace, preparing her for something. Is she ready? The Wood does not seem to care.

Then, one day, as if by accident she arrives at the heart of Þagalwood. She comes upon a holt. It's the only elevation in the dark, even floor of the Wood that she's encountered anywhere, a hill with a flattened top.

The bone-white trees, with their distorted, expressive features, apparently grow outward in a whorl beginning at the base of the hill, spiraling away from it. She might be looking at the heart of the whole world; at the very least it's the heart of Þagalwood.

Without hesitating, Zhanedd climbs the hill. Beside her, the ground is carved with thick white runnels, as if a pure lava has overflowed the hilltop at some point and painted the ground. A glance back down shows her that the white lava circles the base of the hill, and a thin stream of it reaches directly all the way to that first malformed tree.

Reaching the top, she has to shield her eyes. A pulsating white circle caps it—it's the very opposite of Hel, and she cannot imagine this is accidental. The circle exerts a pull upon her that feels like an invitation aligned with the whispering voice. She is welcome to wade into it if she wishes. She does not. This, she suspects, is either the true entrance to or exit from Hel, and somewhere between the two points, she is now certain, lies a gateway into the Unseelie. The invitation to enter that domain is akin to an invitation to embrace death. There can be no returning. The offer is there but she will not accept it any more than she would throw herself over the lip of the well of eternity in the plaza. Not yet, anyway.

Squinting, she can make out misshapen shadows within the blinding white—remnants of *teinds*? But none of them survive, do they, and in any case would consist of barely a few particles at this point.

From her first morning as a changeling she has followed the slow, progressive disintegration of the *teinds* as they fall. Only now she can't help wonder whether they emerge here as something new, a part of the collective Wood perhaps. What if Nicnevin's sacrifices are what replenish the Wood? There must be tens of thousands.

She is compelled to touch the burning white, compelled but not quite ready.

Zhanedd returns to the pool of light again and again. She comes to think of it as Hel's twin. Nothing ever emerges from it, although it feels as if such an emergence is imminent. It's as if something is about to be answered, while she does not yet even know what question is being asked. The voice whispers for her to wait. All will be revealed in time.

Then one day she kneels beside the brilliant pool. She stares into the light, her golden eyes unfocusing, and falls into a trance very like what she experienced as she was recovering from her wound.

She dreams again of the penetrating blue gaze of the idiot boy she dreamt while the symbiont took root in her. The child changes, ages, but those piercing eyes never look away. He grows tall and black-bearded, until finally she is staring into the face of Robyn Hoode awake on his pallet in the cloister. All unfolds exactly as it did: He stabs her and all but kills her before Bragrender hauls her through the gate. Boy and man, the blue eyes are the same.

She comes to her senses with one hand immersed in the white pool. She snatches it back. Pure whiteness from fingers to wrist spreads beneath her skin. Threads wriggle across her torso and into the symbiont.

What does it mean that the boy and the man are one? Who is he and how is any of that meaningful to her? Is it possible that in her dreaming she saw her human family, the one left behind when she was brought here? But she never met them. How could she have? Still, in hunting Robyn Hoode has she been pursuing a relative all this time? Can they be so joined? That idiot boy, brother to her mother, this family she never knew—all would be centuries dead by now. Zhanedd feels no lingering allegiance to any of them. They are strangers she never met. But still, her avowed enemy would thus be her uncle. Queen Nicnevin was her family once, promising her a special place in the hierarchy of Ailfion, which she then proceeded to undermine at every turn. There was always an excuse, an explanation.

Your past returned a hundredfold, the voice reminds her.

Zhanedd scrambles up. She doesn't desire this knowledge, didn't ask for it. Þagalwood may have its own agenda where she's concerned, but that doesn't mean she has to agree with it any more than she agrees with Nicnevin's. No, she is not ready for this.

Tottering, she descends the hill and walks a crooked course back out to the main path. How long will she have been gone this time? The voice of the Wood sighs in her head, another attempt to entreat her, but she is done listening to those who would advise her. She draws her ördstone, opens a gate, and vanishes all in a few moments. Þagalwood stills.

PART THREE:
SPY GAMES

XXII. From Rheims to Paris

Bernard Seys was in a hurry. The information he'd gotten off the Spanish agent in the Paris embassy needed to reach Walsingham as soon as possible. Sir Francis had been right when he'd written to Bowes in Scotland that some great and hidden treason not yet discovered was even now unfolding. If anything, what Seys had just learned made matters worse. Morgan and Paget, the French, and the Spanish—everyone was in on the plot that made Ridolfo a stroll in the Tuileries Garden with Catherine de' Medici by comparison.

He turned away from the foul reek of the slaughterhouse neighborhood around the Châtelet and started across the Pont au Muniers, heading for the Île de la Cité, and in so doing caught sight of two men he had spotted previously upon leaving the Spanish embassy. The openness of the bridge he hoped would offer him a degree of safety. Surely, if they didn't catch up with him, they would do nothing out in the open, but he had a ways to go before he would reach the relative security of the embassy. King Phillip's intentions to invade needed to be communicated and revealed.

Head down, Seys doubled his speed, now just shy of a full run. They had to know already that he'd seen them. It wasn't as if they were even attempting to be secretive in their pursuit.

Then, out of nowhere ahead of him, a brawl seemed to manifest.

Two other men emerged from between two houses. One stumbled as if drunk. The two immediately began yelling curses and threats at one another. The other inhabitants on the bridge acted as shocked as he was, and immediately changed their course, giving the two brawlers plenty of space. The argument, whatever it was, came quickly to a head as the men drew their rapiers. They slashed at each other, paying no mind to the screaming, fleeing citizens nearby, paying no mind to anybody at all.

Seys slowed, looked on, checked the location of the two in pursuit of him. What was the best course? To go back now meant confronting those two who were definitely following him. If he could get around these other fools ahead, he would be fine. Perhaps they would even interfere with the pursuit.

Then as abruptly as it had begun, the brawl seemed to end. In a lull the two arguers separated, even turned their backs to each other, and laughed. The fight seemed to have been nothing but a ridiculous squabble. Along with other people, Seys hurried forward.

He came abreast of them, at which point the two combatants wheeled about and ran him through as if he were an afterthought to their argument. So shocking, so surprising was the move, that people nearby actually jumped. Someone screamed. It might have been Seys. He fell back against the rail above the Seine, and glimpsed the two who'd killed him make a sign to the other two who'd been in pursuit.

All in it together, he thought, dying. Just like what he needed to report to Walsingham.

His grip on the railing loosened and he slid the rest of the way to the ground. His killers and the two following after had already evaporated down alleyways or back into the insalubrious neighborhood surrounding the Châtelet.

The English ambassador, Sir Henry Cobham, wouldn't learn of Bernard Seys's fate for days. By then, Seys's unidentified informant had been fished out of the Seine as well.

Thomas entered the English College under the name of Creighton, a Jesuit student who had barely escaped arrest and imprisonment at home in Ipswich, a backstory cobbled together from any number of actual fugitive tales Sir Francis knitted together, easy to fabricate and easy for Walsingham's nascent network to corroborate, should anyone inquire.

He'd shaved off his beard and trimmed his hair closely. Only the intensity of his blue eyes might have alerted the spymaster to his identity. Without the beard he looked younger than he had. The role of a Jesuit striving for perfection was easy enough for Thomas to adopt. Poverty, chastity, and obedience—the triumvirate of Jesuit dedication—were ways he knew and had lived at various periods in his impossibly long life.

Upon arrival, he was introduced by Thomas Watson to the two men who'd spearheaded the college since its founding in 1568, Doctors Parsons and Allen. They required young men brave or mad enough to be willing to return to England as missionaries, spies, or even armed rebels when the time came for rebellion, as it surely must. If caught, those young men faced almost certain death, and Parsons in particular, his blue eyes sparkling with zeal, spared no opportunity to remind them that their actions, including martyrdom, were sanctioned, blessed by Pope Gregory XIII himself. Martyrdom, he assured them, was a worthy fate.

Even before he was presented to them by Watson, he'd heard the chirr of the Yvagvoja that controlled Parsons. There were enough young recruits being introduced that same evening that he had time to prepare for the inevitable face-to-face moment with Parsons. The doctor reached out to take his hand, and he became as a mute, silent. Parsons moved from him to the next in line without the slightest indication of sensing anything unusual about him.

After that, he made a point of avoiding Parsons beyond his lectures, where a dozen others in the room brought their own noise with them. What Walsingham had told him of Parsons made sense then: the voja was the one who was preparing and conditioning fanatics to carry out the Yvags' plans. Thomas couldn't kill Parsons—too much of what they were doing depended upon his system of recruitment and disbursement.

Understanding that, Thomas spent a good deal of his time watching Parsons and compiling lists of and reports on fellow students in the college, notably the ones who departed and, if he could finesse the information with Watson's help, where they were going. To that list he added another of noted visitors and lecturers, especially those arriving on Parsons' behalf. He did this while pretending utter disinterest in the political sphere. He was a student overwhelmed by his studies—he and Watson were *juris studiosi*—students of law. There was so much to learn, in fact, that Watson joked that they were eternal students, too, because they could never learn it all. Dr. Allen lectured on Bartolus and Baldus, whose reformation of Italian jurisprudence captured Watson's interest. Thomas let his enthusiasm speak for the two of them.

Some of the students departed with great fanfare, with Allen or Parsons speaking of their noble character or accomplishments to come, while others—mostly those close to Parsons—simply vanished overnight, their destinations unmentioned. Those he made special note of in his lists, for they seemed the likeliest members of Parsons' rebellion plot on English soil. He couldn't be sure, however; it was also possible that some when confronted with the actuality of sailing off into martyrdom simply fled. Parsons would never have let on. Priest hunters, like witch hunters, traveled across England and Scotland in search of such secreted missionaries, who could count themselves lucky if, upon discovery, they were merely deported. With so much secrecy, there were also rumors that Parsons had sent some of his "graduates" off to Spain, from where they might sail to the New World or China or elsewhere.

The tricky part was smuggling these lists out to Walsingham. By his own admission, Sir Francis's network in Rheims was thin, and given the short notice Thomas often had, arrangements to pass the information to an agent outside the college could prove next to impossible. Thomas did the only thing he could think of. He would choose an unoccupied or disused chamber, even a closet, where he could open a portal to Tower Hill, invariably deserted at night, and from there hurry the short distance to Seething Lane. Disguised in the glamour of a different student each time, he presented Creighton's and Watson's latest notes for Sir Francis before racing back down the street, often to the graveyard of All Hallows Barking church, where he opened a new gate back to the same space he'd left. Watson believed that he had slipped out of the college to meet with various messengers, and prepared to cover for him, though no one ever did ask after him, he was gone so briefly. He could only hope that the information arrived with plenty of time to have someone ready and waiting to follow the newly coined fanatic when they debarked.

Other than Parsons, Thomas encountered no Yvags in the college, only the occasional lecturer or other acquaintance of Parsons. That was hardly surprising. It would have been a waste of a limited resource to turn any of the students at the college into skinwalkers: They were already doing the work of the elven, sprinkling the landscape with fanatical believers who, in complete ignorance, would make sacrifices and commit atrocities for the elven cause. Of course, such had already happened: the St. Bartholomew's Day Massacre that he and Walsingham had witnessed in Paris had been one such; another had occurred six years prior when two hundred youths, directed by agents from the college, stormed into Belgium to kill "all the heretics." Thomas couldn't help but speculate that it had been a trial run to prove that Parsons's agents would organize and strike effectively when ordered to do so.

Otherwise, Thomas tried as best he could to learn the location of the Yvag that occupied Parsons. So far as he could tell, it was not nearby. In fact, he speculated that it might be hidden where the college had located originally in Douay, possibly in a crypt at the university there. As he could not hope to mete out justice to the fiend without undermining Walsingham's entire program here, he just added Parsons to his list of those he would deal with when the day of reprisals came.

And then there was the matter of the *teind*.

As deeply as he wanted to disrupt another abduction and steal away the Yvags' kidnapped sacrifice, within the college he could not even begin to coordinate events to achieve it. The new ördstone, still unattuned to him, simply did not yet provide that information. Even if it had, he could not work out how he would go about it. His weapons, both bow and arrows, were being kept by Walsingham in London. He couldn't jump from here to Seething Lane and then to Yvagddu, disrupt a procession, snatch the intended *teind* away somewhere, return the weapons to Seething Lane, and then sneak quietly back into the college when hours if not days would have passed. It was an unworkable scenario.

Frustrated but helpless, he had to resign himself to doing nothing about the *teinds* and take small comfort in the idea that by not interfering with the taking of numerous *teinds* over a period of years, he might convince the Yvags that their latest foe had perished and they could stop looking for him. He hoped the elves would conclude that somewhere was a family or village or—who knew?—a college devoted to their destruction and that periodically sent out opponents.

Nevertheless, after two years of being a mere observer of Dr. Parsons' schemes, he could not help wanting to get away from the college, and it was a blessing when word came from Walsingham that

Thomas was to depart the college and travel to the embassy in Paris, there to meet with England's ambassador, Sir Henry Cobham, and secure himself a position with the embassy staff.

It wouldn't help him with *teinds*; only repeated attuning of the ördstone would change that. With the first one, it had been a full century before he comprehended what the stone was showing him. How long it had been providing information prior to that, he did not know. Now, save for the jumps to and from Tower Hill, he drew upon the stone only to keep Parsons from sensing the Yvag aspect of him, using it to seal him in a net of silence.

Preparatory to seeing him off, Watson told him, "Walsingham in his note expressed amazement at all the names we have provided in our time here. It sounds like more than I even knew about." He cocked an eyebrow as if Thomas might explain it to him. "And you're right, we can't remain here too long, else we begin to look suspicious. We may be *juvenis studiosi*, but we can't be that forever, hey?"

Thomas laughed. "Apparently, *you* can."

Watson grinned. "Not even I, not for much longer. I'll be gone as soon as Walsingham provides a replacement. New blood, you know. Now, do you have your travel money?"

"Yes, Mother," answered Thomas.

Watson stared at him in mock indignation. "Well, one of us has to be, and you're certainly ill-equipped. For instance, here are your travel papers, and these"—he drew a sealed letter from his black cassock— "are Walsingham's instructions for you in Paris."

Thomas tucked the note away.

Later that night, with Watson's aid, Thomas slipped out a side gate to depart the English College, he hoped, for good.

"I wish to see Sir Henry Cobham," Thomas said in French to the young man in the entrance to the English embassy in Paris. "He has asked for my services."

"You?"

"Just so."

The secretary sniffed and looked him over critically: tight black cassock with white ruffs at collar and cuffs, and his four-cornered scholar's cap—then finally got to his feet behind the small table as if arising were a chore, and walked across the tiled floor and out.

After another minute he returned and gestured for Thomas to follow him along a short hall with windows in the left wall, to an open door. There, he turned and stepped aside to allow Thomas to pass.

Inside the sparsely furnished room, a man sitting behind a table large enough to seat six for dinner stood up. He made a welcoming gesture and bid Thomas enter, then said, "Pillows, Weatherby," to the departing secretary. Off to one side of the table were a large travel trunk and other assorted items of luggage.

Sir Henry Cobham was slender and slightly shorter than Thomas. His trim beard was close-cut, his mustachios curved like a smile above his lips. He was dressed stylishly, his green ruff substantial. A cloak of fox fur draped his shoulders.

Cobham gestured for him to come sit in one of the chairs opposite the table, then sat down himself. "You've traveled some distance to hear this confession, curé."

Thomas shook his head. "You mistake me, sir. I have no parish."

"You dwell among parsons, then."

Thomas relaxed. The code Walsingham had referenced had been spoken. Each knew the other to be true now.

They paused then as the secretary returned with two large embroidered pillows. "Those will do nicely, thank you, Weatherby."

The secretary bowed and retreated, closing the door behind him.

Cobham leaned forward. "If no one comes along the hall, he might listen at the keyhole," he explained quietly.

"For the French?" asked Thomas.

"Or the Spanish. Or even for the Queen. Sir Francis has his agents, and Cecil has his. They talk to each other. They meet publicly with similarly placed civil servants of other embassies. Mendoza has his spies. Castelnau has his. I receive daily reports and must assume the same information has been made available to my French and Spanish coequals."

"Everyone knows everything," Thomas said, then after a moment's thought added, "Or no one knows anything at all."

Cobham nodded. "You understand the situation perfectly."

Thomas thought the situation might make for fertile hunting. In some ways it was not much different from the English College, where Parsons and perhaps Allen knew what was transpiring, while various students picked up bits of information, hints, distortions, and often reached opinions based on no more than that. Students came and went, taking that information and misinformation with them. He would have been inclined to shut the school down (and preferably by killing Parsons and his Yvagvoja), but Walsingham left it alone, watching for patterns and connections to the world outside.

"But you have come, good frere, to hear my confession before departure." He picked up the two pillows Weatherby had left, and carried them to the floor beneath the windows.

"Departure?"

"Oh, yes. My time here is up. I am recalled and a new ambassador is on his way. Sir Edward Stafford."

Thomas shook his head. "I do not know him." He followed the ambassador across the room away from the door.

"You shall meet him soon enough, I'm very sure."

They knelt side by side on the pillows and facing the wall. From there no one could overhear anything said between them.

Cobham began by explaining that their best agent had been waylaid and murdered in what appeared to be a street brawl. "'Twas no such thing," he said. "Too conveniently executed. And he must have known such might befall him as he had sent word by separate route that he'd learned of a plot involving both Spain and France. Now, he had just come from a meeting with two well-known Catholic exiles living in Paris, Thomas Morgan and Charles Paget, whose names you may know, but if you don't, soon enough you will, I can promise you."

"Paget was a guest of Parsons' awhile back."

"No doubt he brought him some useful intelligence. He and Morgan report directly to Mary of Scotland through her secretaries, Claude Nau and Gilbert Curle. It's a quartet devoted to scheming on her behalf. If any plot manifests, you can be certain they are in it if not orchestrating it."

He nodded, and memorized the names. He would add them to his list of potential Yvags, save for Paget. Paget had not been Yvag. "So, this quartet you name determined Seys was a spy and dispatched him?"

"That is our assumption," Cobham said to the wall.

"How will it be any different if I approach them?"

"Know you a man named William Parry?"

Thomas shook his head.

"He is an agent for Burghley, or so he proclaims. There is good evidence—a suggestion—that he is also doubling on both."

"Some evidence," Thomas repeated doubtfully.

Sir Henry shrugged. "Nothing in this business is certain, neither allegiances nor outcomes. Walsingham and I would recommend you look into Parry as your point of entry into Paget and Morgan's circle. In any case, Sir Francis travels to Paris at month's end to hear a lecture by an obnoxious young Dominican who has garnered attention for his memory system or some such. Walsingham would have you attend, though out of this cassock rather than as a member of the order. You have money for clothing?" He drew a pouch from his doublet. "A stipend from Walsingham."

Thomas took it. "I will make do with this."

"And you shall need a place to stay. We have several safe houses—"

"Begging your pardon, Sir Henry. Did Seys make use of your safe houses?"

"Of course."

"Then I believe I will seek a room on my own for now that no one but me knows of. Given the full picture you present, I must assume I will be followed upon leaving here. If I go directly to such a house, I'm likely to invite the same trouble as Seys. Better that I live the ascetic Jesuit existence for now."

Cobham thought that through. He tugged lightly on one side of his mustache. "Sir Francis was right, you are well-suited to this life, I think."

In reply, Thomas said nothing. After all, he had been leading "this life" longer than Cobham had been alive.

XXIII. Bruno

The guest speaker was a diminutive Dominican with curly hair and a thin mustache. Thomas sat beside Sir Francis Walsingham and his young cousin, Thomas Walsingham, though he had picked his chair first and gave Walsingham the same deferential acknowledgment he would have granted any stranger—and from the look the spymaster gave him, shaved and shorn as he was, he was very nearly a stranger to him. It seemed that whatever Thomas did to change his appearance, even without glamouring now, it only reinforced Walsingham's idea of him as having theatrical skills.

Sir Francis had come to Paris on the premise of hearing this priest talk about memory. "The little Dominican claims to have developed a revolutionary system of connecting memorized facts. The French king was so intrigued by this that he paid to hear a series of thirty lectures by the man."

Thomas without glancing his way, replied, "So Cobham informed me before he departed."

The friar said to the audience, "I will tell you, King Henry at first believed my skill was pure sorcery—how he put it to me, which it is not and nor has ever been. It is organization but of a specific nature, what I call 'the methodology of loci.' Memory in its place, you see, in relationship to the cosmos and to God." He held up a small book. "My *De Umbris Idearum* reveals the shadow world of thought relative to the solid world it would know, although that solidity is itself an illusion as the great Hermes Trismegistus foretold. His works I have studied, too, for the arcane knowledge they contain that has yet to be equaled.

"The Egyptians, I'm sure you are all aware, were far advanced beyond even our current philosophies. They found the divine *everywhere*. In the seas and rivers. Even in fruit. In garlic."

The talk went on in this way, one idea seeming to connect with the next, such that the whole of the talk was itself to Thomas a perfect example of the speaker's illusion of solidity—a clever assemblage of concepts laid out so as to complete a circle. There was, he thought, finally nothing there to hold onto, leaving him with an impression that this speaker, this Giordano Bruno, was someone who thrilled to the sound of his own voice.

Thomas's attention drifted and he looked over the scholarly Parisian audience, wondering if any of the listeners here was Yvag, perhaps even a skinwalker. He noted the French ambassador to England, Michel de Castelnau, was himself present, having presumably traveled from the French embassy in London to hear this talk. Others he recognized included the Duc de Guise, and the new English ambassador, Sir Edward Stafford.

Then Bruno caught his attention once more. "It is so that even the planets and the constellations might be deities. The stars we see are but other suns with their own Earths, and out there must be other beings, other intelligences, possibly even our superiors."

Now some members of the audience jeered and hooted. Walsingham leaned closer to Thomas and without turning from watching Bruno, added, "What think you, might these intelligences even be our mortal enemies, hmm?" Thomas suppressed the urge to corroborate Walsingham's amused notion. After all, he had beheld the weird sky and red sun that bathed Yvagddu in its weak light. On some instinctive level he had always known he was standing on some other world, rather than in some hidden realm of this one.

Afterward, the two Thomases stood together off to one side of the lecture hall while Sir Francis chatted pleasantly with Friar Bruno.

"What is he up to?" Thomas asked Thomas Walsingham. In this way it did not appear as if he and Sir Francis communicated at all.

The somewhat roguish younger Walsingham smirked and said, "Recruitment."

"What, Bruno? What will he do, memorize whole documents?"

"Actually, I would not be surprised if that is precisely what Sir Francis has in mind. The little priest boasts his prodigious memory wherever he goes. I know Francis is not interested in the philosophical talk of Ficino, nor all the astrological works cited. He's no use for astrology unless it actually predicts something."

"And it does not?"

"In Uncle Francis's experience, no. But best ask Dr. Dee about that." He added, "Of course, methinks the recruitment has more to do with the matter of de Castelnau's patronage of the little friar. The ambassador is bringing him to England, did you know? Another string of lectures is being arranged even now in Oxford, but for the duration it's planned that he'll live at the French embassy."

Thomas understood then. "Another spy in the enemy's house."

"And if successful, one whom they're adding themselves."

He could see how, if Walsingham were able to turn the priest, it would be something of a coup. He said as much, adding, "So tell me. Sir Francis invited me to leave the college and attend this lecture. I must assume he has a part for me to play in this latest stratagem."

"Oh, indeed. He would like you to replace Bernard Seys, carry his work forward."

"Seys, the fellow who was murdered?"

Thomas Walsingham finally fell silent rather than answering with whatever it was he thought.

"What am I to do, then? Meet with the same two agents who likely had him killed?"

"Paget and Morgan, yes." He leaned closer and whispered, "Seys must have said something, inadvertently given himself away to them. The kind of mistake that *gets* you killed."

"But none of us knows what that mistake was. Do we?"

The cousin had to agree. "True. Nevertheless, my uncle is certain a Jesuit priest would be regarded as far more trustworthy than a mere conspirator."

Thomas had to stifle a laugh. "I've yet to encounter a conspirator who wasn't suspect. Cobham was likely the most reliable individual I've spoken to in many a year. He admitted what he didn't know and didn't pretend he might be some grand expert on topics about which he knew little to nothing. And *he* has sailed home."

Young Walsingham blushed as if he understood that he'd just heard a critique of himself in those words.

Thomas, his point made, continued. "This new ambassador,

Stafford, is hardly cut from that cloth. Cobham doubted him, but he's the one I'll have to deal with. What can you and Sir Francis tell me of him?"

Thomas Walsingham smiled bleakly and looked at the floor. "In our opinion, he is not to be relied upon. We've intelligence that he has already sold information to the Duc de Guise. And possibly Spanish ambassador Mendoza."

Thomas sighed. It was exactly the situation Cobham had described.

Thomas Walsingham added, "He's been quite busy forging alliances."

"I can imagine, since that is precisely what I will need to do. Sir Francis would have me ingratiate my way into the company of these two enemy agents in Paris while sharing nothing of actual importance as proof of my usefulness to them." He shook his head slowly in some disbelief. "This network continues to seem a little threadbare."

"True allegiance is difficult to purchase."

"Now you're quoting him, aren't you?" Young Walsingham admitted the source of the quotation. "All right, then, tell me of everyone at the embassy. I must needs find a way into your molehill."

The younger Walsingham said softly, "Sir Francis would have you look into a fellow named Parry."

XXIV. Paget & Morgan

The trick for Thomas was to convince William Parry to make the introductions to Messrs. Paget and Morgan on behalf of Thomas Creighton. Parry had worked his way deep into the spy network in France and England. However unreliable his allegiances might be, he'd endeavored to be well connected.

Originally he'd arrived in Paris as a spy for Lord Burghley in order to escape from creditors back home. Sometime later he'd returned to England, whereupon he ran up still more debt and compounded his troubles by savagely attacking the creditor in the Inner Temple. Arrested for the unprovoked assault, Parry was found guilty and sentenced to death. However, relying upon his relationship with Burghley as a spy, he found himself pardoned by the Queen and set free. And despite finding sureties for his debts in the aftermath, he had the sense to flee again to France where, still given to spending extravagantly, he acted now as a double agent, secretly working for the Catholic cause. Or perhaps he always had been—no one seemed entirely sure of Parry.

And now both Cobham and Walsingham had mentioned Parry in discussing Paget and Morgan. Given his unreliable and volatile nature, he seemed to Thomas to represent a weak link that Thomas could exploit.

In order to do that, he tracked Parry to a Paris club where Parry played cards, notably Primero. Parry, looking disheveled, was already in his cups. Thomas bought him some wine, and blearily Parry thanked him. Thomas took a seat beside him, and in introducing himself to this supposed stranger, mentioned that he'd just graduated from the English College in Rheims.

Parry brightened at the mention of it. "Oh, yes, yes," he said. "I've been there. Read Dr. Allen's writings. Know many of the exiled men thereabouts, too—like Charles Neville and Copley."

Thomas exclaimed, "Why, I know Copley!"

"You do?"

"And last I heard he was in Flanders and not terribly well."

"That's what I mean." Parry poked at the air. "Exiled by the cruel queen. The man is ill and he has petitioned Cecil and the Queen repeatedly but been ignored for all that. I mean, what threat can he possibly pose to Her Majesty, hmm? What can any of them?"

"Well," Thomas replied, "Neville did lead a prior uprising in the North, did he not?"

"Oh, yes, yes, but more'n a decade ago. His lands and fortunes all were confiscated. Lives in utter poverty now. He was attainted! At this point all he wants is to return home to his wife." Parry leaned in closer. "I even proposed to Neville that we could dispatch the Queen between the two of us." He seemed to recognize suddenly that this was not a good direction for the conversation. He took a drink. "Who else do you know, young priest?"

"Truth be told, I'm seeking to meet two of whom I've heard unlikely stories, Charles Paget and—"

"Thomas Morgan! Yes, of course. I'm well acquainted with them."

"I met Paget at the College, when he visited Dr. Parsons."

"Oh, yes? Well, I can get you an audience with them, no trouble at all. Count on me, young priest." He threw an arm around Thomas's shoulders. "Now, would you happen to have some ready cash upon you. I was doing very well at Primero, but I've lost a few hands and the house is disinclined to advance me any more cash. Hey?"

Thomas reached into his doublet for his purse.

Thus did William Parry promote Jesuit Thomas Creighton to the inner circle of Morgan and Paget, from which every network connected to promoting Mary of Scotland and eliminating Elizabeth intersected. That he had come from the English College spoke far more for his trustworthiness than Parry's praises. Thomas got the impression that both men recognized Parry's capricious nature. Parry was already talking about returning to London to set in motion his own assassination plot against Elizabeth that he meant to carry out with Edmund Neville.

Nevertheless, suddenly it seemed they were all part of a team invested in plotting to assassinate Elizabeth. Walsingham had said that he felt certain some great and hidden treason as yet undiscovered was brewing. Thomas had stumbled into its epicenter: Everything flowed through here, from letters to visitors.

Paget, who had a beaky nose and short gray-brown hair, seemed the more social of the two. Morgan, with his trim reddish beard and skewering mustaches, was the fastidious one who assembled the caskets of letters that were sent out to Mary of Scotland, or more precisely to Gilbert Curle, one of her secretaries and a name Cobham had provided. Neither man was Yvag, but he knew already they were connected to Parsons and Allen, so Yvags were within their ambit as well. His next step would be to find a means to follow the letters from Morgan to their destination. His opportunity came shortly, with the arrival of a traveler who had spent three years moving across Europe.

Francis Throckmorton and his entourage were on their way back to England when they visited the two conspirators. Throckmorton's family were all prominent Catholics in the north of England. His father had even acted as a witness to Mary's will.

Throckmorton had an innocent face, framed by curly brown hair and a trim beard. He regaled his hosts with stories of his audience with Pope Gregory, of receiving the Pope's assurances that a way would be found to defeat the heretical Elizabeth. "He knew all of you and praised the work you are doing." Of course, that could hardly be true, thought Thomas. The Pope knew nothing of him at all.

Throckmorton was intending to carry the bundle of letters himself. Thomas had to figure a way around that. They were to leave early the following day.

When that morning he and Parry arrived, it was just as Morgan was preparing the casket of letters for Throckmorton. "What think you of this one?" Morgan asked, and passed it to Paget, who handed it to Parry.

Parry snorted. He gave the letter to Thomas. It was titled "A Merchant of Newcastle, regarding the disposition of a certain merchant of London and the merchant's wife."

"It's a code," Thomas remarked.

"Just so," explained Morgan. "Mary is the merchant of Newcastle, Elizabeth the merchant from London, and Walsingham is the merchant's wife. Everything in it is about trade goods, you see. For instance, the price of meat at the Leadenhall market refers to the financing Phillip has promised for the invasion. Quite clever, provided you have the key." They all were pleased. Other sealed letters in the packet utilized a code alphabet that Curle and Nau could decipher on their end.

Morgan took back the "merchant" letter, folded, then sealed it with wax. At any moment Throckmorton would descend the stairs and join them.

Thomas thought it was now or never. He said to Parry and Morgan, "You may know, I have made the acquaintance of Richard Hakluyt, chaplain and secretary of the ambassador, Edward Stafford, yes? According to Hakluyt, alas, our Throckmorton has been under surveillance for some time and the rumor is, he will be arrested the moment he sets foot in England."

"*What?*" Paget exclaimed. "How?"

Thomas shook his head. "We all know the English embassy leaks like a pudding. It's full of spies everywhere, for us, for Spain, for the Pope. Even Stafford himself sells the occasional document or secret for profit and seems to play no favorites." Morgan and Paget had certainly relied upon those same leaks. Nevertheless, Thomas got the impression they both suspected Parry of being involved. Understandably, his often erratic behavior did him no favors.

"If Throckmorton's known, then who shall carry the letters?" asked Parry.

Before Thomas could make the case for himself to transport the letters, Paget traded a look with Morgan, and Morgan said, "Henri Fagot." A nod from Paget. Thomas did not have to pretend to be confused.

Morgan explained, "Castelnau sometimes employs him, and he happens to be returned to Paris from Bastogne now that the matter of Seys no longer presents a problem."

"The matter of Seys" could mean only one thing. Thomas speculated on the name—was Fagot an actual if odd name or a code name? If the latter, then the assassin saw himself as incendiary, an entity who started fires.

Paget dashed off a note, sealed it, then sent for someone to deliver it while the others waited. "We should hear from him soon enough," he assured them, and smoothed back his short gray-brown hair.

Indeed, hardly forty minutes later a servant ushered into the room a dark-haired man, swart of complexion, wearing a brown doublet with gold trim, billowed black pantaloons, and dark green tights. A stiffened, gathered black cap was tugged down, perhaps intended to be rakish, on his head. A rapier hung at his side. His bearing was minatory as he scrutinized the faces he did not know, as if half expecting that this was a trap of some sort and he should be ready to strike.

As the man looked them all over, including young Throckmorton, Thomas heard the quietest of thrumming. Well, he hadn't expected *that*. Another name for his list. He closed himself off quickly.

Paget explained the situation to Fagot, who lost his threatening look in response. Fagot replied, "You are in luck, then, for I was myself about to embark to London at Castelnau's request. It will be as nothing to add a few letters to my equipage. I will place them in his hands, you may rest assured."

"Good, that's settled," said Morgan. "With apologies to Francis, we have our courier." Beaming, he handed over the packet of letters in their little box that Fagot was to deliver.

Thomas must figure out some other way to take possession of the casket of letters, and that could not be accomplished in the company of Parry or the others. On board the ship it would be Fagot alongside Throckmorton and his group. Hardly any room for maneuvering there.

He stood. "I am so very fortunate to be a part of this endeavor. Parry, you and I can speak later about this plot of yours, though my own inclination would be to tell you to delay it while other plans are in motion. You should listen to other opinions, of course." He bowed to the others. "Mr. Throckmorton," he said. "Gentlemen." As he spoke this, he turned for the door.

Fagot stepped in his path, though not as a challenge so much as to engage him. "Allow me to accompany you, Fra Creighton. I am unacquainted with you, and I like to know everyone in our little circle."

Thomas could only welcome him to walk along. But they had hardly opened the door before Parry came up behind them to say,

"Fagot, would you mind another traveler? As I intended to return to London anyway in the coming days, I see no reason to delay my return and deny myself such excellent company, in which case I have some quick packing to do."

"We can *all* go if you like," Fagot suggested in what sounded like a critical swipe. Parry blushed at the comment. Thomas wondered what he was up to, inserting himself in this manner; perhaps the conspirators had good cause not to trust him with information.

Trading a glance with Fagot, Thomas said, "Lay on, then."

They walked briefly along the Rue de Bièvre. Parry wanted to know where and when Fagot's coach would leave.

"From the Château de la Tournelle, at three this afternoon," replied Fagot. "Or you can simply be here when I collect Throckmorton's party."

Parry said he must take care of some business matters first if he was to join them. He bid both farewell and strode off.

After a moment, Fagot asked, "Do you trust him?"

"Parry? Let's say I am not certain I know where his allegiances lie. More than that, I'm not certain that he knows, either. My suspicion is, if he's in a hurry to leave for London, he owes money to someone in Paris."

Thomas and Fagot walked along awhile before Fagot spoke again. "You arrived here from the English College?"

"How did you know that?"

"I am acquainted with both Parsons and Allen and the school's essential purpose."

Thomas smiled. "Jesuit missionaries."

"Indeed. Ah, but here is where I depart. We must meet and talk again when I return."

Fagot extended a hand. Thomas faced him and gripped it. He sensed the Yvag's probing, but kept himself absolutely still. If anything leaked through, it wasn't obvious in the assassin's expression. He studied Fagot's face carefully, then watched as Fagot walked away. Parry was going to be a complication; all he could hope was that he would be his usual, unreliable, and tardy self.

"The Château de la Tournelle at three," he muttered as he turned away.

XXV. The French Embassy

Thomas was outside the château an hour early. He walked its perimeter. The Château de la Tournelle had a doorway that jutted forth from its face, and was flanked by a tower and the main part of the building, itself a curving wall that curled around a slight peninsula of land and seemed to hang out over the Seine. He picked three places where the complex structure offered deep shadows and spaces invisible from the courtyard. Once Parry arrived, there would be no swapping places with Fagot; he would have to board the ship as someone else again and hope for an opportunity that he did not expect. He would be a stranger to all of them and therefore suspect.

This had to happen quickly and quietly.

The coach arrived early. The driver got down and crossed the yard into the château. Thomas stood out of sight past where the wall curved.

Fagot came out with a large traveling chest and followed the driver around to the rear. He placed the chest on the rear of the coach. The driver cinched it into place. Fagot informed him they were waiting for one more passenger. The driver returned to his seat on the coach.

Fagot turned and headed back across the yard to the main building. The moment he was out of the driver's sight and in the deep shadows, Thomas struck.

But either Fagot sensed him or sensed his movement: he reached for his rapier and sprang back. In that moment he discovered that it was himself he faced, and for a second he froze. Then he lunged and thrust, and Thomas twisted side-on, curving his spine out to avoid being skewered. The blade slid along the front of him.

He kicked Fagot's forward knee, and the Yvag collapsed but pushed off the ground, swatting with the rapier to keep Thomas at bay. Unsteadily but urgently, he thrust again. The blade stabbed between Thomas's arm and body. Thomas hooked two fingers into its pas-d'âne rings and pulled hard. Fagot, already plunging forward, lurched into him, and impaled himself upon Thomas's barbed dagger. Thomas cut up and across. His brown doublet tore, and black blood poured out. Thomas tore the sword from the assassin's loosening grip and let it roll across the stones, while Fagot collapsed and rolled down the incline toward the Seine and into the deeper shadows beneath the château.

Thomas followed. The belt and loose rapier sheath, the rings and the cap Fagot wore, would complete the look, in a few minutes.

Dying, Fagot stared helplessly up at him, no doubt wondering who had stolen his identity and why. Thomas could feel the chirr trying to penetrate, to connect with whoever he was. "Who . . . who are you?" the Yvag asked silently. As it did so, it lost its hold on its own human face. Golden eyes with rings of tiny pupils bored into Thomas. Its gills wheezed as it drew slowing breaths. Lips drew back on needle-sharp teeth the way a rabid dog might snarl.

Thomas thought the answer: "Too complicated to explain. Let's just say I gave you more of a chance than you did Bernard Seys. Took four of you by all accounts, even though only two of you stuck him. But no need to worry at your failure here. Nicnevin will have no awareness of it. At least, *I* won't tell her." The Yvag tried for one final lunge at him, but Thomas anticipated the move, and caught the Yvag's arm as it attempted to thrust the dagger from its baldric into him. Thomas tore the dagger from its hold. "Thank you for this, too."

The head lolled back then, the expression softened, the golden eyes dulled. If left there, he might reanimate, though the wound was much the same as he'd inflicted upon Zhanedd long ago.

Thomas didn't even consider trying to cut off his head—not with a rapier and mere dagger to hand. As it was, he'd been lucky that no one else emerged from inside and the driver didn't come around the coach.

He stripped Fagot of his cloak, cap, baldric, and his purse. The latter proved satisfyingly heavy. After buckling on the belt, he retrieved the rapier. He'd only bent the cage a little in pulling on it. Then he grabbed the transformed body by both arms and dragged it the rest of the way around the jutting tower wall to where it hung out over the Seine. A tiny peninsula of land jutted out below the tower, and he knelt there to stuff a few rocks into the Yvag's doublet to weigh the body down, then stepped into the shallows and pulled it off the bank and into the river.

The body sank from sight. Eventually, someone might come upon it, but what would they have other than a demon? Certainly not Henri Fagot. After all, he'd ridden off in a coach just this afternoon.

Parry arrived a quarter hour later. Thomas awaited him on the coach.

They took the coach back to Paget and Morgan's, where Throckmorton awaited them along with his belongings and the small wooden casket of letters. Thomas used the opportunity to test out his impersonation of Fagot with them. He spoke very little, but no one reacted peculiarly to him. Both Paget and Morgan said they looked forward to his safe return. "Your ruthlessness proves essential to our success," Paget told him sotto voce as he departed.

The coach took him and Parry to an inn on the coast at Calais. Fortunately, the real Henri Fagot had made all the necessary arrangements. The innkeeper clearly knew him on sight. Thomas wondered how often the assassin traveled this route.

The most hazardous time for him was potentially while asleep, because unconscious he could not maintain his glamour, and he and Parry and Throckmorton must all share a chamber. However, he had discovered decades earlier, while locked in a gaol cell with others, that the ördstone would maintain his appearance while he slept. How it accomplished this, he did not comprehend any more than he understood how it held memories of others alive within itself. He could not ask and receive an answer from it. But he had long since concluded that he likely knew less than half of what the stone could do. Nevertheless, his first night in their company he worried that the new stone would not protect him in the same way and that he would wake in the morning to find both men pointing weapons at him. However, his fears seemed to be unfounded and he could only hope that meant he and the new ördstone were growing ever more compatible.

They sailed the next morning. Again, his alter ego seemed to be well known to the ship's captain. When he asked quite seriously, "Now, what price did we agree upon?" the captain laughed at his joke. It was one Fagot apparently made all the time.

It was Thomas's intention to carry the letters directly to Walsingham to copy before delivering them to Castelnau at the embassy. However, the ship was met at Dover by men in Castelnau's employ; no one was there waiting to arrest Throckmorton, of course, and he allowed as "that Jesuit" did not know what he was talking about, though it was obvious he was greatly relieved. Thomas had no choice but to accompany his escort to London's French embassy at Salisbury Court.

Michel de Castelnau, the French ambassador, was a full head shorter than Thomas. He had a bulbous nose, short-cropped curly hair, and wore a ring in his right ear. His mustaches were long and waxed, the goatee of his beard as sharp as a cleaver. He greeted "Fagot" warmly, reminding him of a previous time they had encountered each other, which Thomas could only pretend to corroborate. Castelnau announced that an afternoon meal had been prepared for the traveler Throckmorton and his companions. Thomas observed how the ambassador and Parry pretended not to know each other at all.

Castelnau explained that he wished to add more letters to the little casket, and that the Spanish ambassador, Mendoza, had some as well, noting, "He will join us for dinner this afternoon."

Walking through the embassy, they shortly encountered the little priest, Giordano Bruno, whom Thomas had seen speak in Paris. Castelnau extolled Bruno's prodigious memory, then insisted on a demonstration, treating the priest like a trained bear. Thomas took the letter of introduction Morgan and Paget had so proudly constructed, and suggested he use that. Castelnau started to object, but Thomas explained, "It's written in a code he won't understand, so it can mean nothing at all to him."

Bruno read it over, then handed it to the ambassador. He then recited it back without error.

Caught up in the fanfare, Castelnau applauded Bruno. "You see? Remarkable. Ah, but we have so little time. Please excuse me, Henri, Throckmorton. I have my own letters to Queen Mary to write."

Parry had some proposal he wanted to float past Throckmorton, and the two of them drifted off, leaving Thomas on his own. He approached the little priest. He said, "I saw you speak in Paris. I sat with Sir Francis Walsingham." Bruno's gaze shifted with disquietude, as Thomas had expected. "No, I'm not here to identify you to them, quite the opposite." He passed the casket of letters to Bruno, who gazed from it to him. "We have but a few hours before Mendoza arrives. And Throckmorton leaves in the morning."

The little priest nodded in understanding, and slid the small box up inside a voluminous sleeve.

Bruno arrived on Walsingham's doorstep a little after four. He handed the casket to Sir Francis with the words, "These come to you from Henry Fagot."

"Who?" Walsingham asked.

"You do not know him?"

"Not by that name."

"He tells me he was in your company in Paris when I spoke there." Walsingham's expression clouded. "He is well esteemed by Castelnau."

"Is he? Describe him for me."

"Sir Francis, time is of the essence. I bring these at great risk. I have memorized a letter I was not allowed to bring, which I can recite. These others I must return in a few hours, no more. They will be missed as will I."

"Yes, yes, all right." Walsingham led the way through his house, calling for Thomas Phelippes as he went. Bruno followed, intrigued at what he saw.

A short, blond man with a pockmarked face hurried to him and Sir Francis handed over the little letter casket. "You have two hours. Get Gregory to unseal them. Copy what you can, we shall decipher later."

Phelippes squinted up at him, took the letters and, with a nod, turned and seemed to merge back into the shadowy house.

"Now," Walsingham said. "This Henry Fagot."

Bruno said, "Castelnau treats him as someone who seems acquainted with various plans here and in France. I had his name heard in conversations regarding your embassy in Paris." He went on to describe the swarthy messenger in detail.

Walsingham shook his head. "But for your description, I would have suspected I knew his true identity. I cannot believe even a master of disguise could so completely transform his true appearance."

"True appearance?"

"Not your concern. You say you have a letter to dictate?"

"Yes. Fagot tricked them into having me memorize it to demonstrate my skills at remembering. I realize now how clever he was being."

Less than three hours later, with his recitation transcribed and all the contents of the cache copied and resealed, Bruno returned to the French embassy. No one had noticed, or at least thought anything of, his absence in the interim. He was prepared to explain that he'd needed to make arrangements for his third foray into "the ignorant backwaters of England," which those present knew would be taking place in less than two weeks. The simple truth was that, while Castelnau championed him and his strange philosophies, almost everyone in the embassy found him annoying, and they delighted in his absences.

He returned the casket of letters to Thomas, who, following a dinner with the Spanish ambassador, Bernardino de Mendoza, handed it over to Throckmorton for safekeeping. Mendoza had a note of his own to add. Throckmorton would depart the next morning, and carry the letters on to Mary. The assassin Henry Fagot opted to remain behind to become better acquainted with his friend Castelnau and take in some of the city of London, at least until the network in Paris or elsewhere had another agent or two who needed killing, a comment that generated a good deal of mirth.

XXVI. Of Assassins
& Witchfinders

Bragrender enters the dimly lit circular chamber. The main illumination comes from the immense gem in the center of the ceiling, which intensifies the gathered light, casting the interior in a red-gold glow.

Directly below the gem, the body lies upon a dais, its metallic hair matted and mixed with ooze. Ooze also befouls the tights and torn brown and gold doublet.

Queen Nicnevin sits at the head of the dais, her winged throne having expressed from out of the floor. Members of her council sit or stand in a cluster around the body as well.

Approaching the dais, Bragrender recognizes the corpse upon it as Salamerjaan, one of his mother's former consorts. He recalls her explaining with delight that "he is such a good dancer. He masters both the carola and the rondet," as if the dance were reason enough for intimacy. In the end, however, Salamerjaan grew so bold as to try to master Mother, which put an end to their dancing days—and, really, he should have known better. As a consolation (and to remove the ambitious consort from court), she offered Salamerjaan a voja's position. When he politely declined that honor, Salamerjaan found himself sent to the World-to-Be to live in glamoured exile among the humans . . . but, remarkably, thrived there, successfully embedded among the society of exiles in France, in particular working with two humans whose dedication to murdering the English queen rivaled even Nicnevin's. Whatever else one could say of Salamerjaan, the knight was sly and careful, offering the French supporters of Queen Mary essential services—in particular those of courier and assassin. Salamerjaan had made exile seem almost a prize to be sought, so the corpse here on the dais is something of a surprise.

Of course, in death, Mother now grants Salamerjaan honor she would never have in life. The knight certainly won't be reanimating to try and rule her again. His curiosity about this unexpected development tempers Bragrender's disgruntlement at being pulled away from pursuing his own agenda, though he's not about to reveal that to the council.

He asks, "Why have I been summoned this time? Seek you a eulogy for your former pet?"

"Oh, are you offering to speak on their behalf?" Nicnevin asks, seemingly half amused at his show of outrage. She seems to know he is posturing.

"What could I say for Salamerjaan that I would not first say for Ritarenda? Two who performed their tasks well, yet suffered defeat against—"

"Yes, and how is your pursuit of answers coming, child?"

His shifting visage flickers angrily. *Child.* She calls him that only to provoke him, to remind him that she has survived millennia as queen. By comparison he is hardly minutes old. And he must respond.

"I have made little progress, no thanks to anyone here. All of you so grave over this one death as if Salamerjaan deserves glory for thriving in banishment. Forget not the banishment amidst the accolades. Or has dancing superseded ambition in Ailfion?"

"Outrageous!" responds another of the counselors, Valtuustmaj.

"You think to dictate how we honor our dead?" asks counselor Panguramin.

"I measure them, measure them all. One more eternal death." Bragrender nods to the corpse. "In honoring, I weigh Salamerjaan against Ritarenda, and Taistellejan and two escorts. All of them slain, I profess, by a single human hand. Did you, any of you, bother to inquire into that?"

"Five?" says counselor Valtuustmaj. It appears to be the first time this has been brought to the attention of the counselors.

"Oh, so you *are* capable of thought," Bragrender replies.

Nicnevin ignores his goading as she says, "Salamerjaan makes it six." *She* hasn't lost sight of the losses.

Counselor Valtuustmaj argues, "But Salamerjaan hasn't been shot full of arrows. I can tell that from here. Thus, not slain by the same hand."

Nicnevin says, "What say you to that, offspring? Still determined that the deaths are connected?"

"All deaths are connected, even as death itself is unnatural to us. We die only when some successful opposing force is trained upon us. A *true assassin*, for instance."

"Oh, but Salamerjaan was a true assassin with half a dozen kills to his credit."

Rather than reply, Bragrender gestures toward the body. "May I?"

"It is why I interrupted your inquiries, Bragrender. Were you not so inclined to fulminate, you might recognize a courtesy being done you."

Bragrender and the Queen lock eyes for a moment. There is, has always been, an element of madness in her overly large golden stare. Then he tilts his head, and walks serpentine among the counselors, enjoying as always their immediate discomfort at his nearness, his ever-changing aspects, mostly borrowed from their thoughts—his shifting faces a composite of their memories, sometimes wondrous, but mostly grotesque like the rest of his weirdly articulated body, all to unsettle them.

He notes that the ninth counselor, the one killed previously by Zhanedd for following her, has rejuvenated and sits among them again. It's only now that he takes stock of her absence. He wonders if anyone at all among this group has descried Zhanedd since last she attended the Queen. He sought her himself briefly, but without luck. Deliberately avoiding him, no doubt. He is beginning to regret his part in resurrecting her.

Bragrender leans over Salamerjaan's body, runs his hands over the torso until he finds an opening, inserts two fingers through the rent in the body's costume, then traces the upward-and-across gash that sharply and abruptly cuts straight down; he leans over and studies the cuts to the material of the doublet, fingertips mapping the jaggedness of the wound's edges across the tubular gills. He has come across this exact butchery once before, putting him in mind of Zhanedd once more. She experienced it directly. The lack of arrows or *kanerva* as the means of delivering death does not rule out for him the possibility that the same perpetrator is behind this killing as well. They're still seeking him in London, but he has gone away. Gone away and not died. Every time he goes dormant awhile, they convince themselves he's died.

He recalls Nicnevin remarking how assassination seemed the natural course to eliminating the targeted queen. He supposes that is true providing your own assassins go about killing the target you want dispatched. Not so true if some hidden assassin sets about killing your killers. Not at all a satisfactory outcome.

Finally, Bragrender steps back and wipes his hand on the cloak of the nearest counselor who, though outraged, says nothing and barely glances his way. "Salamerjaan has been cut, Majesty, by one of our daggers," he says, "possibly it was his own in an enemy's hand, but decidedly by someone familiar with its cutting power. And assuming that Salamerjaan was glamoured as one of them at the time, then we have a killer familiar with our physiognomy. Can we even say we're certain a human would know to do this?" He shakes his head. Zhanedd killed all the Robyn Hoodes, didn't she? It became her raison d'être for many cycles here, and more than a hundred years in the World-to-Be. He understood *that* Zhanedd, though he disagreed with her notion of rogue changelings living in Þagalwood or somewhere no one could find them. Their successful concealment required too much good fortune. Yet this wound does seem to be the handiwork of an Yvag. How did the original Hoode learn to cut them thus? Who taught him?

Bragrender scrutinizes the counselors again. Factions within this group? He tries to imagine any of them plotting together to be rid of Nicnevin as they participate in mortals' plots to remove a monarch in the World-to-Be. It's too absurd. They would fail, every one of them. But Zhanedd might not.

"You'll want me to float this body to the mortuarian in the undercity, I imagine," he says. "That is, assuming you are all satisfied with whatever honors you've bestowed on . . ." He restrains the impulse to say "this idiot" and just says, ". . . dear Salamerjaan."

"Yes, yes," says Nicnevin. "We release him into your custody." She considers the council. "Yes?" she says.

They make no reply, and she is about to dismiss him, when

Counselor Valtuustmaj interjects, "One point. Before adjourning, I should like to know the status of our so-called witchfinders."

Confused, Nicnevin replies, "What witchfinders do you speak of, Valtuustmaj?"

The counselor sits smugly, saying nothing but just staring at Bragrender.

The Queen looks back and forth between her offspring and the counselor, finally asks, "Of what does Valtuustmaj speak, Bragrender?"

He has commandeered their toys without asking permission, and they are just petty enough to smear him for it. To be fair, it's as a result of Valtuustmaj's information regarding the assassin called Gerard, so the counselor really has no one else to blame.

"Bragrender."

"Majesty," he responds. "Simply, we have used three *dights* to create three Yvagvoja witchfinders dispersed across England."

"Three *precious dights*?" Her exasperation is such that she nearly levitates out of the throne.

He wants to say that *dights* are not half so precious as they once were, that with the shifting religious and political landscape they have significantly reduced reliance upon the *dights*, instead focusing upon increasing the quantity of humans being persuaded to act in accordance with their desires. The Parsons *lich* has made great strides with that. That's not the way to go here, however; he must approach the matter delicately. "The mortals' queen, you may recall, enacted something called a Witchcraft Act some years ago in their time. It allows for the creation of a position called *witchfinder*—mortals tasked with hunting for and arresting individuals who appear to be in league with supernatural forces, demons and devils, charged with doing evil. *Maleficium*, they call it. This is not new. These laws, and their adherence to them, rise and fall."

Nicnevin waves this aside. He is not answering her question. "They are ignorant and superstitious. We've always known that. The Act you mention was deemed of no consequence."

"True, provided we take some precautions to mask our own activities, we continue to go unnoticed."

"Yes?" she says impatiently.

Bragrender takes a moment to give Counselor Valtuustmaj a black look before continuing. "To return to the subject of Salamerjaan, it is evident he was slain by someone who knows our physiognomy even when that physiognomy is not presented. It is clear to me now, as it is to Zhanedd were she on hand to account for herseslf, that we have for some hundreds of their years now been under assault by a force or forces unknown hidden amongst the mortals of the World-to-Be. Either this force comprises the so-called mad changelings that you and Zhanedd propounded in the past, and who—if they exist at all—must lurk in the depths of Þagalwood—"

"I no longer hold opinion they exist, Bragrender. If ever they did, then the Wood has taken them long ago."

"And I concur with you, my Queen. Therefore, we are left with the proposition that, hidden in the World-to-Be, there exists an enemy force of mortals who have extraordinary powers."

"Powers, such as . . . ?"

"Such as defeating our champions and killing our assassins; such as confronting our knights when they select a *teind*—sometimes in Þagalwood, but more recently brazenly right here in Ailfion."

"You imagine multitudes, do you?"

"Possibly." And here came the needle he had to thread. "Respectfully, my Queen, for countless years we have given Yvagvoja enormous latitude on the mortal plane."

Counselor Valtuustmaj, who has been an Yvagvoja, says, "It's not laxity. It's a compulsion impossible to ignore. The mortal conveyance is aware of its tiny lifespan, and thus seeks desperately to reproduce. You cannot appreciate this compulsion until you have yourself possessed and been possessed by one of them."

Thank you, Counselor. "There is your answer, Majesty. A primal urge to procreate through their inhabited *lich*. The voja know full well the unlikelihood of procreating in their true form here, so few of them are viable candidates."

"I am not comprehending your point, Bragrender," says the Queen. He is almost sure this is a lie.

He pauses to look them all over. "Who here has kept track of mortals impregnated by our vojas?"

The Queen stands. "Bragrender, you go too far."

"Really?" he says. "Do you deny the existence of Zhanedd, in whom you've taken such a personal interest?"

Her face contorts with fury. Oh, yes, she has understood the implication of Zhanedd's birth all along and ignored it. Although he is the Queen's offspring, in that moment Bragrender knows he's come very close to being throttled. He remains silent and still.

"Zhanedd..." she finally manages to say, "is unique."

"Only in the sense that we knew her lineage before we snatched her for a changeling. While there are surely others among your changelings, that's not the question. My question is, how many other lecherous vojas have mated with mortals, producing offspring to which we've paid no attention at all? Offspring we did not sweep up for changelings."

Nicnevin looks at her counselors, most of whom cannot meet her gaze. Silently, she sits down.

"Yes," says Bragrender, "the answer is we don't know. All I have done is to adapt this law the mortals passed, creating a trio of witchfinders to swoop in should they or their human counterparts encounter true magic, which is to say discover any... let us say, *gifted* indigenes." Now that he has silenced them all, he continues. "Thanks to Counselor Valtuustmaj, I myself nearly caught and slew one named Gerard, who fits my premise. I believe he changed his form at will. He managed both to elude me and murder four sent to take him. And then he vanished completely. This is a recurring pattern, going back hundreds of years in the World-to-Be. We've been speculating forever on this, but we have never had enough information to make a determination. You, Zhanedd—who is wrong of course. Others."

Nicnevin focuses upon him again. "So, not changelings, but creatures possessing the latent *astralis* of a changeling."

"Correct. They might all exhibit the same tendencies, or their true natures might express differently in each of them. Some of them might even be sempiternal. How would we know?"

Now the counselors erupt in disagreement.

Ignoring them, the Queen nods, understanding the point he's made. She says to him, "Their own kind would brand them as witches."

"Witches, saints, demons—what does it matter? They're a superstitious lot. The witchfinders will identify all of these."

"Majesty. Surely not," objects Counselor Panguramin.

Ignoring the counselor, she asks, "Should I be concerned?"

It's evident that she isn't. No doubt what she wants more than anything is to return to whatever pastime she was enjoying before

Salamerjaan turned up dead: dancing or hunting or another game of jeu de mail. To her the notion of a mortal assassin or two is hardly significant—at most there's a gadfly to be dispensed with, and he, having brought it to her attention, is to deal with it.

"Very well, Bragrender," she says at last, "you have our blessing. Prithee, continue with your witch hunt and keep us informed."

That ends the meeting of the counselors.

Bragrender would like to know who found Salamerjaan's body, and under what circumstances, but he elects not to ask any more questions of the utterly useless council.

He steps beside the dais and touches its surface beneath the body, which rises into the air beside him on a clear panel as did Ritarenda's before, and he accompanies it out of the round ceremonial chamber and into the larger space that adjoins it. At the far side of the chamber, the changeling pool flickers. Would that he could simply immerse Salamerjaan in the pool to restore life. In this instance too much of the blood of Salamerjaan is lost somewhere, probably in the Seine and unrecoverable. Again, he has the sense that whoever slew Salamerjaan was aware of their capacity for regeneration.

Across the plaza, and Bragrender is thinking how the time is approaching for the taking of the next *teind*. If his witchfinders prove unsuccessful in locating someone with an Yvag's powers, he may have to bait a different trap instead.

XXVII. Arrests & Misdirections

The swarthy "Henri Fagot" handed the sealed letter to Francis Throckmorton in his study, a room with elaborate floral paper on the walls, books on shelves, and carpets upon the floor.

"From Castelnau?" asked Throckmorton.

"I believe so," Thomas replied. "I do not know its contents." This wasn't exactly true. Thomas had been on hand when Castelnau received the communication from Morgan in Paris that had set things in motion. The French ambassador had quickly composed his coded message, though not without Thomas glimpsing it. He had been around the coding of messages to and from Mary enough now that he recognized some elements. For instance, the letter *E* was α and *O* represented the word *day*, he knew. From what he saw, the letter warned that their network—Throckmorton in particular—had been compromised.

Folded and sealed, the letter went into a slender, gilt-edged wooden casket with other letters. Throckmorton ran a hand through his curly hair. "I must needs write to our 'Merchant of Newcastle.' Would you be so good as to deliver these to Mendoza for me, Fagot?"

"But of course."

"Then, please forgive me, I have a lot to do."

Thomas bowed and saw himself out. He crossed the road and started walking, but not back to the French embassy. Normally he would have returned there and passed the box on to Giordano Bruno to deliver, but everything about this particular letter suggested speed was of the essence. Eventually, having walked along Tower Street, he turned up Mark Lane and into the church of St. Olave. Only once inside the dark church, did he, unseen, shed his glamour. Then he crossed the nave and exited at the top of Seething Lane as himself for a change. He'd been Henri for so long, he had ceased to notice the tautness of his body. Now he relaxed, and his tense muscles almost trembled with relief.

A servant led him inside Walsingham's house; he thought it was someone he hadn't encountered previously. Sir Francis, seeing him, only allowed himself an arched eyebrow of reaction. "Why, Monsieur Henri Fagot, unless I am mistaken."

Thomas gave a slight bow.

"I've heard tales of your exploits, mostly from Bruno. Still more theatrical effort on your part, Creighton?"

"Quite," Thomas replied. He'd no intention of trying to explain how he changed his appearance. "I would have let this travel by our usual route"—he held out the gilded casket—"but my sense is we haven't the luxury. It's from Throckmorton to Mendoza, and I need to deliver it quickly."

"I see. Come." He took the casket, turned, and headed along the hall to the ciphers and codes room. "Phelippes! Arthur, all of you." The short Phelippes had leapt to his feet. The other half dozen people stopped what they were doing. Walsingham held up the casket. "We need these copied and reassembled as quickly as possible. Decipher what you can after."

He handed the newest letter to Arthur Gregory, who sat down with it and his delicate tools. He used heat to slightly soften the wax. Each seal came loose with excruciating slowness, but in the end he had pried loose the wax without breaking it or tearing the letter. Then he opened it, careful of the order of the folds, and handed it to Phelippes, who looked over the code and immediately began copying it. As he did, he remarked, "This is for Ambassador Mendoza."

Thomas said, "The whole cache of letters is for Mendoza." He looked over Phelippes's shoulder. "That's the code employed by Morgan and Paget."

Phelippes gave him a look. "Yes, I do know that," he said. "Reads like a bill of lading. We've seen this pattern before. Here's a number of kegs promised by their French merchant—that will be soldiers. And a date of delivery. A proposed invasion?"

Walsingham came up beside Thomas. "Have we time to alter those numbers? Increase them, promise double. And change the date, make it later? I would unbalance their plans."

With a few careful strokes of a quill, Phelippes altered the numbers, then handed the letter to another agent. She studied the paper closely before selecting a similar quality of stock and a particular bottle of ink. She then began to reproduce the altered letter with painstaking accuracy.

The rest of the letters, once Arthur Gregory had unsealed them, were copied out verbatim and nothing or little was changed. It was more critical to know from or to whom the letters were going, and the details contained therein. Phelippes was muttering the translation as he copied the code, he'd become so accustomed to the coded language. Thomas found himself amused by the realization.

In a mere fifty minutes, the casket of re-sealed letters was returned to him to deliver to Mendoza.

"I think here we close the doors upon the main actors in this stratagem," Walsingham told him. "After today they shall find no exits. Now, off you go, monsieur. We will handle the letter writer. I expect you'll receive news soon enough. Please come and see me once you do." He smiled then, more broadly than Thomas had seen him do in quite awhile. He wondered what Walsingham had read in this batch that prompted him to action. But as Fagot it was best if he was as surprised as everyone else.

The pounding on the door brought the petite housekeeper. Its source proved to be a small yellow-haired man with a pox-pitted face and a grim expression. He introduced himself as Thomas Phelippes. With him was the taller Arthur Gregory, who gave the housekeeper a friendly smile, though there was nothing about the scene of a remotely friendly nature. Behind Walsingham's operatives four soldiers stood, two bearing partisans. They were all dressed for the cold of November.

Phelippes told the servant, "We are come for Francis Throckmorton. You will please step aside."

Swallowing, the small woman backed out of the way as the six men entered the house. In the street a few people had stopped to watch.

Three rooms in, they found Throckmorton seated at a writing table near a warm hearth. He was writing upon one sheet of paper while looking to another placed above it, one that contained keys to the code he was using. Upon seeing them, he threw down his quill and tried to get up and gather the second paper, managing to crumple it into a loose ball that he then flung at the grate. But Phelippes batted it aside.

Throckmorton then tried to throw the half-completed letter into the fire. He stumbled over one of the protruding legs of the table. The nearest soldier swatted Throckmorton's forearm with the partisan, making him drop the letter. To keep him from trying again, the short blade of the partisan aimed at his throat.

Brown-haired Gregory picked up the crumpled sheet and smoothed it against the table. He read it over, nodding, then offered it to Phelippes, who looked it over before setting it aside. Briefly he sifted through the other papers on the table. Finally, he pulled open the two drawers and flipped through the papers therein. He emptied both drawers.

Finally, with the hilt of a dagger, he tapped at the drawers, listening. Throckmorton looked on helplessly.

Phelippes flipped the dagger around again and then stuck its point into a seam in the bottom of the righthand drawer. The bottom came up, revealing a deeper compartment, one from which he removed a handful of small square letters, folded and sealed. "Here we are," he told Gregory.

"Who the devil? How dare . . . ?" Throckmorton tried to express his outrage but fear creased the lines around his eyes.

Phelippes told him, "Francis Throckmorton, you are hereby arrested on suspicion of treason against Her Majesty. You will accompany us now to the Tower, if you please."

"No, there's a mistake, you are mistaken. I love the Queen. Ask anyone."

"Oh, we will, I'm certain, including all of those to whom you've written your undisclosed letters." He held up the one that Throckmorton had been in the middle of coding, and smiled ruefully. "But we have made no mistake, sir. Rather, the mistakes have all been yours."

Among the papers Philippes and Gregory collected were lists of Catholic coconspirators and plotters, and details confirming that a coordinated French invasion was in the works—which matched information in the letters Thomas had delivered to Walsingham. The documents traced Paget and Morgan's deep involvement on the one end and that of their counterparts, Claude Nau and Gilbert Curle—Mary of Scotland's secretaries—on the other, although their names were found nowhere in the text. The letters and lists revealed that former enemies Spain and France were working together on this. The "great and hidden treason" that Sir Francis had imagined was clearly outlined.

He laid the proof before the Queen, then requested and received more money in order to expand the ranks of his agents to enable him to assign an agent to each of the conspirators on Throckmorton's lists. For good measure he saw Throckmorton himself tortured and interrogated. Although a small player in the grand scheme, Throckmorton had made himself an essential link in the chain. Under torture he gave up everyone. Members of his family were hauled to the Tower as well. Some would never see another home.

The plot had cracked. Word traveled quickly back to Paris. The proposed invasion dissolved. Paget and Morgan were left confused that their carefully orchestrated plan had collapsed.

While Bernardino de Mendoza enjoyed full diplomatic immunity from prosecution and coercion like that applied to Throckmorton, he was easily and swiftly expelled from England, and the Spanish embassy closed permanently.

At Sheffield Castle, Mary of Scotland's jailor, Sir Amias Paulet, a cold and unsympathetic Calvinist, knew full well that for all he did to block it, correspondence both reached and was sent out by Mary and her two secretaries. Paulet had taken small revenge by making her stay there as uncomfortable as possible. He'd put Mary in a cold, moist room where her rheumatism and arthritis flared up. And he ensured that the changing of the guards took place at 5:00 a.m. each morning. Guards beat their drums just outside her door during that formal ritual.

Now, at Walsingham's instruction, he hunted down and closed off every route whereby correspondence reached Mary at both the castle and manor house, but with one exception: He pretended to be unaware of a particular beer keg in among the stored tuns and hogsheads with a hidden compartment in its side. Paulet ignored the keg while another of Sir Francis's agents embedded among the staff, and utilizing Arthur Gregory's methods, intercepted, opened, and transcribed every letter placed in that secret compartment. Paulet's obliviousness of the content of the letters was real. He deliberately never saw one.

Eventually, some of the letter writers were also arrested, housed in the Tower, grilled and, in some cases, let go. Walsingham always decided their fate, and as always, he preferred to let the lesser players run free. Some of them led him to other players; some, along with the lists of names Thomas had provided, revealed hidden Jesuits and families secretly nurturing grievances.

Even the composer William Byrd, because of association he'd had with Charles Paget's brother, the Baron Paget, found himself questioned regarding his loyalty to Her Majesty, and his membership to the Queen's Chapel Royal suspended.

Months passed while Walsingham investigated everybody. Thomas remained in the embattled French embassy, and continued to provide Sir Francis with intelligence.

Finally, in May of 1584, a much-depleted Francis Throckmorton was taken from his cell in the Tower and beheaded.

At the end, he claimed that most of what he'd confessed was false. He had been tortured into saying whatever Walsingham wanted to hear. That Walsingham had established the existence of an intricate network of which he was a part made no difference, he insisted. None of his part in it was true. In the end Throckmorton's head joined those of other traitors on the south gate of London Bridge.

In the French embassy, Castelnau was threatened with expulsion, and allowed to remain in the city only provided he signed the Act for the Surety of the Queen's Person. Passed by Parliament, the act made any coplotters attempting to bring harm to Her Majesty guilty of treason however small their part. More importantly, the act stated that whether or not she even participated in the plot in question, Mary of Scotland would be deemed the guilty party in it. Castelnau chose to remain, putting an end to his active participation in the plots, at least for a time.

"Henri Fagot" had fulfilled his part. It was time for him to disappear.

Thomas was more than happy to be rid of that alter ego. He informed Castelnau that he was returning to Paris. All further communication with him would run through Paget and Morgan as before.

Within five minutes of leaving the embassy at Salisbury Court, he had cast off the burden of that swart glamour and was on his way to Seething Lane. As had been the case the previous time he'd shed that disguise, his body seemed to dissolve toward relaxation, away from a bearing he had embraced almost without noticing, a part he had been playing, rendered indissoluble by the ördstone, for over four years.

Thomas Gerard the plague doctor was gone, dead, and now at last so was the assassin and agent Fagot. Fagot's mysterious disappearance would be discussed in Paget and Morgan's circles for months. They would conclude he had been waylaid at some point by agents of Walsingham's, and possibly drowned during the crossing.

To become himself once more was an enormous relief to Thomas, even if he was now without a name or identity. Gerard, Creighton, Fagot—all of them were finished: Gerard obliterated by the Yvags; Creighton, an embedded Jesuit presumed arrested or executed by Walsingham's forces along with the other Jesuits the spymaster had nabbed; Fagot, an assassinated assassin.

More than five years had passed since Thomas had last disrupted the taking of a *teind*. The news on that front was that the new ördstone had begun to flicker with signals familiar to him. The scheduled taking of the *teind* was nearly within his grasp again.

Surely, after so long, the Yvags would have become complacent, secure in their belief that their enemy had died or fled for good. Before Walsingham concocted some other scenario in which to embroil him, it was time to remind the elves that they still had a nemesis.

XXVIII. Sprung Trap

Thomas sat at a table in the Bull Inn in Shoreditch. Alone and unglamoured, he ate a light supper of salted beef slices with mustard, and cheeses accompanied by some brown bread, which he washed down with the inn's strong ale.

Off to one side of the room a young man played a virginal that had been placed on one of the tables. The tune was almost familiar, something by Tallis, he thought. A few people appeared to know the words and were singing, or at least muttering, along. He might have asked someone its title but had no wish to draw attention to himself, not even harmless attention. Once dinner was done, it would be time for him to go.

Even now he was sensing the ördstone in his thoughts like the shadow of a sundial's gnomon as the critical time approached. It had been long enough since he'd known the sensation that he'd come to believe it was out of his grasp forever.

Only in the past few weeks, as Fagot's participation in Paget and Morgan's latest scheme had dwindled to nothing, he'd come up with an absurd idea regarding the stone, and one night by himself had opened a gate to Old Melrose and stepped through.

In the darkness, the ruins had looked like so much rubble. Anything resembling the monks' habitats and the original abbey were gone. Somewhere beneath that hillock of rocks and small trees lay the crypt where Alderman Stroud had dissolved. What it was that drew him here, he could not say, but within moments, the ördstone was pulsing, both on his palm and in his mind. It was as if he and it had returned to the wellspring of its power and his connection to that power. The tiny gems ran through some mad sequence he could not follow.

Perhaps a quarter of an hour he stood there while they flickered at him, lighting him and all around him in a shifting blue glow. And then all at once they stopped. The glow rose and fell, almost as if the stone were breathing, asleep.

He'd cut another gate back, to Finsbury Field as he'd done long ago, stepped through and sealed it up. From that moment forward, the new ördstone had begun communicating with him much as the original one had done.

In the Bull Inn, he studied the crowd, wondering as always if there hid an Yvag among them. Save for chittering skinwalkers or Yvag knights brushing up against him, he could not tell human from elf, could not even speculate without first drawing the stone, and aiming it at them, one by one, which would surely get him branded as a witch, while ensuring nothing about the nearness of an Yvag.

He had to admit to a little nervousness as he sat there: He hadn't intervened in the Yvag kidnapping of a *teind* in so very long, he could about convince himself that he was inadequate to the task any longer. Even with the ördstone's shadow pinpointing the juncture, there were so many other variables to consider: Where would the *teind* be seized? Where would the victim be taken to? Would this prove to be one of their grand ceremonies, with Nicnevin on hand for some elaborate processional, or would it be a quick and expedient capture and execution? He knew nothing about why the method varied so much, although he speculated that it seemed to do with the relationship between Yvag and the Wood, Yvag and Unseelie.

Meanwhile, the world from which the elves could pluck their victims continued to expand. What was he going to do when the whole of the so-called New World opened up to them as well? He would be delusional to think the elves wouldn't invade right alongside the human explorers, both sides merciless in their exploitation of whatever they found.

That at least was a concern for some other time. This night he was returning to his personal war before Walsingham could intrude. He hoped he could surprise the Yvags once again.

After finishing his ale, he paid for the meal and then left the inn. Outside, against the slowly darkening sky, he stared at the torchlit polygonal shape of the Curtain playhouse nearby. Now that he resided in Shoreditch, he really ought to take in a play. Sir Francis had proposed as much. Soon, he would do it soon. Perhaps something refreshing, performed by the Lord Chamberlain's Men.

Returning to the Shoreditch safe house, he lit a few candles from the embers of the hearth, then checked the ten arrows he'd stood on their nocks against the dining chamber wall. As he'd anticipated, the iron tips were dry now. He'd used the last of the Yvag poison in his possession on them. After this, if he wanted more, he was going to have to reenter the depths of Þagalwood. He could only hope it would let him in again.

Glamouring was one thing—a quick pocket of shadow was all he needed in order to transform. Cutting open a gate to Yvagddu was another matter. The last thing he wanted was to open a gate where he lived, which would effectively invite the elven to invade his home anytime they liked. Or so the case had been before he'd acquired the weird glove. Now at least he could imagine creating and dissolving a gate in so little time that it left the Yvags no opportunity to follow. That said, tonight he would not risk it. He could not draw the bow while wearing the glove, and in any case, he would never chance leading his enemy back to the Shoreditch house.

Thomas took off his clothes and put on the new Yvag armor he'd acquired. Like others before it, the suit flowed of its own accord up and over his body like a second skin, the spiky helm making him look like the devil himself. The "new" additions, edged in silver at his shoulders, elbows, and knees, presented no hint of their tensile-shifting capacity. He pushed at the helm and it shed its spikes and receded, pooling around his throat. At that point he gathered up his discarded clothes and placed them in the traveling chest on top of the jeweled glove, all except for a few sovereigns that he stuffed into one of the hidden pockets in the armor. It always paid to have the fare for a coach or a ketch on him. Next he inserted an Yvag dagger into a built-in sheath in the armor, and belted on the quiver. He took up his bow. He felt as strange as ever he had. It had been so long since he had last dressed for such a battle. With one foot, he pushed the traveling chest behind the bed.

After blowing out the candles, he paused to glamour, providing himself a shoulder cape, doublet, and a small green ruff at the collar. With his bow unstrung and held like a walking stick, he exited the house.

He strolled to Bishopsgate Road and up past what had once been St. Mary Spital Priory. He could recall when the church and the other buildings had been there; almost none remained, long ago disassembled by forces of Henry VIII. At Hog Lane he turned and headed out across Finsbury Field. It was becoming his default location for departures and returns. At night it was almost invariably deserted. He could see a good distance there, all the way across Bunhill Field as well.

Holding the image of the road through Þagalwood in his mind, he took out the pulsating ördstone and sliced open the night. The resulting gate hung before him like a dull rose window edged with spitting greenish fire, and he quickly stepped through it, turned and sealed it up behind him. If anyone had witnessed it at a distance, they would reach this spot only to find no trace remaining, a vanished will-o'-the-wisp, what the old poet and seer Taliesin would have called *canwyll yr ysbryd*.

But he saw no one running up as the last of the seam vanished. The night, left behind, fell silent and still.

In Yvagddu, it's what passes for daytime, although with the dimness of the red sun in the sky above, day remains a dark, shadowy state of being, a perpetual twilight. The first jump places him on the road he and Waldroup once walked, a broad path surrounded by the eeriest of trees, their thick white trunks marred by cavities and cankers that produce the effect of distorted, skeletal faces grown out of the ground and watching his progress. No breeze ever seems to stir here, but the woods whisper nonetheless. The air is thick and hard to breathe; he'd forgotten how much so. By now, if the Queen and her entourage are engaged in acquiring the *teind*, he would expect them to be on the road behind him—as when Onchu and he were brought to the city of Ailfion.

Thomas has always wanted to understand if his brother's selection was merely random chance. What if they hadn't found him, would they have picked the first person who came along? The likely randomness of the act makes it, if anything, that much worse to contemplate.

He sheds his glamour. Raises the helm. Now, spiked, he could be any Yvag knight.

When, after maybe an hour of walking along the wide pathway, he encounters no one, he takes the ördstone in hand once again and slices the air, creating another green fiery gate, this one opening upon a different part of Yvagddu—a hillside inside the city of Ailfion itself.

He steps through. He is above a bowl-like depression. It's a hill he has stood upon previously. Midnight-blue grass twines around his legs. He strings the bow, then climbs the rest of the way up, as he has done a few times now, until in the distance the city of Ailfion lies glistening like many vertical strings of jewels everywhere ahead. Some are stepped ziggurats, some needle-sharp points that seem to reach for the star-shot sky that is like no other sky he has ever seen, a spray of stars strewn across a quilted canopy—stars that remain in the dim daylight. He wonders are they projections, and if so what might exist beyond them. He doubts he will ever have opportunity to ask.

From the hill he can see the numerous plazas of dull yellow brick or at least portions of the plazas between various towers. They look ruddy in the half-light. What he does not see is anything resembling the procession of the *teind*. Granted that time is mercurial between his world and that of the elven, but the ördstone is all but chiming the hour, that shadow gnomon in his head pointing directly to the event. It practically speaks to him, not even pulsing now. There *has* to be a procession here. He turns about, glamours himself as an expression of the landscape, as he has done before. He is grass and thick night sky, a living mirror.

Then, down the hill from where he stands, a spot of green fire ignites. In anticipation he draws an arrow. The flame expands into a line, flexes and opens, and the first of three Yvag soldiers emerges from it. In the center between them their captive shuffles, tall and gaunt, stripped naked. Curiously, the knights radiate fear, turning and turning to glance all around themselves as if they know to expect him.

An all-but-transparent ghost, Thomas descends the hill toward them. He fires his first arrow, his second, and third, grabbing three more arrows as the first volley hits its marks. The escorts all drop, leaving the seemingly dull-witted, ensorcelled victim alone on the hillside. Thomas continues down the hill, but responding to some uncanny instinct, he turns, scanning the tall grass for any other suits of black armor. Something...

The chirring communication throbs in his head—and one word: *Strike!*

The grass and sky ripple above him. The Yvags have glamoured themselves exactly as he has done, transformed into reflections of the landscape itself. They're all around him. *They knew!*

He circles, looking for any way down the hillside, but they've left him nowhere to flee except into the nearest plaza below, while the *teind* he came to rescue simply ripples like a dog throwing off water, becoming the thing he beheld for the first time at Robert Hodde's limetree in Barnsdale Wood and at Kirklees Priory, where it snatched his would-be killer away.

Bragrender.

With one deformed arm the grotesque creature waves away the threat of his bow. "You haven't enough arrows, and reinforcements none." The grinding voice hurts to hear. "In seconds we'll slay you. Put the bow down, uncloak yourself, and admit you've met a superior force in me." When he fails to move, Bragrender says, "No?" His shifting aspect becomes more manic. He waves his arm again. "Loose the hobs to strip him of his glamour!"

Some word, some signal is given, for in one plaza below, a mass of the little monstrosities suddenly takes to the air. At this distance they look like a swarm of hornets.

Thomas fingers his ördstone. There is nowhere for him to go. No gate he can slice open before they take him. No shape change that will make any difference. He has taken the bait and now stands at their mercy. Well, he's had a good run to have made it this far. The instant he unglamours, Nicnevin will know him. Bragrender, too. Their imagined enemy force will be reduced to one.

The air beside Thomas flares, a ball of red-and-green fire from which a straight cut zips down. Even before it fully opens, a bone-pale hand and silver forearm reach through the gap, wraps around him, and yanks hard enough to pull him off his feet and right through the half-made gate.

Thrown, he lands on his backside. The hand that grabbed him sweeps right back, closing the hole with a large, pale ördstone. It all happens so fast that no one on the other side has a chance to react before the gate seals and, with a little *pop*, disappears from existence.

He's sprawled on a different slope. Ailfion is twinkling lights in the far distance, a brightness maybe an hour away.

Above, the ghostly pale face leans toward him, its oversized golden eyes more striking than ever. "Well, this is unexpected. Quick now, get up. We've one more jump to make to avoid their pursuit."

He knows this voice, too. He has heard it in dreams. Listened to it as he reflected upon the events in Nottingham and at Kirklees Priory.

"Zhanedd," he says, and rolls to his feet, ready to fight.

"Shush, not now. They come. And you can dispense with your mirroring glamour. It doesn't hide you from me."

Her slender hand opens yet another gate. The larger stone cuts a gate at least twice as fast as his own ördstone might. She twists back to him. "Go through," she orders.

Next to her a new point of fire has just appeared: Bragrender and his forces have followed the traces of her half-completed gate.

Her stone flares, and the gate she just sealed simply disintegrates, collapsing in on itself. The attempted pursuit sputters and vanishes, too.

"They will try again, and they'll succeed." Zhanedd glances his way. "Move!" She shoves him.

He stumbles back. The gate is raised off the ground and he trips on the lip of it and falls through the opening to land on a hilltop beside a pool of blinding white, brighter than the sun. He catches himself on its edge, his fingertips immersed in the whiteness. The surface ripples out from him, agitated; like liquid light some of it dribbles into runnels down the side of the hill. His fingers burn as from intense cold and still icier voices echo through him. The rippling surface as he breathes upon it looks like a multitude of faces.

Zhanedd leans over and tugs his hand from out of the blinding light. He can only stare up at her, his thoughts overcome by impressions of lives lived and hopes lost, images, moments, thoughts flitting past. Where have they come from? In amid them all, there's one voice that calls "Tommy?" It's so soft, so distant, he's not sure he's heard it at all.

Dazedly, he watches her seal up and obliterate the second gate she's created exactly as he might have done with the jeweled glove if he'd brought it. All around them are the trees of Þagalwood as far as he can see in the gloom.

Zhanedd looks down at him and tilts her head as she studies his features. "So, Uncle," she says, "all these centuries, and you have hardly changed a bit. What *is* your secret?"

XXIX. The Niece

Throughout this escapade of jumps, Thomas has managed to hang onto his bow. He's gauging whether he can nock an arrow when she calls him *uncle*. He gawps at her. And then she does the most unexpected thing of all: she smiles at him.

It's not sly nor malicious nor triumphant. Were it not for those needle-sharp teeth it might even seem friendly.

She tucks the stone away, then extends a hand to pull him to his feet. She grips his hand, looks at the white color fading from his fingertips.

He says, "You've rescued me. Why?" After all, this Yvag has hunted him, interrogated him, probably coupled with him, and ultimately attempted to drag him back to Yvagddu where she intended to watch him die.

"First of all," she says, "I was not rescuing you as much as I was interfering in Bragrender's stratagem." She places one palm against his chest, takes his hand that she still holds and places it against hers. Under his hand, beneath the fluid silver armor she wears, something soft and wet shifts. "However, it is also true that blood must speak to blood. Doubly so in this instance."

His blood speaking to her, and hers to him? *Uncle?* He recollects long ago, in Nottingham, that she had reminded him of his sister. He'd thought she snatched the image out of his memory. Now he can't even remember exactly what Innes looked like. He asks instead, "Where have you brought me?"

"To the heart of Þagalwood. You understandably doubt my intentions."

She points to his fingers. They still tingle, and the pale tips remain numb.

"What did you feel, in the well?" she asks.

He answers uncertainly, "Voices? Or not voices exactly, more like..."

"Souls." She says it as if certain.

"That...might be so." What would he compare them to? He glances at the Wood around them, the way the eerie white trees grow in an outward spiral away from this mound. "What is this wellspring? It's so much like the other, like Hel."

She agrees. "I do not know if it is the far end of Hel or simply an expression of it, Hel inverted. No one else in Ailfion seems to know of it at all. But no one else walks the Wood unmolested. There are times when the trees are harvested to make new strange assemblers, when a way in is allowed, at least for a distance, but no one is ever brought here." Her golden gaze bores into him.

"I believe I might have followed you into the Wood once. I followed someone. Discovered a path, tried to walk it. Þagalwood itself turned me out in the end."

"And you would have attempted to slay me with one of those if I'd returned and caught you then." She points at the quiver on his hip. "You have poisoned arrows."

There seems no point in lying about it. She's been his enemy for too long to believe any other story. "I would have tried, yes."

Instead of answering, she peels away the Yvag armor and stands naked before him, pale rose-colored throat and belly ringed with muscle, the mottled skin, now paler than any Yvag he's seen before. Her side gills flex open and closed. An enormous rent in her torso has been filled in with what looks like matter from the skeletal trees of Þagalwood. "You *have* tried already," she says.

"That wound—"

"You gave it me." She states this simply, without any suggestion of accusation. "I should be dead but that Þagalwood preserved me." She presses fingertips to the whiteness in herself. It moves. This is what he felt beneath her armor. For an instant, her expression drifts into something like longing.

All he can think to say is ridiculously obvious. "It has changed you."

"Oh, yes." Her golden eyes lock upon his again. "You don't yet appreciate that you are responsible for this transformation." She sits beside the white wellhead, then calmly inserts her whole forearm into the well. A look of ecstasy alters her features. "I hear you," she whispers, but not to him. "All of you." Her eyes roll up in her head.

He hears nothing, not even the chirr of Yvag communication, but as he looks on, Zhanedd's skin becomes almost incandescent. Her jaw seems less distended, the spikes or thorns adorning her Yvag flesh less prominent. It's as if the changeling in her is recovering its original self.

She withdraws her arm from the wellspring, and the glow fades. Focuses on him again. "Long have I wondered who you are, to have crossed my path time and again over too many cycles, centuries. To glamour as we glamour. No human can do that. She did this to you, yes? The Queen."

Not the Queen. Nicnevin would never have given him power. He did this to himself, unknowingly. "The Pool," he says.

"Ah. Then have we that in common, too." She rises, puts her silver armor back on, says, "Come, we must leave this grove, else time will devour us completely."

"What do you mean?" he asks, although he has an inkling of the answer.

"This is the heart of Þagalwood. It slows time more than anywhere else in either of our worlds. Yours right now whirls and whirls past."

Zhanedd starts off and he follows, but she draws up to tell him to "pick a new flower," indicating a spray of *kanerva* just off their path. "Who knows when you'll have another opportunity." He carefully plucks one, then hurries to keep up.

"You behold me differently than any other does," she calls back to him. "You see my mother in me."

"I thought so before, but then I suspected you had threaded her from my thoughts to gain advantage."

"The Unseelie . . ." she starts to say, but seems not to know where to go from there. "I once believed there were rogue changelings dwelling here in the Wood—that your actions, occurring over centuries and thus could not be those of any single human against us, were proof of their existence. I did not understand the nature of you. I was Yvag and you human. We were enemies. It was no more complicated than that."

Her spiral path returns them to the main road through Þagalwood. He is as disoriented as the last time he followed a path of hers. She turns to face him, more pallid than before. The burning white of the arm she submerged has diffused throughout her.

"The Unseelie," she says again, this time continuing: "I have communed with Þagalwood."

"That's what you were doing?"

She nods. "I beheld the Unseelie War with the People—the Wood has opened my eyes to it, told me much that was hidden."

"What was hidden?"

She shakes her head. That is not something she means to share. "Also it has told me who I am, who you are," and adds, "*I* am the rogue changeling I imagined."

"How are you . . . how are you rogue?"

"I belong to no world any longer."

He laughs. "Would that you knew how often I've shared that very same thought."

"Yes, of course you have." She draws the large ördstone from her armor. "Tell me, did my mother ever speak my true name to you?"

He thinks back to the night he crept into her room in Castle MacGillean. She'd been ensorcelled into seeing that she had a son, whom she'd named Dougal. She had never known about the girl child they'd stolen away, nor had he.

"I'm sorry," he says, unable to come up with a believable lie. "I can only imagine that she might have named you after our mother, whose name was Sìne."

Zhanedd repeats the name.

"What was she like, my mother?"

He recollects her in Baldie's keep, half out of her mind. That's not how he wants to remember her, much less the image he would share. He says, "She was a laughing girl. I was . . . damaged. She cared not, loved me anyway."

"My uncle."

"Thomas," he replies.

Zhanedd silently repeats his name. "I must send you back, then, Thomas. You will have missed some time now. If the opportunity arises, I might aid you again how I can."

"Why? We've sworn to kill each other, and come very close to succeeding."

Her ringed pupils swell, as though the notion excites her. "That we have. But the enemy of my enemy is my friend. Potentially, at least."

He thinks of Isabella Birkin, who he has always believed was turned by Zhanedd. He is not sure he could ever give her quarter. "What about the *teind* I meant to rescue?"

She shakes her head. "There was no *teind*. Bragrender changed the rules of play and had the captive already secured in a cell. You could save no one, no matter how you came at it. You were deceived."

"He deserves to die."

"He believes himself the superior life-form, greater than any of the People, greater than me, certainly greater than your entire race. His hubris leads him in all things."

He starts to speak but she shushes him.

She presses a hand to the slowly shifting white mass in her core. "This, that you've touched, was but an experiment for him. He expected my loyalty in return for the accident of keeping me alive. He looks for me because he believes he is owed something for his trouble."

"And what is it he's owed?"

"He expects me to support his bid to replace Nicnevin. There is, you see, no room in Bragrender's world for anyone but Bragrender."

She turns back to the way ahead, then slices down, opening a new gate. The far side is an open landscape, with a windmill so close he can hear the creaking of the vanes. She has returned him to Finsbury Field, which is too much of a coincidence: She must have been watching him all the time he thought he was being clever and unobserved.

"Goodbye, then, Uncle. If I see you again, let us hope it is not on a battlefield."

He reaches over, clasps her luminous white hand in his. Her Yvag voice thrums in his head. They remain on opposite sides of a war, loyalties divided. This reciprocity between them doesn't change that, nor how she's used, abused, or tried to deceive him in the past. Each has, at one time or another, tried very hard to kill the other.

He stares into her strange golden eyes. "Sìne," he says by way of departing.

Then he steps through, and draws a shockingly cold deep breath of the winter air of home. Even before he can turn around, she has sealed up the gate and gone.

XXX. Enter a Playwright

A light coating of snow dusted Finsbury Field. Underdressed for the weather, Thomas strode fast across the field, heading for a familiar inn on Hog Lane. He knew where he was, but had no idea when.

By the time he reached Beaumont's Tavern, he could barely feel his fingers. Inside, a lovely fire warmed the low-beamed-ceiling room, but the handful of customers all stopped what they were doing as he stood inside the doorway to thaw out. He had glamoured himself with a cloak, and the Yvag armor acted as insulation against the cold to an extent, but he was still carrying a strung bow and arrows, not to mention a queer purple flower that should not have existed in this weather, never mind in this world, carefully held by the stem in his free hand.

Nobody in their right mind would have been about practicing archery on such a night, and no doubt the clientele's first impression was that an escapee from nearby Bethlehem Hospital had arrived, armed, in their midst. He made a point then of walking quietly over to a small table in a relatively isolated corner where he could set aside the bow and quiver. The other clientele watched him, nevertheless.

There were two boys scurrying about as servers. From the elder of the two he ordered a mug of ale and whatever warm meal they were serving with it, which proved to be a thick barley soup, accompanied by a hunk of warm black bread pasted with salted butter. It tasted like heaven, and he ate with fiendish intensity, finishing by wiping the bowl clean with the bread.

After that, Thomas just sat awhile, and let the food bring him back to life.

He bought a second mug of ale. Whatever his perceived mental state might be, his coin worked just fine here. When the older boy brought him the drink, he offered up one of the sovereigns, and the boy's eyes widened. "Yours, if you can tell me the day and year."

The boy squinted at him, trying no doubt to figure the true nature of this trick question. Who but a madman would part with so much money in this fashion?

"Twenty-eight December," the boy cautiously told him, "1585."

"Nearly a *year*?" Thomas said in astonishment. He came halfway off his bench. A few people glanced his way, and, self-conscious, he sat down again. "She did not lie," he muttered to himself.

"Who?" the boy looked around.

"'Tis nothing. I made a bet and lost it. Here." He slid the coin across to the boy, who picked it up in wonder and quickly departed.

What Zhanedd had tried to explain was now clear: The heart of Þagalwood imposed a greater distortion upon the passage of time than the equivalent spent in Ailfion itself. The spiraling Wood or, more likely, that white mound in its center increased the already-distorted speed with which time passed . . . Perchance it was the very source of discrepancy, and so worse the nearer he got to it.

Eventually, he felt sufficiently warmed, his belly full. He got up and left the tavern.

The safe house on Aldersgate Street stood dark. The key to the drunk man's lock on the front door still remained behind a stone in the garden wall.

He entered cautiously, but the little house proved to be cold and silent, uninhabited. No fire had burned in its recent past. It appeared that nobody was making use of it at the moment. However, kindling and a few logs lay in the hearth, suggesting that someone had occupied it at some point in his absence; in the dark he located the striking flint and struck it with his Yvag dagger, sending sparks into the wood. It took him ten minutes, but he managed to start a fire.

All the while, he was thinking that this could be the perfect opportunity to go his own way without having to see or explain anything to Walsingham. He could simply take his possessions, cross the channel again, and go somewhere where this war of Yvags, Catholics, queens, and spymasters wasn't playing out.

He'd made up his mind to do so by the time he discovered that his traveling chest was gone from behind the bed and was nowhere else in the house, either.

Panic rose in him, but he forced it down. The absence of the chest made a certain sense. To Walsingham's network, he had vanished without a trace, and many months had passed with no sign of him, and no communication. Walsingham would likely assume he was dead, possibly at the hands of the very people they had been monitoring—Paget and Morgan if not the Spanish or the French ambassador or the demon Yvags. There would be no cutting ties just now. And he hoped to God it *was* Sir Francis who'd laid hands upon his traveling chest. He thought of the damage that could be done by anyone else. Not to mention that his fortune lay in the bottom of that chest in the form of sealed letters of credit.

Like it or not, tomorrow he would have to visit Seething Lane. Tonight, all he wanted to do was sleep.

Sir Francis Walsingham's reaction when he was ushered in was as icy as the day outside. "Where have you been in all this time with no word?" Before Thomas could answer, he continued, "And is it still Creighton, or have you adopted yet another name?"

"Creighton if you like, or any other you prefer. I haven't been... here."

Walsingham waved the explanation away as superfluous.

As before, the interior of the house was as busy as a hive, with some people deciphering codes and others mimicking them in ink. Thomas Phelippes, looking up as they passed, met his gaze with raised brows.

Once in Walsingham's room, Thomas explained that, having done his part in foiling Throckmorton and the French ambassador's plot, he'd dispensed with his disguise and gone after other Yvags with the intention of rescuing one of their human tithes, but failed in his attempt. Instead, he had become trapped in their world until he could escape—easier than explaining how time ran differently. Walsingham had enough to digest in accepting the reality of the demons and that Thomas could travel to their realm and back again. He had very nearly been killed—that was what mattered.

"Which," said Walsingham, "conveniently no one can disprove. You have provided such good results that I do wish to embrace your version of your absence, but so much has to be taken on faith, and that is in short supply just now. You do see my dilemma."

He did, of course, and regretted the need to ask, "What might I do then to prove my allegiance still?" Words that would surely put him back in harness.

Walsingham had an answer. "For one, you might sign the Bond of Association, whereby you swear never to engage in acts against Her Majesty, else forfeit your life. Somehow we overlooked that before you became . . . unavailable."

"That all plays trippingly off the tongue. By all means, Sir Francis. Bring me ink and page and I shall sign it."

"Very good." Walsingham sent a servant for the bound volume.

While they waited, Thomas asked, "What all has happened in the time since Henri Fagot vanished?"

"It has been so long a time that I am now uncertain of the precise date of your departure. So, let me cast back." Throckmorton, a fabulist in the end, confessing, and then recanting every single thing to which he had admitted, had been executed. Throckmorton's coded letters had damned Mendoza as well, and the Spanish embassy remained shuttered. "Castelnau in the French embassy lives now under threat of blackmail and ejection."

The book arrived. The servant left it. Walsingham got up, wearily, and opened the book to a page well filled with signatures already. He pointed to where he wanted Thomas to sign. "This is part of the Act for the Surety of the Queen's Person. Essentially, I now have a document that ensures the guilt of Mary of Scotland in any plot to harm the Queen whether she knew of it directly or not. I can now charge her as an instigator of any and all plots," he announced proudly. "I will have her."

Thomas made a point of studying the quill awhile. Then having dipped it in the ink, he hesitated. "But what name do I sign for you, Sir Francis? Gerard or Creighton? Surely not Fagot?"

Now Walsingham studied him. "Ah, yes, *there's* a problem unique to you. Who are you and who will you be upon some future date? Was Gerard your first? I now very much doubt it. And so will Creighton be your last? Have you not abandoned him already?"

"He had to remain behind in Rheims."

"Naturally. You are like an actor upon a stage, changing your very identity, assuming a new rôle every night till your true name be lost for all time."

They traded a look, one that suggested Sir Francis knew more of him than had been broached.

Walsingham said, "I suggest you should sign it 'Number Four.'"

Thomas stared down at the page awhile.

Behind him Walsingham said, "That is the sobriquet I am now assigning you. Your code name, if you will. However many names you pluck for yourself, for me it shall remain a point of reference. I will know of whom I speak when I say it."

Thomas and he stared at each other awhile before he finally leaned forward and wrote.

Walsingham turned the volume and read: "Number Four." He glanced up, curious. "Now you may have all the alternate names you wish; I know what to call you in every instance."

Thomas had set down the quill. "You say the Spanish embassy is shuttered now."

Walsingham replied, "That is correct. Oh, and you knew William Parry, did you not?"

"'Knew' suggests that Parry is dead."

Dour Walsingham nodded. "He has been executed for treason."

"Parry? But he was so . . . ineffectual. I thought he was working for both you and Cecil. Was he not? I did not think him a Catholic agent."

"Of course you didn't, Number Four. You weren't meant to. Part of his skill was misdirection. He accused Edmund Neville—I believe you met him also through our French embassy. Neville alerted us first that Parry was planning an assassination attempt. He had proposed to Neville that they ride alongside Her Majesty's coach, one on each side, and at some predetermined time would draw their pistols and shoot the Queen between them."

Thomas replied, "More likely they would shoot each other. Don't tell me you believed him."

Walsingham frowned at Thomas. "Understand that I do not care to be second-guessed by one I employ who evaporates when and as it suits him." He let that hang in the air a moment before continuing calmly. "In fact, I offered Parry every opportunity to reveal himself as plotting in order to attract conspirators, in particular Neville. He failed to do so, whether too foolish to understand how dire his situation was, I do not know. But at the most crucial time he chose to offer no other explanation."

This was the concern Thomas had expressed from the beginning with the spymaster: that to deceive those who plotted against the Queen, an agent might have to live the life of that very enemy, and do it so well that it would be impossible to distinguish the truth of him. He must *be* the enemy to lure the enemy.

"And Neville?"

"We dare not assure ourselves of his allegiance, either, given his past failures. He has far more reason to put the blame on another. For his trouble he resides now in the Tower." He closed the signed book. "It is perhaps just as well you were absent or you might also have been dragged into all of it."

"Then I am happy to have been elsewhere." Uneasily, he turned to the question he'd not yet asked. "As regards the house at St. Martin's le Grande, Sir Francis, I found that my travel chest and its contents have been removed from it. Did you by chance—"

"Take it and bring it here? Yes, after you'd gone missing for months and we feared your death as a result of the expulsion of Mendoza, given that both seemed to occur simultaneously. And I wished to make use of that house. Your chest remains under lock and key. You may have it back whenever you like."

He breathed a sigh of relief. "Well, that is one less worry," though really it was more than that, more than he could express to Walsingham: He had not lost his travel chest, and he hadn't been captured by Nicnevin and thrown back into her prison, which no doubt he would not escape from again.

"Then we should perhaps celebrate your return to the fold. There is a single performance today at Burbage's Theatre of Lyly's *Campaspe*. The Children of Her Majesty's Chapel performed it at Blackfriars last year, but in the wake of the latest bout of plague, they've taken it and themselves upon the road. Burbage is allowing Hunsdon's Men to present it, mostly, as I understand it, so that he might assay the part of Diogenes, who, it is almost unnecessary to add, has all the best lines. Might I interest you in accompanying me before we return to the business of saving England? There is someone in the company there you should meet."

His possessions in Walsingham's keeping, Thomas could but agree. The spymaster had him again.

Thomas had only viewed Burbage's Theatre at a distance. It was a three-story octagonal building with two enclosed exterior staircases bulging from its sides, and topped with a bright yellow flag and pennants.

Walsingham's coach brought them up Shoreditch Street to a low brick wall that edged the lane for quite a ways to either side of the theater. Various garden patches, a large barn, and a cattle pen shared the walled-off plot of land. An opening in the wall aligned with the theater, and a crowd milled about in the wide yard around it.

As the two of them walked into the yard, a trumpet blast sounded from the top of the structure. The crowd shifted; suddenly they were all moving to go inside.

Walsingham, leading the way, entered the nearest stairwell. Inside, he seemed to identify a short, scruffy fellow, to whom he gave sixpence. The short man turned and led them up to the second level and into an open gallery. They were directly across from the stage, the gallery above it. The attendant hailed someone else, who came running over with two cushions that he placed on the bench for them. From there they had a perfect view of the stage. Below was the crowd, the so-called groundlings, many of them dressed in the flat caps and blue garb of apprentices on break from the Inns of Court—at least, that was Walsingham's expressed opinion.

After perhaps fifteen minutes the trumpets sounded again and the audience fell quiet.

A white-robed figure walked alone onto the stage. He opened a scroll, held it up, and read: "They that fear the stinging of wasps make fans of peacock tails, whose spots are like eyes." This, the prologue, continued for a few minutes, after which two figures in Greek armor stepped forward from behind a curtain and began discussing the conqueror Alexander and his honor. In the midst of their discussion a group of women arrived, guarded by a few other soldiers. The women, Thomas knew, were all boys or at least the youngest men in the troupe. The one playing Campaspe seemed particularly striking—to Alexander as well as to Thomas—wearing a flowing pink gown, belted round with blue ribbon, and with a shorter second chiton of olive green wrapped over the first. The conqueror had much to say regarding "her" beauty, before a group of philosophers came forward, gathering to speak with Diogenes, who lived in a tub and spoke his sharp and witty lines from within it. Eventually, Alexander confessed to his general, Hephestion, that he was in love with the girl Campaspe. The general (who seemed enamored of her himself) tried to convince the conqueror not to continue with this courtship. Alexander could not seem to help himself. He hired a painter, Apelles, to paint Campaspe, but from the start it was clear that the artist, too, was smitten with her beauty and wit.

The play brimmed with sharp dialogue and repartee, especially whenever Diogenes was on hand to toss out his comic catechisms. Apelles and Campaspe discussed the many ways Jupiter had cruelly deceived and abused both goddesses and mortal women as if he thought he had to do so. Finally, Campaspe admitted that she had never been in love. Apelles replied, "It's not possible that a face so fair and a wit so sharp, both without comparison, should not be apt to love." In the end, Alexander, having much the power of Jupiter in this situation, recognized that Campaspe had herself fallen in love with the painter, and unlike a god, stepped aside and ordered them to marry.

The play included songs, some quite bawdy. Apelles's song of Campaspe revealed just how deeply he had fallen in love with her. He sang:

> Cupid and my Campaspe played
> At cards for kisses, Cupid paid;
> He stakes his quiver, bow, and arrows,
> His mother's doves, and team of sparrows;
> Loses them too; then, down he throws
> The coral of his lip, the rose
> Growing on's cheek (but none knows how),
> With these, the crystal of his brow,
> And then the dimple of his chin:
> All these did my Campaspe win.
> At last, he set her both his eyes;
> She won, and Cupid blind did rise.
> O love! has she done this to thee?
> What shall (Alas!) become of me?

When the play concluded, the audience erupted in cheers. Thomas thought the leading actors all exceptional. He asked who they were. Walsingham again identified Diogenes as Burbage, and Burbage's son, Richard, as Apelles, the artist.

"And Alexander?" asked Thomas.

"Ah, I told you there was someone here whom you must meet. And that is our Alexander. Come with me."

"Tell me, who's the boy playing Campaspe?" Thomas asked as Walsingham turned away. "He's most remarkable, I think. Why, the whole audience must have swooned over his presence. I could feel the passion in these men, ignited by him. That is, I myself forgot entirely that she is, in fact, he."

"Oh, I concur, but know not the name of the actor. We shall ask our friend."

Along the corridor behind the gallery they circled the theater, then descended a level, which placed them backstage in the large dressing room, separated by a curtain. The actors, chattering away, milled about in celebration, James Burbage squeezing shoulders and telling them, "Immaculate performances, one and all."

Burbage caught sight of Thomas and Walsingham, and abruptly changed course to come hurrying over. "Sir Francis!" he called loudly. Others' heads swiveled—they all knew what a patron of the theater he was. He was instrumental in the selection of the Queen's Men, the ever-transforming "best of" company who would entertain the Queen at Placentia Palace and were well rewarded for it. Everyone wanted to be among those players. "We are honored to have you in our audience today."

Walsingham brushed the comment aside. "Not at all. Having seen the boy troupe perform Lyly's play at Placentia, how could I deny myself the pleasure of your group's interpretation?"

"And do we transcend?"

"Oh, you should ask my associate here what he thinks. I will tell you, he was *most* taken by Campaspe herself."

Burbage clasped his hands together. "He has proven to be a real find, such that your man will have to compete with half the actors in this room tonight. They all be in love with Simon."

"Simon?" asked Thomas. He glanced about.

"There he is. Simon! Come here, come here. This is one of our royal patrons, Sir Francis Walsingham, and this his associate . . ." He reached as if to snatch the name off Thomas.

"Lindsay, Thomas Lindsay," he said, to himself oddly shy as he gave the name. How long it had been since he'd called himself that! "Your performance was exquisite."

Campaspe blushed. He still wore the black wig of coiled hair, with a long cylindrical fall spilling over one shoulder. Thin, not yet bearded, and of medium height in aspect, the actor bowed to him, but with a dark blue gaze that seemed to be searching Thomas's face as if seeking some connection or secret hidden there.

Before either could say more, another man burst through the curtain at the rear of the chamber and shoved his way past some of the actors. Beholding Campaspe, the man charged straight for them. Two others, armed with partisans and looking menacingly official, followed in his wake.

"I am here," announced the man, "to arrest *her*!" He thrust an accusing finger at Campaspe and said, "Witch!" His other hand drew his wheellock pistol but did not cock the dog. He seemed to seek who might be in charge, settling on Walsingham and Burbage as likely targets. "I have been tracking this female all the way from Horsham. She is a witch and I am duly appointed under the Witchcraft Act of 1563 as witchfinder to take her into custody." He said it defiantly as if daring anyone to object or contradict him.

Burbage started to do just that, but Campaspe held up one hand to stop him, then reached up, removed a long pin from the black fall of hair, and drew off the wig. Beneath it lay a head of short, dark hair. A few of the other players chuckled. With the removal of the wig, the actor's face, long and slightly equine, seemed to transform. Despite its coating of makeup (or perhaps because of it), it now seemed obviously the face of an older boy. "Campaspe" picked up a cloth and started wiping the dark makeup alongside his nose, placed to make the line of nose appear thinner and sharper than it was; then he wiped the red from his lips, which became less full, and the kohl-black edging of his eyelids that made his eyes seem larger than they were. With each swipe of the rag, he looked less and less like Campaspe and more like a pretty young man, as if each time the cloth passed across his face, he was reshaping it.

In the end, the actors were snickering at the witchfinder. Campaspe, now clearly revealed as Simon, undid his costume finery and shoved the dress down off his thin shoulders. He stepped out of it, revealing a bum roll tied around his hips over his braies. He untied and removed the roll, then stood there slim-hipped and tightly muscled. In his own voice, an octave below that of Campaspe's, he asked the witchfinder, "You tracked me from where, sir?"

Everyone laughed at the witchfinder then. He flushed crimson, spluttered, "But this is just more witchcraft!" He waved the gun about.

Burbage finally spoke up. "I insist you put your gun away, sir! If you knew anything at all about the theater, my dear fellow, you would know that we employ *no* women on the stage, else we would be closed down for indecency. Right here stands the Queen's own Secretary of State to vouch for us, and for this nearly naked boy."

Walsingham sternly addressed the witchfinder. "That is so, and I fear you are an unfortunate and unintended consequence of the act upon which you so heavily depend. You are whom?"

"D'Arcy," the man replied.

"Mr. D'Arcy. You may very well have tracked *some* witch from Horsham to London, to that I cannot speak. Here, however, I believe you have mistaken an actor in costume for your bargainer with the devil."

"No, no, I can assure you—"

"In point of fact you cannot. Shall I have him take his braies down all the way merely to satisfy you further? No, I shall not. Why, in another moment you will be blaming this actor and theater for the terrible earthquake of 1580." That prompted more laughter. With a pointed glance at Thomas, he added, "We have among us right here experts on the subject of supernatural beings. And you will find none such here. You must shoulder your arms and look elsewhere."

No doubt Walsingham's name carried weight with the witchfinder, who looked between him and Thomas while stepping back at last, bumping into Alexander the Great, whose smooth, full-cheeked face and nicely formed mouth might have suggested that beneath his beard and makeup, he, too, was a woman. His hazel eyes gazed upon D'Arcy with distaste. "You had best go," he suggested to the witchfinder, "and contemplate your biblical folly elsewhere. Our behavior"—he reached over to the "philosopher" beside him, and draped an affectionate arm around his shoulders—"would only shock you into shooting some perfect innocent."

D'Arcy again blushed, and finally squeaked, "But I'm not wrong." Even so, he turned at last and pushed his way out of the backstage room, followed by his two guards.

The actors roared at his departure and fell back into chattering once more.

Burbage said, "Try shall I once more to introduce you to our Campaspe. This is young Simon Wyntour."

"Wyntour?" repeated Thomas. The name carried an odd familiarity.

Wyntour hastily changed into a shirt and doublet, pulled up tights, and drew loose slops over them. Meanwhile, he spoke to both Thomas and Walsingham. "I did, in fact, come to London from Horsham, though it used not to be a crime." He looped a baldric supporting a sheathed dagger around his hips, finally pulled on his boots, and placed a cap upon his head. To Thomas he said with a gesture at Walsingham, "He implied you're an expert in supernatural beings. I should like to hear more of what you know on that subject, but another time, I think." Wyntour turned as if to leave, then paused to add, "Oh, and I should tell you that you are refulgent in red, sir."

The actor attempted to leave then, but other members of the company engaged him before he could escape the room, and the happy cluster of them headed off together, no doubt to some nearby alehouse.

Burbage commented, "He has a great future with us so long as his voice holds out. We've one or two a few years older and already confined to male parts, for their falsettos play them now false."

Perplexed in that he wore no red at all and intrigued by Simon Wyntour's allusion to Walsingham's comment, Thomas made to follow after, but Walsingham caught him by the arm and pulled him aside. "Not quite yet, my good fellow. This," he said, barely audible over the din in the room, "our Alexander, is the person I wished you to meet in coming here. Christopher Marlowe, student, poet, and—of more importance to you—a spy in my employ."

PART FOUR:
SYNDONY

XXXI. Maleficium

Following the performance of *Campaspe*, Thomas, Walsingham, and Marlowe dined alongside the rollicking actors at a victualing house, the Dolphin Inn on Houndsditch Street. The late afternoon was warmer than it had been the other night. Walsingham made introductions: Christopher Marlowe was twenty-one years old, and freshly arrived from Cambridge, where Walsingham had recruited him. "He steps into the world of theater as smoothly as he has done that of espionage. Between the two of you, I anticipate there is no secret that does not unravel." Thomas and Marlowe observed each other as if neither really trusted that description or perhaps each other—certainly not yet. Thomas would have paid more attention to the conversation, but he was keeping one eye on Simon Wyntour at the tables across the tavern, as he reexamined their earlier conversation, no less frustrated for the effort.

Walsingham went on. In the year Thomas had been absent, Marlowe had made inroads in the English College in Rheims, following much the same path that Thomas had charted before him alongside Watson. "Would you be surprised were I to tell you, this path led him straight to Paris and the personages of Paget and Morgan?"

Those names snapped him back into the conversation. "I thought we demolished that plot when we arrested Throckmorton," Thomas replied, adding, "Otherwise I would not have gone off on my own business." He wasn't entirely sure that was the truth, but it made for a defensible excuse.

Sternly, Sir Francis said, "We shattered *a* plot. The fragments spun away from where we struck. But e'en a piece of pottery, once smashed, retains a memory of the shape it once knew."

Somewhat chagrined, Thomas asked, "Did we achieve anything, then? Other than fitting Throckmorton's head on a spike."

"Of course we did," Walsingham assured him. "However, that hardly means we have vanquished our enemies. They must always gather themselves and try again. And again. Until from this Earth we expunge them all." He glanced at the play's Alexander. "What say you, Marlowe?"

The young poet continued to chew his salted ham and seemed to be giving this some thought. He wiped one hand on the napkin thrown over one shoulder, then said, "Were either of you aware that the city of London allows no more than forty taverns? Yet there's no limit to the number of churches. I believe I am outraged."

It was so casually blasphemous that Thomas had to stifle a laugh while glancing sidelong at Walsingham to see how he reacted. He, as if he'd heard nothing, concentrated upon his roasted conies.

It was decided that the two of them were to meet at Seething Lane in the morning to make arrangements, presumably for a return trip to Rheims or Paris. Walsingham paid the bill and left enough coinage to cover more ale if they chose. Then, tall and solitary as a ghostly shadow, he departed.

"What do you think of him?" Thomas asked Marlowe.

"He is Lucifer," came the reply.

Thomas laughed. "I had the very same thought when first I met him."

Marlowe drank more ale. "One day I shall find a place for him in some drama." He glanced over at the other actors while he spoke. "I am curious about you. Sir Francis in his incessant praising of you claims you have a remarkable facility for disguise. How does one develop such a skill and not be of the theater culture?"

That was a question for which Thomas had no ready answer. He said only, "People see what they wish to see, and what they're expecting."

"Well, yes, and that's the secret of every one of us who treads the boards, especially of those donning women's clothing and mannerisms for their part."

The comment caused Thomas to glance away from Simon

Wyntour. He apprehended that Marlowe had been studying him during the meal.

"You do know that every one of them is in love with Simon, yes? In his performance, half the company see the perfect woman. The other half worship his beautiful self and the matter of his sex counts as nothing."

"Which are you?"

"Oh, I'm the one who watches, amused by 'em all." He waved a hand in the air. "Let Jupiter dandle Ganymede on his knee in full view of everyone. I will not turn away nor feel shame beholding that half-forbidden expression of love."

"Only half-forbid?" When Marlowe only smiled slyly, he said, "A spectator, then."

"Until I find myself a willing participant. As John the Baptist was with Jesus—which is Christianity's Jupiter and Ganymede, though I certainly will be damned for suggesting it." He watched Thomas closely for his reaction. "Do I shock or offend thee?"

Thomas cocked an eyebrow. "I have seen and known too much for such harmless contemplation to shake me, Master Marlowe."

"But you are what, a decade my senior? Not that much more could you have witnessed, surely." His teasing was an attempt to draw Thomas out. Marlowe blasphemed as a way to measure people, to draw out their prejudices and prevarications. Thomas refused to give him the reaction he wanted.

Then Simon Wyntour stood up from the tables at the far end and made to leave. Thomas quickly gathered himself together and got to his feet. "Have we paid our bill?"

Marlowe replied, "We have. And I shall join you, at least so far along Bishopsgate as you go."

"You needn't."

"Well." He gave Simon Wyntour a sidelong glance. "Mayhap I would vie for a tumble of my own. There are numerous houses along Bishopsgate."

It was impossible to tell how much he meant any of his words and how much was his targeting a weak spot to work. In any case, the young actor at the center of the discussion was exiting the inn. There was no more time. "Fine," he replied. Whatever Marlowe said now, Thomas would let it pass. It was a distraction.

On the way to the door, another actor hailed Marlowe—a lean young man, no more than Marlowe's age, with a ring in his ear, and his beard trimmed short like Thomas's. He'd played one of the philosophers. "How goeth *Dido*?" he called. His gaze took in Thomas as well.

"In all things I am behind, but rest assured there's a part for you." He gestured at Thomas. "Here is a friend of Walsingham's."

"The devil has friends now? This is news."

"And this," Marlowe said to Thomas, "is Will Shakespeare. Actually, you both have in common that Walsingham believes you can play anything."

"Truly." Shakespeare leaned back as if to reassess him. "What company are you in?"

"None," Thomas replied. "Marlowe exaggerates."

"Oh, he does that as often as he exhales the air."

Thomas looked to the door and back. "Forgive me my rudeness, but in haste I must go." He pushed past Shakespeare.

Marlowe explained, "*Campaspe* stole his heart." He winked, then followed Thomas out of the inn. He had on pattens to protect his good shoes, and so clopped out onto the pavers.

Although it was not terribly late, the cold sky was crepuscular. Simon Wyntour had turned to head north on Bishopsgate Street.

Marlowe, coming up behind Thomas, declaimed, "'As for myself I walk abroad o'nights! And kill sick people groaning under walls.'"

Headed off in pursuit of the actor, Thomas asked, "What's that?"

"It's from a play I'm writing e'en now."

"Well, feel free to continue, provided you can walk faster while you emote." He increased his stride up the incline. The young actor was still visible ahead in the gloom.

Marlowe went on, "Sometimes I go about and poison wells. And now and then..."

Simon Wyntour had just come abreast of Bedlam Hospital when three figures stepped out of the shadows of Fisher's Folly across the road and into the light cast from within Bedlam. The leading figure wore a heavy dark cloak and a lighter, perhaps gray, capotain, and had a spade beard. The two flanking him wore heavy leather doublets over galligaskins but no cloaks. They each carried a long-handled glaive.

Even before the lead man spoke, Thomas sensed a buzzing communication taking place. It vibrated in his skull. The trio were Yvags; more than that, the leading figure himself was an Yvagvoja. The elves were dedicating a precious resource to this encounter.

The leader proclaimed, "Under the Witchcraft Act of 1563, I hereby arrest the witch who goes by the name of Wyntour for acts of *maleficium* committed in league with the devil!"

Upon sight of the trio, Marlowe had ceased reciting. He came up beside Thomas. "Our lovely Simon accosted by two witchfinders in one afternoon? That seems excessive. I could ride an hour in any direction from here and encounter none at all. Other than his beauty what is *so* extraordinary about him?"

"This is something else, I fear," Thomas replied, and continued forward. But Marlowe grabbed him by the arm and swung him about.

"And you are *drunk*, I say!" Marlowe announced loudly. One look at Marlowe's winking expression and Thomas knew what he was doing.

In reply, he bellowed, "'Tis not I who indulged, you knavish coxcomb!" He shoved both hands against Marlowe, who obligingly pretended to be pushed up the road toward the witchfinder. The trio had paused to watch the spectacle of two oblivious drunkards lurching their way.

Shoved again, Marlowe turned and shambled toward them, arms out to implore the witchfinder. "God's light, do you hear how this apple-squire accosts me? Heh? You, sir, will you bear witness?" He went straight for the witchfinder as if unaware of the armed guards.

Without hesitation, the man stepped quickly back and flung aside the edge of his cape. Beneath it, he held a wheellock pistol. "Begone!" he yelled and raised the gun.

Thomas had already drawn his rapier as if to run Marlowe through, but was too far away to do anything other than make a leap forward. The gun wavered; the witchfinder couldn't quite decide which of them to shoot. That gave Marlowe a moment to straight-arm the man's weapon aside. Held at an angle, the pistol's obliging wheel spun and the gun fired, but its ball missed everyone and embedded in the outer wall of the hospital.

As if the shot were a signal, both guards lowered their glaives and charged. Marlowe, still holding onto the witchfinder, shoved him in their way. The nearest guard crashed into him and both fell.

The other guard avoided collision and charged straight at Thomas. Coming near, he thrust his glaive hard. Thomas twisted sideways to dodge the curved blade, arms up, and as the guard drew it back for a second attack, Thomas thrust low and stabbed his rapier alongside the glaive, running the guard through.

He turned in time to see the witchfinder scramble to his feet, only to be met as he stood by Simon Wyntour's rondel dagger, thrust at close quarters. The second guard sprang to his feet and with his glaive swatted Simon in the head. The young actor went down hard.

Marlowe struck the guard in the face, causing him to stumble back. Thomas ran him through. The guard pitched forward and lay face down.

Marlowe glanced at him, then blinked and looked a second time. He reached down and took the guard by the shoulder, rolling the body over.

Looking from the guard to Thomas and back to the creature lying there, Marlowe exclaimed, "But, it's a *demon*. Look at it!" The "guard" had become a gray and spiky thing with silvery hair and needlelike teeth. Its eyes, already seeing nothing in this world any longer, were golden and not at all normal. Its costume of leather doublet and paneled galligaskins remained, as did its weaponry. The Yvags weren't wearing their usual black armor beneath their disguise: They had anticipated no trouble in arresting Wyntour.

"Lindsay, *look*," insisted Marlowe, but Thomas did not need to look. He knew what they were. He was far more concerned about Simon Wyntour, but the actor was moving slowly, coming around. His face, mostly in shadow, appeared . . . but no, it must be a trick of the light.

"You are all right?" Thomas asked.

"I will be directly."

At that point the stabbed witchfinder, who had slowly crawled back toward the darkness of Fisher's Folly, succumbed to its wound. Face down, its body gave a great shake, and its skin turned bruised, spotted and discolored like the week-old corpse it was. Thomas knew they were near St. Botolph's. He would have liked to race there to catch what he was sure would be an Yvag clawing its way out of a tomb, but he would not be separated from Wyntour now. Marlowe was right: For some reason the young actor was being hunted by the Yvags. Simon's dagger was what anyone abroad at night might carry for protection, but it might also signify his awareness of being hunted.

As if to add weight to that idea, once Simon got to his feet, he gave the rotten corpse a hard kick. It was clear from his expression he wanted to do far worse than that. He wiped the rondel dagger clean on the finder's cape before resheathing it.

Marlowe was going from body to body, studying the elven knights and, finally, the rotten corpse that had only moments ago been alive and threatening. Along the way he picked up one of the glaives. "This is all magic, that is, *real* magic. At Cambridge I read a volume about the German magician Joannes Faustius. A pederast and dark magician who bargained with demons exactly like these. The faces, the eyes, those spikes, the—"

"We need to finish it quickly," Thomas said.

"Finish it?"

"If you remain a few minutes, these guards likely will reanimate for you."

The other two stared at him. Marlowe barked a laugh. "No," he said.

Thomas walked over and gently took the glaive from him, then turned, stepped over to the nearest guard, and with one swing cut off its head. The body jerked and kicked for a moment. Blood as black as pitch poured from it. The other two moved back from the inky blood.

"What are you doing?" Marlowe asked.

"Minimizing our risk," he replied, and beheaded the other guard.

The fleeing voja would immediately report to Nicnevin, but events had all happened quickly and in semidarkness. With any luck, the creature would have little to tell. They had already known the identity of Simon Wyntour, so nothing was gained or lost there, but they could only speculate on the two "drunkards" who had come to his rescue. They might blame someone from Burbage's company of players, but even then could they be sure?

"We've killed nothing human here but defended ourselves against monsters."

"Demons are *real*," Marlowe mused to himself. "Imagine if Faustius were to call..."

"Kit," Thomas said.

Marlowe blinked a few times.

"You'd best be on your way. Better we're not all together if any others of their kind have been alerted. And if arrests should be made, you'll be so good as to alert Walsingham or Burghley?"

Marlowe balked at leaving. "Yes, but . . . But you will tell me how it is you knew of these demons." He shook a finger at him. "At least once we set sail on the morrow?"

"I will tell you what there is to tell."

Marlowe stared at the grotesque scene as if he was memorizing every aspect of it, finally gave his head a nod, then walked away with increasing speed, past Thomas and Simon, up Bishopsgate Street and toward Shoreditch.

Once he was far enough off, Thomas told Simon, "You do not dare go home. They'll have found out everything about your comings and goings." He thought of Van der Paas's ruff shop, and how the Yvag had swiftly laid a trap for him there. "I've a house they likely know nothing about. I would urge you to come with me. We must discuss how you intend to survive here now the elven are hunting you."

Simon replied, "They've been hunting me since Roffey. It's what sent me here."

Roffey. That was the moment he remembered everything: the Lazarus-house, the mother a plague victim he tried to aid, and her children, Mathias and . . . not a brother but a sister named Syndony. So, who then was Simon? A cousin? Much too young to be Mathias. Thomas wanted to hear the story. He thought it remarkable that his path had crossed that of the Wyntours again. And that comment, that he was "refulgent in red," put him in mind of the strange sister. *Red* was all she'd said to him.

Simon was looking at him curiously now, a sidelong glance like that of a nervous horse, as if at any moment the lad might bolt. Thomas reached over and gripped Simon's shoulder as though to reassure him, but in reality to open himself and listen. Within was the silence he'd have expected of any normal person, but behind it and far less obvious than the persona of an Yvag was something like a shadow—as if a second identity lay folded deep within the first. Not Yvag, no, but certainly unusual.

"Come," he said.

"But these bodies?" Simon asked.

"Where better to have them found than at the door of Bedlam?

Madmen reporting dead demons and a rotting corpse. It will hardly be credited."

"Where are we—" asked Simon.

"It's this way."

The young actor hesitated, almost ready to bolt. Thomas gave him time to decide which he would do.

Finally, together, they walked down the deserted street.

XXXII. Lust of the Voja

The safe house was sure to be safer than Roffey and, after tonight, safer than where Simon had been lodging among the other actors.

Thomas placed new kindling beneath logs in the grate and set them alight. Once it was going, the two of them stood near the fire to warm themselves. He saw no reason to put off asking the key question.

"You know me, don't you?"

Simon bowed his head; his lips quirked. "Dr. Gerard. I remember how you were going to come visit us, but you never did."

"That's true. Life grew . . . unexpectedly complicated. But who is 'us'? I saw to the safety of Mathias and his sister, Syndony, and their mother. Are you a relative of theirs?"

"Yes, and no."

"Well, how did everyone fare?"

Simon answered, "Mother lived another year."

"Ah. I'm sorry it was not more," he replied.

"Mathias remains in Roffey. It's his farm now, but the witchmen aren't hunting for him."

No, they were expressly looking for a woman. For Syndony, no doubt. But in that case . . . He asked, "What exactly happened?"

"You mean with the witchmen?"

"I do. They seem to be expending resources to seek you. And where is Syndony? I have to assume she's the one D'Arcy and the possessed one thought they were hunting."

"Possessed." Simon's deep blue eyes met Thomas's gaze straight on; the young actor then let out a heavy sigh, and rippled like something fluid, liquid. In that moment, Thomas realized what he should have been able to guess.

The transformation itself was subtle—the loose doublet seemed to expand only a little in accommodating her breasts. The baggy slops by their nature hid any change that might have taken place in the shape of her hips. Her face lost some of its equine cast, becoming smoother and rounder, her lips more full, closer to how they had seemed painted as Campaspe. Her dark hair remained short. What he remembered most, however, were those expressive cobalt-blue eyes. They were unmistakable and he couldn't believe he had overlooked that one feature. But, then, she had been *glamouring*!

"Syndony," Thomas said.

She folded one arm and made a bow. "Doctor," she answered.

"Not any longer, I was forced to bid him adieu, and for reasons akin to your situation. He became hunted."

"Yet you're him just as he was when last I saw him. You've not aged a day. Is your art like mine, then? Do you reshape by will? Hide your true appearance?"

"I can, yes," he admitted. "Although it's generally to hide that I haven't changed."

"Can you—will you show me?"

He considered for a moment.

Then he concentrated while watching her face as he imagined himself into Kit Marlowe. From her expression, he captured Marlowe well. He released the glamour and rippled back into himself.

There was something like reverence in Syndony's expression: The face of someone who's been seeking another like herself for so long that she has long since given up hoping ever to find one.

"Yours is quite the cleverer disguise," Thomas told her. "A woman masquerading as an actor who then pretends to be a woman. You've found the perfect means to confound most any witch hunter. As Simon, who do you embody, then? Is it—"

"My brother. I know how he looks, how he carries himself, how he sounds. My voice," she said, "is the least malleable aspect."

"True for us both as it is for the Yvags when they cloak themselves as us," he agreed. "Glamouring tricks the eye, not the ear. Still, you lowered your voice enough to unstring D'Arcy."

"But not the other, the apricot one," said Syndony.

"I'm not certain I understand. Apricot?"

"In the same way you are red," she explained.

Head tilted, she half-lidded her eyes as she looked at him.

"There's a crimson nimbus that edges you—and did thus when first you encountered us." With her fingers she traced an outline shape around him.

"But what does it mean, this nimbus?"

"I cannot say, save that yours is unique. I've ne'er seen another one your color anywhere."

"But you see other colors?"

"Most people are a sort of dull tan or lavender, a soft halo. Now and then I've beheld those with yellow outlines, as if the sun is glowing around them. Those guards you dispatched in the road there wore *that* glow."

Glamoured Yvags. Was she saying she could identify Yvags hidden among humans on sight? "And the apricot?"

"The witchfinder I stabbed. His outline was that color, much more intense." Her expression hardened. "He was one of *them*."

"Them?" he asked. He knew what that meant to him but not to her.

Whatever memory she was looking at, it made her scowl. "Too many'a them."

He could see there was no pursuing that train of thought with her just now. "So you can glamour yourself as I do, and you recognize disguised elven demons on sight. How do you come to have these abilities?"

She frowned distantly. "Mathias should tell it you."

Thomas said, "But he is not here." By now they were warm enough to move off from the fire. Thomas invited her to sit on the bench beside it. He kept a bottle of wine on the cupboard, and retrieved it. No telling if it was potable, but he unsealed the cork and with a knife opened it, taking care not to stir up the liquid within. "This will undoubtedly be full of sediment, so you'll want to let it sit before you try drinking it."

She set it down as he suggested. He sat beside her with a cup of his own.

"What story would he tell if Mathias were here?"

"He would tell you the story of our father," she said. "He was a merchant tailor, a freeman of London, who traveled to fairs a good part of the year, measuring and selling cloth, meeting others of his livery. This meant that our mother was left alone frequently.

"There was another member of Father's livery company, a man of much higher rank named Gibson, who would come around when he'd gone. At those times this man would express his interest in Mother, claiming deep concern for her well-being, left alone with us as so often she was. She was quite beautiful, at least Gibson thought so, told her so. Mathias didn't think she teased or led him on, but Mathias was only three and knew nothing about how men and women could be together. And all the while, of course, this man claimed to be our father's good friend.

"Eventually—it was a year or more—our father left for many days, and Gibson came visiting in order to have his way with Mother. Once he had, it was as if he could not let her be. She was his obsession.

"Before long, she became with child. All the while Gibson returned again and again for more of her. He threatened that if she spoke out, and she dared denounce him, he would defame her. Meantime, our father came and went several times. At first he seemed to suspect nothing. At some point either he recognized that he could not'a been the father of the child she carried—of me—or else she could keep silent no longer, though speaking the words was sure to destroy them. She confessed to him what had happened, and what Gibson did to her each time my father went away, for his tastes were cruel.

"To satisfy himself of the truth of the situation, our father made a great show of going off to a fair in Oxford, but crept back home at first opportunity and waited. Hidden, he watched Gibson arrive and take charge. Where she put up a struggle, he threatened Mother exactly as she'd told Father he would.

"Then Father revealed his presence and offered Gibson no quarter, but struck him a fatal blow wi'an ax.

"Gibson did not die as anyone might expect. He burst like that witchman did in the street, but worse. His blood shot out of him and his body just rotted right before them. Mathias saw it, too. He said it scared him so that he would not sleep alone for months and months after. Mother screamed as the rotten thing collapsed on the floor of our house.

"After, the livery company didn't know quite what to do about

Gibson. This must be him dead an' all, but everything about it was wrong. No one could accuse Father of killing something what had obviously been dead for many years. Witchcraft was surely involved. Had a curse been placed upon Gibson or upon us? No one knew nor could sort it, and so they made it that Gibson had fled from his crimes. Was far easier to tell stories of how he had run off and it mattered little if these even contradicted one another, for it turned out our mother wasn't the only woman after whom the fiend had lusted. Within days many a man wanted to hang his corpse. But our mother was the only one with child because of it."

Thomas said, "He was a *lich*. It's a corpse to which one of the elven demons has attached itself. The witchfinder was such. The creatures, when they take control of a body in this way, they seem to lust after carnal pleasures, as though they've never known such pleasures before. That said, you are the first offspring of such a union I've heard of who wasn't gathered up by the Yvags as a changeling. I'm left wondering how it is they overlooked you."

"I'm told my birth coincided with a resurgence of plague, a bad year. People sequestered, and didn't trust one another. Fled the city where they could. 'Course the plague retreated the way it always does. Following so much death, though, Gibson became forgotten."

Thomas replied, "And no one came for you. They overlooked you."

"From that one's conquests, I seem to be the only offspring. It's possible the other women hid the truth of their being with child or took care of their state.

"This gift or curse of reshaping didn't present itself until after you'd left us in Roffey. I discovered it by accident. One day, while Mathias was speaking to me, I just became him. I didn't even know I'd done it." She looked down, then up at his eyes. "You're the first I've met who shares my . . . nature."

"As you are to me." He thought of Zhanedd, but he'd never encountered her as a human; the Yvags had already whisked her away by the time he learned of Innes's fate. Yet there it had been, right in front of him all this time—Balthair MacGillean, one of the first skinwalkers he'd ever encountered, a drowned corpse, had sired a daughter on his sister. "I have to say, this gives me small hope that there might be more like you and me of whom we know nothing, but who also might have eluded the nets the demons cast."

"If they escape those, they'll still have the witchmen hunting them same's I do."

"I think you and I are the very reason for the Yvag witchmen."

"Yvag."

"It's what the elven race call themselves. Any other offspring, if they survived, must be as cautious as you. If not, they'll be found, taken from this world. Tell me, can you not see your own color?"

"No," she answered. "Everyone *but* myself."

"So, how is it the witchfinders got on to you in the first place?"

She drank some wine. "I remembered how you laid your hands upon my mother and she was much better afterward. I found that I could do something akin to it, and that people often felt better or threw off their fever afterward."

He nodded. "And, of course, eventually someone told."

"A neighbor I couldn't help, and they blamed me instead, said I'd killed their child they'd asked me to cure. But I couldn't cure him. I could do nothing."

"Inevitable, I think," he said. "As a physician treating plague victims, I was sometimes blamed for their getting worse. Even for remaining free of the plague while I treated them. Everything is dark magic when you know nothing. And we are all ignorant men, pretending to recognize remedies for imbalanced humors we've fabricated."

"But how did *you* come to be this way?"

"Well," he said, "my tale's a bit more complicated than yours."

He then provided her a condensed version of his story. As he spoke, he was reminded of the night he'd explained himself to Isabella Birkin so very long ago in the heart of Sherwood Forest. At the end of his telling, she stared wide-eyed and exclaimed, "Four hundred *years*?"

"Approximately."

She looked worried. "Is that going to happen to me?"

"I know not. It would seem that you're aging as most anyone would thus far. Whether that changes, slows, I can't say. I have nothing to compare you to." That was certainly true. She was like him not only in terms of her ability to glamour; she wanted revenge on these creatures for how one of them had cruelly used her mother. It made no difference that she was the by-product of that rape, just as he could not be dissuaded from taking revenge on the Yvag race for their casual destruction of his brother and father, and the punishment inflicted upon his sister.

For awhile they sat in silence. He contemplated her situation and the very real likelihood that another Yvag witchfinder would follow this one, and probably be more cautious if not more lethally inclined now that the "witch" had proved herself capable of fighting back. They would surely blame her in part if not entirely for the three deaths.

Thomas said, "They might hunt for me, for Marlowe as well, but we'll be away at first light. Your company of actors might protect you, but I worry at the ease with which one of them might be replaced. Even if you recognized the change in their aureola, they might trap you."

"I think I must flee again," said Syndony. "I can't be in the others' company every minute. Eventually, the masquerade of being Simon exhausts me and I need time as myself to recover."

So, he thought, glamouring wore her out the way reshaping wore down an Yvag or him. He leaned forward. "With your gifts, though, you at least have the advantage of them. You can identify an Yvag before it even gets near you. They still have no awareness of your capability." Even as he said it, he could imagine it failing to protect her. Eventually, another witch-seeking trio might find her alone in the theater, recovering from being "Simon" all day. And this time they would come expecting a fight.

He ought to clear what he wanted to suggest with Walsingham and probably Marlowe, too, but he didn't see how he could at the moment. "What would you say to not returning to Burbage's players just now, but traveling with me and Marlowe instead?"

"I shouldn't. You have affairs to conduct, matters I know nothing of."

Thomas nodded. "True, we do have business to conduct. However, these demons *will* come seeking you again and that theater is a fixed location. They have only to watch it and bide their time. And now they're on their guard. I've eluded them in a similar way, traveling long enough for them to give up hunting me. If you come with us, no one among the players will know where you've gone. No doubt they'll object to your absence, but they won't be able to tell anyone where to find you. If you return to the theater later, you can always say you were kidnapped by pirates."

She looked him in the eyes and broke into a smile.

Thomas added, "Before you decide for certain, understand that we might be gone weeks or months. There is a scheme unfolding, the size and nature of which no one can say just yet. Your skill with the dagger might come in handy, too. I know your ability to see these elven creatures will."

"And when we come back, 'Simon' need not appear again?"

"A decision to make when the time comes, though I think whoever he is he will not be called Simon anymore."

The Yvags were hunting this magical woman, even if they didn't know quite what they had hold of. He hoped he did.

All he had to do now was to convince Marlowe of it. With luck maybe they wouldn't have to tell Walsingham at all.

XXXIII. A Plethora of Poleys

"Things have changed," Walsingham told them. Thomas and Marlowe exchanged a worried glance.

They had arrived at Seething Lane, expecting to be sent off immediately to Rheims. Instead, Sir Francis invited them to walk with him.

Outside, the air was quite brisk, clouds scudding across the blue sky on a breeze that whisked away the more fetid aspects of the streets. It soon became apparent that they were heading to the Tower, and that earned another traded look. A concerned Thomas strained to listen for chirring on the off chance that the spymaster had been replaced in the night. To his relief, there was none.

"This remains between us for now," said Sir Francis. "Put simply, the influence of Morgan and Paget has reached into Seething Lane. You may know that, not so many months ago, my daughter, Frances, wed Sir Philip Sidney, and subsequently—while Sir Philip is fighting in the Netherlands—has been living under my roof along with various attendants of the Sidneys, including one by the name of Robert Poley. I learned last night that this same Poley has sent word to Morgan of his position in my house, with a promise to deliver any and all gathered intelligence directly to him. Poley carries correspondence back and forth between Frances and Sir Philip, and as such is free to come and go."

Marlowe asked, "Can you not turn him?"

Walsingham frowned. "It is perhaps early days—hours, really—but I do not expect much joy there. I had Robert Poley imprisoned previously in Marshalsea, and while he insists he would carry intelligence for me, he almost certainly lies and would deliver for Morgan and Paget."

"What would you have us do?" asked Thomas.

They approached the West Gate, where the soldier on duty stiffened at their approach. Walsingham passed him without acknowledgment and entered the Tower. Inside, they climbed three flights of steps to where many cells lined the corridors.

He drew up before a studded door, had the guard unlock it and pull it back. Inside, prostrate on a small bed, lay Robert Poley. "He has been exhausted by his visit with the Duke of Exeter's Daughter," Walsingham said darkly.

Thomas knew what that meant. Poley would be fortunate that his shoulders were still attached.

He walked over to Poley to observe him closely. Marlowe and Walsingham followed. The room contained a small table and stool, and a slops bucket. On the table lay paper, quill, an inkpot, and a candle. Nothing had been written on the paper.

Poley was a small man, thin and lightly bearded, his brown hair pasted to his forehead. Thomas imagined glamouring himself as Poley. He would have difficulty maintaining so diminutive an illusion.

At his back, Walsingham said, "You ask what I would have you do. It is this: You and Marlowe will return to the English College in Rheims. Now that Poley has sent word to Morgan, there will be some repercussion, ripples if you will, throughout that network, and you need to be in place to learn of these ripples. With Poley locked away here, we will in all likelihood have a single small opportunity to make use of our information."

After a moment, Thomas said, "And what if someone were to replace Poley?"

Walsingham smiled indulgently. "I admire your skills, Four, but surely even the greatest artist of disguise cannot shrink himself so substantially as this. Neither of you is small enough to pass."

"No, not I."

"Who, then?"

Thomas made no reply, but Marlowe caught his eye and must have read his thoughts, uttering a disbelieving, *"No."*

Walsingham studied them both as if he might be able to perceive what they were pointedly not saying.

Thomas said, "Allow me—allow us—to return here in two hours and we will show you. It will prove much simpler than any attempt to explain."

Walsingham tapped together his fingertips. "Very well. Two hours."

On the way out, Marlowe said to Thomas, "Why does he call you 'Four'?"

Thomas answered, "I've used up my first three lives."

Previously, Thomas had promised to tell Marlowe everything about the Yvags. As they strode through the city to the safe house again, and at Marlowe's insistence, he made good on that promise, receiving in return half a dozen amazed or skeptical glances. His depictions of their world, their schemes, and their involvement in English affairs of state left Marlowe eyeing him sidewise.

Upon hearing an abbreviated version of Syndony's story, however, Marlowe burst out laughing. "Oh, this is exquisite," he said. "A woman treads the boards of the Theatre, faery-glamoured as a man who plays women for his livelihood. The Lord Mayor would hang the entire company if he found out. It's a mad enough tale you tell—demon creatures stealing babies and replacing people in order to manipulate matters of state."

"And yet you've seen some tiny fraction of it for yourself."

"I am aware. Then again, it takes no convincing me at all that at least half the reigning powers of this world are corrupted and deranged. That fool who assassinated Willem van Oranje only after he'd retired, was he one of these?" Of course, Thomas didn't know. "Well, Van Oranje was shot with a wheellock the same as I almost was last night."

"The most I can say about that is, the age of pistol assassinations and gunpowder plots has arrived." He thought of the caliver in Deptford that was almost the Queen's undoing.

"As I like to say, you must be proud, bold, pleasant, resolute. And now and then stab, as occasion serves. But to what end does all this transpire? What do these elvish demons desire so hotly?" Marlowe asked.

"Ultimately, to transmute the world to please them and choke us out."

"Then they're alchemists, your demons," said Marlowe. "And we are what, their base metals?"

"If you like."

"And you and she, you are both threats to their plans?"

"Potentially. And should they learn that you know this, you will now pose a threat as well. Syndony has a way of identifying them at a distance. She is the only person I've ever met with such a gift, though there may be others."

Marlowe thought about it a moment, then said, "And thus will our Simon aid Walsingham."

"If, once he beholds her, he doesn't have her arrested for witchcraft." They walked on in silence the rest of the way.

To Syndony, Thomas explained how the situation had changed overnight. "You would be working as we are, to protect the Queen and undermine all attempts to replace her with Mary of Scotland, but you'll be on your own for much of it. People you interact with won't know your true identity at all, while you'll know theirs, not to mention given your gifts whether or not they're humans, glamoured creatures or skinwalkers imitating people. It's the same as it was with the actors. It won't be for—"

"I'll do it," she said without hesitation.

"Oh." She startled him being so direct. "Aye. That's good. There is but one detail. We must reveal this ability of ours to Sir Francis Walsingham first."

Marlowe, behind him, stood leaning against the wall, shaking his head at the madness of the suggestion. "I do swear, he will shop you both to the witchfinders."

"Let us hope not, for the good of England and us. However, if he does, we need to be prepared to leave and not come back." To Syndony, he added, "Be sure you have an identity in mind to shift into."

"'Away with her to prison presently!'" Marlowe proclaimed.

"You're not helping."

"And thou art mad, both of you," Marlowe said.

"One thing more," Thomas said to Syndony. "You should be Simon this last time. I hope Walsingham will embrace our skills, but doubt he would ever consent to a woman performing onstage."

Nevertheless, at the appointed time, the three of them returned to the Tower. Thomas introduced "Simon" to the spymaster, who happily identified Burbage's Campaspe.

Walsingham remarked, "Four has convinced you to play Poley for us?"

Thomas replied only, "Let us go see."

Walsingham grudgingly assented and led the way again up the steps to the cells.

Poley was awake now. When the door opened, he stood up from the stool with some difficulty and warily observed the four people entering his tiny chamber. "Who's this boy?" he asked of Syndony, but no one answered him. She walked all the way around him, then nodded to Thomas. They went back out, and a guard closed and locked the door again before being dismissed.

"Performed you that for my benefit?" Sir Francis asked. "You are about the right size, lad, I grant you. But otherwise—"

Thomas took a position between the spymaster and Syndony. She closed her eyes. A tremor ran through her. She opened her eyes again, and Thomas stepped aside to give Francis Walsingham a full view of Robert Poley, standing in the corridor outside his locked cell.

For once even the spymaster was staggered. He approached, leaned in and studied her closely, then crossed to the studded wood door, opened the viewing panel in it. From within the tiny room the real Poley looked at him with weary eyes. By the time Walsingham turned back, Thomas, concentrating as she had done, had transformed himself into the swarthy assassin Henry Fagot.

Walsingham looked him up and down as recognition slowly shifted his expression. The space grew thick with tension, but he did not call for the guards. His eyes expressed calculation. "So," he said, "that *was* you in the embassy."

Thomas nodded. "And, with your permission, Sir Francis, Syn— Simon can be your Poley."

"How does he sound in the part?"

Deepening her voice, she said as Poley had, "'Who's this?'" It wasn't an exact match by any means, but then it didn't have to be. Morgan and Paget had never met Poley in person.

Walsingham nodded slowly to himself, as if imagining the entire chain of events yet to come. "I shall be accused of consorting with demons. Then again, I've been compared to the devil himself, so who else would I consort with?" To Thomas, he said, "When Bruno described you to me as someone who'd been at my side in Paris, I began to suspect, but could not understand how you changed shape, size, as well as color. But now I've the whole picture. If I may ask, what are you two? Certainly not witches as we countenance them. This is no magic that Dee or other necromancers have ever described and 'tis no trick of the light nor sleight of hand."

"True. It's no witchcraft. I would tell you we are both victims, but that would imply we have suffered and had all agency stripped from us by the elven, which is not quite true, although 'tis how they would prefer it."

"Your golden-eyed Yvags again."

"The same. We have suffered changes to our selves, but with the result that we are left, let us say, gifted now with abilities that can prove useful to you and your network—have already so proven, in my case."

Walsingham, as he often did whilst thinking, tapped his fingertips together. To Marlowe, he said, "And you knew this but said nothing?"

"I only learned it all myself just prior to arriving here."

"That is so," agreed Thomas.

"This being your exordium, what now will you do, if you both go off with Marlowe?"

"We will do as you described, Sir Francis. Robert Poley will arrive on Morgan's doorstep with some manner of information on your household and a promise of far more to come—you will have to give them something, some verifiable fact to secure his value to those two. We will hope that Morgan entrusts him with something, even as a test—a message, a letter. Marlowe and I will stand guard from the vantage of the English College, he as Marley and I as a new student he has recruited at Cambridge. We can use that as an excuse to introduce me to everyone, allowing us to enumerate who now resides there, and who should be watched. I anticipate we'll be present when Morgan and Paget send their next messages north."

Walsingham allowed himself a rare smile. "Number Four, as I have expressed upon occasion, you have a mind for subterfuge. This you describe we must do," he agreed. "All of it."

XXXIV. Treble Agents

Syndony Wyntour arrived in Paris, dressed in the clothing of Robert Poley taken from Walsingham's house: a patterned reddish doublet with elaborately slitted sleeves, cut to accommodate the codpiece stitched in a matching pattern amidst padded hose in a darker bloodred, and all beneath a dark gray cloak and matching velvet cap.

Approaching Morgan's home, she found herself gripped by intense fear that might have driven any number of people to turn away or flee to some safer ambit, but here the actor in her took over; this fear she knew well from the many plays in which she had already performed. It accompanied her to the curtain and out onto the stage. The audiences for *Campaspe*, for *Sapho and Phao*, had proved to her that while such fear might be warranted, it could not keep her from executing her part flawlessly. She thought of a line Alexander spoke in *Campaspe*: "Where do you first begin, when you draw any picture?" Lyly, the playwright, understood perfectly what an actor did. They started with something small and essential, then built out from there until they had fashioned a whole person who was not them. She reminded herself of Thomas's words in briefing her: "Neither Morgan nor Paget has ever met Poley. Yours will be the defining version of him. They will be far more convinced once they see what you've brought them. The opportunity of having you placed within the very household of the spymaster himself is too great a treasure for them to pass up. You are a unicorn," he said, and squeezed her arm.

Recalling that touch, she all but shivered. Despite that they had known each other only a few days, she felt an affinity for him beyond words. He was the doctor who had rescued her mother and brother, who had seen her unnaturalness and not been terrified or angry, who for all that he'd cut the heads off two demons right in front of her, seemed remarkably gentle and thoughtful. They had slept two nights in the same bed in his house and he hadn't once tried to touch her or have his way. Of course, he knew her history now . . . and that was the other thing they shared: the desire to punish if not destroy the Yvags as he named them. The deep-seated anger he carried with him was a match for her own. Those close to them had been abused by the elves, and they could not avenge themselves sufficiently to be satisfied that they'd done enough. Granted, it was also possible that he simply preferred boys or men, but unless she was deceiving herself, she sensed his attraction to her *as* herself. He was respectful.

A few minutes later, she was at the door on Rue des Augustins. It was opened by a thin-faced man with short, receding reddish-brown hair, a sharp nose, and the distrusting eyes of a bird of prey. She introduced herself. At the name, his thin eyebrows raised slightly— the most interest he would reveal—and he stepped back to let her enter.

In Rheims, "Marley" was greeted warmly by Doctors Allen and Parsons, the more so for the new convert he had brought along, a shaggy-haired and bearded blue-eyed man named William Colerdin from Cambridge. An "excellent candidate" in Marlowe's assessment. "Colerdin" discoursed fervently in particular upon Jeanne d'Arc in explaining his desire to actively pursue the Catholic cause. The way he spoke of her, it was almost as if he'd known her, spoken with her.

Allen remarked that Colerdin reminded him a bit of another student they'd had perhaps four years earlier, a young Jesuit who they feared had been caught by Wallsingham's forces, for they'd never heard from him again.

The College itself was humming with more excitement than either Thomas or Marlowe had seen before: A group of travelers had arrived from Rome. They were the first here to have had an audience with the new pope, Sixtus V. Parsons in particular wanted to know how Sixtus was going to compare with Gregory XIII. These pilgrims were led by young Anthony Babington, a slender, boyish-faced believer in their cause who seemed to be of the curious opinion that Mary of Scotland awaited him in particular. Allen explained that Babington had once before acted as a courier of letters to Mary in 1580, after befriending Thomas Morgan, while she was held by his former master, the Earl of Shrewsbury; when they moved her to Tutbury and her gaoler changed, however, security tightened and he was no longer able to reach her.

Nevertheless, Babington made his odd claims. Mary knew he was coming, and he was going to rescue her where all others had failed.

In answer to Parsons' questions, he remarked that, upon ascension, Pope Sixtus had immediately responded to the lawlessness that had grown within the Papal States under Gregory. Because of his iron hand, thousands of brigands had already been arrested and dealt with. "There are more heads on spikes across the Ponte Sant'Angelo than you'll find ripe melons in the market. Under him, I'm assured we *will* finally bring Mary to the throne." That prompted a cheer.

Marlowe and Thomas circulated among the group of travelers. Allen took Marlowe to meet a newly appointed deacon among the gathering named Gilbert Gifford. Gifford was pale, dark-haired, and spoke with a slight lisp. He had a short chin beard. Allen informed Marlowe and Thomas that "Gifford was expelled from our college in Rome; consequently, I initially opposed his readmittance. However, his cousin, Dr. William Gifford, who does teach for us now, spoke up on his behalf, and prevailed on Dr. Parsons in his favor. He has been ordained as a deacon, though I confess, as a student of theology, his close friend Christopher Hodgson has proven much more satisfactory."

Allen assigned Gifford to introduce Marley to other new students about. Quite a number of new faces had arrived in the short time he had been absent. Thomas took care to take note of any who'd come from Cambridge and might be suspicious of Colerdin, but no one appeared to find his presence worth questioning, perhaps as a result of Marlowe keeping the focus upon himself with his little blasphemies. As Colerdin, Thomas stayed as close as possible to Parsons in order to eavesdrop on the bombinating dialogue between voja and *lich*.

Gifford bragged to them that he had carried letters for Mary in the past and would do so again, as if he was in competition with Babington.

Another of Babington's traveling companions, named John Savage, intended to act as Mary's right hand to "swat the gadfly queen" when the opportunity arose. He proclaimed that he would personally assassinate the excommunicated Elizabeth. The room pulsed with such zealotry.

Back in their room, Thomas and Marlowe compared notes. Savage, Gifford, and the high-strung Babington were the three they both agreed bore closest scrutiny.

Marlowe told him, "Savage was a soldier before this, serving under Farnese and fighting the Calvinists up and down the Spanish Road. I asked in reply if that meant he had set aside his weapons of war to train as a Jesuit. He laughed and said that weapons of war encompassed more than swords and guns. Words could be the sharpest weapons of all."

"Hardly a foolish soldier, then."

"Marry, almost the response of a poet," said Marlowe. "All of them revere Morgan as if he's the great strategist. Verily he may be, for somehow in this subversive tapestry those two in Paris have woven together the Pope, the French, the Spanish, and the Catholic lords of the north."

Thomas replied, "Mendoza, Castelnau, Paget and Morgan—the very same players as before, if anything, revived and hungrier," Thomas replied. He shook his head. "I worry now I've thrown Syndony into a lion's den."

"E'en it's so, no doubt have I that she will come through," Marlowe reassured him. "She's too brazen to fail. In any case, I've learned that Babington and his little society are following Father Ballard back across the waters in a few days."

"Ballard."

"A priest here in Rheims, one with a great deal of influence."

"We must find excuse to join them on their journey."

"Yes, but Deacon Gifford is not going with them, so he says."

"Staying here, is he?"

Marlowe replied, "I don't yet know."

"Yes, we received your message," Charles Paget said to Syndony. He had short gray-brown hair, pouchy blue eyes, and a beaked nose, giving him an incongruously jovial look. "You've become a member of Walsingham's household. However was that managed?"

Phlegmatic Morgan appeared to be half asleep on the nearby bench as he held the letter that had preceded her arrival. She doubted he was anything close to dozing at all. His aura was too lively.

Keeping her voice raspy, she said, "My cousin, Christopher Blount, secured my position there, sir. He is a close friend of Sir Philip Sidney, who recently married Walsingham's daughter, Frances. The letter explains that, and how it is that I am trusted among the household."

"Trusted enough to leave it without notice," Morgan said. Only now did he look up. "You did not join Sidney in his war with the Spanish in the Netherlands. You prefer to *avoid* action?"

"I am assigned to the household of Lady Frances, not to the battlefield. That said, I carry letters between the two of them, which allows me a certain flexibility in traveling." Underneath the questions, posed almost as afterthoughts, she had a growing sense that Morgan didn't believe her story at all. She began to fear that he had met the real Poley before and knew she was false. Still, what else could she do but stick to the story they had worked out at Seething Lane? At least Morgan and Paget were both mortals and not elves, and she had read a copy of the letter Poley had smuggled out to them, so she knew what to emphasize and how to phrase it.

Then Morgan abruptly sat upright, hard eyes wide open, and set the letter down beside him. "We happen to know that a group charged with bringing rebellion against Elizabeth is even now meeting at the English College. Friends of ours, who would greatly benefit from information provided by a person in your position. I will write you a new letter of introduction. As it happens, we have a packet of letters to be delivered to Mary of Scotland at this very moment. At the College, introduce yourself to a man named Gilbert Gifford and inform him you are our new go-between, embedded right in the middle of Walsingham's nest of spies."

"Gifford."

"If Gifford doesn't know what to do with you, I'll make garters of his guts. In the meanwhile, stay and entertain us with tales of the spy headquarters of which old Walsingham is so proud." He ran his sharp reddish mustaches one after the other between thumb and forefinger. "We would all of us know his secrets."

XXXV. Babington

And so, some few days later and late in the afternoon, Robert Poley arrived on horseback at the English College and was taken directly to Dr. Parsons, who wore his short gray beard brushed and was never seen about without his scholar's cap. With Parsons were Anthony Babington and a few other students. Poley's immediate reaction upon being introduced to Parsons was to take a step back, as if Parsons' persona overwhelmed him.

Poley wore the same reddish outfit he'd worn arriving in Paris. He explained to them, nervously, that he had come from Paris with correspondence he was to present only to a Gilbert Gifford. Allen asked to see this casket of letters, but Poley politely refused, and maintained his distance. "They are for no one else but Gifford," he said adamantly. "That is my remit."

Young Babington condescended to smile, though somewhat resentfully in that Poley's materials were not being shared with him, either. He inserted himself by saying, "Pardon me, Doctor," and then addressing Poley before anyone could interrupt him, "You were sent by the two who are one?"

Poley studied him carefully before replying. "I am. And bound for the one who is all."

Babington smiled more broadly, and turned about as if taking everyone else into his confidence. "There. That is the proper code. He is who he claims." As if that had been at issue.

They sent for Gifford then. By chance, accompanying him were the two recent arrivals from Cambridge, Marley and William Colerdin.

Poley stared hard at Colerdin, as if he might make Colerdin hear his thoughts.

In front of them, Poley repeated that he was carrying letters he could give to no one but Gifford. Gifford clasped his hands almost as in prayer. "You see, it is as I said. I have been entrusted with our queen's correspondence before and so I am once more." He held out a hand. Poley drew the wooden casket of letters from beneath his cape and handed it to Gifford. "You have done your job now and can be at ease," Gifford said.

Poley replied, "I cannot, in fact, sir. I must return to the household of Sir Francis Walsingham so as not to raise suspicions and thereby limit my future utility to you all."

After that, everyone wanted to know what Robert Poley could tell them of Seething Lane. Gifford said, "Dr. Allen, might someone show our new friend where he can lodge?"

Babington pressed forward eagerly. "Please, allow me," he said, and hurried over to escort Poley out. Thomas as Colerdin moved as if to stop him but Marlowe held him back.

"Wait now. She can handle herself," he whispered. "She's got past Paget, Morgan, and Parsons already, has she not?" Thomas glared but allowed Marlowe's reasoning to govern him.

That evening, plans were finalized for Babington and his group to return to England alongside Father John Ballard, a Catholic priest of Rheims, to whom he had allied himself. Tall, dark-complexioned Ballard, in his blue-black robe with a rosary at his waist, flat-brimmed hat upon his head, and a staff in hand, looked the part of someone who had made many journeys, some deep into Scotland to gather supporters to the Catholic cause. He asserted that he would connect Babington and the others with an extensive network he had built among the Northern gentry, which would act as a spider's web, drawing together and sticking to the likes of the Walsinghams and Cecils and even Elizabeth herself. He and Parsons stayed close and chatted throughout, although most of the time they just seemed to be sitting side by side. Even at the distance of half the dining hall, Thomas listened to the buzzing whispers being traded back and forth.

Babington hardly had to insist for Ballard to add Robert Poley to their group of travelers—simply one more nondescript pilgrim was no inconvenience.

Gifford, however, refused to accompany them. He and his cache of letters were bound for Rye, he said. It was well known that Walsingham had spies everywhere at Dover. Just to be safe, Gifford's letters would take a different route, using the busy pilgrims' arrival as camouflage.

This gathering at the College set the wheels of the intertwining plots in motion. Although Mary had been shunted from the relaxed security of Sheffield Castle to the more tightly controlled Chartley Manor, Gilbert Gifford insisted he had the means to deliver the letters to her via a safe route undiscovered by either Walsingham or Cecil. "There is a beer keg with a secret compartment in it," he explained to them all. Thomas and Marlowe kept perfectly straight faces while Gifford detailed his cunning delivery method. Thus communication with their chosen Queen would shortly resume.

Ballard would have his supporters in the north at the ready and awaiting a signal to strike. That signal was to come in the form of John Savage's murder of Elizabeth at a spot he had chosen near St. Giles in the Fields. The conspirators thereafter talked of nothing else but how they would bring down her reign. Every detail was worked out and in conversation embellished. Savage extolled the late William Parry, who had devised the simplest of plans, with himself and one other accompanying her coach ostensibly as guardians, drawing their pistols and firing into the coach from either side. How regrettable that Parry had not had the opportunity to carry out this execution. "It is," remarked Savage, "very much the model for my own stratagem."

Through all of it, Thomas could barely sit still. He was compelled to speak with Syndony before they went separate ways again. Tomorrow they would be in the company of Ballard and his followers, and after that were off to different destinations again for who knew how long. The difficulty was getting her away from Babington, who had, for whatever reason, clearly become infatuated with Poley. Marlowe helped him arrange to meet her in the empty room where canon and civil law were taught in the day. Marlowe would keep Babington entertained meanwhile, no doubt with a few of his blasphemies to hold everyone's attention by stirring up his devout followers. The room contained three rows of eight angle-topped desks and accompanying narrow benches, all directed at the front of the room, where the master's seat stood like a large pulpit or throne. What little light there was came through two arched and mullioned windows.

Arriving first, Thomas took a seat on a bench off to one side, where he had often sat while attending lectures on canon law during his previous infiltration of the College.

A few minutes later, Robert Poley entered surreptitiously, pausing at the door until able to make out the shape of Thomas where he sat. He stood up, and she crossed the room quickly and embraced him. Thomas found himself holding her close, as well. Until that moment, he hadn't admitted to himself exactly how worried he was for her.

She stepped back. "Liaisons are difficult if not perilous here."

"True, but we're unlikely to have any other opportunity to confer."

Eyes wide, Syndony told him, "There are two of *them* here. You warned me of Parsons, but that other priest is also one."

"Father Ballard, yes, I know. He's newly arrived. I can hear his passenger and Parsons conversing, like a field of crickets. At least you only have to see their emanations." He smiled, trying to make a little light of the perilous situation.

She told him, "It's all further complicated because Babington is in love with Poley, or so he professes. He refers to me already as *his Robyn*. I need do nothing in order to intoxicate him."

Thomas suppressed his own ire at Babington's infatuation, and asked simply, "How serious a complication is it?"

"Thus far I can manage him. But it also may be an opportunity. From others in his group, I know he has a wife at home. He married young, and part of his undertaking of pilgrimages and the like stems from him not wishing to address her. His nature, let us say, is otherwise persuaded. He's both rash and insecure. He reminds everyone constantly of his close bond with Queen Mary."

"You doubt him?"

"Only because he is compelled to say so at every opportunity. Although I'm no seasoned spy, I know enough to call Babington loose-lipped and foolish. So, ay, I trust him not at all and will try to use his flawed character to advantage."

They were calming each other with the conversation. Thomas said, "Seasoned or no, had I not seen you perform on stage, I should say you'd found your calling in this rôle."

She smiled secretly. "I confess it, I do enjoy the frisson of the intrigues at least a little. Morgan, I thought certain, had found me out, but it resolved he plays all parties as if about to accuse them. His way of testing the nerves of everybody." Somewhat shyly, she added, "I do thank you for the part."

He bit his tongue rather than admitting to her that he'd enjoyed none of it and had been on pins and needles until he'd caught sight of her as Poley. He said calmly instead, "Gifford travels to Rye. If there is any way you can communicate to Walsingham's agents in Dover to arrest him there, that will greatly help. In all likelihood you will reach land first."

She asked, "And how do I contact his agents?"

"Convince Babington to pause for an ale at The White Horse, or at very least take yourself there. They will find you. You can say you've been sent by Number Four."

"You *must* follow him?" she asked. She did not mask her own unhappiness at their renewed separation.

"Same as I would say to you of Babington, though I know you must." He ran a hand over the carved surface of the nearest angle-topped desk. "I worry that you and I are each on our own course, and it could well lead us still farther apart, when what I would greatly prefer is for us to be together on our"—he met her gaze—"adventures."

"Oh. And is that all?"

He made a shrug with his shoulders. "What I want to say . . . I wish us not to part."

She answered, "We have been apart since the day you left us in Roffey."

"Yes, but I . . . I never . . ." He could not find the proper shape for what he wanted to say. She finished it for him.

"But that girl was a mere child, who grew up out of sight and mind, while you were already engaged in diabolical intrigues elsewhere."

"A mere child who grew up into a most extraordinary woman."

"Oh, I know," she answered, deadly serious. "One with a beard." He knew then that she was teasing him. "I could show you it."

"Syndony—"

"Shh." She put a finger to his lips. "My name here is Robert." Then she leaned over and kissed him lightly. Her mustache tickled. He drew back, looked at her false face, and kissed her back twice as hard. Then she said, "Once I'm in London, when I can get quit of Babington and his puppy love, I'll come to your safe house. Look for me there."

"And how will I know it's you? You might look like anyone."

"All the more fun for you."

He shook his head. "Perhaps I'm a fool."

"No more than I, dear heart, and of the same deportment." She gave him another kiss. "But an' I remain in this room with you one minute longer, I'm going to lose control of this form, because my true one wants too urgently to come out."

She got up then from the bench, but he caught her wrist. "Wait," he said. Then he drew out the thong from around his neck and took it off. He handed her the pouch. "I've been furious at myself that I didn't give you this before. You must take it now."

"What is it?"

Thomas opened the pouch and slid the contents onto his palm. The stone glittered in her presence. "It's called an ördstone. Wear it around your neck while you're traveling with Babington. When you fall asleep, whatever form you've taken, this will keep your true nature hidden— at least, I hope it will. It does so for me."

Syndony held the stone up. The lights flashed upon her face. With her other hand she rubbed at her temple. "That's a strange sensation it causes."

"Be careful not to show it to any of your companions, especially the apricots. Ballard and Parsons especially would recognize it immediately. Also, it has many other powers and you don't really want to stumble into another world just now."

She looked at him wide-eyed. "You mean that, don't you?"

"I do."

"But if you give it me, what will you use?"

"Once I leave here I'll be traveling alone, and unglamoured. With luck I won't need to glamour before I see you again, whereas you must. Too many in Babington's group for you to drop your appearance. I know it's exhausting for you. The stone might help there, too. I'm not sure."

She leaned down and kissed him once more before leaving the room.

Sitting there on a bench in the dimness, Thomas was both exhilarated and aware that he'd hardly put a dent in his worries for her.

XXXVI. Rye

Babington's group with Gifford in tow departed the next morning for the coast. Gifford wore a brown peascod jerkin with black figures worked into it over a gray doublet and gold-trimmed paned hose, clothing supplied him by Parsons.

Thomas kept himself sealed off from Father Ballard as they rode to Boulogne-Sur-Mer. From there they would travel across to Dover and then Rye.

Thomas and Marlowe watched the Babington group depart. Marlowe said, "You'll have to scramble to catch up. And e'en then, what can you do with 'em? It's not as if you can be twinned in their company."

"Oh, I don't wish to look like him."

Marlowe chuckled. "Not yet, anyway." He curled a finger beneath his chin as if deeply lost in thought. "While I, helpless here amidst heretics, can only await news of your success or failure to tell me when or if I jump, for the next departure will likely be my last from this place. Parsons grows ever less tolerant of absences."

It was close to one hundred miles from Rheims to Boulogne-sur-Mer. Thomas left the English College at midday as if off for a stroll after his meal. Wandering into a thicket not all that far away, he dispensed with the glamour of William Colerdin, emerging, for once, as himself. In the town he acquired a horse and then set off for Boulogne, traveling that first day as far as the town of Noyon. He did not come across Babington's group and was glad of it. The second day, more cautiously, he caught up with them just outside Abbeville near

275

the mouth of the Somme, but pretended to have no interest in them. They were just a group of eight riders.

They stayed the night at the same inn, faced in red and white brick, which put him in mind of Queen Elizabeth's Placentia Palace. Irritatingly, Babington showed repeated physical affection for Robert Poley, finding any opportunity to touch him and speak closely with him. Thomas made eye contact with Syndony a few times, but she, as Poley, had to keep Babington engaged, if only to give Thomas more opportunity to focus on Gifford, and that meant pretending to be charmed by the mustachioed young traitor. Although superficially with them, Gifford remained somewhat aloof with his packet of letters for Mary of Scotland, sitting by himself off to one side at the end of a dinner table, and glancing about as if suspicious of his companions. Thomas wondered if someone among them had attempted already to pilfer the casket of letters. It was conceivable he was not the only agent Walsingham or Cecil had placed here.

Ballard or someone had made arrangements for them at the inn. They occupied all three rooms on the second floor. Thomas found himself assigned a spare bed in a room with John Savage and Thomas Salisbury, the latter a broad-shouldered, saturnine man with curly black hair. Salisbury wore a baldric beneath his belly, supporting both a rapier and dagger, as though spoiling for a fight. But contrary to his outward appearance, he conversed in a friendly manner with Thomas, who admitted he was on his way to Rye. He had a complete story of a wife and child prepared if Salisbury asked, but an admonishing look passed between Salisbury and Savage, after which Salisbury tersely wished him a good night, and then lay down.

Thomas lay back on his pallet, glad now that he'd opted to dismiss the disguise of glamour for this journey; without his ördstone, and in a room with these two, who knew what face he might have revealed as he slept?

At Boulogne, once again Ballard's advance planning and network came into play. The travelers had a ship at quayside and could walk their horses up a ramp onto it for the short crossing to Dover. Thomas had made no such arrangement. Instead, at a nearby stable he managed to sell his horse for half its worth, but he'd no time to haggle or seek a better offer if he wanted to join Ballard's party aboard the same ship.

During the crossing, he kept to himself, ignoring them all.

At Dover, the horses were led down into the shallows and the group rode off. Thomas could only watch Syndony recede. He must remain on board with Gifford.

By midafternoon, he was walking across the beach of Winchelsea and up past the Brede Inn. He could not help but think of the *teind* named Piers he'd rescued and sent off from here—how odd to find himself back where this adventure had more or less begun, but now heading along the path into Rye. Gilbert Gifford, of course, had ridden ahead. He might very well depart Rye before Thomas even got there, but it was late enough in the day that he hoped Gifford would be more likely to rendezvous with others in the town and stay overnight. If Gifford set out immediately, there was nothing Thomas could do about it. Nevertheless, while alone on the path he glamoured himself as the ruff-maker, Van Der Paas, a face he had not seen in years and thus presumably a stranger to anyone here.

Then as he climbed the hill into Rye, he located Gifford's horse tied outside a two-story alehouse with a deeply slanting roof just below the crest of the hill, and allowed himself a smile. The messenger had not yet departed.

Thomas entered the alehouse to find Gifford already engaged in discussion with two men. He recognized neither of them. Both were well dressed, one in a tan doublet with red sleeves, the other in a black jerkin over a white satin doublet with elaborate figures stitched into it. Both men glanced his way as he entered. He immediately crossed to a small table and sat on a stool. He lay down coins, catching the attention of the proprietor, then faced the entrance in such a way that he could see what that trio was doing. His mug of ale arrived a moment later, but he barely had time to lift it to his lips before the two men with Gifford discreetly drew daggers and let their prey notice them.

The three men got up together, Gifford between the others, his eyes wide with barely controlled terror as they exited the tavern. Thomas bid his ale goodbye, stood and followed them out.

They must have seen Gifford arrive, because they knew to take his horse, too. By following so quickly, Thomas showed perhaps too keen an interest. One of the men turned back, his dagger still drawn. Thomas said, "You were sent by the two who are one?"

The man blinked at him, his brow furrowing. He looked to the other man, who shrugged. Had Gifford gone through the same ritual and with the same result? Of course, glamoured Thomas was a stranger to him here, but the way Gifford was staring back at him, he clearly thought Thomas to be the contact he was supposed to meet. Gifford didn't know his network, either.

"From Walsingham, then," Thomas guessed. But by now the two were as interested in him as they were in Gifford.

"Where's your horse?" asked the nearest one in the white satin doublet.

"I had to eat him."

"Best you find a new one quick now, else you're *walking* beside us."

"Excuse me?"

"You're coming with us and 'im, aren't you?"

"What's your name, then?" asked the other.

Thomas hesitated for only a moment. Doubting it would mean anything to them, he replied with the name Walsingham had assigned him. "Number Four," he said. The men reacted as if he'd pronounced himself king, eyes wide and nervous. "Thought you was a story, like," the nearest said. He took the reins of Gifford's horse.

"One moment." Thomas walked over to Gifford. The two with their daggers watched him cautiously. "Hands out," he told Gifford, who complied reluctantly. Thomas had seen where Gifford stuffed the casket of letters under his peascod doublet, and now violently dug his hand in under the stiff pudendal padding. Gifford expressed outrage, and grabbed at Thomas's wrist. Thomas tore his hand away, then slapped Gifford. "Don't," he warned. A moment later, he'd fished out the small casket of letters. "This is what Walsingham wants. This one would've tossed it away when none of us was watching."

"Well, now," the agent said appreciatively.

"Sir Francis didn't tell you that?"

The man shook his head. "All we got was notice to take him."

Good Christ, they would have ridden him to London, by which time the letters would have been lost for good along the road.

The nearest agent held out his hand for the casket. Thomas said, "I think not." He rested his free hand on the pommel of his rapier.

"Fine. Then, let's find you a horse afore 'is real friends catch us up."

Surrounding a crestfallen Gifford, they all continued up the hill.

XXXVII. Awaiting Letters

It was Syndony as Robert Poley working on Babington's insecurities who convinced him that others were receiving all the credit for things he had done to drive plans forward. Throwing Babington's own words back at him, Poley said, "You've done more than anyone, dear sir, to free Mary and place her upon the throne. The least she can do is acknowledge it." As Poley, Syndony threaded the intimacy between them cautiously, forever on the verge of a possible physical relationship with Babington, at the same time hinting that it could not happen before all of "this political subterfuge" resolved and they could travel far from the intrigues to which they were currently bound. Poley would not have him in thrall to both Mary and himself. The matter of Mary Stuart, Ballard, Savage, and the promised Spanish invasion needed to conclude. "Only then," swore Poley, "can I give my heart to someone."

And so the discussion continued to center on receiving his due from Mary of Scotland.

Poley said, "I think your best approach is to enumerate for her all the many things you have done on her behalf. Allow the predominance of your actions to speak for you."

The result, as Syndony had hoped, was that twice a petulant Anthony Babington refused to act as courier for letters from France for Mary. Instead, Poley saw to it that these letters were delivered to Gifford, ensuring also that the letters were decoded by Thomas Phelippes and his team (and occasionally altered) before Gifford carried them northwest to Chartley Manor and deposited them in the false beer keg.

Babington, meanwhile, wrote a letter to Mary detailing all he had accomplished in preparing to put her on the throne.

Poley contacted Morgan, recommending that he or Paget must convince Mary (or someone standing in for her) to write the letter placating Babington. Too much in the coming coup depended upon the participation of those under Babington's influence, and Poley made it clear that he was proving to be unreliable, even unstable. Morgan and Paget had seen enough of Babington to read between the lines.

The carrying of letters back and forth also took time, and Babington was not terribly good at waiting. When no word arrived immediately, Babington's paranoia drove him to ask Poley to expedite getting him and Thomas Salisbury, another of his coconspirators, licenses to travel across Europe. Poley stalled him, in part by expressing some hurt at being passed over for Salisbury. The misunderstanding delayed things further.

Thomas, now acting as Gifford, was no less frustrated than Babington. He, too, wanted to see the end of this affair sooner rather than later, while matters seemed to drag on and on. Every move was like a stone skipped on a pond, creating ripples after ripples.

Walsingham, though he now had ample evidence of the conspiracy itself, insisted on letting Babington, Ballard, and Savage run free a while longer. Thomas found the wait excruciating, and the free conspirators a perpetual threat on the loose.

One evening, Syndony arrived at the safe house with a packet of letters, and practically jumped when Thomas proved to be there ahead of her. That day Babington had intruded upon Poley while he was busy copying one of Mary's letters to deliver to Walsingham, one Syndony would not have opportunity to smuggle out.

Poley had defended himself by explaining that he needed to know what Mary desired but could only read the code by copying it out.

While Babington had accepted this explanation, Syndony doubted he'd swallowed it entirely. Cracks were forming in that perpetually stalled relationship.

"This needs to end," she said. "I need to come in. I'm going to make a mistake, one I can't explain away so easily next time. And 'tis not just Babington now. They are all increasingly frustrated by the dawdling progress made since first they mapped out their plans at the College. They expected to strike right away, but Ballard insists everyone from the Scottish lords to the Spanish must be in place before he gives Savage the signal to strike. The time approaches when he will not be heeded. Should Walsingham wait much longer, he shall find himself pursuing the Queen's murderers."

She was rescued by the contents of the very packet of letters: Mary had at last responded to Babington's previous urgings, writing, *The affair being thus prepared, and forces in readiness both within and without the realm, then shall it be time to set the six gentlemen to work; taking order upon the accomplishment of their design, I may be suddenly transported out of this place . . . Let the great plot commence.*
Signed
Mary.

When Sir Francis Walsingham read that, he sat back in his chair and shook the letter. "At last," he told Thomas, "we have her."

With that, everything shifted and events moved rapidly. Fourteen warrants were issued for Babington and his coconspirators.

The first taken was the Jesuit priest, John Ballard.

He and five other of the conspirators met at the Bear Inn on Basinghall Street to share news from Mendoza sent through Morgan and Paget. Their number included Thomas in the guise of Gifford. He'd warned Walsingham that Ballard, an Yvagvoja, would be capable of affecting the minds, even taking total control, of any two or three men who might attempt to arrest him. "Think of the four in Deptford and how that demonic assassin bent them to his will. Don't make that mistake."

Ballard left the meeting in the company of Henry Donn. The two men got as far as London Wall before Ballard found himself surrounded by eight men with pistols and rapiers. As the circle closed around Ballard, Donn backed away, then ran off down London Wall toward Cripplegate. No one pursued him. The eight closed around Ballard and marched him to the Tower, where he was placed in a corner cell on a nearly unoccupied floor, well away from the cells reserved for his confederates. Only two cells near him were occupied—by the real Robert Poley and Gilbert Gifford, neither of whom had the slightest idea of what had transpired since they had arrived here, much less that they'd been replaced. Ballard, extending his perceptions in their direction, encountered only confusion and ignorance. Listening to that cacophany, however, the Yvagvoja began to understand just how the Babington conspirators had all been played, and by whom.

Back at the Bear Inn, Anthony Babington dined with Thomas Salisbury, Chidiock Tichborne, and Gilbert Gifford. Walsingham had given Thomas clear instructions on what to do next. And so at one point during the meal, he made an excuse to go relieve himself, but left behind at his place a folded-up document. Babington glanced at it. Wasn't that his own name written across it? As the others conversed, he reached over and with one finger dragged the paper toward himself. He unfolded it. Written by Sir Francis Walsingham himself, the document proved to be a memorandum regarding an arrest warrant for Babington and a substantial sum to be paid to someone referenced only by the code name of "Number Four."

Babington stood up. The others paused in their conversations and looked at him. He had gone pale and acted as if seeking a carver. "Forgive me, but I must...I think I must return to Dethick immediately." He lurched across the room. The others traded confused looks. Tichborne dragged the memorandum to himself, and after a moment said to Salisbury, "We are all undone. Hurry now!" They stood and gave chase after Babington. They caught up with him fleeing down Basinghall Street. Babington bent over, hands on thighs, winded and helpless to run any farther. Thomas, watching from the shadows, listened to their terrified voices. Babington was practically babbling. Salisbury, however, seemed to have kept his head. "To St. John's Wood, then," he said. "Bring what provisions you can gather. From there we'll determine our course!"

They all hurried off. Thomas returned to the Bear Inn to retrieve Walsingham's memorandum. It had produced exactly the reaction the spymaster had desired: The conspirators were fleeing for their lives, and at his disposal. They could not hide in the wood for long.

Thomas tucked the document away. He was tired of playing the part of the letter-ferrying Gifford—tired really of playing all of these parts for Walsingham. He was ready to take flight himself...the moment he reunited with Syndony.

"We have all fourteen of the conspirators in custody," proclaimed the ever self-possessed Walsingham, although for once Thomas caught the barest hint of something like smug satisfaction in Sir Francis's manner. "Babington in his correspondence with Mary laid out in detail what their plans were. John Savage's plan was to kill the Queen at St. Giles in the Fields, so the gentlemen shall be taken there specifically to be hanged, drawn, and quartered. Gifford—the real Gifford—having been made aware of this, is now providing most helpful information. And Babington is blaming everything on Ballard."

"What does Ballard say?" Marlowe asked.

"That he forgives his young friend."

"Then he's the better man."

Thomas and "Simon" said nothing. Walsingham already knew that Ballard was possessed, like the body he'd beheld at the Lazar-house—or at least, he'd been told. Thomas would have preferred to deal with Ballard himself, the first name on a list of Yvags he intended to dispatch.

"What of Mary Stuart?" he inquired.

"Even now I have a warrant being drawn up for her execution. Lord Burghley and I believe the Queen must sign it."

"Eventually," Thomas muttered.

"Oh, no, no, Mary's complicity is this time undeniable. Her Majesty *must* sign, particularly in light of Spain's preparations to go to war with us. I have received dispatches from Standen in Madrid, which make that absolutely clear. And we make preparations as well. Plans have been instituted to rebuild Dover harbor. We will be ready, and we shall triumph."

"Of course. We've no doubt, Sir Francis," said Thomas. "Have we, fellows?"

"None at all," replied Simon.

"Oh, none," Marlowe agreed. He gave everyone a smile.

"Well, then," Walsingham said as prelude to dismissing them. "Executions to carry out, very busy. Oh, but Marlowe, could you stay a bit? I should like to discuss future employment of you on something new elsewhere."

Thomas said, "Sir Francis, you've done me the kindness of keeping my travel chest quite some time now. I think it's time I took it off your hands. Don't you?"

Distracted, Walsingham called for a servant to assist Thomas. He opened a drawer, took out a key, and handed it to the servant.

At that point, short, round Arthur Gregory, the skilled counterfeiter who opened sealed envelopes for Walsingham, entered the study with a sheet of paper covered in writing, and a small pouch of coal dust.

Walsingham said, "Yes, Arthur?"

"The, ah, invisible writing method I mentioned to you earlier?" He shook the paper.

"Yes, of course. Marlowe?" Walsingham gestured his dismissal to Thomas. There lay beneath that cursory dismissal an edge of unease, which Thomas interpreted as the discomfort of the spymaster in the presence of two shape-shifters. In that sense, Thomas suspected, they remained a bargain he'd made with the supernatural and would never quite be able to resolve.

Marlowe nodded agreeably. As Gregory moved in to demonstrate his invisible writing method, Marlowe turned and, exasperated, whispered to Thomas and Syndony, "This is hell nor am I out of it. I shall have to catch you up later. At the Theatre, perhaps?"

"The Theatre, then," Thomas replied as Marlowe went back inside Walsingham's study and closed the door. He and Syndony followed the servant to another room, one full of boxes and crates. Thomas identified his locked travel chest, picked it up, and then quickly exited before either he or Syndony could be reeled back in.

XXXVIII. Best-Laid Plans

Once back at the St. Martin's le Grande house, Thomas had hardly set down the travel chest before Syndony was upon him. His own passion was urgent, but no match for hers. They undressed in a clumsy rush. Her clothes were still those of a man right down to the braies, and he tugged and all but tore them off her. Both of them had been seeking someone like themselves; each had been lonely longer than they could say, alone in their own way, and now of a sudden had a partner—the equal that they'd long since resigned themselves to never finding.

Naked, they could not touch each other enough, and each of them rode multiple waves of arousal and rapture.

Afterward, they lay in each other's arms without words. Thomas admired the smooth hillocks of her breasts. He lightly brushed a palm over the tips and took a lazy pleasure in watching the nipples stiffen. He thought he would never tire of watching that response to his touch.

In between tumbling about, they rested and carried on a conversation of sorts.

At one point Syndony said, "That man will keep us on our leashes until the Spanish war is finally fought. Marlowe's right. We'll never get away."

He nuzzled her neck. "We have all we need now to elude him. And to be honest, I believe he wants us to do so but will not say it aloud. I see it round the edges of his glances, the desire to have us gone. My sense is, he will make no effort to pursue us. We are his pact with the devil, which amuses me because that is how I characterized him when first I met him."

She turned on her side so that their lips could meet.

Drawing back, he said, "Do you know, I think this is the first time I've kissed you without your having a mustache."

She grinned wickedly. "I could reimagine it for you." She squinched up her face as if about to transform.

"Don't you dare!" And he pulled her on top of him.

The rest of the afternoon they spent like that, laughing and unwilling to let go of one another. Whenever one made to get up, the other would wrestle them both down into the bedclothes. Eventually, the light began to dim, and Syndony complained that she was famished. "You feed my soul," she told him, "but my belly wants your attention just now."

"All right," said Thomas. He was no less exhausted than she was. "Let us take ourselves to the Panier alehouse for a meal."

After getting out of bed, Syndony sponged herself off, then did the same to Thomas. He retrieved the leather thong and pouch he'd given her and hung the ördstone around his own neck again. No longer would they need to disguise themselves in order to traverse London if not the world. Surely, enough time had passed in both their lives that no one would be looking for either of them, and that meant it was time to make good their escape. But he reminded himself that at first opportunity, he needed to provide her with one of the spare ördstones.

Because they intended to meet Marlowe at the theater later, Syndony dressed once more as a young man, in a green doublet, baggy slops, and cape, with a matching flat cap set upon her head. She added the baldric and dagger that she liked to carry. Thomas wore red trunk hose and a plain black jerkin over his light gray, banded doublet. He, too, wore a cap in his black hair. Together they looked like a tradesman and his apprentice.

The Panier was bustling, but they managed to secure a table in one corner. As they crossed the room, she looked all around. Thomas asked if she saw any colorful haloes. She did not. No Yvags hid among the clientele of the inn. They could at least enjoy their meal in peace.

A small basin and cloth was brought so that they might wash their hands, after which they were left a plate of salted radish slices to nibble on while their meal was prepared. Their ale arrived first, fresh and a little sour. For the meal they shared a stew of spiced cabbage and onion, followed by fried potato cakes and a capon slow-cooked in a wine currant sauce.

Insatiable after their afternoon of pleasure, they ate like starved prisoners. While they attacked the food, they found themselves immersed in conversations about the executions of seven of the traitors that had taken place that day.

The most shocking seemed to be the initial drawing and quartering of John Ballard. Someone described him as "bursting" when the executioner cut into him, after which it was as if his body lost its shape altogether. Another witness described it as an unholy death.

Thomas wiped his mouth. "A pity. He was at the top—"

"—of your list," she said.

"*Our* list now, I think," he replied. "We each have suffered and had those close to us suffer at the hands of these creatures."

The conversations continued. Like two people in a bubble, they were assailed with gory details of the executions that had taken place.

Ballard must have died instantly. Thomas knew how such deaths went. Nothing like that had happened with the remaining six executed that day, some of whom had endured far too long, groaning, roaring, screaming, and whimpering in agony as they were eviscerated. The Queen had found the punishments so terrible that she insisted all other conspirators must be hanged until dead before being drawn and quartered. These were people whose company Thomas and Syndony had shared not long before. Strange to think of them in such circumstances—he had only recently watched them fleeing down the street after Babington, all ultimately for nought.

Syndony sighed and pushed the bowl of food aside. Thomas continued eating a little longer, until she said, "I am thinking that you and I ought to forge a partnership."

Although he had been thinking along the same lines, he asked her what she meant.

"You have begun your list of—what do you call them?" she asked.

"Voja. Skinwalkers, like the man Gibson you told me about, and—"

"Ballard himself."

"A pity we couldn't mete out justice there, but at least it was served." He drank some ale. "Once we've left Walsingham and his machinations behind, I mean to continue robbing the Yvag of their sacrificial victims where and when I can."

"Surely I can help there as well."

"Possibly," he replied, "but I don't want you taken in their place or put at risk."

"Thomas," she said sharply, causing him to raise his head. She placed her long dagger on the table between them in a gesture of mock-fealty. "We are, both of us, committed to the cause against these devils. And, forgive me, but it is not your place. Whatever we are to each other, you are not my protector, nor will I be told to sit quietly by. That's no partnership I want a part of. I've lived in the world as a man, and I appreciate how differently the world treats me as a woman. And while neither of us wants the other taken, remember, you may hear them, but I'm the only one who can see these monsters well before they reveal themselves to you or anyone else."

He looked her up and down. "You're quite right. I won't ask you to sit quietly by. You've as much reason as I to hunt the elven. Please remind me of that should I forget again." Finally, he slid her dagger back to her. "In my travel chest I've another dagger for you. And also a suit of armor."

"You can fit a suit of armor into that small chest? But surely, it will be too large for me in any case."

"On the contrary, I think you'll be surprised how well it fits."

He stood up to pay the bill.

"Come, let's go home," he said. "Later, we can stroll out to the Theatre and bid Marlowe a final farewell."

He took her arm and walked with her. She leaned her head against him. "I believe I shall love you, Thomas Rimor," she told him.

"And I you, mademoiselle. And I you."

Thomas dragged his wooden travel chest out from beside the bed. He lifted it by its side handles and set it on the small table near the bed. The key he'd kept in a pocket of his breeches and now employed, unlocking and removing the padlock to lift the central hasp. He flipped open two smaller pin clasps to each side of the central hasp, then opened the angled lid.

Syndony leaned in close to see the contents. He took the opportunity to kiss her again.

"Now," he said, "let's see what we have."

He removed a folded gown and doublet. Beneath them lay the real treasures he'd acquired over time: the stone phial of poison into which he dipped his arrows came out first. He set it aside carefully. That was followed by the strange red glove that could disintegrate whole buildings.

Syndony made to put it on, but he stopped her. "I'm not entirely certain you want to do that," he said. "I am not fully conversant with how to control it just yet."

She regarded it doubtfully, then lay it down on the bed.

"Here we go." He lifted out one of the suits of Yvag armor.

She held it up. It was shiny black with portions of silver trim. "'Tis almost a skin."

Syndony began undressing. Meanwhile, Thomas reached into the chest again. He brought out a gold ring, topped with a small square-cut stone. "Now, this I acquired from Seething Lane one day. Hold out your hand."

She paused to do so, and he slid the ring onto her middle finger. "Let it be a promise ring from me. But see here." Thomas reached around the base of the stone until he found the secret latch. Then he carefully flipped the stone open. It had been ground almost hollow. Protruding out of the middle of the ring was a tiny needle. "Be careful with that, it's been dipped in the same poison as my arrows."

She paused to look at it closely, but snapped the stone closed before letting the ring slide around her finger. "I'm afraid it's too large for me," she told him. She drew it off and handed it back.

He slid it onto the middle finger of his own left hand. "Well, we'll have it resized for you later."

Syndony, naked now, stepped into the Yvag armor. "What do I—" she started to ask before the suit slid up her body, under her feet, down her arms and fingers. The helmet enclosed her head. She gasped and then began to laugh. Thomas pushed at the helm and it withdrew, forming a rolled collar around her throat.

"Perfect fit," he said. "Here." He held out one of the black barbed daggers. This he slid into the front seam of the armor. It clicked into place. "There's another hidden slot for the ördstone I'll give you."

"What else is there?" she asked with childlike wonder. "Ooh, what's this?" She lifted out a small green pyramid covered in indecipherable markings.

Quickly, Thomas snatched it away from her. "This is another

dangerous device of the Yvags. You want to be extremely cautious even touching it. I don't know any way to turn it off once it's engaged. And the effect it would have on you is too terrible to contemplate." He put it back into the chest.

Syndony walked about in the armor. "It hardly weighs anything," she said, amazed.

"Not only that, it repairs itself if cut or torn."

He took everything out of the chest and put it on the bed. Syndony danced around the bed and out into the main room.

Thomas checked the false bottom, ensuring that the letters of credit still resided in their compartment. Then he began replacing the various objects, ending with the gown on top, covering everything.

"Syndony," he called. "It's time to take off the armor. We need to pack up."

When she didn't reply, he glanced up. "Syndony?"

Thomas closed the chest. He drew his dagger, crossed the bedroom, and went out the door. He had just enough time to comprehend the sight of the hulking monster that held Syndony in place in front of the fireplace, before something flashed beside him—the long, flat blade of a glaive. It struck him on the side of his head even as the name "Bragrender" formed on his lips.

XXXIX. The Spinner

Thomas came to on his back. The Yvag knight, not even bothering to glamour, stood over him looking bored. Across the room, Syndony stood stiffly before Bragrender, stripped of her Yvag armor. Her expression was blank. Thomas knew she'd already been spelled. A second knight with glaive stood beside her.

Bragrender turned as he sat up, and the knight next to him stepped nearer.

"There you are." Bragrender's voice was like metal against metal. "It seems like centuries since we've seen each other. Come to think of it, it *has* been centuries, hasn't it, and yet here you lie, looking not one day older than you did at the priory. Tell me how it is that Robyn Hoode lives on."

When Thomas made no reply, Bragrender gestured dismissively. "You *are* going to tell me. Not here, perhaps, but certainly in Yvagddu. By the time you are limbless, eyeless, and planted in Þagalwood where you belong, I'll have heard every detail of every memory you possess."

Thomas didn't move but asked, "What of her?" He gestured at Syndony. "Why not let her go?"

Bragrender's flickering visages jittered, the equivalent of a sneer. "Ah, well, there's a problem, you see. I know you acted the part of Gilbert Gifford."

"Who?"

Bragrender laughed. The sound threatened to shake the foundations. "Let me save you the trouble of lying. Your Walsingham had our Yvagvoja's *lich* imprisoned in the Tower between Gilbert

Gifford and Robert Poley. When the *lich* was executed—that would be John Ballard to you—the released voja came straight to us directly, immediately, to warn that Gifford and Poley had been imprisoned all the time they were active in Babington and Savage's schemes. Therefore someone with our abilities was imitating them. Now, you..." Bragrender came closer. "You played Gifford. But who was it acted Poley's part?" With one clawlike hand, the Yvag brushed Syndony's cheek, and watched Thomas's reaction. He tried not to show anything, but his body tensed. The creature read him clearly. "I think it was she. You can tell me now or later. Either way, she is a *teind*, and once the Queen's council and I have interrogated her thoroughly, off she will go to feed the hungry maw of Hel like all the rest."

Thomas sat up straighter. "What if—"

"Oh, you have no 'what ifs.' Tell me directly how many of your kind there are."

"My kind?"

"The hidden offspring of voja."

The elves, it seemed, had begun speculating about the very same thing he and Syndony had discussed. "Is that what I am?"

Bragrender replied, "As I said, you will tell me everything in the end."

"Then ask me something I can answer."

Annoyed, Bragrender leaned toward him. "How does the Wood let you in? How do you obtain *kanerva*?"

"Now, that would be telling," answered Thomas.

Bragrender sighed, dismissed him. "Enough of your games. It is time for her to go. Say goodbye if you like, though she won't hear you."

"Syndony!" he yelled. The knight beside him pressed down on his shoulder with the glaive to keep him seated. He noted that a jewel lay in the center of the blade, and he suspected the weapon did more than merely cut—all of their devisings seemed to be powered by stones or jewels. Syndony did not acknowledge him, but he had known she wouldn't. He knew how it was with the *teind*. He wanted Bragrender believing this was a certain narrative.

Bragrender drew his large ördstone and sliced the air in front of the hearth. As the spitting green-fire gate opened, Thomas wondered how they had arrived here to begin with. Had they opened a different portal while he was showing Syndony the contents of the travel chest?

Or had they been waiting, hidden, their chittering thoughts cloaked? And how had they found him here of all places?

The hearth vanished behind the portal. Through it, the hills of blue grasses overlooked Ailfion's distant towers and spires, all glimmering like stars.

"Take her," Bragrender ordered the nearest knight, which nudged her with its glaive. Then the guard walked past her and she followed him as if pulled along on a rope, like every *teind* he'd ever beheld. They walked into the grasses and up over the hill.

Bragrender said, "Now your turn," and his head filled with the intoxicating thrum of Yvag enchantment, the same weird and voiceless spell that had once bound him to Alderman Stroud in the ruins of Old Melrose. But that was before he had immersed in the Changeling Pool in Ailfion.

He stood between the monster and the knight. He let his face go slack, his eyes dull, and stood as if waiting for orders to move.

Bragrender nodded in satisfaction, communicated to the knight, "Take him. I will follow to present him to the Queen."

The blade of the glaive directed him through the gateway and he shuffled forward. His thumb flicked open the ring he still wore. He had carefully rotated it on his finger so that the stone hung in line with his palm; then, as he passed Bragrender, he reached over and gripped the Yvag's arm.

Bragrender reacted to the sting of the needle by snatching his hand away. His golden eyes glared at Thomas, while the creature's voice echoed in his head, "What treachery is this?" Even as Bragrender projected his outrage, the poison spread through him. Thomas could well recall how quickly the poison had dropped him in Barnsdale Wood. Bragrender fell into Thomas and the knight.

Thomas grabbed the creature and shoved him against the knight. The two crashed down together. They fell against the table, and in the moment of confusion, Thomas wrestled the pole weapon out of the knight's hands, reversed, and swung it up all in one movement. The ferrule slammed into the knight's chin hard enough to lift the creature off its feet and send it tumbling away. Bragrender hit the floor and lay still. The knight tried to sit up.

Thomas took two swift steps and stuck it with the exposed needle, too. How much poison remained, he didn't know, but the knight went limp and its eyes rolled up. He struck it with the glaive for good measure. The knight fell back and didn't move. Paralyzed Bragrender could only stare at it.

Thomas knelt for Bragrender's ördstone. "An infuriating sensation, isn't it, not being able to do anything at all? Lasts a good while, too. You had me in the back of that wagon for hours on the way to the priory. What do you think—three hours?"

He looked through the gate. There was no sign of Syndony and the other guard. He knew, if he left this open, something would come through it—some of those obnoxious little fae or an onslaught of Yvag knights. As much as he didn't want to lose the connection, he couldn't come at Syndony this way. He would never make it across the plaza, much less collect her and escape from Nicnevin's clutches.

He sealed up the gate.

Thomas left Bragrender on the floor and hurried into the bedroom. He dug around in the chest again, and brought out what he wanted. It was a mad plan, but he could think of no other way that offered him even a chance of success.

He came back to the table, set everything down, then bent over, lifted Bragrender like an enormous rag doll, and set him in the nearest chair. Bragrender leaned against the table, dull eyes watchful but still almost expressionless. Thomas slid the green *dight* up beside him where he could see it. The ring of pupils in those golden eyes enlarged—the only indication that the creature understood what he was seeing.

"I've hung onto this for such a long time, not knowing why I kept so dangerous a thing nearby. Now I understand. I would never be able to get near Nicnevin or Syndony, would I? Not a chance of it. But you—you can go anywhere. In fact, they're expecting you for the interrogation as you said, so my hope is that I learn how to make use of you somehow. If I don't, well, you won't be here to complain, however this goes, but I want you to comprehend everything that's happening to you, too."

Thomas took the *dight* and turned it onto its point.

"We would never not be enemies, would we, nor ever stop hunting each other down."

He stared hard into the golden eyes.

"Goodbye, Bragrender." He spun the *dight* and stepped away.

XL. Into Hel

While the *dight* spun, Thomas remained in the bedroom and watched the flash of the green light as it whirled. He'd been in Oak Mill as another *dight* had spun—as it drank up the miller's soul—but he could not be certain how the device would work in the presence of Bragrender. For all he knew, the grotesque Yvag might prove immune to it and the thing latch onto whoever else was near. This entire plan he was pulling together out of pieces of things he knew.

Bragrender had made it clear that the interrogation of Syndony could not conclude until he had participated, and Thomas prayed that was so. Even then, the escape route he imagined was full of unresolved and untested inferences.

The green *dight* spun down finally, leaving just a flickering glow against the section of the wall he could see through the doorway, or so he thought. When he stepped into the outer room, he was surprised to find a new gate hovering in the air and, standing in it, Zhanedd. She looked from Thomas to Bragrender and back again. From her expression he could not tell if she was furious, horrified, or both.

Despite their détente, he slid an Yvag dagger up his sleeve before stepping out.

Zhanedd crossed to where Bragrender slouched against the table, absolutely still but not dead. He might simply have been paralyzed by the poison still.

Zhanedd placed a hand upon the depleted *dight*. She said, "I came once it was obvious that Bragrender had caught you. Your . . . witch was led across the plaza and we were all informed that he would be along soon with Robyn Hoode."

She paused. Held up the *dight*.

"This comes from Palavia Parva, doesn't it? You kept one back all those years ago."

"That's true. At the time I didn't know why. How could I?"

She set it down again, leaned close to study the creature's empty expression. "Your experiments and machines can't help you anymore, can they, Bragrender? All that posturing and this is where it brought you. Superior to everyone, dismissive of all. You won't be vying for kingship of Ailfion now." To Thomas: "This will hardly win you back your witch. And I certainly won't occupy him for you. We remain enemies, you and I, even if we've attained an understanding of sorts."

Thomas kept himself from saying they had reached no understanding on anything. He would never stop hunting the Yvag. But that discussion must wait, because he needed her assistance one last time.

"It's not you I'm asking," he said.

She comprehended what he meant immediately. "What you are proposing, Uncle, no one has ever had opportunity to try. Assuming you could even achieve it, you could be lodged in him forever."

As if the proposition wasn't made already.

"Is she really worth that to you?"

"Yes, Sìne, she is."

She stared at him in silence awhile. "Well, I will help you in this endeavor because it furthers my own plans, but understand, this is the last time blood speaks to blood between us."

"All right," he said. "How do I attempt it?"

"Your lifestone makes it possible. I know you have one."

"Had," he replied. He drew the pouch from its thong and took out the ördstone. "The previous one died."

She held out her hand for it. "You do enjoy taking risks, don't you?" She held it up against him, watched its lights flash in sequence. "It is nearly attuned to you, well enough for this if it's going to work at all." She handed it back to him. They stood like that until she said, "Well, point it at him."

"Oh." He did so, and the blue jewels became agitated, sparkling through a faster and faster sequence. Bragrender's expressionless head glowed blue as if the stone was lighting it from within.

Thomas experienced a momentary displacement, a near-dizziness as if he occupied two separate spaces simultaneously.

In the next moment he found himself leaning against the table. Peripherally, he saw Zhanedd laying his body down upon the floor beside the unconscious knight. She looked up at him as she took the ördstone from his body's fist. "So, you arrived."

He started to answer, but the sound of his voice shocked him into silence.

"Try standing up," she told him.

He had to think of what he wanted to do before he did it: Turn your head in order to look around; raise your hands to look at his clawlike appendages, the extra-articulated fingers; turn them over to look at the other side, feeling the oddness of his joints, but also the powerful strength of his body. Finally, he climbed to his feet. Wobbly at first, he held onto the edge of the table while a wave of vertigo threatened to overwhelm him. He fought down the inclination to tip, and remained standing as it retreated; he studied the sensations coming from joints that belonged to an Yvag rather than a human. When she directed him to walk around, he took a first tentative step, not trusting his own muscles to hold him up, because after all they weren't his muscles. The signals were strange. Then he shuffled the first few steps, conscious of his balance, of what he had to do to make his strange legs walk him around and around the room. Soon he was balanced enough to lift his feet, to turn in a circle as he walked. He took larger strides. It was as if all of him was flowing out to fill the new shape he occupied—and he was glad for the few times he had reshaped previously. The sensation was not dissimilar.

He tried again to speak. Bragrender's voice emerged, of course, raw and torn, not his. "I'll have but one opportunity," he said, "to present myself to Nicnevin."

Zhanedd answered, "You have one advantage. No one wants to look at you. Let us hope that will suffice. But there is one other element in this we must consider."

He had already been thinking of it. "The open gate," he said. Zhanedd nodded.

"That will be critical."

"Your father was Yvag," says Queen Nicnevin.

Syndony replies, "No." She has tried not to answer anything but is compelled to by the spell cast upon her. In the perpetual twilight of

Ailfion, she is aware of everything around her, including the distant helical towers, and sharp spires that seem to poke at the sky.

The regal creature sits stiffly upon her winged throne, which is extruded out of the plaza itself. She's dressed as Elizabeth might be, all in purple, with vertical falls of jewels, and a V-shaped bodice topped by reticella lace. Her hair is red and worked into curls around her inhuman face. It's as if she's making fun of the Queen.

A dozen tiny bat-like fae perch along the throne wings, and just beyond it stands a waist-high well of some sort, its top glowing, pulsating.

The Queen's council sit on smaller extruded seats nearby. They have referred to the well as Hel and to her, Syndony, as "our *teind.*" Yet they speak without speaking. Their words buzz through her head. They are all gray-faced, spiny, and golden-eyed.

Her presence—her very existence—has excited or alarmed them. One of the first things the Queen did was order her to glamour herself as one of them, choosing one named Panguramin. Syndony resisted, but the spell she's under saps all her resistance. She doubled the creature with ease, and the counselors all gasped as one. They're all haloed in bright yellow save for the Queen, whose aura shades toward the same red as Thomas's glow. Elves, all of them.

The Queen replies, "No? Your father was no Yvag?"

"Not my father. The one that raped my mother."

"The voja," says the Queen with emphasis as she meets the gazes of her council. "At last here's evidence that our sleepers have fathered offspring through these random encounters with humans. If there is one, there are certainly others, also with the power to glamour, to remain hidden from us."

Panguramin seemingly does not want to have to look at her and asks that she change back. The counselor then asks, "Majesty, what if we placed her in the Changeling Pool? Would she perhaps cross over entirely? Be trainable as a changeling?"

"More likely she would contaminate it again."

"But surely the ritual—"

"Yes, yes, the ritual. We do not know what would happen."

Panguramin seems about to ask another question when a spot of green fire spits and crackles in the air near the glowing well, drawing everyone's attention. The fire grows into a line, then unfolds into a circle. Some of the fae flutter up into the air and flit toward it.

Through it, Syndony can see bone-white skeletal trees in a dark reddish night. Out of the circle emerges the monster that captured her and cast its spell upon her. It's encumbered by various items it's carrying, including a bow and quiver, and a pole weapon similar to what its guards had; but most of all encumbered by the body it drags along after it.

Even spelled, she can feel her heart freeze. It looks like the body of Thomas.

The creature wears a suit of black armor just like the one taken off her. By comparison with all the others on the plaza, the creature is huge.

Curiously, however, the creature's aura has changed color, become deep orange shot with filaments of red. It's not the color of a typical Yvag, and not exactly the color of a skinwalker, either. And then there's the body of Thomas, which glows a fading yellow. Yet, she senses that no one else present notices these discrepancies. No one else seems to see the auras at all.

Thomas leaves the gate open behind him; between the body and the weapons he carries, he has no means of closing it, as he intended. No one seems to be concerned by this.

Nicnevin arises and descends from her throne. "What have you brought me, Bragrender?" she asks in unspoken words.

He replies in that deep, creaking voice of his, "Majesty." It sets the nerves of all her counselors on edge. The words have to be in his forethoughts, prepared. He doesn't want any of the court to hear the chatter between him lying in Þagalwood and the remotely guided monster. He benefits from their inclination to shy away from Nicnevin's grotesque offspring. "I give you the mortal who has plagued us. Who went by the name of Gerard but in times past was called Robyn Hoode." As he speaks, he loops the bow across his torso to free up his hands.

Zhanedd has glamoured the paralyzed guard perfectly with her ördstone. The Queen, mere inches from him, stands over the body. After fiddling with the bow, he sets down the glaive. They are shy one knight, but then Bragrender did not share information about his forays into the World-to-Be.

Nicnevin peers at the face. Shaggy black hair and trim black beard. "This is Hoode?"

"The same," he says.

"Show me his eyes."

He leans down, clutches the body, pulls back an eyelid: bright blue eyes, barely aware, staring at nothing.

"Mayfly?" says Nicnevin. "Is it possible? Panguramin, is this not the one who escaped from our prison cycles and cycles ago?"

The rotund counselor and others approach, so intent upon the body that they barely notice how Bragrender is not flicking through his usual assortment of faces to terrify. His single split visage is disturbing enough. Peering down at their prisoner, the counselors bombinate between themselves:

"'Tis him, Thomas the Rhymer."

"The same that we conjured and cursed through the ballads we constructed."

"He has been a true nemesis. Defeated Adalbrandr, that one. Forced us to seal up Malros, the first gate."

Nicnevin says, "And you mean to say he was Robyn Hoode as well?"

"And others, I suspect," Thomas tells them.

"But no match for Nicnevin," insist the counselors.

Sneering appropriately, Thomas says, "No match for *me*." Having listened to the creature's thoughts, he knows full well that Bragrender would not share credit with all those he considered inferior—which is everyone.

He sidles away from the body upon which they're all so intent and closer to Syndony. He wonders how much of the proceedings she is aware of, hopes that she will recognize who he is, but has no way to be sure.

One of the other counselors turns from the gathering and walks over to close the portal he's left open. He has only moments left now.

Nicnevin addresses the council. "This would seem to rewrite our history, our knowledge. There may be more of these creatures, but in this one we have had a single enemy for many cycles, brought down finally by Bragrender." She faces him. "You do us proud, child."

He genuflects loosely, hardly paying it any mind, his focus upon judging distances and positioning himself. Then as quietly as possible, he says, "Thank you, Jumalatar Nicnevin Ní Morrigu. Remain."

The Queen, immobilized by his words, stares at him in surprise.

He turns back as if to address the council, but instead wraps one arm around Syndony and the other around wide-eyed, furious Nicnevin. Then before any among the counselors or guards can react, he bounds straight ahead and springs over the lip of Hel.

The three of them fall through the lightning-shot incandescence and into the depthless blackness below.

XLI. Exit, Pursued by a Bear

As they plunge through the incandescence, strings of lightning jump across and core the first tiny burns through them. They fall in utter silence, at least until the naming spell evaporates and Nicnevin bellows, "You condemn us all, you fool!"

In response, Thomas releases his hold on her, pushing himself off, away from her. His other hand clings to Syndony. With his freed hand he manages to reach the seam pocket in his armor and squeezes out his ördstone. It almost slips from his grasp. A violet streak flashes and burns another hole in him. He hisses, and droplets of his blood spill past.

The Queen flails, and catches hold of his foot. Thomas ignores her, doubles over and slices the blackness.

A circular gate flexes into being below Syndony: bloodred darkness and the skeletal trees of Þagalwood. Thomas guides her through the portal.

Meanwhile, he's about to fall past it. The Queen pulls herself up his calf. He reaches up with both clawlike hands and clutches the rim of the gate. The gate, though it seems to be falling as well, is stationary. The harder he holds onto it, the more the forces of Hel tear at him, trying to wrest him free.

The Queen shouts at him to stop, to rescue her. When he continues to ignore her, instead pulling himself up until he can almost fold over its lip, she screams, "Who are you? You're not Bragrender!"

"Thomas!" he shouts back. "Thomas Lindsay Rimor de Ercildoun, Your Majesty." He kicks at her.

"You! I should have swapped you for your pathetic brother. I should have squashed you like the insect—"

His heel connects with her jaw. Her head snaps back, and the red wig she wears falls away. Beneath, silver hair sprays out, long and straight and shining like metal. In that moment she could be any Yvag. He kicks again and her grip releases. She falls away at the same time that he tugs himself the rest of the way over the edge of the gate and into its separate reality.

He lands on his back hard enough to knock the air out of him, finds himself staring up at an archway of white branches overhead against a bloodshot sky. He is lying on the main pathway through Þagalwood. He manages to raise his head and look all around; then he rolls over, pushes himself up on one hand. There is the gate, offering a view of Nicnevin falling ever farther away, down and down into Hel. He groans as he gets up. Then with the ördstone he seals off the spitting fiery gate into the pit. A single straight zip up and Nicnevin is gone.

A short distance away, Syndony lies sprawled on the path, too. He pushes himself to his knees, whereupon he discovers three blackened holes burned into him by Hel's lightning. The wounds sting like ice but his restorative powers are already shrinking them. He gets up, unsteady now on his Yvag legs, and lurches toward Syndony where she lies.

She remains spelled, silent. He counts four similar blackened and bleeding wounds on her, burned by the energies of Hel, one straight through her face. He can't be sure yet she heals the way he does. He gathers her up and starts walking. In Bragrender's arms, she weighs almost nothing.

Not far along the path he comes to the end of the first gate, and steps into a second one, one of the misty red tunnels that he and Waldroup once walked along. He enters it, turns and seals up Þagalwood behind him. This was Zhanedd's precaution, the second gate; if they'd found the means to pursue him, it offered an additional layer of protection.

After passing through, he seals it as well.

It's only moments before he spots Zhanedd far ahead, standing guard over his own body.

As he nears, Zhanedd says, "And Nicnevin?"

"If there's any justice in the universe, she will fall forever."

Zhanedd smiles in satisfaction. "It's not how Hel works, but 'twill suffice for now. Harp and carp, Thomas. Come along."

Zhanedd opened two more gates before casting her last one into the safe house at St. Martin's le Grande. The fire had burned down completely in the hearth, and outside dawn was breaking. Otherwise everything looked the same as when they'd departed. Thomas guessed one, possibly two nights had passed.

As Bragrender, he carried Syndony across the threshold and into the outer room. Zhanedd sealed up the gate after him, then used her stone to erase all traces of various gates that had penetrated into the safe house, including one that Bragrender had secretly opened to invade.

Thomas laid Syndony down upon the table, then picked up the used *dight*. Did he know for certain it didn't have more life in it? He could not be sure. He started for the bedroom, but Zhanedd held out her hand for it.

When he hesitated to give it to her, she said, "It's used up, and you won't be needing it again ever, while I cannot have so powerful a toy lying about here in your world. I would prefer you gave it over of your own free will."

For a moment, they stood like that. Her golden eyes stared hard at him. She was being polite, but she would take it off his corpse if need be. Finally, he handed it over to her.

"And Bragrender's ördstone."

Reluctantly, he drew the larger and more elaborate stone from his armor and placed it in her palm.

"I'm letting you go, Uncle, but you understand I cannot have you equipped with armaments you've accumulated to fight us. We—you and I—continue to live at cross-purposes. We will remain enemies. An I become Queen, I will tolerate none of this going forward. Our pact is completed here. We've each gotten what we desired."

Thomas unlooped the bow from across his torso, ducking his head through the half circle of it. He could not help but wonder to what extent she had played him. She had presented him with the *kanerva* blossom. Had he done exactly what Zhanedd wanted in hollowing out Bragrender? Were they not also adversaries? Was Thomas her puppet, doing the very thing she would not do herself? It didn't matter, he supposed. It had been the only way to recover Syndony. He'd have risked the destruction of the entire world to save her. He asked, "May I put away the bow and arrows at least?"

"By all means," she told him. He went into the bedroom. Where the chest still sat upon the bed, he laid down the bow, took off the baldric and quiver, and placed them beside it. He then reached into the seam of his armor and drew out the red glove, his own ördstone, and one of the Yvag daggers. With a glance, he made sure she hadn't followed him in, and then dropped the glove and dagger inside the chest, picked up the pouch he wore round his neck, and returned his own ördstone to it. He picked up his folded clothing and placed it all back inside on top of the Yvag items, drew the key from where he'd hidden it previously under the bedding, then closed and locked the chest again before sliding it back beneath the bed and replacing the key.

Back in the outer room, Zhanedd seemed to be making ready to depart. As she faced him, she glamoured herself into a man in yellow doublet and hose whose identity he did not recognize.

"Wait," he said. "What about me? How do I wake Syndony?"

"Your lifestone should suffice to remove the spell of the *teind* from her."

"And this, what do I do with this?" He gestured at himself, the whole of Bragrender.

"I told you that you might wear that shape longer than you intended. As I would not inhabit Bragrender for you then, neither will I murder him for you now. Whatever else he was, he did find a way to keep me alive that no one else would have done. I am here because of him, and I owe him some small accommodation for that, whereas you tried your best to kill me and I you. If you pursue your path of vengeance against my kind, a time such as that will come again. But worry not; meantime, I'm sure you'll find someone to dispense with you. Wake her, and I wager she grabs a dagger first thing and kills you herself." Then she added something he did not quite understand. "You end your line just as the English queen ends hers, without offspring."

At the door, she paused to give him a final look back.

"For the last time, I think, goodbye, Uncle. When next we meet, it will be in battle." She opened the door and went out.

❀ ❀ ❀

Kit Marlowe approached the house at St. Martin's le Grand with trepidation. Neither Thomas nor Syndony had turned up at the Theatre last night, and while that had proved to be a wise choice on their part, their absence concerned him. Even with all the members of the Babington plot hanged, that still left men like Robert Poley and Nicholas Skeres on the loose—reasons for Sir Francis to require his services again.

The sudden appearance of a complete stranger emerging out of the deep shadows of the courtyard and heading toward Aldersgate only increased his unease. Who could it be? Blond, mustachioed, and wearing yellow attire and a black conical hat, it was definitely no one Marlowe knew. Some instinct told him this was not someone familiar to Creighton, either. Marlowe was tempted to follow him just to find out where he went next, but the desire to discover what the stranger might have left behind took precedence. He turned into the yard and marched straight for the door. Unconsciously, his right hand reached across and slid closed around the grip of his rapier.

He opened the door and stepped quickly inside, only to be met by a shocking scene. A hulking monstrosity wearing some strange and gleaming black armor stood over the naked and unconscious body of Syndony Wyntour, who was laid out upon the dining table. Across the room on the floor lay the body of his friend Thomas, almost certainly dead by the look of him.

Marlowe already had his rapier out. "Devil!" he proclaimed. "Do your worst. I'll live in spite of you!" The creature turned to face him—and it was truly horrible to behold, with such distorted features that it seemed to present the halves of two faces. In a voice excruciating to hear, it said his name, but by then Marlowe had already lunged and run the monster through.

It fell back against a chair. Then, roaring in pain, it pushed itself onto its feet again and came at him. He'd no choice but to stab it a second time. The blade flexed and nearly failed to penetrate the armor. Marlowe jumped back. When the creature took yet another step for him, he thrust the sword again. This time he aimed for and punctured its unprotected throat.

The creature rocked back, then collapsed upon a chair. Much to his surprise, it raised a hand and croaked wetly, "Thank you."

Its torso shuddered and a dark mist erupted out of it, hung a moment in the air, and then evaporated like steam.

The monster doubled over and fell to the floor then. Marlowe kept his dripping blade at the ready, but the creature didn't move after that.

Behind him, Thomas abruptly inhaled a ragged breath. Marlowe swung about. Thomas's body convulsed, then lay still. Finally, he blinked, blue eyes taking in Marlowe upside down. "Thank you, Kit," he said.

"I don't . . . Prithee, what just happened?"

"You . . . saved me." Thomas attempted to stand but fell back. He lowered his head. "It's remarkably disorienting."

"What is?"

Thomas merely shook his head. "How is Syndony?"

Marlowe looked back at her. "She might be dead."

Thomas reached out. "Help me up, then. I need to free her."

"Free her?"

"A spell. She's been ensorcelled. Quickly."

"By that monster?"

"What? No, no. By—"

"The man who just left here."

"That's right." Thomas waved his arm, and Marlowe finally sheathed his rapier and then pulled him to his feet.

Thomas went to her. "We should perhaps find her some clothes."

Marlowe strode into the bedchamber. He called out, "I see only a green doublet and slops here."

"Those are hers," Thomas answered. While Marlowe was in the bedchamber, he retrieved his ördstone from the body of Bragrender. Finally, the pouch was around his own neck again. He held the stone up beside Syndony. The gem flickered to life.

Marlowe, returning with her clothing, stopped to press one hand to his head. "What is it that stings me?"

Thomas ignored him. He watched Syndony's eyes roll back and forth beneath their lids, which opened at last. She saw him above her, and softly said, "Oh, thank God."

"Actually, it's thank Kit Marlowe. Without him I would still be Bragrender." He tucked the ördstone away.

"I knew that was you. I could see and hear all that was spoke, even words that never touched lips." She sat up and realized at once that she was naked. Marlowe held out her doublet and she dragged it across herself.

"Of what does she speak? Words that never touched lips?" Marlowe asked.

"The world of elves, Kit, who snatched her away. It's the reason we never arrived at the theater."

"You were in their world? Oh, I would marvel to behold that."

"You wouldn't, trust me. You would be lucky to get out alive."

"And that kept you from Burbage's Theatre last night?"

"That's right."

"No matter how terrible, it's just as well that it did. Walsingham turned up and was looking for you. He insisted no one was here, the fire burned down, and asked what I knew, which was nothing, fortunately. But 'tis why I've come so early this morning."

"Walsingham."

"Him. Says he has another assignment for you. A 'grave task,' as he put it."

Thomas and Syndony traded a glance. She ignored all decorum, and climbed down off the table. Naked, she grabbed up her clothes and hurried back into the bedroom. She called out, "My shirt, where's my—ah, there it is!"

Thomas smiled to Marlowe. "Kit, could I trouble you to go to Cheapside Street and find us a small coach or wagon? Tell them we're going to the Custom House quay. No idea when the ferry to Gravesend—"

Marlowe put up his hands. "No more, no more. Please tell me nothing. If Walsingham asks, I want to be able to say I've absolutely no idea where you've gone." He hurried out the door.

Thomas went into the bedchamber. Syndony was belting her baldric and dagger. "Pack what will fit and cannot be replaced," he told her.

She wrapped her arms around him and they kissed long and hard before collecting the rest of their things.

In the early afternoon, with the tide going out, the long ferry departed from the Custom House docks with thirty-seven passengers, headed for Gravesend. The sun cast diamonds upon the water.

As the ferry approached Rotherhithe, a handsome couple in their cloaks, hats, and ruffs stood together at starboard side and watched Sussex's Bermondsey House go by.

Thomas commented, "Perhaps we'll find a house as grand as that old abbey for ourselves in Italy."

"Is that our destination, then? Italy?"

"Or Greece, or wherever you like."

The ferry sailed up around the large bend in the river and then past Deptford. Glamoured, Thomas watched the creek pass by where his adventures with Walsingham had all but begun. It was now devoid of dead Yvag assassins.

"Wherever I like is where there are no skinwalkers or elves lurking about," she answered. She had established already that none had accompanied them on the ferry.

A tiltboat scooted past, heading for a tavern dock.

"Not long now before we pass Greenwich and Placentia Palace."

Syndony asked, "Should we make an excursion and visit the Queen?"

"Only if we insist on ensuring that everybody we need to avoid knows where we're going."

"As to that, for how long, my love?"

"Until we're so fiercely bored that facing down an army of Yvag knights sounds like fun."

"A very long time, then," said she.

He continued to watch as the Queen's Palace passed by. Her barge was there, secured near the steps out into the river. Thomas gave it a wave, as though believing someone there was watching for his signal.

A long while they stood like that; she pressed against the rail and he squeezed his arms around her. Her scent seduced him all over again, and he sighed.

Syndony remarked, "I have to say, some of what I heard the Queen and her minions discussing while they interrogated me I found confusing."

"You're speaking of the Yvag queen, Nicnevin."

"Of course."

"Yes, I didn't think Elizabeth had gotten hold of you. In any case, I remain fairly certain Nicnevin will not be hunting you, or me for that matter. But I'm curious. Were you confused by what they intended to do with you? What was expected to happen to you in Hel, or would have happened if I was unable to open a gate inside its cosmic gulf?"

"No, I understood all that well enough. But there was something one of them mentioned, which sounded like it might be important."

"And what was that?" he asked.

"I think they called it the Changeling Pool. Do you know of it?"